PRAISE FOR ALI HAZELWOOD

"A literary breakthrough. . . . *The Love Hypothesis* is a self-assured debut, and we hypothesize it's just the first bit of greatness we'll see from an author who somehow has the audacity to be both an academic powerhouse and [a] divinely talented novelist."

—*Entertainment Weekly*

"Contemporary romance's unicorn: the elusive marriage of deeply brainy and delightfully escapist. . . . *The Love Hypothesis* has wild commercial appeal, but the quieter secret is that there is a specific audience, made up of all the Olives in the world, who have deeply, ardently waited for this exact book."

—*New York Times* bestselling author Christina Lauren

"With her sophomore novel, Ali Hazelwood proves that she is the perfect writer to show that science is sexy as hell, and that love can 'STEM' from the most unlikely places. She's my newest must-buy author."

—Jodi Picoult, #1 *New York Times* bestselling author of *Wish You Were Here*

"Ali Hazelwood is the queen of smart rom-coms. . . . Filled with snappy banter, clever characters, and crackling tension (and lots of chess!), this is the perfect rivals-to-lovers romance. *Check & Mate* will have you swooning, laughing, staying up all night, and smiling so much your face hurts. This book is my new obsession. Who knew chess could be so romantic?"

—Alex Aster, #1 *New York Times* bestselling author of *Lightlark*

"Funny, sexy, and smart. Ali Hazelwood did a terrific job with *The Love Hypothesis.*"

—*New York Times* bestselling author Mariana Zapata

"Gloriously nerdy and sexy, with on-point commentary about women in STEM."

—*New York Times* bestselling author Helen Hoang
on *Love on the Brain*

"STEMinists, assemble. Your world is about to be rocked."

—*New York Times* bestselling author Elena Armas
on *Love on the Brain*

"This tackles one of my favorite tropes—Grumpy meets Sunshine—in a fun and utterly endearing way.... I loved the nods toward fandom and romance novels, and I couldn't put it down. Highly recommended!"

—*New York Times* bestselling author Jessica Clare
on *The Love Hypothesis*

"The reigning queen of STEMinist rom-coms returns with a tale set in the cutthroat world of elite academia full of delightful humor, realistic emotions, and the messy search for self-acceptance."

—*Booklist* (starred review) on *Love, Theoretically*

"A decidedly quirky and thoroughly charming tale.... Geeky science jokes, humorous student emails, and expertly delivered snarky banter enhance the narrative. Readers will cheer for Jack and Elsie and their bumpy road to happily ever after."

—*Publishers Weekly* (starred review) on *Love, Theoretically*

ALSO BY ALI HAZELWOOD

The Love Hypothesis
Love on the Brain
Love, Theoretically

ANTHOLOGIES
Loathe to Love You

NOVELLAS
Under One Roof
Stuck with You
Below Zero

YOUNG ADULT NOVELS
Check & Mate

BRIDE

ALI HAZELWOOD

BERKLEY ROMANCE
NEW YORK

BERKLEY ROMANCE
Published by Berkley
An imprint of Penguin Random House LLC
penguinrandomhouse.com

ISBN: 9780593817001

The Library of Congress has cataloged the Berkley Romance
trade paperback edition of this book as follows:

Names: Hazelwood, Ali, author.
Title: Bride / Ali Hazelwood.
Description: First Edition. | New York: Berkley Romance, 2024.
Identifiers: LCCN 2023019644 (print) | LCCN 2023019645 (ebook) |
ISBN 9780593550403 (trade paperback) | ISBN 9780593550410 (ebook)
Subjects: LCGFT: Novels. | Paranormal fiction. | Romance fiction.
Classification: LCC PS3608.A98845 B75 2024 (print) |
LCC PS3608.A98845 (ebook) | DDC 813/.6—dc23/ eng/ 20230503
LC record available at https:// lccn.loc.gov/ 2023019644
LC ebook record available at https:// lccn.loc.gov/ 2023019645

First Edition: February 2024

Printed in the United States of America
1   3   5   7   9   10   8   6   4   2

Book design by Daniel Brount

To Thao and Sarah. I could knot do this without you,
and I wouldn't even want to.

PROLOGUE

This marriage, it's going to be a problem.
She is going to be a problem.

THIS WAR OF OURS, THE ONE BETWEEN THE VAMPYRES AND the Weres, began several centuries ago with brutal escalations of violence, culminated amid flowing torrents of varicolored blood, and ended in a whimper of buttercream cake on the day I met my husband for the first time.

Which, as it happens, was also the day of our wedding.

Not quite the stuff of childhood dreams. Then again, I'm no dreamer. I only ever contemplated marriage once, back in the gloomy days of my childhood. Following a few too-harsh punishments and a poorly executed assassination attempt, Serena and I concocted plans for a grand escape, which was going to involve pyrotechnics-based diversions, stealing our math tutor's car, and flipping off our caregivers in the rearview mirror.

"We'll stop by the animal shelter and adopt one of those shaggy dogs. Pick up a Slurpee for me, some blood for you. Disappear forever into Human territory."

"Will they let me in if I'm not Human?" I asked, even though that was the least of our plan's flaws. We were both eleven. Neither of us could drive. Interspecies peace in the Southwest region relied, quite literally, on me staying the hell put.

"I'll vouch for you."

"Will that be enough?"

"I'll marry you! They'll believe you're Human—my Human wife."

As proposals went, it seemed solid. So I nodded solemnly and said, "I accept."

That was fourteen years ago, though, and Serena never married me. In fact, she's long gone. I'm here alone, with a giant heap of expensive wedding favors that'll hopefully fool guests into overlooking the lack of love, genetic compatibility, or even previous acquaintance between me and the groom.

I did try to arrange a meeting. Suggested to *my* people that they suggest to *his* people that we could grab lunch the week before the ceremony. Coffee the previous day. A glass of tap water the morning of—anything to avoid a "How do you do?" in front of the officiant. My request was escalated to the Vampyre council, and resulted in a phone call from one of the members' aides. His tone managed to be polite while heavily implying that I was a cuckoo nutbird. "He's a Were. A very powerful and dangerous Were. Just the logistics of providing security for such a meeting would be—"

"I'll be marrying this *dangerous* Were," I pointed out evenly, and a bashful throat was cleared.

"He is an Alpha, Miss Lark. Too busy to meet."

"Busy with . . . ?"

"His pack, Miss Lark."

I pictured him in a home gym, tirelessly working on his abs, and shrugged.

Ten days have passed, and I have yet to meet my groom. Instead, I've become a *project*—one that requires a concerted effort from an interdisciplinary crew to look weddable. A manicurist coaxes my nails into pink ovals. A facialist smacks my cheeks with relish. A hairdresser magically hides my pointed ears under a web of dark blond braids, and a makeup expert paints a different face on top of mine, something interesting and sophisticated and zygomatic.

"This is art," I tell him, studying the contouring in the mirror. "You should be a Guggenheim fellow."

"I know. And I'm not *done*," he reprimands, before dipping his thumb in a pot of dark green stain and swiping it over the insides of my wrists. The base of my throat on both sides. My nape.

"What's this?"

"Just a bit of color."

"What for?"

A snort. "I pulled strings and researched Were customs. Your husband will like it." He whooshes away, leaving me alone with five odd markings and a newfound bone structure. I squeeze into the bridal jumpsuit that the stylist begged me not to refer to as a onesie, and then my twin brother comes to retrieve me.

"You look stunning," Owen says flatly, distrustfully, squinting at me like I'm a fake ten-dollar bill.

"It was a team effort."

He gestures for me to follow him. "I hope they vaccinated you for rabies while they were at it."

The ceremony is supposed to be a symbol of peace. That's why, in a heartwarming display of trust, my father demanded an all-Vampyre armed security detail for the ceremony. The Weres refused, which led to weeks of negotiations, then to a near break of the engagement, and finally to the only solution that could make everybody equally unhappy: staffing the event with Humans.

There's a tense atmosphere, and then there's *this*. One venue, three species, five centuries of conflict, and zero good faith. The black suits escorting Owen and me seem torn between protecting us and killing us themselves, just to get it over with. They wear sunglasses indoors and mutter entertainingly bad code into their sleeves. *Bat is flying to the ceremony hall. I repeat, we have Bat.*

The groom is, uninventively, *Wolf.*

"When do you think your future husband will try to kill you?" Owen asks conversationally, looking straight ahead. "Tomorrow? Next week?"

"Who's to say."

"Within the month, for sure."

"For sure."

"One has to wonder if the Weres will bury your corpse or just, you know. Eat it."

"One has to."

"But if you care to live a bit longer, try tossing a stick when he starts mauling you. I hear they love to fetch—"

I halt abruptly, causing a slight commotion among the agents. "Owen," I say, turning to my brother.

"Yes, Misery?" His eyes hold mine. Suddenly, his indolent, insult-comedian mask slips off, and he's not my father's shallow heir anymore, but the brother who'd sneak into bed with me whenever I had nightmares, who swore he'd protect me from the cruelty of the Humans and the bloodthirstiness of the Weres.

It's been decades.

"*You know what went down the last time the Vampyres and Weres tried this,*" he says, shifting to the Tongue.

I sure do. The Aster is in every textbook, albeit with vastly differ-ent interpretations. The day the purple of our blood and the green of the Weres' flowed together, as bright and beautiful as the bloom-ing flower the massacre was named after. *"Who the hell would enter a marriage of political convenience after that?"*

"Me, apparently."

"You are going to live among the wolves. Alone."

"Right. That's how hostage exchanges work." Around us, the suits hurriedly check their watches. *"We have to go——"*

"Alone to be slaughtered." Owen's jaw grinds. It's so unlike his usual careless self, I frown.

"Since when do you care?"

"Why are you doing this?"

"Because an alliance with the Weres is necessary to the surivival of——"

"These are Father's words. It's not why you agreed to do this."

It's not, but I'm not about to admit it. *"Maybe you underestimate Father's persuasiveness."*

His voice drops to a whisper. *"Don't do this. It's a death sentence. Say you've changed your mind—give me six weeks."*

"What will have changed in six weeks?"

He hesitates. *"A month. I——"*

"Is something amiss?" We both jump at Father's sharp tone. For a split second we're children again, again scolded for existing. As always, Owen recovers quicker.

"Nah." The vacuous smile is back on his lips. "I was just giving Misery a few pointers."

Father cuts through the security guards and tucks my hand into his elbow with ease, like it hasn't been a decade since our last physical contact. I force myself not to recoil. "Are you ready, Misery?"

I cock my head. Study his stern face. Ask, mostly out of curiosity, "Does it matter?"

It must not, because the question isn't acknowledged. Owen watches us leave, expressionless, then yells after us, *"Hope you packed a lint roller. I hear they shed."*

One of the agents stops us in front of the double doors that lead into the courtyard. "Councilman Lark, Miss Lark, one minute. They're not quite ready for you." We wait side by side for a handful of uncomfortable moments, then Father turns to me. In my stylist-mandated heels, I nearly reach his height, and his eyes easily catch mine.

"You should smile," he orders in the Tongue. *"According to the Humans, a wedding is the most beautiful day of a bride's life."*

My lips twitch. There's something grotesquely funny about all of this. "What about the father of the bride?"

He sighs. *"You were always needlessly defiant."*

My failures spare no front.

"There is no going back, Misery," he adds, not unkindly. *"Once the handfasting is complete, you will be his wife."*

"I know." I don't need soothing, or encouragement. I've been nothing but unwavering in my commitment to this union. I'm not prone to panic, or fear, or last-minute changes of heart. *"I've done this before, remember?"* He studies me for a few moments, until the doors open to what's left of my life.

It's a perfect night for an outdoor ceremony: string lights, soft breeze, winking stars. I take a deep breath, hold it in, and listen to Mendelssohn's march, string quartet rendition. According to the bubbly wedding planner who's been blowing up my phone with links I don't click on, the viola player is a member of the Human

Philharmonic. *Top three in the world*, she texted, followed by more exclamation points than I've used in my cumulative written communications since birth. I must admit, it does sound nice. Even if the guests glance around, confused, unsure how to proceed until an overworked staffer gestures at them to stand.

It's not their fault. Wedding ceremonies are, as of a century or so ago, exclusively a Human thing. Vampyre society has evolved past monogamy, and Weres . . . I have no clue what Weres are up to, as I've never even been in the presence of one.

If I had, I wouldn't be alive.

"Come on." Father grips my elbow, and we start down the aisle.

The bride's guests are familiar, but only vaguely. A sea of willowy figures, unblinking lilac eyes, pointed ears. Lips closed over fangs, and half-pitying, mostly disgusted looks. I spot several members of my father's inner circle; councilors I haven't met since I was a child; powerful families and their scions, most of whom fawned over Owen and were little shits to me when we were kids. No one here could even remotely qualify as a friend, but in defense of whoever came up with the guest list, my lack of meaningful relationships must have made seat-filling a bit of a challenge.

And then there's the groom's side. The one that emanates a foreign kind of heat. The one that wants me dead.

The Weres' blood beats quicker, louder, its smell coppery and unfamiliar. They are taller than Vampyres, stronger than Vampyres, faster than Vampyres, and none of them seems particularly enthused at the idea of their Alpha marrying one of us. Their lips curl as they eye me, defiant, angry. Their loathing is so thick I taste it on the roof of my palate.

I don't blame them. I don't blame anyone for not wanting to be here. I don't even blame the whispers, or the catty comments, or the fact that half the guests here never learned that sound carries farther than shit.

"*. . . she used to be the Collateral with the Humans for ten years, and now this?*"

"*I bet she likes the attention . . .*"

"*—blade-eared leech—*"

"*I give her two weeks.*"

"*More like two hours, if those animals—*"

"*. . . either stabilize the region once and for all, or cause full-out war, again—*"

"*—think they're actually going to be fucking tonight?*"

I have no friends on the left, and only enemies on the right. So I ground myself and look straight ahead.

At my future husband.

He stands at the end of the path, turned away from me, listening to what someone is whispering in his ear—his best man, perhaps. I can't get a good look at his face, but I know what to expect from the picture I was given weeks ago: handsome, striking, unsmiling. His hair is short, a rich brown cut to a buzz; his suit is black, well fitted across his broad shoulders. He's the only man in the room not wearing a tie, and yet he manages to look elegant anyway.

Maybe we share a stylist. As good a starting point for a marriage as any, I suppose.

"*Be careful with him,*" Father whispers, lips barely moving. "*He is very dangerous. Do not cross him.*"

What every girl wants to hear ten feet from the altar, especially when the hard line of her groom's shoulders already looks cross. Impatient. Annoyed. He doesn't bother glancing in my direction, as though I'm inconsequential, as though there are other, better things for him to do with his time. I wonder what the best man is whispering in his ear. Maybe a mirror copy of the warnings I got.

Misery Lark? No need to be careful. She's not particularly dangerous, so feel free to cross her. What is she gonna do? Chuck her lint roller at you?

I snort out a soft laugh, and that's a mistake. Because my future husband hears it, and finally turns to me.

My stomach drops.

My step falters.

The murmurs quiet.

In the photo I was shown, the groom's eyes looked an ordinary, unsurprising blue. But as they meet mine, I realize two things. The first is that I was wrong, and his gaze is actually an odd pale green that borders on white. The second is that Father was right: this man is very, *very* dangerous.

His eyes roam over my face, and I immediately suspect that he must not have been given photos. Or maybe he just wasn't curious enough about his bride to check them out? Either way, he's not pleased with me, and that's obvious. Too bad I've cut my teeth on disappointing people, and I'm not about to start caring now. It's on him if he doesn't like what he's seeing.

I square my shoulders. A small distance separates us, and I let my eyes pin his as I close it, which is how I see it all happen in real time.

Pupils, widening.

Brow, furrowing.

Nostrils, flaring.

He watches me like I'm something made of maggots and takes one deep breath, slow. Then another, sharp, the moment I'm delivered to the altar. His expression widens into something that looks, for an instant, indecipherably shaken, and I knew it, I *knew* that Weres didn't like Vampyres, but this feels beyond that. It feels like pure, hard, personal contempt.

Tough shit, buddy, I think, lifting my chin. I step forward, again, until we are standing in front of each other, this side of too close.

Two strangers who only just met. About to get married.

The music wanes. The guests sit. My heart's a sluggish drum, even slower than usual, because of the way the groom looms over me. Leaning forward to study me like I'm an abstract painting. I watch his chest heave hungrily, as if to . . . *inhale* me. Then he pulls back, licks his lips, and stares.

He stares and stares and *stares*.

The silence stretches. The officiant clears his throat. The courtyard breaks into bouts of puzzled mumbles that slowly rise to a sticky, familiar friction. I notice that the best man has unsheathed his claws. Behind me, Vania, the head of my father's guards, is showing her fangs. And the Humans, of course, are reaching for their guns.

All through that, my future husband still stares.

So I step closer and murmur, "I don't care how little you like this, but if you want to avoid a second Aster—"

His hand comes up lightning fast to close around my upper arm, and the warmth of his skin is a shock to my system, even through the fabric of my sleeve. His pupils contract into something different, something *animal*. I instinctively try to wriggle free of his grasp, and . . . it's a mistake.

My heel catches on a cobblestone and I lose my balance. The groom stops my fall with an arm snaked around my waist, and a combination of gravity and his sheer determination wedges me between him and the altar, his front pressing against mine. He cages me, pins me, and stares down at me like he forgot where he is and I'm something to be consumed.

Like I'm *prey*.

"This is highly— Oh, *my*," the officiant gasps when the groom growls in his direction. Behind me I hear the Tongue and English— panic, screams, chaos, the best man and my father snarling, people yelling threats, someone sobbing. *Another Aster in the making*, I think. And I really should do something, I *will* do something to stop it, but.

The groom's scent hits my nostrils.

Everything recedes.

Good blood, my hindbrain hisses, nonsensical. *He'd make for such good blood.*

He inhales several times in rapid succession, filling his lungs, pulling me in. His hand moves up from my arm to the dip of my throat, pressing into one of my markings. A guttural sound rises from someplace low in his chest, making my knees weak. Then he opens his mouth and I know that he's going to tear me to pieces, he's going to maul me, he's going to *devour* me—

"You," he says, voice deep, almost too low to hear. "How the fuck do you smell like this?"

Less than ten minutes later he slips a ring around my finger, and we swear to love each other till the day we die.

CHAPTER 1

It's been storming for three days straight when he finally returns from a meeting with the leader of the Big Bend huddle. Two of his seconds are already inside his home, waiting for him with wary expressions.

"The Vampyre woman—she backed out."

He grunts as he wipes his face. Smart of her, *he thinks.*

"But they found a replacement," Cal adds, sliding a manila folder on the counter. "Everything's in here. They want to know if she has your approval."

"We proceed as planned."

Cal huffs out a laugh. Flor frowns. "Don't you want to look at the—"

"No. This changes nothing."

They're all the same, anyway.

Six weeks before the ceremony

SHE SHOWS UP AT THE START-UP WHERE I WORK ON AN EARLY Thursday evening, when the sun has already set and the entire bullpen is contemplating grievous bodily harm.

Against me.

I doubt I deserve this level of hatred, but I do understand it. And that's why I don't make a fuss when I return to my desk following a brief meeting with my manager and notice the state of my stapler. Honestly, it's fine. I work from home 90 percent of the time and rarely print anything. Who cares if someone smeared bird shit on it?

"Don't take it personally, Missy." Pierce leans against our cubicle divider. His smile is less *concerned friend*, more *smarmy used car salesman*; even his blood smells oily.

"I won't." Other people's approval is a powerful drug. Lucky me, I never got the chance to develop an addiction. If there's something I'm good at, it's rationalizing my peers' contempt toward me. I've been training like piano prodigies: tirelessly and since early childhood.

"No need to sweat it."

"I'm not." Literally. I barely own the necessary glands.

"And don't listen to Walker. He didn't say what you think he did."

Pretty sure it was "nasty bitch" and not "tasty peach" that he yelled across the conference room, but who knows?

"It comes with the territory. You'd be mad, too, if someone did a penetration test against a firewall you've been working on for weeks and breached it in what, one hour?"

It was maybe a third of that, even counting the break I took in the middle after realizing how quickly I was blowing through the system. I spent it online shopping for a new hamper, since Serena's damn cat seems to be asleep in my old one whenever I need to do laundry. I texted her a picture of the receipt, followed by *You and your cat owe me sixteen dollars*. Then I sat and waited for a reply, like I always do.

It didn't come. Nor had I expected it would.

"People will get over it," he Pierces on. "And hey, you never bring lunch, so no need to worry someone'll spit in your Tupperware." He bursts into laughter. I turn to my computer monitor, hoping he'll peace out. Boy, am I wrong. "And to be honest, it's kind of on you. If you tried to mingle more . . . Personally, I get your loner, mysterious, quiet vibe. But some read you as aloof, like you think you're better than us. If you made an effort to—"

"Misery."

When I hear my name called—the *real* one—for a split, exceptionally dumb second, I experience relief that this conversation is going to be over. Then I crane my neck and notice the woman standing on the other side of the divider. Her face is distantly familiar, and so is the black hair, but it's not until I focus on her heartbeat that I manage to place her. It's slow like only a Vampyre's can be, and . . .

Well.

Shit.

"Vania?"

"You're hard to find," she tells me, voice melodic and low. I briefly contemplate slamming my head against the keyboard. Then settle for replying calmly:

"That's by design."

"I figured."

I massage my temple. What a day. What a fucking day. "And yet, here you are."

"And yet, here I am."

"Why, hello." Pierce's smile gets a notch slimier as he turns to leer at Vania. His eyes start at her high heels, travel up the straight lines of her dark pantsuit, stop on her full breasts. I don't read minds, but he's thinking *MILF* so hard, I can practically hear it. "Are you a friend of Missy's?"

"You could say that, yes. Since she was a child."

"Oh my God. Do tell, how was baby Missy?"

The corner of Vania's lips twitches. "She was . . . odd, and diffi-cult. If often useful."

"Wait—are you two related?"

"No. I'm her father's Right Hand, Head of his Guard," she says, looking at me. "And she has been summoned."

I straighten in my chair. "Where?"

"The Nest."

This is not rare—it's unprecedented. Excluding sporadic phone calls and even more sporadic meetings with Owen, I haven't spoken with another Vampyre in years. Because no one has reached out.

I should tell Vania to fuck off. I'm no longer a child stuck on a fool's errand: going back to my father with any expectations that he and the rest of my people won't be total assholes is an exercise in futility, and I'm well aware of it. But apparently this half-assed over-ture is making me forget, because I hear myself asking, "Why?"

"You'll have to come and find out." Vania's smile doesn't reach her eyes. I squint, like the answer is tattooed on her face. Mean-while, Pierce reminds us of his unfortunate existence.

"Ladies. Right hand? Summon?" He laughs, loud and grating. I want to flick his forehead and make him hurt, but I'm starting to feel a frisson of worry for this fool. "Are you guys into LARPing or . . ."

He finally shuts up. Because when Vania turns to him, no trick of the light could hide the purple hue of her eyes. Nor her long, perfectly white fangs, gleaming under the electric lights.

"Y-you . . ." Pierce looks between us for several seconds, mutter-ing something incoherent.

And that's when Vania decides to ruin my life and snap her teeth at him.

I sigh, pinching the bridge of my nose.

Pierce spins on his heels and sprints past my cubicle, running over a potted benjamin fig. "Vampyre! *Vampyre*—there's a— A Vampyre is *attacking* us, someone call the *Bureau*, someone call the—"

Vania takes out a laminated card with the Human-Vampyre Relations Bureau logo, one that grants her diplomatic immunity in Human territory. But there's no one to look at it: the bullpen has erupted into a small panic, and most of my coworkers are screaming, already halfway down the emergency stairs. People trample each other to get to the nearest exit. I see Walker dart out of the bathroom, a strip of toilet paper dangling from his khakis, and feel my shoulders slump.

"I liked this job," I tell Vania, grabbing the framed Polaroid of me and Serena and resignedly stuffing it into my bag. "It was easy. They bought my circadian rhythm disorder excuse and let me come in at night."

"My apologies," she says. Unapologetic. "Come with me."

I should tell her to fuck off, and I will. In the meantime, I give in to my curiosity and follow her, straightening the poor benjamin fig on my way out.

THE NEST IS STILL THE TALLEST BUILDING IN THE NORTH OF THE City, and perhaps the most distinctive: a bloodred podium that stretches underground for hundreds of feet, topped by a mirror skyscraper that comes alive around sunset and slides back to sleep in the early hours of the morning.

I brought Serena here once, when she asked to see what the heart of the Vampyre territory was like, and she stared open-mouthed, jarred by the sleek lines and ultramodern design. She'd been expecting candelabras, and heavy velvet drapes to block the murderous sun, and the corpses of our enemies hanging from the ceiling, blood milked from their veins to the very last drop. Bat artwork, in honor of our winged, chiropterous forefathers. Coffins, just because.

"It's nice. I just thought it'd be more . . . metal?" she mused, not at all intimidated at the idea of being the only Human in an elevator full of Vampyres. The memory still makes me smile years later.

Flexible spaces, automated systems, integrated tools—that's what the Nest is. Not just the crown jewel of our territory, but also the center of our community. A place for shops and offices and errands, where anything one of us could need, from nonurgent healthcare to a zoning permit to five liters of AB positive, can be easily obtained. And then, in the uppermost floors, the builders made room for some private quarters, some of which have been purchased by the most influential families in our society.

Mostly *my* family.

"Follow me," Vania says when the doors swish open, and I do, flanked by two uniformed council guards who are most definitely not here to *protect* me. A bit offensive, that I'm being treated like an intruder in the place where I was born, especially as we walk parallel to a wall that's plastered with portraits of my ancestors. They morph over the centuries, from oils to acrylics to photographs, gray to Kodachrome to digital. What stays the same are the expressions: distant, arrogant, and frankly, unhappy. Not a healthy thing, power.

The only Lark I recognize from personal experience is the one closest to Father's office. My grandfather was already old and a little demented by the time Owen and I were born, and my most vivid memory of him is from that one time I woke up in the middle of the night to find him in my bedroom, pointing at me with trembling hands and yelling in the Tongue, something about me being destined for a grisly death.

In fairness, he wasn't wrong.

"In here," Vania says with a soft knock to the door. "The councilman is waiting for you."

I scan her face. Vampyres are not immortal; we grow old the same as every other species, but . . . damn. She looks like she hasn't aged a day since she escorted me to the Collateral exchange ceremony. Seventeen years ago.

"Is there something you need?"

"No." I turn and reach for the doorknob. Hesitate. "Is he sick?"

Vania seems amused. "You think he'd call *you* here for that?"

I shrug. I can't think of a single other reason he'd want to see me.

"For what? To commiserate? Or find solace in your filial affection? You have been among the Humans far too long."

"I was thinking more along the lines of him needing a kidney."

"We are Vampyres, Misery. We act for the good of the most, or not at all."

She's gone before I can roll my eyes, or serve her that "fuck off" I've been meaning to. I sigh, glance at the stone-faced guards she left behind, and then walk into my father's office.

The first things I notice are the two walls of windows, which is exactly what Father wants. Every Human I've talked with assumes that Vampyres hate light and relish darkness, but they couldn't be more wrong. The sun may be forbidden to us, toxic always and deathly in large quantities, but that's precisely why we covet it with such intensity. Windows are a luxury, because they need to be treated with absurdly expensive materials that filter everything that might harm us. And windows this large are the most bombastic of status symbols, in a full display of dynastic power and obscene wealth. And beyond them . . .

The river that slices The City into North and South—*us*, and *them*. Only a few hundred feet separate the Nest from Were territory, but the riverbank is littered with outlook towers, checkpoints, and guard posts, heavily monitored twenty-four seven. A single bridge exists, but access to it is closely surveilled in both directions, and as far as I know, no vehicle has traveled across it since well before I was born. Past that, there are a few Were security areas, and the deep green of an oak forest that stretches south for miles.

I always thought it smart of them not to build civilian settlements next to one of the most sanguinary borders in the Southwest. When Owen and I were children, before I was sent away, Father walked in on us wondering why the Vampyre headquarters had been placed so close to our most lethal enemies. "To remember," he explained. "And to remind."

I don't know. Twenty years later, it still seems pretty fucked up to me.

"Misery." Father finishes tapping at the touch screen monitor and stands from his luxury mahogany desk, unsmiling but not cold. "It's good to see you here again."

"It sure is something." The past few years have been kind to Henry Lark. I examine his tall frame, triangular face, and wide-set eyes, and I'm reminded of how much I take after him. His blond hair is a little grayer, but still perfectly slicked back. I've never seen it anything but—never seen Father less than impeccably put together. Tonight the sleeves of his white button-down may be rolled back, but meticulously so. If they're meant to trick me into thinking that this is a casual meeting, they've failed.

And that's why, when he points at the leather chair in front of his desk and says, "Sit," I decide to lean back against the door.

"Vania says you're not dying." I'm aiming for rude. Unfortunately, I think I just sound curious.

"I trust that you're healthy, too." He smiles faintly. "How have the last seven years treated you?"

There is a beautiful vintage clock behind his head. I watch it tick eight seconds before saying, "Just peachy."

"Yes?" He gives me a once-over. "You'd better remove them, Misery. Someone might mistake you for a Human."

He's referring to my brown contacts. Which I considered taking out in the car, before deciding not to bother. The problem is, there are many other signs that I've been living among the Humans, most not so quickly reversible. The fangs I shave to dull points every week, for instance, are unlikely to escape his notice. "I was at work."

"Ah, yes. Vania mentioned you have a job. Something with computers, knowing you?"

"Something like that."

He nods. "And how is your little friend? Once again safe and sound, I trust."

I stiffen. "How do you know she—"

"Oh, Misery. You didn't really think that your communications with Owen went unmonitored, did you?"

I clench my fists behind my back and seriously debate slamming the door behind me and returning home. But there must be a reason he brought me here, and I need to know it. So I take my phone out of my pocket, and once I'm sitting across from Father, I lay it face up on his desk.

I tap on the timer app, set it for exactly ten minutes, and turn it toward him. Then I lean back in the chair. "Why am I here?"

"It's been years since I last saw my only daughter." He presses his lips together. "Is that not enough reason?"

"Nine minutes and forty-three seconds left."

"Misery. My child." The Tongue. *"Why are you angry at me?"*

I lift my eyebrow.

"You should not feel anger, but pride. The right choice is the one that ensures happiness for the largest number of people. And you were the means to that choice."

I study him calmly. I'm positive that he really does believe this bullshit. That he thinks he's a good guy. "Nine minutes and twenty-two seconds."

He looks briefly, genuinely sad. Then he says, "There is to be a wedding."

I jerk my head back. "A wedding? As in . . . like the Humans do?"

"A marriage ceremony. Like the Vampyres used to have."

"Whose? Yours? Are *you* going to . . ." I don't bother finishing the sentence—the sheer thought is ludicrous. It's not just *weddings* that have gone out of fashion hundreds of years ago, but the entire idea of long-term relationships. As it turns out, when your species sucks at producing children, encouraging sexual walkabouts and the search for reproductively compatible partners takes precedence over romance. I doubt Vampyres were ever particularly romantic, anyway. "Whose?"

Father sighs. "Yet to be decided."

I don't like this, not any of it, but I'm not sure why yet.

Something prickles in my ear, a whisper that I should get the hell out now, but as I'm about to stand, Father says, "Since you chose to live among the Humans, you must have been following their news."

"Some of it," I lie. We could be at war with Eurasia and on the verge of cloning unicorns, and I'd have no clue. I've been busy. Searching. Scouring. "Why?"

"The Humans recently had an election."

I had no idea, but I nod. "Wonder what that's like." A leadership structure that's not an unattainable council whose membership is restricted to a handful of families, passed down from generation to generation like a chipped china set.

"Not ideal. As Arthur Davenport was not reelected."

"Governor Davenport?" The City is divided between the local Were pack and the Vampyres, but the rest of the Southwest region is almost exclusively Human. And for the last few decades, they've chosen Arthur Davenport to represent them—as far as I can recall, with little hesitation. That jerk. "Who's the new guy?"

"A woman. Maddie Garcia is the governor-elect, and her term will start in a few months."

"And your take on her . . . ?" He must have one. Father's collaboration with Governor Davenport is the driving force behind the amicable relationship between our two people.

Well. *Amicable* might be too strong of a word. The average Human still thinks that we're gagging to suck their cattle dry and mind-scramble their loved ones; the average Vampyre still thinks that Humans are cunning but feckless, and that their main talent is for procreating and filling the universe with more Humans. It's not like our species hang out, aside from very limited, highly artificial diplomatic events. But we haven't been overtly murdering each other in cold blood for a while, and we're allies against the Weres. A win is a win, right?

"I have no opinion," he tells me, impassible. "Nor will I have the opportunity to form one soon, as Ms. Garcia has refused all my requests for meetings."

"Ah." Ms. Garcia must be wiser than I am.

"However, I am still tasked with guaranteeing the safety of my people. And once Governor Davenport is gone, in addition to the Were threat that we constantly face at the southern border, there might be one at the north. From the Humans."

"I doubt she wants trouble, Father." I pick at my nail polish. "She'll probably just leave the current alliance as it is and cut down on the ceremonial bullshit—"

"Her team has informed us that as soon as she takes office, the Collateral program will be no more."

I freeze. And then slowly look up. "What?"

"We have been formally asked to return the Human Collateral. And they will send back the girl who's currently serving as the Vampyre Collateral—"

"Boy," I correct him automatically. My fingertips feel numb. "The current Vampyre Collateral is a boy." I met him once. He had dark hair and a constant frown and said "No, thank you" when I asked if he needed help carrying a stack of books. By now he might very well be as tall as me.

"Whatever it might be, the return will happen next week. The Humans have decided not to wait for Maddie Garcia to take office."

"I don't see . . ." I swallow. Gather myself. "It's for the best. It's a stupid practice."

"It has been ensuring peace between the Vampyres and the Humans for over one hundred years."

"Seems a little cruel to me," I counter calmly. "Asking an eight-year-old to relocate alone inside enemy territory to play hostage."

"'Hostage' is such a crude, simplistic word."

"You hold a Human child as a deterrent for ten years, with the mutual understanding that if the Humans violate the terms of our alliance, the Vampyres will instantly murder the child. That seems crude and simplistic, too."

Father's eyes narrow. "It's not unilateral." His voice grows harder. "The Humans hold a Vampyre child for the same reason—"

"I know, Father." I lean forward. "I was the previous Vampyre Collateral, in case you have forgotten."

I wouldn't put it past him—but no. He might not recall the way I tried to hold his hand as the armored sedan drove us north, or me trying to hide behind Vania's thigh when I first got a glimpse of the Humans' oddly colored eyes. He might not know how it felt, growing up with the knowledge that if the ceasefire between us and the Humans broke down, the same caregivers who'd taught me how to ride a bike would come into my room and drive a knife through my heart. He might not dwell on the fact that he sent his daughter to be the eleventh Collateral, ten years a prisoner among people who hated her kind.

But he does remember. Because the first rule of the Collateral, of course, is that they have to be closely tied to those in power. Those who make decisions concerning peace and war. And if Maddie Garcia doesn't want to throw a member of her family under the bus in the name of public safety, that only makes me respect her more. The boy who took over when I turned eighteen is the grandson of Councilwoman Ewing. And when I served as the

Vampyre Collateral, my Human counterpart was the grandson of Governor Davenport. I used to wonder if he felt like I did— sometimes angry, sometimes resigned. Mostly expendable. I'd sure love to know if, now that years have passed, he gets along with his family better than I do with mine.

"Alexandra Boden. Do you remember her?" Father's tone is back to conversational. "You were born the same year."

I sit back in my chair, unsurprised by the abrupt change of topic. "Red hair?"

He nods. "A little more than a week ago, her little brother, Abel, turned fifteen. That night, he and three friends were out partying, and found themselves near the river. Emboldened by their youth and feeble-mindedness, they challenged each other to swim across it, touch the riverbank that belongs to Were territory, and then swim back. A show of bravery, if you will."

I'm not invested in the fate of Alexandra Boden's bratty brother, but my body goes icy cold nonetheless. All Vampyre children are taught about the danger of the southern border. We all learn where our territory ends and the Weres' begins before we can speak. And we all know not to mess with anything Were.

Except for these four idiots, clearly.

"They're dead," I murmur.

Father's lips curl up in something that looks very little like compassion, and a lot like annoyance. "It's what they deserved, in my frank opinion. Of course, when the boys couldn't be found, the worst was assumed. Ansel Boden, the boy's father, has strong ties to several council families, and petitioned for a retaliatory act. He argued that their disappearance would justify it. He was reminded that the good of our people as a whole comes before the good of the one—the basic principle Vampyre society relies on. Birth rates are at our lowest, and we are facing extinction. This is not the time to stoke conflict. And yet, in an unbecoming display of weakness, he continued to beg."

"Disgusting. How dare he grieve for his son."

Father gives me a scathing look. "Because of his relationship to the council, he came close to having his way. Just last week, while you were busy pretending to be Human, we were closer to an interspecies war than we've been in a century. And then, two days after their dull-witted stunt . . ." Father stands. He walks around the desk and then leans back against its edge, the picture of relaxation. "The boys reappeared. Intact."

I blink, a habit I picked up while pretending to be Human. "Their corpses?"

"They are alive. Shaken, of course. They were interrogated by Were guards—treated as spies, at first, and then as unruly nuisances. But they were eventually returned home, whole and healthy."

"How?" I can think of half a dozen incidents in the past twenty years in which borders were breached and whatever was left of the offenders got sent back in pieces. It mostly happens outside city limits, in the demilitarized woodlands. Regardless, Weres have been merciless to our people, and we have been merciless toward Weres. Which means that . . . "What changed?"

"An intelligent question. You see, most of the council assumed that Roscoe was growing tender in his old age." Roscoe. The Alpha of the Southwest pack. I've heard Father talk about him ever since I was a child. "But I've met Roscoe once. Just once—he was always clear about his disinterest in diplomacy, and people like him are like skull bones. They only harden with time." He turns toward the window. "The Weres are as secretive as ever about their society.

But we do have some ways to obtain intel, and after sending over some inquiries—"

"There was a change in their leadership structure."

"Very good." He seems pleased, as though I'm a student who mastered the transitive property well ahead of expectations. "Maybe I should have chosen you as my successor. Owen has shown little commitment to the role. He appears to be more interested in socializing."

I wave my hand. "I'm sure that when you announce your retirement he'll stop carousing around with his councilman heir friends and become the perfect Vampyre politician you always dreamt he'd be." *Not.* "The Weres. What kind of change?"

"It appears that a few months ago, someone . . . *challenged* Roscoe."

"Challenged?"

"Their succession of power is not particularly sophisticated. Weres are most closely related to dogs, after all. Suffice to say, Roscoe is dead."

I refrain from pointing out that our dynastic, hereditary oligarchies seem even more primitive, and that dogs are universally beloved. "Have you met them? The new Alpha?"

"After the boys were returned safely, I requested a meeting with him. To my surprise, he accepted."

"He *did*?" I hate that I'm invested. "And?"

"I was curious, you see. Mercy isn't always a sign of weakness, but it can be." His eyes take a sudden faraway bent, then slide to a piece of art on the eastern wall—a simple canvas painted a deep purple, to commemorate the blood spilled during the Aster. Similar art can be found in most public spaces. "And betrayal is born of weakness, Misery."

"Is it, now?" Always thought betrayal was just betrayal, but what do I know?

"He is not weak, the new Alpha. On the contrary. He is . . ." Father pulls back into himself. "Something else. Something new." His eyes settle on me, waiting, patient, and I shake my head, because I cannot imagine what reason he might have to tell me all of this. Where I could possibly come into play.

Until something worms its way through the back of my head. "Why did you mention a wedding?" I ask, without bothering to hide the suspicion in my voice.

Father nods. I think I must have asked the right question, especially because he doesn't answer it. "You grew up among the Humans, and did not have the advantage of a Vampyre education, so you may not know the full history of our conflict with the Weres. Yes, we have been at odds for centuries, but attempts at dialogue were made. There have been five interspecies marriages between us and the Weres, during which no border skirmishes were recorded, nor Vampyre deaths at the hands of Weres. The last was two hundred years ago—a fifteen-year marriage between a Vampyre and his Were bride. When she died, another union was arranged, one that did not end well."

"The Aster."

"The Aster, yes." The sixth wedding ceremony ended in carnage when the Weres attacked the Vampyres, who, after decades of peace, had become a little too trusting, and made the mistake of showing up to a wedding mostly unarmed. Between the Weres' superior strength and the element of surprise, it was a bloodbath—mostly ours. Purple, with a sprinkling of green. Just like an aster. "We don't know why the Weres decided to turn on us, but ever since our relationship with them irreparably broke down, there has been one constant: we had an alliance with the Humans, and the Weres did not. There are ten Weres for every Vampyre, and hundreds of Humans for both our species combined. Yes, Humans may lack Vampyres' talents, or Weres' speed and strength, but there is power in numbers. Having them on our side was . . . reassuring." Father's jaw clenches. Then, after a long time, relaxes. "Certainly, you can see why Maddie Garcia's refusal to meet with me is a concern. Even more so because of her relative warmth toward the Weres."

My eyes widen. I may be a bit checked out of the Human cultural landscape, but I didn't think diplomatic relationships with the Weres would be on their statecraft bucket list for the year. As far as I know, they've always ignored each other—not too difficult, since they don't share important borders. "The Humans and the Weres. In diplomatic talks."

"Correct."

I remain skeptical. "Did the Alpha tell you this when you met?"

"No. This is intel we obtained separately. The Alpha told me other things."

"Such as?"

"He is young, you see. Around your age and built of a different stock. As savage as Roscoe, perhaps, but more open-minded. He believes that peace in the region is possible. That alliances among all three species should be cultivated."

I snort out a laugh. "Good luck with that."

Father's head tilts to the side, and his eyes zero in on me, assessing. "You know why I chose *you* to be the Collateral? And not your brother?"

Oh, no. Not *this* conversation. "Tossed a coin?"

"You were such a peculiar child, Misery. Always uninterested in what went on around you, locked in a vault inside your head, hard to reach. Withdrawn. The other children would try to become your friends, and you'd stubbornly leave them hanging—"

"The other *children* knew that I'd be the one sent to the Humans, and they started calling me *fangless traitor* as soon as they could form full sentences. Or have you forgotten when I was seven, and the sons and daughters of *your* fellow councilmen stole my clothes and pushed me out in the sun right before midday? And those same people spat on me and mocked me when I returned from ten years serving as *their* Collateral, so I'm not—" I exhale slowly, and remind myself that this is fine. *I* am fine. Untouchable. I'm twenty-five and I have my fake Human IDs, my apartment, my cat (fuck you, Serena), my . . . Okay, I probably don't have a job right *now*, but I'll find another soon, with 100 percent fewer Pierces. I have friends—*a* friend. Probably.

Above all, I've taught myself not to care. About anything.

"The wedding you mentioned. Whose is it?"

Father presses his lips together. Several moments tick by before he speaks again. "When a Were and a Vampyre stand in front of each other, all they see is—"

"The Aster." I glance down at my phone, impatient. "Three minutes and forty-seven seconds—"

"They see a wedding between a Vampyre and an Alpha that was supposed to broker peace, but ended in death. The Weres are animals, and always will be, but we are on the road to extinction, and the good of the most must be considered. If we let the Humans and Weres form an alliance that excludes us, they could completely wipe us out—"

"Oh my God." It suddenly dawns on me, the crazy, ridiculous place where he's heading, and I cover my eyes. "You are joking, right?"

"Misery."

"No." I let out a laugh. "You . . . *Father, we cannot marry our way out of this war.*" I don't know why I've switched to the Tongue, but it takes him aback. And maybe that's good, maybe this is what he needs. A moment to think this madness through. "Who would agree to this?"

Father looks at me so pointedly, I know. I just know.

And I burst into laughter.

I only ever laughed out loud with Serena, which means that it must have been well over a month since I last did it. My brain nearly hiccups, startled at these newfangled, mysterious sounds my voice box is producing. "Did you drink rotten blood? Because you're unhinged."

"What I am is charged with ensuring the good of the most, and the good of the most is the furthering of our people." He seems somewhat offended by my reaction, but I cannot help the laughter bubbling in my throat. "It would be a job, Misery. Compensated."

This is— God, this is *funny.* And mental. "No amount of legal tender would convince me to— Is it ten billion dollars?"

"No."

"Well, no *lower* amount of legal tender would convince me to marry a Were."

"Financially, you will be set for life. You know the council's pockets are deep. And there is no expectation of a real marriage. You'd be with him in name only. You'll be in Were territory for a single year, which will send the message that Vampyres can be safe with Weres—"

"Vampyres *cannot.*" I shoot to my feet and begin pacing away from him, massaging my temple. "Why are you asking *me*? I cannot be your first choice."

"You aren't," he says flatly. He has plenty of faults, but lack of honesty was never among them. "Nor our second. The council is in agreement that we must act, and several members have offered their relatives. Originally, Councilman Essen's daughter agreed. But she had a change of heart—"

"Oh, God." I stop pacing. "You're treating this as a Collateral exchange."

"Of course. And so are the Weres. The Alpha will send a Were to us. Someone important to him. She will be with us for as long as you are with him. Ensuring your reciprocal safety."

Bonkers. This is absolutely *bonkers*.

I take a grounding breath. "Well, I . . ." *Think everyone involved has lost their mind, and whoever shows up to that wedding is going to get slaughtered, and I cannot believe your sheer presumption in asking this of me.* ". . . am honored that you eventually thought of me, but no. Thanks."

"Misery."

I walk to the desk to pick up my phone—one minute, thirteen seconds left—and for a brief moment, I'm so close to Father, I feel the rhythm of his blood in my bones. Slow, steady, painfully familiar.

Heartbeats are like fingerprints, one of a kind, distinctive, the easiest way to tell people apart. Father's was pressed into my flesh on the day I was born, when he was the first person to hold me, the first person to care for me, the first person to know me.

And then he washed his hands of me.

"No," I say. To him. To myself.

"Roscoe's death is an opportunity."

"Roscoe's death was murder," I point out evenly. "By the hand of the man you'd have *me* marry."

"You know how many Vampyre children were born this year in the Southwest?"

"I don't care."

"Fewer than three hundred. If the Weres and the Humans join forces to take our land from us, they will wipe us out. Completely. The good of the most—"

"—is a cause I've already donated to, and no one is showing me much gratitude." I meet his eyes squarely. Slide my phone into my pocket with determination. "I've done enough. I have a life and I'm going back to it."

"Do you?"

I stop halfway through turning around. "Excuse me?"

"Do you have a life, Misery?" He looks at me when he says it, pointed, careful, like he's pushing a sharp weapon a mere millimeter into my neck.

I need you to care about one single fucking thing, Misery, one thing that's not me.

I push the memory away and swallow. "Good luck finding someone else."

"You feel unwelcome among your people. This could rehabilitate you in their eyes."

A frisson of anger runs through my spine. "I think I'll hold off on that, Father. At least until they have rehabilitated themselves in mine." I take a few steps backward, cheerfully waving my hand. "I'm leaving."

"My ten minutes aren't up yet."

My phone chooses that very moment to beep. "Exquisite timing." I flash him a smile. If my blunt fangs bother him, that's his problem. "I can safely say that no amount of time will change the outcome of this conversation."

"Misery." A pleading edge is creeping into his tone, which is almost entertaining.

Too bad. So sad. "See you in . . . seven years? Or when you decide that the key to peace is a joint Were-Vampyre MLM scheme and try to sell me dietary supplements. Do have Vania fetch me at home, though. I do *not* look forward to reorganizing my résumé." I turn around to find the doorknob.

"There won't be another opportunity in seven years, Misery."

I roll my eyes and open the door. "Goodbye, Father."

"Moreland is the first Alpha who—"

I slam the door shut, *without* first walking out of the office, and turn around, back toward Father. My heart slows to a crawl and thuds in my chest. "What did you just say?"

He straightens up from the desk, full of confusion and something that could be hope. "No other Were Alpha—"

"The name. You said a name. Who . . . ?"

"Moreland?" he repeats.

"His full name—what's his *first* name?"

Father's eyes narrow suspiciously, but after a few seconds, he says, "Lowe. Lowe Moreland."

I look down at the floor, which appears to be shaking. Then at the ceiling. I take a series of deep breaths, each one slower than the other, and then run a trembling hand through my hair, even though my arm weighs a thousand pounds.

I wonder if the blue dress I wore at Serena's college graduation would be too casual for an interspecies wedding ceremony. Because, yeah.

I guess I'm getting married.

CHAPTER 2

He used to think that all Vampyres' eyes looked the same. He may have been wrong about that.

Present day

S UCH AN UNFORTUNATE, DESOLATE CHOICE. WHAT LOVING parent would choose to name their child Misery?"

I don't consider myself a sensitive person. As a rule, I'm not opposed to people implying that I am a disappointment to my family and my species. But I do ask for one thing: that they keep that shit away from me.

And yet, here I am. With Governor Davenport. Leaning on my elbows over the balcony that overlooks the courtyard where I just got married. Biting back a sigh before explaining:

"The council."

"Pardon?"

Gauging intoxication levels in Humans is always a struggle, but I'm fairly sure the governor is not *not* drunk. "You asked who gave me my name. It was the Vampyre council."

"Not your parents?"

I shake my head. "That's not how it works."

"Ah. Are there . . . magic rituals involved? Sacrificial altars? Seers?"

So self-centeredly Human, the assumption that everything that's *other* must be shrouded in the supernatural and the arcane. They nurse their myths and legends, in which Vampyres and Weres are creatures of magic and lore, capable of curses and mystical acts. They think us able to see the future, to fly, to make ourselves invisible. Because we're different from them, our existence must be governed by otherworldly forces—and not simply, like theirs, by biology.

And maybe a couple of thermodynamics laws.

Serena was like that, too, when I first met her. "So crucifixes burn you?" she asked me a couple of weeks into our cohabitation, after I failed to convince her that the viscous red liquid I kept in my fridge was tomato juice.

"Only if they're, like, *very* hot."

"But you guys do hate garlic?"

I shrugged. "We don't really eat food in general, so . . . sure?"

"And how many people have you killed?"

"Zero," I told her, appalled. "How many people have *you* killed?"

"Hey, I'm *Human*."

"Humans kill all the time."

"Yeah, but indirectly. By making health insurance too expensive or stubbornly opposing gun control. You guys suck people dry to survive?"

I scoffed. "Drinking directly from a person is kinda gross and no one ever does it." It was a bit of a lie, but at the time I wasn't sure *why.* All I knew was that a few years earlier Owen and I had walked into the library to find Father latched onto the neck of Council-woman Selamio. Owen, who'd been more precocious and less of a social pariah, had covered my eyes with his hand and insisted that the trauma would stunt our growth. He'd never explained the reason, though. "Plus, blood banks are right there. So that we don't need to hurt Humans." I wondered if it had more to do with the fact that killing someone would be a lot of exhausting work, what with the thrashing around, and the burying of the corpse, and the Human police potentially showing up in the middle of the day, when all we want is to crawl into a dark space.

"What about the invitation business?"

"The what?"

"You need to be invited into a room, right?" I shook my head, hating that she looked disappointed. She was funny, and direct, and a little odd in a way that made her at once awesome and approachable. I was ten, and I already liked her more than anyone I'd ever met. "Can you at least read my mind? What am I thinking about?"

"Um." I scratched my nose. "That book you like. With the witches?"

"Not fair, I'm always thinking about that book. What *number* am I thinking?"

"Ah . . . seven?"

She gasped. "Misery!"

"Did I get it right?" Holy *crap*.

"*No!* I was thinking of three hundred and fifty-six. What *else* is a lie?"

The thing is, Humans and Weres and Vampyres might be different species, but we're closely related. What sets us apart has less to do with the occult, and more with spontaneous genetic mutations thousands of years down the line. And, of course, the values we developed in response. A loss of a purine base here, a repositioning of a hydrogen atom there, and ta-da: Vampyres feed exclusively on blood, are wimps with the sun, and are constantly on edge about extinction; Weres are faster, stronger, (I assume) hairier, and they worship violence. But neither of us can whip out our magic wand and lift a sixty-pound suitcase on top of a rack, or find out the Powerball numbers in advance—or turn into bats.

At least, Vampyres don't. I don't know enough about the Weres to get offended on their behalf.

"No naming rituals," I tell the governor. "Just a busybody council. No one wants five Madysons in the same class." I hold for a beat. "Plus, it seemed fitting, since I *did* kill my mother."

He hesitates, unsure how to react, and then lets out a nervous laugh. "Ah. Well. Still, as a name, it's very . . ." He looks around, as if grasping for the perfect word.

Oh, fine. "Miserable?"

He finger-guns at me and I shiver, either because I hate him or because it's starting to get way too cold for my Vampyre needs and my lace jumpsuit.

The gathering can only be defined as "a party" with *lots* of generosity. About one hour in, I decided that I had finally had enough. If my husband—my *husband*, who was on the edge of murdering me at our altar of connubial bliss because I stink—could be off somewhere discussing important matters with my father, I, too, could sneak away.

I made my way up to the mezzanine balcony to be alone. Unfortunately, the governor had the same idea, and brought along a watering can's worth of alcohol. He decided to join me—heartbreaking—and seems intent on making conversation—a fucking cataclysm. His eyes keep straying to Maddie Garcia's table, as though he's trying to incinerate her ahead of her inauguration next month. I should probably join him in his resentment toward the Human governor-elect, since her choices are what made this sham of a marriage necessary, but I cannot help admiring the way she has been expertly avoiding my father. She's definitely a smart woman. Unlike the bumbling idiot next to me.

"It's very brave, what you're doing, Miss Lark," he tells me, patting my shoulder. He must have misplaced the memo: Vampyres don't touch. "*Very* brave, in the face of great danger."

"Hmm." The reception is going as cartoonishly poorly as expected. Weres and Vampyres are seated at tables on opposite sides of the hall, exchanging hostile looks while the most unappreciated viola player in the world spends some quality time with Rachmaninoff. The Weres and the few Human guests have been served food prepared by a world-renowned chef, and make a valiant attempt at eating it despite the ugly atmosphere. "*Revolting,*" I overheard the daughter of Councilman Ross say in the Tongue as I slunk up here. "*Unsocialized beasts. They feed in public, shit in public, fuck in public.*" I refrained from pointing out that it's called "eating," and that the last two are illegal in the Human world. I'm just glad I managed to explain to the planner that one doesn't *sip blood at a party*, that feeding is a private act for Vampyres, never communal or recreational, and that no, serving blood cocktails with little umbrellas in them was not a "fun idea." When she asked, "What will the Vampyres do, while the Weres eat?" I guessed "Glare at them?" Boy, was I right.

"*Especially* brave, you are." The governor takes another swig. "What an interesting life you have led. A Vampyre raised among Humans. The famous Collateral. The Weres, it seems to me, have *two* reasons to hate you."

I distractedly run my tongue over my regrown fangs, wondering if a fight will break out. The hatred in the room is thick, suffocating. The Human guards, too, sharkle around, a little too eager to strike, curb, defend. A gust of wind could make this coiling tension snap.

"Then again, Moreland gave up a lot for this arrangement. The Collateral they're sending . . . The councilman's daughter for the Alpha's mate. Sounds like poetry, right?"

My head whips around. The Governor's eyes are glazed. "The Alpha's what?"

"Oh, I shouldn't have mentioned her. It's a secret, of course, but . . ." He chuckles deep in his throat and tips his glass at me.

"Did you say 'mate'? Like a spouse?"

"I'm not at liberty to divulge, Miss Lark. Or should I say, Mrs. Moreland?"

"Shit," I mutter softly, rubbing the bridge of my nose. Was Moreland married before? If that's the case, I cannot comprehend how pissed he must be at the prospect of being shackled to *me* while his wife is far away, first in line to the slaughter. Maybe that's why he flipped earlier?

That, and how I apparently smell like rotten eggs.

Well, tough shit, I tell myself as I push away from the railing. He and Father are the masterminds of this marriage. *I* am the masterminded. Hopefully he'll remember that and not direct his anger at me. "A pleasure chatting with you, governor," I lie, waving goodbye.

"If you decide to change it, call my office." He makes the phone hand gesture, the one old people use. "I can speed up the paperwork."

"Excuse me?"

"The name."

"Ah. Yes, thank you."

I head downstairs, in search of Owen. I think I saw him deep in conversation with Councilman Cintron earlier—gossiping, which he can do like a pro. I bet he can find out more about this *mate* business. Chances are, he already knew but didn't say anything because he found the thought of this poor woman jumping up in the middle of the ceremony to object *hilarious*, and wanted to see a rabid wolf eat my pancreas for being a home-wrecker in front of the upper crust of Vampyre society.

"—never heard of anything like it."

I halt abruptly, because—

My husband.

My husband is here, at the bottom of the stairs.

He got rid of his jacket, and the sleeves of his white shirt are rolled up. Two people stand with him: a Were with a ginger beard—the best man, if I'm not mistaken—and another, older, gray-haired, with a deep white scar on his neck. Their expressions are somber, and Moreland's arms are crossed on his chest.

It's a scene I've come across before, with my father: a powerful man, hearing important information from people he trusts. The last thing I want is to walk past them right now, in close competition with the second to last—reprising my conversation with the governor. Still, I'm ready to go back and hear more about the failures of my given name, until:

"—the consequences, if it really is *her*," the best man continues.

It's the *her* that stops me in my tracks. Because it feels like it might be referring to . . .

Moreland presses his lips together. His jaw clenches and he says something, but his voice is deeper, lower than his companions'. I cannot make out the words over the background noises.

"It must have been a moment of confusion. She cannot be your—" The string music suddenly soars, and I inch closer, just one step down the stairs.

Lowe's broad back stiffens. I'm afraid he heard me move, but he doesn't turn. I relax when he says, "You think it's a mistake I would make?"

The older man freezes. Then hangs his head, apologetic. "I do not, Alpha."

"We need to change our plans, Lowe." The ginger. "Find other accommodations. You shouldn't live with—" A commotion erupts in the hall, and their heads lift in its direction. When I follow suit, my stomach drops.

A short distance away, two children are bawling. They are toddlers, one with dark skin and lilac eyes, the other pale and blue-eyed. A Vampyre and a Were. Between them lies a dark blue superhero action figure, broken in two at the waist. And next to them, clutching their respective sons, are a Vampyre father and a Were mother. Who, for reasons I cannot divine, thought that bringing *children* here would be a good idea, and now are showing their fangs at each other. Growling. Drawing the attention of the other guests, who start to gather around them protectively. Or maybe aggressively.

The music stops when the noise in the room rises to a panicked pitch. A small crowd surrounds the kids, and the Human guards join it, drawing their weapons and bringing firearms into the mess. My heart thumps dully in my chest as the tension grows fat and sticky, the start of another massacre that will go down in the history books—

"Here."

Lowe Moreland kneels between the children, and the room

drops to a deafening silence. The Vampyre's father, whom I now recognize as Councilman Sexton, pushes his son behind his legs, upper lip peeled back to reveal his long canines.

"It's all good," Moreland says. Calm. Reassuring. Not to the father, but to the child. As he holds out the intact action figure— not broken, after all.

The boy hesitates. Then his hand darts out from between his father's knees to collect his toy, mouth widening into a toothy smile.

Several of the guests exhale in relief. Not me, though. Not yet.

"Anything you'd like to say?" Moreland asks, this time to the Were child. The boy blinks several times before looking at the ground with a pout.

"Sorry," he mumbles, the *r*'s rounded into *w*'s. He looks on the verge of crying, but then dissolves into laughter when Moreland ruffles his hair and picks him up, effortlessly wedging him under his arm like a football. He turns around, giving his back to the group of Vampyres assembled around the Sextons, and returns the little Were to his table.

Just like that, the tension relaxes. Vampyres and Weres return to their seats with a few lingering looks of distrust. The music resumes. My husband makes his way back to the bottom of the stairs, without lifting his eyes or noticing me, and I finally let out the breath I was holding.

"Make sure it doesn't happen again. Tell the others, too," he quietly orders the ginger and the older Were, who nod and leave to mix with the guests. Moreland sighs, and I wait for a handful of seconds, hoping he'll join them and clear my way.

Two handfuls.

What feels a lot like a minute.

A minute and *more* handfuls—

"I know you're there," he says, not looking at anyone in particular. I have no idea who he's addressing until he adds, "Come down, Miss Lark."

Oh.

Well.

This is nicely mortifying.

There are about ten steps separating us, and I *could* crawl my way down in shame. But our species have been mortal enemies since electricity wasn't a thing, which might put us beyond embarrassment. What's some eavesdropping among foes?

"In your own time," he adds wryly.

Given the . . . incident a couple of hours ago, I'm hesitant to go stand next to him. But perhaps I shouldn't have worried: when I reach his side, his nostrils twitch and a muscle jumps in his jaw, but that's about it. Moreland doesn't look my way, nor does he seem too tempted to mangle me.

Progress.

Still, I have no idea what to say. So far we've only exchanged recited promises that neither of us means to keep, and some commentary on my body odor. "You can call me Misery."

He's quiet for a beat. "Yeah. I probably should."

We fall into silence. In the far corner of the courtyard, what seems to be another small ruckus involving a Were and Vampyre nearly pops up, but it's swiftly curbed by a Were woman I vaguely remember standing by the altar.

"Do we have another interspecies brawl?" I ask.

Moreland shakes his head. "Just some idiot who drank too much."

"Not from a Were, I hope."

I regret the words the second they're out of my mouth. I'm not usually a nervous blabberer, because I'm not usually *nervous*. One doesn't serve as the Collateral for a decade without learning a baffling number of anxiety management strategies. And yet.

"Did you just joke about *your* people drinking *my* people dry?"

I close my eyes. Death would be nice, right now. I'd welcome it with open arms. "It was in terrible taste. I apologize." I look up at him, and there they are. Those eerie, unearthly, beautiful eyes, glowing at me in the dim lights, a chilling green that borders on feral. I wonder if I'll get used to them. If one year from now, when this arrangement is complete, I'll still think them bizarrely lovely.

I wonder what Serena thought when she first saw them.

"They're expecting us," Moreland says curtly. My apology dangles, not accepted, not rejected.

"Who?"

He points at the orchestra. The viola player lifts her bow in the air for a beat, and then the music switches gears. Not Rachmaninoff, but a slow, instrumental rendition of a pop song I've heard in line at the grocery store. Did Moreland approve of this? I bet the planner went rogue.

"First dance," he says, holding out his hand. His voice is deep, precise, economical. A man who's used to giving orders and having them answered. I look at his long fingers, remembering how they closed on my arm. That moment of fear. Thing is, I don't *feel* a lot, and when I do—

"Misery," he says, a trace of impatience in his tone, and my name sounds like a different word in his voice. I take his hand, watch it engulf mine. Follow him onto the dance floor. We had no photographer at the ceremony, but there are a couple here. When we reach the center of the hall, Moreland's palm splays on my back, where my jumpsuit dips low. His fingers briefly travel down my wrist, brushing against the marking, then wrap around mine. We start swaying to a peal of sparse, half-hearted applause.

I have never slow-danced before, but it's not too difficult. Perhaps because my partner is doing most of the work.

"So." I glance up, attempting conversation. In these shoes I push six feet, but there's no towering over this man. "I smell like sewers or something?" It cannot be easy for him, being this close to me.

He stiffens. Then relaxes. I think he won't reply until his terse "Or something."

I wish I could commiserate, but Vampyres don't comprehend scents the way other species do. Serena used to point at flowers and spin wild tales of beautiful fragrances, then act shocked that I couldn't tell them apart. But plants are insignificant to us, and I was just as shocked that she had no awareness of people's heartbeats. Of the blood coursing through her own veins.

It's a pity that I smell foul to Moreland, because his blood is nice. Engulfing. Healthy and earthy and a bit rough. His heartbeat is strong and vibrant, like a caress to the roof of my mouth. I don't think it's just a Were thing, because the others here at the wedding seem less inviting. But maybe I just haven't gotten close enough to—

"Does your father hate you?"

"Excuse me?" We're still swaying. Cameras click around us like insects in the summertime. Maybe I misheard.

"Your father. I need to know if he hates you."

I meet Moreland's eyes, more baffled than offended. And perhaps a little peeved that I cannot insist that my one living parent gives a shit about me. "Why?"

"If you're going to be under my protection, I need to know these things."

47

I cock my head up at him. His face is so . . . not handsome, even though it is, but striking. All-consuming. Like he invented bone structure. "Am I? Under your protection?"

"You're my wife."

God, it sounds weird. "In name, maybe." I shrug, and it makes my body brush against his. His eyes do an odd thing, the pupils acting out, contracting and expanding of their own volition. Then they settle on the markings painted on my neck. He seems unwarrantedly taken by them. "I think I'm just a symbol of goodwill between our people. And Collateral."

"And being a Collateral is your full-time job."

I can't even counter that, since Vania got me fired. "I dabble."

He nods thoughtfully, turning me around. New couples are starting to join us, none looking enthused—likely marched to the dance floor by our zealous wedding planner. My eyes meet Deanna Dryden's; she held me down and stuffed my mouth with feathers when I was seven, disappeared from my life for ten years, then called me a Humanfucker in front of a crowd of dozens when we next crossed paths. We nod at each other politely.

"Let's see, Misery." My name is pointed—at what, I'm not certain. "You were formally announced as the Collateral when you were six, and then sent to the Humans at eight. You had twenty-four seven protective detail—all Human guards—and yet over the following decade, you suffered several assassination attempts by anti-Vampyre extremist groups. All failed, but two came *very* close, and I'm told you have the scars to prove it. Then, when your term as the Collateral finally ended, you briefly returned to Vampyre territory, then chose to adopt a fake identity and live among the Humans—something Vampyres are forbidden from doing. If you were a member of my own family, I would never have allowed any of it. And now you've signed up to marry a Were, which is the most dangerous thing someone in your situation could do, with nothing to gain and no obvious reason—"

"I'm flattered that you skimmed my file." I bat my eyes up at him. He does seem to have the whats and the wheres, if not the whys. "I read yours, too. You're an architect by training, right?"

His body tenses, and he pushes me away for—no, he's just whirling me around to the music. "Why is your father so remiss when it comes to your survival?"

His blood really *does* smell nice. "I'm not some kind of victim," I say quietly.

"No?"

"I agreed to this marriage. I'm not being forced into anything. And you—"

His arm snatches abruptly around my waist, and he pulls me closer to avoid another couple. My front plasters against him, his scorching heat a shock to my cool skin. He really is foreign. Different. Incompatible with me in every possible way. It's a relief when he puts some distance between us and we're again comfortably apart. The thought of him already being in a relationship flits into my head once more, intrusive and unprompted, and I have to track down my abandoned sentence. "And you are putting yourself in the exact same situation."

"I'm the Alpha of my people." His voice is hoarse. "Not a white-hat hacker who only miraculously made it to twenty-five."

Ouch, and fuck you. "What I am is an adult woman with agency and the tools to make choices. Feel free to, you know, treat me accordingly."

"Fair." He hums agreeably. "Why *did* you consent to this marriage, though?"

Have you ever heard the name Serena Paris? I nearly ask. But I already know the answer to that, and the question would only give him something to hide. I have a plan, a painstakingly drawn one. And I'm going to stick to it. "I like to live dangerously."

"Or desperately." The music plays on, but Moreland halts, and so do I. We stare, a hint of challenge swirling between us.

"I'm sure I don't know what you mean."

"You don't?" He nods. Like he wasn't going to say what's coming next but doesn't mind continuing. "The Vampyres don't claim you as one of them unless they have something to gain from it. You chose to be among the Humans, but you had to lie about your identity, because you're not one of them. And you're definitely not one of *us*. You truly belong nowhere, Miss Lark." His head dips closer. For a terrible, head-splitting second, my heart pumps with the certainty that he's going to kiss me. But he bends past my mouth, to the shell of my ear. Through a landslide of what has to be relief, I hear him inhale and say, "And you smell like you know all of this very, *very* well."

That hint of challenge solidifies, heavy as concrete, into something cities could be built on. "Maybe you should stop breathing in so much," I say, pulling back to look him squarely in the eye.

And then everything happens much too quickly.

The glint of steel at the corner of my view. An unfamiliar, rage-filled voice yelling, "You Vampyre *bitch*!" Hundreds of gasps, and a sharp blade making its way toward my throat, my jugular, and—

The knife stops a hairbreadth from my skin. I don't remember closing my eyes, and when I open them my brain cannot seem to catch up: someone—a Human, dressed as a waiter—came at me with a knife. I did not notice him. The guards did not notice him. My husband, on the other hand . . .

Lowe Moreland's palm is wrapped around the blade, less than an inch from my neck. Green blood trickles down his forearm, its rich scent crashing into me like a wave. There is no sign of pain in his eyes as they hold mine.

He just saved my life.

"Nowhere, Misery," he murmurs, lips barely moving. In the distance, Father is barking orders. Security finally reacts, pulls away the thrashing waiter. A few guests gasp, scream, and maybe *I* should scream, too, but I don't have the wherewithal to do anything until my husband tells me, "For the next year, let's make sure to stay out of each other's way. Understood?"

I try to swallow. Fail the first time, do a great job the second. "And they say romance is dead," I say, pleased not to sound as dry throated as I feel. He hesitates for a moment, and I could swear he inhales again, deep, storing up . . . something. His hand tightens on my back for a second before finally letting go.

And then Lowe Moreland, my husband, stalks off the dance floor, a trail of forest-green blood tracking his path.

Leaving me blissfully alone on the night of our wedding.

CHAPTER 3

He is under siege in his own home.

THE VOICE IS YOUNG AND SULLEN. IT WORMS ITS WAY UNDER my pillow and into my ears, nudging me awake in the dead middle of the day.

"This used to be my room," it says.

The floor is hard underneath me. My brain is blurry and my ears are made of cotton and I don't know *where* I am, *why*, *who* would commit this ignominy upon my person: wake me up when the sun is bright in the sky and I am sapped of all strength.

"Can I hide in here? She's grumpy today."

I gather six months' worth of energy and unearth myself from under the blankets, but run out of steam when it comes to lifting my eyelids.

No, we Vampyres don't pulverize in the sun like glitter bombs. Sunlight burns us and it *hurts*, but it won't kill us unless the exposure is unfiltered and prolonged. However, we *are* pretty useless in the middle of the day, even inside. Lethargic and weak and crawly and headachy, especially during late spring and summer, when the rays hit at that pesky steep angle. *"This crepuscularity of yours is really cramping my brunch lifestyle,"* Serena used to say. *"Also, the fact that you don't eat."*

"Is it true that you don't have a soul?"

It's goddamn *noon*. And there is a *child* here, asking me:

"Because you used to be dead?"

I crane my eyes to a semi-open slit and find her right here, in the closet where I made my bed early this morning. Her heartbeat hops happily around, like a pent-up fawn. She's round faced. Curly haired. American Girl dolled.

Very annoying.

"Who are you?" I ask.

"And then you were forced to drink someone's blood?"

She is, I would estimate, anywhere between three and a young thirteen. I have no way of narrowing this down any further: with this one, my staggering indifference toward children meets my twenty-five-year-old determination to avoid anything Were. And on top of everything, her eyes are a pale, dangerous, familiar green.

I don't like this. "How did you get in here?"

She points at the open closet door like I'm a little daft. "And then you came back to life, but without your soul?"

I squint at her in the near darkness, grateful that she hasn't pulled the curtains. "Is it true that *you* were bitten by a rabid dog and are now a furry who froths at the mouth during the full moon?" I'm trying to be a bitch, but she lets out a peal of laughter that has me feeling like a stand-up comedian.

"No, silly."

"Well, then. You have your answer. While I still don't know how you got in here." She points at the door again, and I make a mental note to never have children. "I locked that." I'm sure I did.

I'm positive that I did not spend my first night among the Weres without locking my damn door. I figured that even with their super strength, if one of them decided to wolf me down, a locked door *would* keep them out. Because Weres would build Were-proof doors, right?

"I have a spare key," Were-child says.

Oh.

"This used to be my room. So if I had nightmares, I got to go to Lowe. Through there." She points at another door. Whose doorknob I didn't try last night. I suspected who the adjoining room would belong to, and I didn't feel like processing that kind of trauma at five a.m. "He says that I can still go, but now I'm across the hallway."

A tinge of guilt penetrates my exhaustion: I've evicted a three-(thirteen?)-year-old from her room and am forcing her to cross an entire hallway in the grip of horrific, recurring nightmares to reach her . . .

Oh, crap. "Please tell me Moreland's not your father."

She doesn't reply. "Do you ever get nightmares?"

"Vampyres don't dream." I mean, I can deal with separating true lovers or whatnot, but an entire family? A child from her . . . Oh, *shit*. "Where is your mother?"

"I'm not sure."

"Does she live here?"

"Not anymore."

Fuck. "Where did she go?"

She shrugs. "Lowe said that it's impossible to tell."

I rub my eyes. "Is Moreland—is Lowe your dad?"

"Ana's father is dead." The voice comes from outside the closet, and we both turn.

Standing in the light seeping in from the hallway is a red-haired woman. She's pretty, strong, fit in a way that suggests that she could run a half-marathon with no notice. She stares at me with a mix of worry and hostility, like my kink is burning crickets with kerosene.

"Many Were children are orphaned, most of them at the hands of Vampyres like you. Best not ask them about the whereabouts of their parents. Come here, Ana."

Ana runs to her, but not before whispering at me, "I like your pointy ears," entirely too loud.

I'm too bone-tired to deal with any of this at midday. "I had no idea. I'm sorry, Ana."

Ana seems unperturbed. "It's okay. Juno's just grouchy. Can I come over to play with you when—"

"Ana, go downstairs and get a snack. I'll be there in a minute."

Ana sighs, and rolls her eyes, and pouts like she was asked to file a tax return, but eventually she does leave, sneaking me an impish smile. My sleep-addled brain briefly considers returning it, then recalls that I let my fangs regrow.

"She's Lowe's sister," Juno informs me protectively. "Please, stay away from her."

"You might want to take this up with her, since she still has a spare key to her old room."

"Stay away," she repeats. Less worried, more threatening.

"Right. Sure." I can live without hanging out with someone whose skull hasn't even properly closed yet. Though Ana *is* technically my BFF in Were territory. Slim pickings over here. "Juno, right? I'm Misery."

"I know."

I figured. "Are you one of Lowe's seconds?"

She tenses, crossing her arms to her chest. Her eyes are hooded. "You shouldn't."

"Shouldn't?"

"Ask questions about the pack. Or strike up conversation with us. Or walk around unsupervised."

"That's a lot of rules." To give to an adult. For *one year.*

"Rules will keep you safe." Her chin lifts. "And keep others safe from you."

"That's a very honorable sentiment. But it might reassure you to know that I lived among the Humans for nearly two decades, and murdered . . ." I pretend to check a note on my palm. "A whole zero. Wow."

"It will be different here." Her eyes move from mine and trace the contours of the room, still a mess of moving boxes and piles of clothes. Her gaze hiccups on the bare mattress, now stripped of the sheets and blankets that I dragged inside the closet, then stops on the only thing I put up on the wall: a Polaroid of me and Serena looking away from the camera during that sunset lake tour we did two years ago. Some guy took it without asking, while we were dangling our feet in the water. Then he showed it to us and said he'd only return it if one of us gave him our number. We did the only logical thing: caught him in a headlock and forcibly took the photo.

All that self-defense we learned, as it turns out, works for offense, too.

"I know what you're trying to do," Juno says, and for a moment I'm afraid that she read my mind. That she knows I'm here to search for Serena. But she continues, "You can try to paint yourself as a pawn, say that you only agreed to this in the name of peace, but . . . I don't believe it. And I don't like you."

No shit. "And I don't know you enough to make a judgment.

Your jeans are cool, though." Riveting conversation, but I'm about to pass out. Thankfully, with one last withering look, Juno leaves.

The corner of my eye catches a hint of movement. I turn, half expecting Ana to make a comeback, but it's just Serena's goddamned fucking cat, stretching his way out from under the bed.

"*Now* you show up."

He hisses at me.

———— ✦ ————

DURING OUR FIFTEEN-YEAR FRIENDSHIP, I AMASSED HALF A MILlion small, big, and midsize reasons to love Serena Paris with the intensity of the brightest stars. Then, a few weeks ago, one came to obliterate all of them, driving me to loathe her with the strength of a thousand full moons.

Her damn fucking cat.

As a rule, Vampyres don't do pets. Or pets don't do Vampyres? I'm not sure who started it. Maybe they think we smell yucky because we're obligate hemovores. Maybe we rejected them because they get along so well with Weres and Humans. Either way, when I began living among the Humans, the concept of a domestic animal felt supremely foreign to me.

My first caregiver had a little dog that she sometimes carried around in her purse, and honestly, I'd have been less shocked if she'd combed her hair with a toilet brush. I eyed him suspiciously for a few days. Showed him my fangs when he showed his. Finally, I found the courage to ask the caregiver when she was going to eat him.

She quit that night.

Animals and I went on to do absolutely great ever since, giving each other wide berths on sidewalks and exchanging the occasional dirty look. It was pure bliss—until Serena's damn fucking cat came into the picture. I tried my best to dissuade her from adopting it. She tried her best to pretend she didn't hear me. Then, about three days after taking home thirteen pounds of asshole from the shelter, she vanished into the ether.

Poof.

Growing up collecting attempted murders like milk teeth tempered me and taught me to be calm under pressure. And yet I still remember it, that first churning twist in my stomach when Serena didn't turn up to my place for laundry night. Didn't reply to my texts. Didn't pick up the phone. Didn't call in sick to work, and simply stopped showing up. It felt a lot like fear.

Maybe it wouldn't have happened if we'd still been living together. And honestly, I'd have been okay sharing an apartment. But after spending her first few years in an orphanage and her second few years as the companion of the best-monitored Vampyre child in the world, she'd only wanted one thing: privacy. She'd given me a set of spare keys, though, and it had felt like such a precious, beautiful honor bestowed upon me; I'd carefully hidden them in a secret place. That by the time she disappeared, I'd long forgotten.

So that day I broke into her apartment using a hairpin. Just the way she taught me when we were twelve, and the TV room was off-limits, and one movie per day wasn't quite enough. Reassuringly, her rotten corpse was not folded in the chest freezer, or anywhere else. I fed her damn fucking cat as he meowed like he was approaching starvation *and* hissed at me at the same time; checked that my brown contacts were in place and my fangs still properly dulled; then went to the authorities to report a missing person.

And was told: "She's probably hanging out with her boyfriend somewhere."

I made myself blink, to look extra Human. "Can't believe she told *you* about her love life and not *me*, her closest friend of fifteen years."

"Listen, young lady." The officer sighed. He was a lanky, middle-aged man with more heart rate turbulence than most. "If I had a nickel for every time someone 'disappears,' and by that I mean, they leave and neglect to tell someone in their social circle where they're going—"

"You'd have how much?" I lifted an eyebrow.

He seemed flustered, though not enough for my taste. "I bet she's on vacation. Does she ever take trips on her own?"

"Yes, often, but she always warns me. Plus, she's an investigative reporter for *The Herald*, and did not take days off." According to their system. Which I hacked.

"Maybe she was out of vacation days and still wanted to, I dunno, drive to Las Vegas to see her aunt. Just a misunderstanding."

"We had plans to meet, and she's an orphan with no family or friends who doesn't own a car. According to her banking portal, to which she gave me access"—kind of—"no cash withdrawals or on-line payments were processed. But maybe you're correct, and she's bouncing to Las Vegas on her pogo stick?"

"No need to get testy, honey. We all want to think that we're important to the people who are important to us. But sometimes, our best friend is someone else's best friend."

I closed my eyes to roll them behind my lids.

"Did you two maybe have a fight?" the officer asked.

I crossed my arms on my chest and sucked my cheeks in. "That's not the point—"

"Ha."

"Okay." I frowned. "Let's say Serena secretly hates me. She still wouldn't leave her cat, would she?"

He paused. Then, for the first time, he nodded and picked up a notepad. I felt a spark of hope. "Cat's name?"

"She hasn't gotten around to naming him yet, though last we spoke she'd narrowed it down between Maximilien Robespierre and—"

"How long has she had this cat?"

"A few days? She still wouldn't let the little asshole starve," I hurried to add, but the officer had already dropped his pen. And even though I went back to the station three times that week, and eventually managed to get a missing person report filed, no one did anything to find Serena. The hazard, I guess, of being alone in the world: no one to care that she was safe, and healthy, and *alive*. No one but me, and I didn't count. I shouldn't have been surprised, and I wasn't. But apparently I still had the capacity to feel hurt.

Because no one cared whether *I* was safe, or healthy, or alive. No one but Serena. The sister of my heart, if not of my blood. And even though I'd been *plenty* alone, I'd never felt so lonely as after she was gone.

I wished I could cry. I wished for lacrimal ducts to let out this horrible terror that she'd left forever, that she'd been taken, that she was in pain, that it was my fault and I'd driven her away with our last conversation. Unfortunately, biology was not on my side. So I worked through my feelings by going to her place and taking care of her damn fucking cat, who showed his gratitude by scratching me every single day.

And, of course, by looking for her where I shouldn't have.

I had the keys, after all. Because the key to everything is but a line of code. I was able to rifle through her bank statements, IP addresses, cell phone locations. *Herald* emails, metadata, app usage.

Serena was a journalist, one who wrote about delicate financial stuff, and the most likely option was that she'd gotten embroiled in something fishy while working on a story, but I wasn't going to exclude other possibilities. So I went through everything, and found . . . nothing.

Absolutely *nothing*.

Serena's poof had been quite literal. But one cannot move in the world without leaving digital traces, which could only mean one thing. One terrible, blood-curdling thing that I couldn't even put into words in the privacy of my own head.

And that's when I did it: I kneeled in front of Serena's damn fucking cat. He was playing like he always did after dinner, pawing at a crumpled receipt in a corner of the living room, but managed to squeeze a couple of hisses into his busy schedule just for me. "Listen." I swallowed. Rubbed my hand on my chest and then even slapped it, trying to dull the ache. "I know you only knew her for a few days, but I really, really . . ." I scrunched my eyes shut. Oh *fuck*, this was hard. "I don't know how it happened, but I think that Serena might be . . ."

I opened my eyes, because I owed it to this asshole cat to look at him. And that's when I got a good view of it.

The receipt, which wasn't a balled-up receipt at all. It was a piece of paper torn from a journal, or perhaps a notebook, or—no. A planner. Serena's incredibly outdated planner.

The page was for the day of her disappearance. And there was a string of letters on it, written quickly in black marker. Gibberish.

Or maybe not quite. A distant bell rang, reminding me of a game Serena and I used to play as kids, a primitive substitution cipher we made up to gossip freely in front of our caregivers. We'd named it the butterfly alphabet, and it mostly consisted of adding *b-* and *f-* syllables to normal words. Nothing complicated: even rusty as I was, it took my brain only a few seconds to untangle it. And once I was done, I had something. I had three whole words:

L. E. MORELAND

CHAPTER 4

They say keep your friends close and your enemies closer.
They don't know what they're talking about.

SPORADIC BOUTS OF TEENAGE IDIOCY NOTWITHSTANDING, I doubt a Vampyre has been in Were territory for centuries.

I felt it in my bones last night, as my driver sank farther past the river. Serena's damn cat fidgeted in the carrier next to me, and I knew that I was really, *truly* alone. Being with the Humans was like living in a different country, but here? Another galaxy. Deep space exploration.

The house I was brought to is built on a lake, surrounded by thick, gnarly trees on three sides and placid water on the remaining one. Nothing cave-like or underground, despite what I'd have imagined from a wolf-related species, and yet odd nonetheless, with its warm materials and large windows. Like the Weres teamed up with the landscape and decided to build something beautiful together. It's a bit jarring, especially after spending the last six weeks shuttling between the sterility of Vampyre territory and the crowded bustle of the Humans. Avoiding the sunlight is going to be an issue, and so is the fact that the temperature is kept considerably lower than is comfortable for Vampyres. I can deal with that, though. What I was really bracing myself for was . . .

In my third year as the Collateral, at a diplomatic dinner, I was introduced to an elderly matron. She was wearing a sequined dress, and when she lifted her hand to pinch my cheeks, I noticed that her antique bracelet was made of very unusually shaped, very pretty pearls.

They were fangs. Pulled from the corpses of Vampyres—or live ones, for all I know.

I didn't scream, or cry, or attack that old hag. I was paralyzed, unable to function properly for the rest of the night, and only started processing what had happened when I got home and told Serena, who was furious on my behalf and demanded a promise from the caregiver on shift: that I would never be forced to attend a similar function again.

I was, of course. Many, many times, and I encountered many, many people who acted like that sparkly bitch. Because the bracelets, the necklaces, the vials of blood, were nothing but messages. Displays of discontentment for an alliance that, while long established, in many pockets of the population was still controversial.

I expected something even worse from the Weres. I wouldn't have been shocked to see five of us impaled in the yard, slowly bleeding to death. No such thing, though. Just a bunch of syca-mores, and the flutter of my new friend Alex's rabbity heartbeat.

Oh, Alex.

"I know I said this is Lowe's house, but he's the Alpha, which means that lots of pack members come and go, and his seconds who live in the area are, um, pretty much always here," he says, walking me through the kitchen. He's young, and cute, and wears khaki pants with an improbable number of pockets. When I met Juno earlier today, she clearly wanted to shove me under a giant magnifying glass and burn me alive, but Alex is just terrified at the idea of showing a Vampyre around her new accommodations. And yet, he's rising to the occasion: running a hand through his mop of light hair to let me know that "There have been, um, *suggestions*, that you might want to store your, um . . . *things* in the other fridge over there. So if you *please* could . . . If it were *possible* . . . If it *isn't* a bother . . ."

I end his suffering. "Don't keep my gory blood bags next to the mayo jar. Got it."

"Yes, thank you." He nearly slumps in relief. "And, um, there are no blood banks that cater to Vampyres in the area, because, well—"

"Any Vamps in the area would be swiftly exterminated?"

"Precisely. Wait, no. *No*, that's not what I—"

"I was kidding."

"Oh." He pulls back from the verge of a heart attack. "So, there are no banks, and you're obviously not at liberty to just walk in and out of our territory—"

"I'm not?" I gasp, and instantly feel guilty when he takes a step back and fingers his collar. "Sorry. Another joke." I wish I could smile reassuringly at him. Without looking like I'm about to butcher everything that he holds dear, that is.

"Do you, um, have . . . preferences?"

"Preferences?"

"Like . . . AB, or O negative, or . . ."

"Ah." I shake my head. Common misconception, but cold blood is nearly flavorless, and the only things that would influence its taste would disqualify people from donating in the first place. Illnesses, mostly.

"And when do you . . . ?"

"Feed? Once a day. More when it gets really warm—heat makes us hungry." He looks queasy at the mention of blood, more so than I'd have expected from someone who turns into a wolf and mauls rabbits by the litterful. So I wander away to give him a minute to recover, taking in the stone accent wall and the fireplace. Despite the chill, there's something just *right* about this house. As though its place was meant to be here, carved between the trees and the waterfront.

It's probably the nicest home I've ever lived in. Not bad, since there's a nonzero chance that I'll also croak in it.

"Are you one of his seconds?" I ask Alex, turning away from the waves lapping at the pier. "More— Lowe's, I mean."

"No." He's younger, softer than Juno. Not as defensive and buttoned up, but more jittery. I've caught him squinting at the points of my ears three times already. "Ludwig is . . . The second from my huddle is someone else."

His what? "How many seconds does Lowe have?"

"Twelve." He pauses to stare at his feet. "Eleven, actually, now that Gabrielle was sent to the . . ."

Gabrielle, I file away for future perusal. God, is that the mate? Was she his wife *and* his second?

Alex clears his throat. "Gabrielle will be replaced."

"By you?"

"No, I wouldn't . . . And I'm not from her huddle; it'll have to be someone who . . ." He scratches his neck and falls silent. Oh, well.

"Are there any close neighbors?" I ask.

"Yeah. But 'close' is different for us. Because we can . . ."

"Transform into wolves?"

"No. Well, yeah, but . . ." His cheeks have an olive tinge. God, I think he's blushing. Because of course they'd flush green. "Shift.

We call it shifting. We don't become something else. We just kind of toggle between two settings."

This time I do smile, keeping my lips sealed. "Love the coding references."

"You like tech?"

"I like what tech can do." I lean against the counter. Years with the Humans, and I'm still freaked out that houses contain entire huge-ass rooms dedicated to the preparation of *food*. "So, when you guys shift into wolves, do you still think the same way? Does your brain shift with you, too?"

Alex mulls it. "Yes and no. There are some instincts that take over in that form, more than they otherwise would. The impulse to hunt, for instance, is very powerful. To chase a scent, track down an enemy. That's why you maybe shouldn't venture out alone to . . ."

"Skinny-dip at midnight?"

He looks away. He's kind of adorable, in an *I want to tie his shoelaces and blow on his skinned knee* kind of way. "Do you . . . It's probably bullshit, but I just wanted to make sure . . . Vampyres don't, right?"

I tilt my head. "Don't what?"

"Shift into animals. Not that I believe the bat rumor, but just in case you're going to fly away and . . ."

I bet Alex gets along great with Ana. "Nope, I do not turn into a bat. Would be lovely, though."

"Okay, good." He seems incredibly relieved. I decide to take advantage of that, broadcasting a mix of casualness and very mild interest in my surroundings, then say offhandedly:

"Can you shift into a wolf whenever you want? Or is the full moon thing just a rumor?"

"It depends, I guess."

"On what?"

"How powerful a Were is. Being able to shift at will, it's a sign of dominance. Being able to avoid shifting during the full moon, too."

I don't know what possesses me to ask, "What about Lowe? Is he powerful?"

Alex lets out a startled laugh. "He is the most powerful Were I've ever seen. And that my grandfather has ever seen—and he's seen many Alphas."

"Oh." I pick up a ladle. Or a spatula. I forgot which one is which. "Is he powerful because he can shift whenever he wants?"

Alex frowns. "No. That's just part of who he is, but—everyone knew that he had the making of an Alpha." His eyes are starting to shine. A Moreland stan, clearly. "He was the fastest runner, and the best tracker, and even his scent was right. That's why Roscoe sent him away."

"Not a dumb move, since in the end Lowe killed Roscoe."

Alex blinks at me. "He didn't kill him. He challenged him, and Roscoe died through that process."

There must be cultural nuances that I'm not grasping here, not to mention that Roscoe was, by all accounts, a bloodthirsty sadist. Doesn't seem like a huge loss, so I don't press it. "Is my roomie Lowe usually gone during the day?" It's about six p.m., but I can't hear anyone moving about the place. Maybe Moreland is avoiding home because I stank it up? I took a bath when I woke up, and soaked for a long time. Not quite an olive branch, but . . . an olive. "What about Ana?"

"Ana is with Juno." Alex shrugs. "Lowe is off to deal with the sabotage that happened this morning, and . . ."

I cock my head, and it's a mistake—too much broadcasted interest. Alex takes a step back, clearing his throat. "Actually, they're out on a run," he says, and he must be the worst liar I've ever seen. I'm tempted to pat his back, let him know that he's doing great and won't go to hell for making stuff up.

Instead, I push harder. "Have you ever seen Humans in this house?"

"Humans?" His brow furrows. "Like who?"

Serena's face flashes through my head. She's rolling her eyes because I'm wearing a galaxy T-shirt I got for free when I bought a lava lamp. *Who wears this, Misery? No—who buys a lava lamp?*

"Any Human." I shrug artfully. "Just curious."

I don't think he buys it. "I've never seen a Human in Were territory." He gives me a suspicious look. I've played my hand too heavily. "And this is the Alpha's home. A place for Weres to feel safe."

"Except, now I live here." I play with my silver wedding band—a habit I've picked up in less than twenty-four hours. I've never been much for jewelry, but maybe I'll keep it when I find Serena and this is over. Or buy one of those mood rings that think Vampyres are always sad because our body temperature is low. "Why?"

"Um, what do you mean?"

"I'm just surprised Lowe would want me around."

"You're married."

"Not for real, though. Lowe and I didn't meet on a Caribbean vacation and fall in love while getting our scuba diving certificates."

"It's not a matter of love."

I lift my eyebrow.

"Having you live with him—it's about protection. Making a commitment. Sending a message. They know you're not his true wife or his mate or anything."

Ah, yes, the famed *mate*. Who probably used to live in his house. I nod, not quite understanding. Then again, I don't understand Humans or Vampyres, either. I'm sure the Weres have their reasons to do what they do.

Just like I have mine.

"So, I shouldn't head out on my own, but inside the house I can be wherever I want?"

Alex's shoulders relax at the change of topic. "Sure. Maybe stay out of Lowe's and Ana's rooms. And his office."

"Of course." I smile just a little. Fangless. "And where's the office?"

He points at the hallway behind me. "Left, then right."

"Perfect. I just hope I don't get lost." I shrug airily, and plant my first lie: "My orientation skills are pretty bad."

———— ⌇ ————

THE FIRST TIME I SEARCHED ONLINE FOR L. E. MORELAND, I FOUND two things: a semi-defunct GeoCities website promoting a wholly defunct real estate agent, and the infinite vastness of nothing.

So I searched again, the way penetration testers do: with some disregard for doors. I jumped a fence or two, slithered between gates' pickets, took advantage of windows left half open by their owners.

That's when I discovered that the late Leopold Eric Moreland, who died peacefully in his bed in 1999, had previously settled out of court on a lawsuit for negligence in his fiduciary duties, and was obsessed with Yorkies.

And nothing else.

So I took off my white hat. And when I started searching next, there was less stealthing around ajar doors, and more knocking over entire walls. In hindsight, I got a little reckless. But I was getting frustrated, because—no offense to my animal-lover-but-sloppy-worker friend Leopold—no decent records of L. E. Moreland could be found.

With one exception.

Deep in a Human server with ties to the governor's office, hidden in a memo locked behind a bewildering number of passwords, I discovered a communication regarding a summit that had occurred a couple of weeks earlier. Around the time Serena hadn't shown up for laundry night.

Lowe Moreland and M. Garcia are expected to be present, it said. *Security will be increased.*

I like data, and numbers, and thinking things through with logic and pivot tables. I've never been instinctive, but in that moment, I knew—I just *knew*—that I was on the right track. That Lowe Moreland had to be involved in Serena's disappearance.

So I started searching for him twenty-four seven. I took time off work. Called in favors. Stared at security camera footage. Went deep into the dark web, which is even less fun than it sounds. After weeks, I discovered one thing about Lowe Moreland: whoever took care of erasing his digital footprint was nearly as good as I am.

And I'm pretty fucking good.

Once I found out from Father that Lowe was a Were, the secrecy finally made sense. Their firewalls have always been exceptional, their networks hack-proof. I'd love to meet the person who keeps it up so I can either fangirl or deck them. But wandering around Lowe's beautiful home, which is even larger than I thought,

I know that it's not going to be a problem anymore. Because while there might be several things I can't do remotely, if I'm physically in front of a computer? It's happening, baby. And once I'm in, I'm going to scour every single document and piece of communication the Weres have, and I'm going to find Serena, and then . . .

Then.

"What's the plan?" Serena would ask if she were here, even though the little schemes she hatched never worked out. She liked the vibe of organizing more than the actual job of it, and my usually impervious heart clenches a little at the thought that I cannot call her out on it.

I have no plan—just the only person I ever cared about, displaced from my life. And maybe it's a little amateur sleuth of me, all this skulking around through semi-dark hallways in the hope of finding a whiteboard with "List of people Lowe disappeared" written on it. I'm begging for something, anything, while being aware that this entire endeavor melting into nothing is a distinct possibility.

A slightly nauseating one.

"And there she is."

I jump, startled. The good news is, Lowe didn't come home early from something that definitely wasn't a run to find his reeking Vampyre bride pretending she mixed up his office with the linen closet.

The bad is . . .

"You are very beautiful, aren't you?" the Were says.

He's younger than me, maybe around eighteen. When he comes closer, I try to place him, wondering if I remember his short, wiry frame and aquiline nose from the ceremony. But he wasn't there. And I believe he's seeing me for the first time, too.

"I didn't think Vampyres could be beautiful." There's nothing complimentary about his words. He's neither hitting on me, nor attempting to creep me out. Just stating a simple fact, followed by another step toward me, and I'm suddenly very conscious that I'm at the end of a hallway. He stands between me and the exit.

"Who are you?"

"Max," he says, but doesn't elaborate. There is something absentminded, almost empty about him. Disoriented. Like he was going to take a swim in the lake but found himself here without planning on it. "I wonder if Lowe likes seeing you around. Because you're so pretty," he muses numbly.

"I doubt it." I want to put a door between myself and Max, but the only one I can reach is Lowe's office—locked. I glance around for another escape route, but all I find is a giraffe painting of questionable quality.

I might be overreacting.

"Or maybe he hates you, because you force him to remember."

"Remember what?" This is unsettling. "I don't want to startle you, but would you mind if I walked past—"

"Remember what your people have taken from him. It's almost as much as they've taken from me. And yet he's making alliances with them like a common traitor. He married you, and said that you're not to be harmed." Max runs a hand over his dark hair, and then shakes his head in what looks like disbelief. He looks so deeply lost, I forget my unease and ask:

"Are you okay?"

His eyes sharpen. "How could I be okay?" He takes a step farther, nearly cornering me against the wall. The smell of his blood sweeps over me, hot, unpleasant. His heartbeat punches in my ears, booming, impossibly fast. "How could I be okay, when you're here, in my Alpha's home, after your people have hunted my relatives and mounted their embalmed heads to their walls."

The part of me who was once fourteen years old and almost stabbed by an anti-Vampyre activist posing as a gas inspector kicks in. "Then maybe we're even, since *your* people have made wine out of the blood of mine and then mixed it with livestock feed." I slide a hand into the pocket of my jeans, hoping for any weapon. A key, a toothpick, even some lint—nothing.

Shit.

"Tell me." He moves closer. I force myself to stand my ground. "Your father is alive?"

"As far as I know."

"Mine isn't. Nor my older sister." His green eyes are bright and glossy. "She was murdered when I was nine, while patrolling a border in the Northeast that the Vampyres sometimes cross just for fun. She died to protect me and other Were children, and . . ." The words stick in his throat. I feel a surge of compassion. My heart drops, heavy with certainty that he's going to burst into tears.

But I'm dead wrong, and I realize it too late.

He races toward me in a sudden explosion of vicious energy. The impact of his body against mine briefly knocks the breath out of me—briefly. He's a male Were, much stronger, but I'm used to people wanting to assassinate me, and when his hand clutches my wrist, hours of training spring into muscle memory. My knee hits his groin and he wails. I use the distraction to push him away, and it's not easy, it *hurts*, but by the time I can breathe again, my forearm is pinning his throat to the wall, and our faces are only inches apart.

I don't want to hurt him. I'm *not* going to hurt him, even if he's screaming abuse at me—"I will *end* you" and "Murderer" and "You *leech*."

So I peel back my lips, and show him my fangs.

The rumble in his throat instantly dulls into a whimper. His eyes lower to the ground, and the tension in his muscles loosens. I take a deep breath, making sure that he's not faking this, that he's really calmed down and he won't attack me the second I pull back, and—

A pair of hands a million times stronger than Max's yanks me away. What happens next is too blurry to parse, but a moment later, I'm the one sandwiched against the opposing wall. My back digs into the frame of the giraffe painting, and my front presses against something just as unyielding, but warm.

What the fuck, I think, or maybe I say it out loud.

I'm just not sure. Because when I open my eyes, all I can focus on is the way Lowe Moreland is staring down at me.

CHAPTER 5

She is resilient. He tries to imagine how he'd feel if he were in her position—alone, removed, used, and discarded. He has nothing but reluctant respect for her, and that angers him.

UNLIKE MAX'S GRIP, LOWE'S DOESN'T HURT.

It's tight, though. And the way he presses me against the wall, like he's trying to put his big body between me and the rest of the world, makes it difficult to breathe in without plastering my entire front to his.

"Miss Lark," he says. Hoarse. A growl, nearly.

I swallow against the sudden drought in my throat, which makes me realize where his hand is: wrapped around my neck. Almost entirely. His fingers are so long, they touch the valleys behind my ears.

"What do you think you're doing?" he asks, low and deep. Those offbeat eyes of his bore into mine. My heartbeat, which remained miraculously steady during my scuffle with Max, suddenly pounds louder—then whisks into slow flutters when Lowe lowers his head to murmur against my temple, "We haven't even been married for twenty-four hours. Praying mantises have longer honeymoon periods."

Max, I could take, fairly easily. Lowe, no way. It's the difference between a puppy and a dire wolf.

"Just, you know." My words sound wobbly. I'm not proud of that. "Trying to avoid getting killed."

Lowe stiffens for a millisecond, then pushes away. But he sticks close, palms flat against the wall on each side of my head—one still bandaged from yesterday's wound. It feels like a cage. A makeshift prison that he's building, made of his body and his glare, to keep me pinned in place as he turns around to ask Max, "You okay?"

Max looks up and nods, lips trembling. By now there are several Weres gathered around him. Alex, who glances between Lowe and me with an expression so guilty he'd probably admit to mortgage fraud if pressed ever so slightly. But also Juno, thoroughly inspecting Max for any mortal wounds I might have inflicted, and the older man and the ginger from the ceremony, who stare at me as though I just told the orphanage kids that Santa isn't real.

Everyone in this hallway looks very ready to shatter my kneecaps, maybe eat the marrow after. Which, nope.

"Excuse me." I try to dip out of Lowe's cage to leave. He lowers one arm, locking me in more tightly.

"What happened?" he asks me.

Juno beats me to the answer. "She was about to drink him dry. We all saw it." She runs a hand over Max's clammy forehead. He looks briefly adrift, and then stammers out,

"Sh-she was on me. Before I could do anything about it. And . . ." He bends his head, as if lost for words.

Every pair of eyes in the room turns to me. "Oh, come on," I snort.

"Her fangs were so close," he whispers feebly, and now I'm

getting annoyed. Clearly method acting is his passion, but he did try to assault me.

"Yeah, okay." I roll my eyes. "Please, leave me out of your eroto-maniacal delusions—"

"Have a doctor check Max," Lowe barks, and then his hand closes around my wrist, at once gentle and unyielding. It happens so fast, I nearly lose my balance. Before I know it, I'm scrambling to keep up with his longer legs as he drags me inside his office.

I immediately look around. I *am* worried about what he's going to do with me, but this is a great opportunity. He didn't use a key, which means that he must have some kind of smart lock—

"What happened?" Lowe asks. He let go of me, but still stands way too close, when there's plenty of space in the room to not crowd me. It's giving me flashbacks to our wedding, and this time I'm not even wearing heels, which means that he gets to loom over me in a way almost no one ever does.

The door opens suddenly. Juno enters, but Lowe's eyes stay on me.

"Misery," he growls, "how about you fucking answer me, for once?"

"Max came over, saw me, decided to indulge in some light after-noon murder." I shrug. "That, I'm used to. It's the subsequent lying that—"

"Bullshit," Juno says.

I turn to her. "I'm not asking you to believe me. But reason it out—why would I attack a Were, on my first day in your territory, when the consequences would be my death at best, and full-on war between the Weres and the Vampyres at worst?"

"I think you can't help yourself. I think you saw him, and you wanted to feed, and you—"

"—and I was too lazy to stop by the blood-dedicated fridge fifty feet away?" I step in front of her, forgetting all about Lowe. "That's not how feeding works. Let's just acknowledge that we know nothing about each other's species. Max came in, started telling me about how a bunch of people I share some distant DNA with killed his family, that Lowe's a traitor for marrying me, and then he . . . what?"

Juno isn't listening to me anymore. Her eyes meet Lowe's. A whole conversation passes between them in a split second.

Then she looks back at me. Furious. "If you are trying to imply that Max is working with the Loyals—"

"I'm not. Because I have no idea what the Loyals are."

"Max is *not* a Loyal."

"Sure. He's not a brook trout, either. I'm not making any ontological claims on him, but he *did* attack me."

"You are"—she takes an angry step closer—"a *liar.*"

"Leave us." Lowe's sharp voice reminds us that we're not alone in the room. We turn at once. And we're equally shocked to see that he's addressing Juno.

"She's lying," Juno insists. It's getting a little ridiculous, the way she points at me like I'm a mugger who yanked her purse away. "You should punish her."

I snort out a laugh. "Yes, Lowe. Spank me and take away my TV privileges."

"*You blade-eared leech.*"

"Juno. Out."

However the hierarchy works among the Weres, it must be *strict.* Because Juno clearly wants to stay and ground me with her claws, but she dips her head once in something akin to a salute, and then murmurs a soft "Alpha," before stalking out of the office.

79

It feels like respite, the door closing behind her, the blessed quiet. Until Lowe moves closer, and I suddenly mourn not having a third person in the room. The bad, as it turns out, is still better than the worse.

"Misery," he says. There is reproach in his voice, and a bit of a rough edge, and the tone of someone who has lots of problems keeping him busy, and is used to solving most of them with a look and maybe a *tiny* threat of violence.

We regard each other, just me and him, and yes, I feel it loud in my blood: we're alone. For the first time—though not of many to come. I doubt Lowe was planning to spend quality time with me ever again after yesterday.

Aside from a layer of stubble, he looks like he did at the cere- mony, his harsh face all structure. Clearly, as my makeup artist was painting the Sistine Chapel redux, his found nothing to improve on. I notice his eyes dip to my collarbone, where a faint shadow of the forest-green markings still lingers behind the riot of waves left over from the braids. Once again, that muscle in his jaw jumps, pupils get fat all of a sudden.

This situation is a problem. The Collateral is supposed to be a nonplayable character in a video game. For the next year, I need to be invisible, unobtrusive as I search for Serena. Not the kind of nuisance who gets caught murdering a young Were.

God, I bet they call them *pups.*

"You don't believe me, do you?" I ask.

He blinks, like he forgot we were in the middle of a conversa- tion. He clears his throat, but his voice stays gravelly. "Believe what?"

"That I didn't attack Max."

He presses his full lips together. "You were showing him your fangs."

"You jealous?" I bat my eyes at him, not sure where this recklessness comes from. I don't *think* I want to provoke him. "Wanna see them?"

His eyes rocket down to my lips and stay for a beat too long. It's almost funny, how repulsive Weres find our teeth. "What I am is worried that my Vampyre wife will get herself killed. I'd have to bury her corpse in the raised bed under the plumbago, and the next batch will sprout ugly."

I gasp theatrically. "Not the plumbago."

"They are my sister's favorite."

"And she *is* very cute."

He abruptly leans so close, I feel his breath on my lips. "Is this a threat?"

"No." I frown, bewildered. "*No.*" I let out a choked laugh. "There was no 'would be a shame if something happened to her' implied. Despite the fan fiction Max and Juno have been writing about me, I do *not* usually plot the demise of children." I think about my conversation with Alex. Who's probably off somewhere biting his cuticles to little stumps. "Plus, you're the one who decided I should be living here."

His eyebrow lifts. "I'm sure you have some excellent advice on where else I should house the daughter of the most powerful Vampyre in the council, who's apparently a fearsome fighter in her own right."

"Fearsome?" I'm . . . flattered?

"For a non-Were," he adds, a tad begrudgingly, like he regrets the compliment. I bet this man thrives on grudges. He has a questionable temperament, stern and autocratic, and I've always thought of myself as too much of a survivor to be in any way mouthy, but here I am. Nettlesome.

"Still. It feels like committing to the bit a little too much, giving me the bedroom next to yours."

"I'll decide what's too much." He's condescending. And inflexible. A dick, probably.

"By all means, then, let's embrace tradition. Should we slice my palm and drip some blood on the sheets? Hang them from the public square?"

His eyes close briefly and he grits out, "I doubt there are any expectations of virginity on your part."

"Fantastic. I love surprising people."

I see the confusion in his parted lips, before he subdues it and shifts back to his default austere expression.

It's amusing to me, the idea that someone who has skimmed a synopsis of my life would assume I've had any sort of romantic entanglement. With whom? A Vampyre, when they only see me as a traitor? A Human, who would consider me a monster?

The birth control shot I was given before coming here was a joke, not just because Lowe and I are as likely to have sex as we are to start a podcast together, but also because he's a Were and I a Vampyre, and we couldn't reproduce even if we wanted to. Interspecies relationships are unheard of—if not unseen, judging by all the Human-produced porn Serena and I would watch. We'd eat popcorn and laugh at the untalented actors in purple contacts and fake teeth engaging in acts that proudly showcased their ignorance of Vampyre anatomy. Were, too. I'm no expert, but I'm fairly sure their dicks wouldn't get stuck in an orifice like that.

"Where did you learn how to fight?" Lowe asks. Probably to change the topic from sex with his least favorite sentient species.

"Was it not listed in your briefing memo?"

He shakes his head. "I did wonder how you could still be alive, after seven attempts on your life."

"So did I. And there were more than that, though most were half-assed. We got tired of reporting them."

"We?"

"My foster sister and I." I cross my arms, and now I'm mirroring his pose. Here we are, too close once again, my elbows almost brushing his. "We took self-defense classes together."

You know her, don't you? She knows you. Tell me something. Anything.

He does, but not what I want to hear. "No fighting in Were territory."

"Sure. So, next time someone attacks me, I let them help themselves? Then again, *you* could be the next one to attack me. Since you're not exactly a fan."

The pause that follows is not encouraging. "For as long as you live in Were territory, you are under my protection. And under my authority."

I let out a silent, breathy laugh. "What are your orders for me, then?"

He takes one step closer, and the tension in the room instantly changes, shifting to something tighter, more dangerous. Fear stabs my stomach, that maybe I pushed too much. That's why a Were is bending over me: to remind me how insignificant I am and say, "I need you to behave, Misery."

His voice is all hard consonants and narrow eyes, and a shiver runs up my spine, cold and electric. My mind jumps back to Alex's words: *Even his scent was right. Everyone knew that he had the making of an Alpha.* I'm no Were, and if I inhale, all I can smell is clean sweat and strong blood, but I think I know what he meant. Somehow I feel it, the compulsion to nod, agree. To do as Lowe wants.

I have to actively stop myself. And shiver in the process.

"At least you are clever enough to be afraid," he murmurs.

I grit my teeth. "Just cold. You keep the temperature far too low."

His nostrils flare. "Do as I fucking tell you, Misery."

"But of course." My voice is steady, but he knows how rattled I am. Just as I know I'm rattling him. "May I be excused?"

He nods brusquely, and I dart for the door. But then I remember something important I've been meaning to ask.

I turn back to him. "Can my cat—"

I stop, because Lowe's eyes are closed. He's inhaling deeply, as though gathering every possible air molecule within the room inside his lungs. And he looks . . .

Tormented. In pure, absolute agony. He straightens his expression when he notices that I'm looking, but it's too late.

My stomach twists with something slimy and unpleasant. Guilt. "I took a bath. Did that not make it better?"

His stare is blank. "Make what better?"

"My scent."

He swallows visibly. His tone is sharp. "The situation hasn't improved for me."

"But how—"

"What were you going to ask, Misery?"

Oh. Right. "I have a cat."

He scowls like I told him I keep pet centipedes. "*You* have a cat."

"Yup." I stop at that, because Lowe hasn't earned the right to any explanation for my life choices. Not that anything about Serena's damn fucking cat was a choice. "He's currently locked in my room, if your sister didn't let him out with her pilfered key. Can I let him roam around the house, or will Max try to frame him for racketeering?"

"Your cat is welcome among us," Lowe says. If that's not a jab, nothing else is.

"Wonder how that feels," I say breezily, and slip out of the room without glancing at him again.

CHAPTER 6

Being gone is a relief. And sheer agony.

ALL IN ALL, IT'S NOT THE MOST AUSPICIOUS OF STARTS. In the week following my arrival, I spend an unhealthy amount of time mentally slapping myself over the way I handled the kerfuffle with Max. I don't care whether the Weres think I'm a deranged monster, but I do mind that whatever crumb of freedom they might have been inclined to give me has been swiftly vacuumed up.

I'm escorted *everywhere*: as I take a stroll by the lake; to grab a blood bag from the fridge; when I sit in the garden at dusk, just to experience something that's not my en suite. I am but a cornucopia of regret. Because we're all bad bitches—till a scowling Were stands outside the bathroom door while we're washing our hair.

Till we lose our chance to snoop around.

So much time on my hands, and so little to spend it on. It's the Collateral life I'm familiar with, just with significantly fewer Serenas to keep me busy. I should be bored to death, but the truth is, this is not too different from my routine in the Human world. I have no friends, no hobbies, and no real purpose aside from earning enough money to pay rent in order to . . . exist, I guess.

It's like you're—I don't know, suspended. Untethered from everything around you. I just need to see you go toward something, Misery.

There might be something stunted about me. After the Collateral term was over, Serena and I were free to venture into the outside world, to be with people who weren't our tutors or our caregivers, to fall in love and make friends. Serena jumped right into that, but I could never bring myself to. Partly because the closer I'd let someone get to me, the harder it'd be to hide who I was. Or maybe spending the first eighteen years of my life becoming acquainted with the cruelty of all species didn't quite set me up for a bright future.

Who knows.

So I sleep during the day, and spend my nights napping. I take long baths, first for Lowe's sake, then because I grow to truly enjoy them. I watch old Human movies. I walk around my room, marveling at how pretty it is, wondering who the hell thought of this beamed ceiling, sophisticated and cozy and stunning at once.

I do miss the internet. There is a concern that I might want to moonlight as a spy, and to prevent me from transferring classified and confidential information I could come across while in Were territory, I don't really have access to technology—with the exception of my weekly check-in call with Vania, which is heavily monitored and lasts just long enough for her to sneer at me as she ascertains that I'm still alive. Of course, this is not my first rodeo, and I did try to smuggle in a cell phone, plus a laptop and a bunch of pen testing gadgets.

Your honor, I got caught. Whoever went through my stuff had the gall to confiscate half of it—and to pluck out all the antenna points and Wi-Fi cards from the rest. When I realized it, I lay on the floor for two hours, like a thwarted jellyfish beached in the sun.

Lowe is rarely around, and never within sight, although sometimes I'll feel his low voice vibrate through the walls. Firm orders. Long hushed conversations. Once, memorably, right as I slid into my closet for my midday rest, a deep laugh followed by Ana's delighted screams. I drifted asleep moments later, second-guessing what I heard.

On the fifth evening, someone knocks on my door.

"Hi, Misery." It's Mick—the older Were who was talking with Lowe at the ceremony. I like him a lot. Mostly because, unlike my other guards, he doesn't seem to want me to go stand outside and get struck by lightning. I love to think that we bonded when he took his first night shift: I noticed him slumping against the wall, pushed my rolling chair into the hallway, and bam—instantly BFFs. Our three-minute conversation about water pressure was the apogee of my week.

"What's up, friendly neighborhood warden?"

"The politically correct name is 'protective detail.'" There is something off about his heartbeat—something dull, a slight drag that's almost despondent. I wonder if it's related to the big scar on his throat, but I might be imagining it altogether, because he smiles at me in a way that turns his eyes into a web of crow's feet. Why can't everyone be this nice? "And there's a video call for you, from your brother. Come with me."

Any hope I have that Mick will take me to Lowe's office and leave me alone to snoop around dies when we head for the sunroom.

"Ready to come back?" Owen says before "Hi."

"I don't think that's an option, if we want to avoid . . ."

"Pissing off Father?"

"I was thinking full-on war."

Owen waves his hand. "Ah, yes. That, too. How's marital life?"

I'm very aware of Mick sitting across from me, intently monitoring everything I say. "Boring."

"You got hitched to a guy who could kill you any second of any day. How are you *bored*?"

"Technically, anybody could kill anybody, anytime. Your obnoxious friends could pull out a garrote on you tonight. I could have poured triazolopyrimidines in your blood bags a million times over in the past twenty years." I tap my chin. "As a matter of fact, why did I not?"

Something flickers in his eyes. "And to think that we used to like each other," he murmurs darkly. He's not wrong. Before I left for Human territory, every Vampyre child who chose to be a dick about my soon-to-be Collateralship tended to encounter curiously karmic events. Mysterious bruises, spiders crawling in backpacks, mortifying secrets bared to the community. I'd always suspected it was Owen's doing. Then again, maybe I was wrong. When I returned home at eighteen, he seemed less than happy to see me, and he certainly didn't want to associate with me in public.

"Can you please just be terrified to be living among the Weres?" he asks.

"So far, Humans are worse. They do shit like burning the Amazon rainforest or leaving the toilet seat up at night. Anyway, anything you need from me?"

He shakes his head. "Just making sure you're still alive."

"Oh." I wet my lips. I doubt he gives a fuck about whether I continue to exist on this metaphysical plane, but this is a good opportunity. "I'm so glad you called, because . . . I miss you so much, Owen."

A stutter of incredulity flashes on his grainy face. Then understanding dawns on him. "Yeah? I miss you, too, honey." He leans back in his chair, intrigued. "Tell me what ails you."

Every Vampyre in the Southwest knows that we are twins, if only because our arrival was originally celebrated as a dazzling source of hope ("Two babies at once! In the prestigious Lark family! When conception has been so difficult, and so few of our young come by! All hail!") and later briskly swept under a thick rug of truculent stories ("They murdered their own mother during a two-night labor. The boy weakened her, and the girl dealt the final blow—Misery, they named her. More blood flowed on that bed than during the Aster."). Serena had known, too, when I first introduced her to him after she pestered me to meet "The guy who could have been my roomie for years, if you'd played your cards better, Misery." They'd surprisingly hit it off, bonding over their love for roasting my appearance, my clothes, my taste in music. My general vibe.

And yet, even Serena wasn't able to shut up about how unbelievable it was that Owen, with his dark complexion and already receding hairline, was even *related* to me. It's because where I take after Father, he . . . well, I suppose he looks like Mother. Hard to say, since no pictures seem to have survived her.

But whatever the differences between Owen and me, those months sharing a womb must have left *some* mark on us. Because despite growing up with fewer interactions than a pair of pen pals, we do seem to understand each other.

"Remember when we were children?" I ask. "And Father would take us to the forest to watch the sun set and feel the night begin?"

"Of course." Neither Father nor the army of nannies who looked after us ever did anything like it. "I think of it often."

"I've been reminiscing about the things Father would say. Like: *That thing I lost. Do you have any news about it?*" I shift smoothly between English and the Tongue, making sure not to change intonation. Mick's eyes glance up from his phone, more curious than suspicious.

"Ah, yes. You used to laugh for minutes and say, *I have not. She hasn't returned to her apartment—I'll be alerted if she does.*"

"But then you'd get mad because Father and I weren't paying attention to you, and wander off on your own, grumbling about the oddest things. *Let me know if that changes. Have you been talking with the Were Collateral? Has she mentioned anything about Loyals?*"

He nods and sighs happily. "I know you'll never believe it, but I always say: *I have no contact with her. But I'll see what I can do.* Father always loved you best, darling."

"Oh, darling. I think he loves us equally."

Back in my room, I pull out my computer, wondering if I could pilfer a Wi-Fi chip off someone's phone. I fuck around a bit, writing a flexible script to scour Were servers that I might never be able to use. Like always while coding, I lose track of time. When I look up from my keyboard, the moon is high, my room is dark, and a small, creepy creature stands in front of me. It's wearing owl leggings with a chiffon tutu, and stares at me like the ghost of Christmas past.

I yelp.

"Hi."

Oh my *God*. "Ana?"

"Hello."

I clutch my chest. "What the *fuck*?"

"Are you playing?"

"I . . ." I glance down at my laptop. *I'm building a fuzzy logic circuit* seems like the wrong kind of answer. "Sure. How did you get in here?"

"You always ask the same questions."

"And *you* always get in here. How?"

She points at the window. I stride there with a frown, bracing myself against the sill to look out. I've explored it before, in my desperate quest for some unsupervised espionage. The bedrooms are on the second floor, and I've checked multiple times whether I could climb down (no, unless I got bit by a radioactive spider and developed suction cups on my fingers) or jump out (not without breaking my neck). It never occurred to me to look . . . up.

"Through the roof?" I ask.

"Yes. They took away my key."

"Does your brother know you've been climbing like a spider monkey?"

She shrugs. I shrug, too, and go back to my bed. It's not like I'm gonna tattle her out. "Which one is it?" she asks.

"What?"

"A spider monkey. Is it a spider that looks like a monkey, or a monkey that looks like a spider?"

"Hmm, not sure. Let me google and—" I pull my computer onto my lap, then remember the Wi-Fi situation. "Fuck."

"That's a bad word," Ana says, giggling in a delighted, tickled way that has me feeling like an improv genius. She's flattering company. "What's your name?"

"Misery."

"Miresy."

"Misery."

"Yes. Miresy."

"That's not . . . whatever."

"Can I play with you?" She eyes my laptop eagerly.

"No."

Her pretty mouth curves into a pout. "Why?"

"Because." What are we even going to do? Long division?

"Alex lets me play."

"Alex? The blond guy?" I haven't seen him since the Max incident. I'm assuming it was filed as "under his watch," and got him plucked out of jailer rotation.

"Yes. We steal cars and talk with the beautiful ladies. But Alex says that Juno isn't supposed to know."

"You play *Grand Theft Auto* with Alex?"

She shrugs.

"Is that appropriate for a . . . three-year-old?"

"I'm seven," she declares haughtily. Holding up six fingers.

I let that slide. "Not gonna lie, pretty proud that it was within my range of estimation."

Another shrug, which seems like her default response. Relatable, honestly. She settles on the bed next to me and I'm briefly worried that she might pee on it. Does she have a diaper? Is she housebroken? Should I burp her? "I want to play," she repeats.

I'm not a soft person. After living the first eighteen years of my life in function of a long list of very nebulous *others*, I perfected assertiveness. I have no issue with producing a firm, final no and never revisiting a request again. So I must be suffering a major cerebral event when I sigh, and pull up my editor, and quickly use JavaScript to whip up a *Snake*-like game.

"Is this edu . . . Edu . . . ?" she asks, after I'm done explaining how it works. "Edutacional?"

"Educational."

"Juno says it's important that the games are edu . . ."

"I don't know if it is, but at least no major felonies are involved."

There is something disarming about the way she leans against me, soft and trusting, as though our people haven't been hunting each other for sport in the last couple of centuries. Her tongue sticks out between her teeth as she tries to snatch apples, and when a dark curl slips in front of her right eye, I catch myself with my fingers hovering right there, tempted to fold it behind her ear.

"Shit," I mutter, pulling back my hand.

"What?"

"Nothing." I trap my arms between my back and the wall, horrified.

It feels like the middle of the night when Ana yawns and decides it's time to go back to her room. "My cat is waiting for me, anyway."

Wait. "Your cat?"

She nods.

"Does *your* cat happen to be gray? Long hair? Smushed face?"

"Yes. Her name is Sparkles."

Oh, fuck. "First of all, he's a boy."

She blinks at me. "*His* name is Sparkles, then."

"No, his name is Serena's damn fucking cat."

Ana's expression is pitying.

"And he's actually *my* cat." Serena's. Whatever.

"I don't think so."

"You do realize that he arrived when I did."

"But he sleeps with me."

Ah. So *that's* where he disappears to all the time. "That's just because he hates me."

"Then maybe he's not your cat," she says, with the delicate som-

berness of a therapist who's letting me know that I don't have a di-
agnosable disorder, I'm just a bitch.

"You know what? I don't care. It's between you and Serena."

"Who's Serena?"

"My friend."

"Your best friend?"

"I only have the one, so . . . yeah?"

"My best friend is Misha. She has red hair, and she's the
daughter of my brother's best friend, Cal. And Juno is her aunt.
And she has a little brother, his name is Jackson, and a little sister,
and her name—"

"This is not *The Brothers Karamazov*," I interrupt. "I don't need
the family tree."

"—is Jolene," she continues, undeterred. "Where is Serena?"

"She . . . I'm trying to find her."

"Maybe my brother can help you? He's real good at helping
people."

I swallow. I just can't with children. "Maybe."

She studies me for several seconds. "Are you like Lowe?"

"I'm not sure what you mean, but no."

"He doesn't sleep, either."

"I do sleep. Just during the day."

"Ah. Lowe doesn't sleep. At all."

"Never? Is it a Were thing? An Alpha thing?"

She shakes her head. "He has pneumonia."

Seriously? When did he get it? He seemed healthy to me. Maybe
for Weres, pneumonia is not a big— "Wait!" I call when I see Ana
heading for the window. "How about you go through the door?"

She doesn't even stop to say no.

"It would be more fun. You could stop by Lowe's room on your way," I offer. Because if this child dies, it's on *me*. "Say hi. Hang out."

"He's not here. He's gone to deal with the lollipops."

I trail after her. "With the lollipops."

"Yes."

"There's no way he is dealing with— Do you mean the Loyals?"

"Yes. The lollipops." She's already climbing upward, and spider monkey doesn't even begin to describe how agile she is. But *still*.

"Don't. Come back! I . . . forbid you from continuing."

She keeps scaling. "You're a Vampyre. I don't think you can tell me what to do." She sounds more matter-of-fact than bratty, and all I can think of replying is:

"Shit."

I follow her progress, terrified, wondering if this is motherhood: anxiously picturing your child with her skull cracked open. But Ana knows exactly what she's doing, and when she has hoisted herself on top of the roof and disappeared from my view, I'm left alone with two separate pieces of knowledge:

I'm befuddlingly invested in the survival of this tiny pest of a Were.

And Lowe, my husband, my *roomie*, is gone for the night.

I slip inside the bathroom, find one of my hairpins, and do what I have to do.

CHAPTER 7

The scent is growing into more than just a problem. It invades. It swirls. It travels. It sticks to his nose. It concentrates, sometimes.

They rarely touch. When they did, her wrist accidentally brushed against the front of his shirt, and he found himself tearing off the piece of fabric where her smell was most intense. He slipped it in his pocket, and now carries it everywhere.

Even as he leaves to avoid her.

BREAKING IN TAKES LONGER THAN I EXPECTED, BUT NOT BY much. The lock clicks and I stop, wondering if my guard—a no-bullshit Were named Gemma, I believe—will check in on me. After a minute I decide that I'm safe and push the door open.

Lowe's room is as beautiful and interesting as mine, the accent wall and beamed ceiling setting a snug, mellow atmosphere. It has less furniture, though, and even though Lowe must have been living here far longer than me, I see two moving boxes stacked in a corner, and a couple of framed paintings leaning against the wall, waiting to be put up.

The soles of my feet are cold as I step on the herringbone hardwood floors. I know exactly what I'm looking for—a phone, a laptop, possibly a diary titled "That Time I Abducted Serena Paris" with an easily breakable lock—but can't help indulging in some snooping. There are several shelves, lined with classics, fiction, but mostly art books, tall and thick and glossy, the pages full of beautiful sculptures and odd buildings and paintings I've never seen before. The bathroom is spotless all over, except for the corner where a unicorn toothbrush, strawberry toothpaste, and no-tear shampoo have been placed. His closet is martial in its orderliness, every shirt monochrome, every pair of pants neatly folded, always khakis or jeans. The sole exception is the suit he wore at our wedding.

My husband, I discover, wears size fourteen shoes.

I search for electronics, to no avail. I really did not need to know that Lowe Moreland hates clutter, that he's immune to the inevitable accumulation of useless trinkets we're all subject to. He owns what he needs, and all he needs seems to be one charger, a million pairs of interchangeable boxer briefs, and a bottle of silicone-based lube. I find it in his bedside nightstand, pick it up, and immediately drop it like it's a nest of wasps.

Okay. I didn't need to know that he . . . But his lady is off frolicking with my people, and . . . okay. It's perfectly normal. I'm not going to think about this any longer.

Starting now.

There is one single picture on the wall: a younger Ana and a beautiful middle-aged woman who shares Lowe's distinctive coloring and sharp cheekbones. The more I study it, the more I notice that aside from the eyes, Ana doesn't look like her mother at all, nor like Lowe. If they take after their father, they must have grabbed different things.

I search under the pillows, behind the headboard, in the desk. Lowe clearly doesn't keep a laptop in the bedroom, and this entire break-in is starting to feel like a useless endeavor. I've mostly given up when I try the bottom drawer of the dresser and find it shut. Hope gurgles. I run back to my room and retrieve my hairpin.

I'm not sure what I expect from a locked cabinet—maybe Vampyre-fang necklaces, or extra lube he got wholesale, or a drawerful of Wi-Fi cards accompanied by a Hallmark greeting card ("Help yourself, Misery!"). *Not* a set of pencils and a sketch pad. I frown, picking it up and opening it, gently pulling the pages apart to avoid any ripping.

Initially, I think I'm looking at a photo. That's how beautiful the art is, how accurate and painstaking. But then I notice the smudges, the lines that sometimes stretch a little too long, and no. This is a drawing—an architectural drawing of a vault, flawlessly executed.

My heart thuds louder, but I couldn't say why. With trembling fingers, I start turning the pages.

There are sketches of rooms, offices, storefronts, piers, houses, bridges, stations. Large and small buildings, statues, domes, cabins. Some are just the outside, while others include inside layouts and furniture. Some have numbers and vectors scribbled in the margins, others colors woven through them. All of them are perfect.

He's an architect.

I'd forgotten. Or perhaps I never had a clear idea of what it meant. But looking at these drawings, I feel it as something solid and heavy in my stomach—the love Lowe has for beautiful shapes, exquisite places, interesting sights.

He's only a few years older than me, but this is not the work of someone who's untrained. There is expertise here, and passion, and talent, not to mention time, time that I cannot imagine he has to dedicate to beauty and pretty drawings now that he's the Alpha of his pack, and . . .

It's too much. I'm thinking about this—about *him*—way too

hard. I shut the sketch pad too forcefully and place it back where I found it. It causes something that was at the very end of the notebook to slip out.

A portrait.

My heart halts as I scramble to lift it up, expecting—no, *sure*—that I'll find Serena's smiling face on it. The pouty lips, upturned eyes, narrow nose, and pointed chin; they're all so familiar to me that I think it must be her, because who else's face would I know so well? It can only be Serena's, or . . .

Mine.

Lowe Moreland has drawn my face, and then stuffed it at the bottom of his bottom drawer. I'm not sure when he observed it long enough to pluck this level of detail out of me, the serious, detached air, the tight-lipped expression, the wispy hair curling around the cusp of an ear. Here's what I do know: there is something *sharp* about the drawing. Something searing and intense and expansive that's simply not there in the other sketches. Force, and power, and lots of feelings were involved in the making of this portrait. *Lots.* And I can't imagine they were positive.

I frown. I swallow. I sigh. Then I whisper, "I'm not a fan, either, Lowe. But you don't see me doodling you with horns in my diary."

I fold everything back in the drawer, making sure it's exactly how I found it. On my way out, I let my fingers trail on the bookshelves, wondering once more just how bad my next year with the Weres is going to get.

THE FOLLOWING DAY I SLEEP UNTIL LATE AFTERNOON. I'M TIRED enough that I could go longer, but there's something going on outside, on the usually calm lakeshore. It involves screaming laughter and charred smells, and I drag myself to the window to check it out, making sure to avoid the direct light still filtering in.

It's a barbecue, or a potluck, or a cookout—I never quite got the difference, despite Serena's explanations on the nuances of Human social get-togethers. Vampyres don't really build community this way, by assembling without an agenda. Our friendships are alliances. I didn't encounter the concept of hanging out, of spending time with someone for the sake of it, until my Collateral years.

But I can count over thirty Weres. Hanging around the lakefront, grilling, eating, swimming. Laughing. The loudest are the children: I spot several, Ana among them, having a rollicking good time.

I wonder whether I'm invited to partake. What the reaction would be if I made my way downstairs, waved at the guests. I could borrow a bikini from Juno. Pour myself some blood on the rocks, sit at a table in the shade, ask my dinner companions, "So, how about them football players?"

The idea has me chuckling. I settle on the windowsill, still in my pajama shorts and the worn tank I got from a team-building exercise at work two years ago, staring at the gathering. And at Lowe, who has returned home.

My eyes are immediately drawn to him. Maybe because he's . . . well, *big*. Most Weres are tall, or athletic, or both, but Lowe takes it a notch further. Still, I'm not positive his looks are what center him so insistently.

He is . . . not charming, but *magnetic*. His full lips curve into a small smile while he chats with some pack members. His dark brows furrow as he listens to others. The corners of his eyes split into a web of crinkles when he plays with the children. He lets a young girl beat him at arm wrestling, gasps in mock pain when another pretends to punch him on his biceps, shoots a boy into the deep water to his unabashed delight.

He seems beloved. Accepted. Belonging, and I wonder what that feels like. I wonder if he misses his partner, or mate, or whatever. I wonder if he gets to draw much these days, or if the pretty houses mostly stay locked in his head.

He definitely does *not* look like he is just recovering from being ill, but what do I know? I'm no pulmonologist.

I'm about to push myself off the sill and start my night when I spot him.

Max.

He's separate from the rest of the crowd, on the outskirts of the beach, where the sand first turns into shrubs, then thickens with forest trees. At first glance, I don't think much of it: unlike most of the partygoers, he's wearing a long-sleeved shirt and jeans, but hey. I've been a self-conscious teen before, trying to hide with clothes the way I'd shot up about six inches in three months. And melanoma *is* evil, according to Serena.

But then he goes on his knees. Begins to chat with someone much shorter than him. And my entire body stiffens.

I tell myself that there's no reason to be scowling the way I am. Max and I may have had our differences (Difference. One, if major.), but he has every right to be interacting with Ana. For all I know, they're related, and he's been babysitting her since she was in diapers. Not my business, anyway. I'm a very unwanted guest here, and I have my daily hourlong bath to take.

Except. Something pulls me back to the window. I don't like it. The way he's talking to Ana, pointing at someplace I cannot see, someplace between the trees. Ana shakes her head—*no*. But he seems to insist, and . . .

Am I being paranoid? Probably. Ana's literal brother is right there, a few dozen feet away, watching her.

But he isn't. He's playing something with the ginger best man—Cal, his name is Cal—and a few other people. Bocce, if I recognize the game from Serena's bowling-variants period, and boy, do Weres and Humans have things in common. Father might be right to fear an alliance between them. Still, this doesn't concern me, and—

Max's hand takes Ana's, pulling her toward the woods, and my brain short-circuits. Mick's on duty, and I barge out of my room barefoot, meaning to warn him. But his chair is empty, save for a used plate with some traces of coleslaw on it.

He's probably in the restroom, and I consider looking for him there. Then decide there's no time. A couple of stray neural cells lurch awake to point out that this is the perfect time for me to break into Lowe's office and search for intel on Serena. The remaining 99 percent of my brain, sadly, is focused on Ana.

God. I hate, hate, *hate* that I care.

I dash down the stairs, then outside via the kitchen. The heat crashes into me like a wave, slowing me down as the sunlight stabs my skin like a million little shark teeth. Fuck, it hurts. It's way too bright for me to be out.

A couple of Weres see me, but no one *notices* me. Little jagged stones dig painfully into the soles of my feet, but I power through, heading for the forest. By the time I've reached the woods, my flesh is burning, I'm limping, and I've almost lost my balance twice, courtesy of a pile of sand buckets and an arm floatie.

But I see Ana's bright blue swimsuit amid the green, the dark gray of Max's shirt, and yell "Hey!" I wade through the thick of the trees. "Hey, stop!"

Max keeps on walking, but Ana turns, sees me, and grins, gap-toothed and delighted. Her heartbeat is sweet and happy. "Miresy!"

"Not my name, we've been over this. Yo, Max? Where are you taking her?"

He must recognize my voice, because he halts. And when he looks at me, his face is pure hatred. "What are *you* doing here?"

"I *live* here." Fairly sure pine needles are burrowing inside my skin. Also, I might be in flames. "What are *you* doing with a six-year-old in the middle of the forest?"

"Seven." Ana corrects me cheerfully, letting go of Max's hand and holding up six fingers, and *damn* this child.

"Ana, come with me." I offer her my hand, and she happily trots my way, arms open as though she means to hug me—yikes. My heart sinks when Max scoops her up and starts carrying her in the opposite direction. "What the hell are you—"

That's when several things happen at once.

Ana thrashes around and screams.

I charge at Max, ready to free her, ready to tear him to shreds with my fangs.

And about a dozen Weres jump out of the trees surrounding us.

CHAPTER 8

It would be easier if he didn't like her as a person.

IS IT A VAMPYRE THING, SHOVING YOUR POINTY LITTLE FANGS into other people's business and ruining their plans? Or is it more of a Misery Lark passion project?"

I've been nursing my abused soles on the living room couch for less than five minutes, but it's the third time a variation of this question has been asked of me. So I keep my head bent down and ignore Lowe's second—the one who looks like a Ken doll—as I pluck an assortment of detritus from my toe. I need tweezers, but I didn't bring any with me. Do Weres use them? As the original furries, do they find them morally repugnant? Maybe they hold body hair sacred, and any threat to its rightful dwelling on the flesh is considered blasphemous.

Food for thought.

"Let me go," Max whines. Like me, he's sitting on a couch. Unlike me, his hands are tied behind his back, and he's being watched by several guards with the kind of icy treatment one would reserve for someone who tried to kidnap a child.

Which is exactly what Max did.

"You can stop asking," Cal tells him mildly. "Because it ain't going to happen." Out of all the Weres in here, it's clear that he and Ken Doll are the highest ranking. They also appear to have a bad cop, even worse cop thing going on. Cal is affably scary, Ken is snarkily terrifying. Whatever works for them, I guess.

"I want to see my mother," Max re-whines.

"Do you, champ? Are you sure? Because your mother is out there, *humiliated* by what you just did and the company you've been keeping."

"I dunno, Cal." Ken fixes his baseball cap. "Maybe we *should* turn him over to his mother." He leans forward. "I'd love to see his face when she declaws him."

Max growls, but it turns into a whimper when his Alpha comes in, Juno and Mick in tow. I mouth a bashful *So sorry* to Mick, worried that he'll get in trouble for taking a piss and leaving me alone for a minute. He waves his hand at me, and the entire room drops into silence, everyone focusing on Lowe like his presence is a gravitational pull. Even *I* cannot look anywhere else, and abandon my toe to its infected destiny. Lowe looks so stone-cold pissed, I shiver. Though it could be the blast of the AC on my blistering flesh.

"Is Ana okay?" Gemma asks.

Lowe nods. "Playing with Misha." Hands on his hips, he surveys the room. Every pair of eyes is instantly downcast.

Except for mine.

"Who wants to tell me what the fuck just happened?" he asks, staring at me. I expect everyone to explode into rushed explanations, but Were discipline is better than that. A heavy silence stretches, broken only by Lowe coming to stand in front of me. I'm ready to say my final words, but all he does is take off his zip-up hoodie, wrap it around my shuddery shoulders, then admire the result for a beat too long.

Everyone's eyes are still on the ground.

"Cal," he says. It's embarrassing, the sense of relief I feel at not being called on.

"Everything was going according to plan," Cal starts. "As expected, Max was trying to lure Ana away. We were tailing him to see who he would rendezvous with, when . . ."

He turns to me, and suddenly I am the center of the room. My relief was premature.

"I'm sorry." I swallow. "I had no idea this was some kind of cahooty ambushy plan. If I see a guy who's been a total dick to me absconding with a child, it's only natural for me to . . ." To what? Why did I intervene, again? Now that the adrenaline has dried up, I cannot recall what my reasoning was. I'm no hero, nor do I want to be.

Ken Doll snorts. "Were you watching us from the window?"

"I mean . . . yeah?"

"Creepy. You need a hobby."

"You're right. I've heard amazing things about paragliding, or competitive duck herding. Maybe I could—oh, wait. I forgot that I'm *literally* stuck in a one-hundred-and-thirty-square-foot bedroom twenty-four *seven*."

"Read a book, pointy."

"Enough." Lowe stalks across the room to crouch in front of Max, who instantly tries to scramble away. His tone is firm but surprisingly gentle when he asks, "Where were you going to take Ana?" Max doesn't reply, so he continues, "You are fifteen, and I'm not going to punish you like an adult. I don't know who you got mixed up with, or how, but I can help you. I will protect you."

Sweat trickles down Max's temples. He's much younger than I thought. "You're just going to get rid of me. If I tell you, you—"

"I do not hurt my own, especially not children," Lowe growls. "I am not Roscoe."

"No." Max's eyes flick to me. "He'd never have made alliances with the Vampyres or the Humans, would never have taken one in and left her to kill the Weres—"

"You're right. Roscoe liked to kill the Weres on his own." Max lowers his eyes. He's just a boy. "Is an alliance with the Vampyres really worse than more Were deaths at their hands?"

Max seems to grapple with the question, Adam's apple bobbing. Then he remembers his rage, and spurts out, "You're not the rightful Alpha."

It's clearly a *big* faux pas. Because every other Were in the room takes a step forward to intervene—and then stops at once at Lowe's lifted hand.

"Who told you that?" he asks. Menacing, ruthless. "Maybe it's a fair mistake. Maybe they simply weren't there when Roscoe lost the challenge to me. I sent a message to the Loyals, let them know that I'd gladly accept the challenge from any of them. And yet." Lowe stands. "Dissent and discussion are welcome. I'm not Roscoe, and I won't dispose of those who disagree with me. But trying to take a child, sabotage important infrastructure, brutally attack huddles who support me . . . This is violent insurgence. And as long as I'm Alpha of this pack, I'm not going to accept it. Who sent you here, Max?"

He shakes his head. "I don't know."

"Did you forget?" Ken Doll comes to stand next to Lowe. Max recoils. "We have ways of making you remember."

"He's barely more than a child, though," Cal points out.

"He *chose* to work with the Loyals," Ken says, cracking his knuckles.

Cal, to my shock, shrugs. "I suppose you're right." He, too, cracks his knuckles.

I search Lowe's face for a sign that he's not going to let his minions . . . I don't know, waterboard a boy. His expression is detached, happy to delegate. Not what I'd expect from someone who's planning on deescalating this.

"Wait!" I yell. Today must be a *particularly* nosy day for me. "Don't hurt him. I can help you."

All heads whip around to me, with varying degrees of annoyance. "I think you've done enough, leech," Ken says.

I roll my eyes. "First of all, I grew up among the Humans, and leech, parasite, sanguisuge, bloodsponge, tick, sucker, bat bitch—they're *not* the groundbreaking insults you think they are." Vampyres *do* drink blood to survive, and we're not shy about it. "I can find out who sent Max. Without nail pulling or whatever you're planning."

"I dunno," Cal says. "He deserves some harm."

But Max is shaking like a leaf. And I must not be the sadist I fancied myself. "Please," I plead to Lowe, tuning out the rest of the room. "I can help."

"How?" He, for one, seems more curious than irritated.

"It's easier done than said. Here." I stand and brush past him to go to Max. He stops me with his fingers on my wrist. When I crane my neck up to him, startled, he's looking straight ahead. "Why?" he asks, without meeting my eyes. His voice is low, meant only for me.

I'm not quite sure what he wants to know, so I go for what feels right. "Ana has been visiting," I say, matching his tone. "She keeps me company, and even though she's terrible at pronouncing my name and clearly doesn't know whether she's six or seven . . ." I swallow. "I'd rather she doesn't get, you know. Kidnapped and trafficked."

He finally looks down at me. Scans my face for several long moments, and whatever his inspection is about, I must pass muster. He nods and lets go of me. I don't move.

"Actually, could you help me? I'm not *super* good at this." His brows furrow, and I hasten to add, "But good *enough*."

I think? I've only done this with Serena, who insisted I foster my single useful Vampyre trait and practice on her. She'd have me put her under and use our shared cell phone to film videos of her making out with a cabbage; reciting the Pledge of Allegiance with a German accent; confessing to an entire series of dirty dreams with Mr. Lumiere, our French tutor, as the recurring guest star.

Hopefully, I remember how to.

I kneel in front of Max, ignoring his nauseating, fear-drenched heartbeat, the way he hisses at me to get away. "Dude, I'm trying to help you avoid an iron chair, or however it is that your people extract information, so—"

Something wet lands on the front of my tank top.

Because Max spit on me.

"Ew." I gasp, disgusted, but before I can—I don't know, spit *back*?—Lowe's hand presses against Max's chest and pins him to the couch.

"What the fuck did you just do?" he grunts.

"She's a *Vampyre*!"

"She's my—" Lowe's hand jerks up to clutch Max's jaw. "Apologize to my *wife*."

"Sorry. *Sorry*. Please don't— I'm *sorry*." Max starts sobbing.

Lowe turns to me. "Do you accept?"

"Accept . . . the spit?"

"His apology."

"Oh." Oh my God. What is happening? "Sure, why not? It was so . . . sincere and spontaneous. Just, hold his head still, and don't let him move—yes, hands on the chin. Okay, this will take a second, don't let him wiggle away."

I start with my thumb at the base of Max's nose, and my index and forefingers on his forehead. Then I wait for Max to calm down and meet my eyes.

At the fourth attempt, I get a lock. Max's brain is soft, and over-agitated, and easy to sink into. I stitch his mind to mine and then scramble it a little—a temporary interference. I don't stop until I'm extra sure that my hold on him is tight, and when I pull back, his body relaxes at once, pupils suddenly blown wider. Behind me, I hear some murmurs and a soft "What the fuck?" but it's easy to push it out, just as easy as it is to let my eyes do what they're supposed to.

For the thrall.

Humans say that we have magical mind-control powers. That our souls can body-snatch theirs and tie them up like a Thanksgiving turkey. Much like everything else, though, it's simple biology. An additional intraocular muscle that allows us to shift our eyes at high speed and induce a hypnotic state. Vampyres who are talented thrallers, like my father, can do it without touching their victim at all, and much more quickly. But they are rare, and for the mediocre ones like me, who need someone to be restrained to initiate a thrall, it can be an unwieldy practice.

There are some caveats, too. The thrall only works on other species, and not every brain is equally responsive. And, of course, entering people's minds without consent is an act of violence, and deeply unethical. Just because we can, it doesn't mean that we should. But Max did try to hurt Ana, and he might do it again. Plus, my morals are just not that solid.

"Okay." I lean back, vigorously rubbing my eyes. The thrall requires a *lot* of energy. "He's all yours."

Everyone stares at me open-mouthed. And my mind might be playing tricks, but I'm almost positive that they've all taken a step back from me.

Except for Lowe, who's almost too close.

"You guys might wanna hurry. This will only last ten minutes or so." I point at Max's state of unresponsive stupor. "He won't just word-salad his life story at you. You need to go ahead and ask him questions." No one speaks. Did I accidentally thrall *them*, too? "Something like, 'Why were you trying to take Ana, Max?'"

"I was tasked to take her to the Loyals, where she could be used as leverage, to force Lowe to step down as Alpha," he recites tonelessly.

The room explodes in a flurry of panicky, suspicious mutters that have nothing to do with Max's answer. In fact, I'm pretty sure I catch a "Microwaved his brain."

"The thrall," Lowe murmurs.

"Yup. That's it. No deep-frying involved." I stand and grimace at the spit on my shirt. It's starting to seep through—gross.

"I thought it was a myth," Cal whispers. "That our elders used to scare us."

I can relate, since I grew up fairly sure that if I misbehaved, a Were would crawl up the toilet to eat my ass. "It's not. I'm not really good at this, actually." It seems best not to disclose what someone like Father could do.

"You look plenty good to me," Cal says. He actually sounds admiring, while Ken is glaring suspiciously, and Mick frowns, and Gemma shakes her head, and some other Weres exchange looks, and Juno seems, as ever, worried and angry, and Lowe . . .

I've given up on understanding Lowe.

"How do we know you're not planting lies in his head?" Ken asks.

I shrug. "Ask him something I wouldn't know."

"What happened when you asked Mary Lakes out for a date?" Juno says.

"She said no," Max drones.

"Why?"

"Because I had a huge blob of snot coming out of my nose."

It's funny, but no one laughs. The group seems to have gotten over the initial incredulity, and Cal starts grilling Max. "Did Roscoe's mate send you to take Ana?"

"I believe so, even though I did not talk to Emery directly."

Cal shakes his head. "Of fucking course."

"Stop." Lowe interrupts, and the room falls silent again. He turns to me. My breath catches as his arm reaches inside the hoodie he put on me. His palm briefly fits on my waist, then moves north to brush against my breast, and oh my God, what—

He slides his phone out of the inside pocket and pulls back.

My cheeks are on fire.

"Take her to her room, then come back," he orders Mick. To Juno: "Check on Ana, please."

I'm escorted out. I must really be at my most busybody, because I'm tempted to ask if I can stay. Figure out what this strange war within the Weres could be about. Instead I meekly follow Mick up the stairs.

"I hope I didn't get you in trouble," I tell him, "but I saw Max take Ana, and I know you guys don't believe me, but he'd attacked me, so—"

"No one doubted you," he says kindly.

I look at him. "Lowe sure did."

"Lowe knew Max had attacked you first. He is very good at smelling lies."

"Oh. As in . . . literally smelling?"

Mick nods but doesn't elaborate. "He knew Max was up to something, knew it had to do with Ana, and wanted to get as much information as he could out of him. It's a tightrope to walk, for Lowe. He won't go about interrogating every person he doesn't like, or he'll be the same as Roscoe was toward the end. But the Loyals have been hurting their own, and they must be stopped."

"He sure seemed ready to let the others torture Max."

"That was a show, meant to scare Max. And it would have worked, we could all smell it. But you did make it easier with your . . ." He smiles and gestures at my eyes. "Just promise you won't do it to me, okay? You were *scary* in there."

"I would *never*. You're my most beloved jailer." I smile, close-lipped and fangless. "Besides, I'm the one who should be scared."

"Why?"

I point to the scar on his neck. The row of teeth marking his collarbone. "You're the one rolling in here with that, like your favorite pastime is getting into fights." I cock my head. "Is that how you turned into a Were?"

His eyebrow quirks. "We're a legitimate species, not an infectious disease."

"Just making sure that if someone bites me I won't turn into you."

"If you bit someone, would it turn them into a Vampyre?"

I think about it for a moment. "Touché."

He laughs softly and shakes his head, suddenly wistful. "This is my mate's bite."

Mate. The word, again.

"Do they have one, too? Your mate."

"Yes, of course."

"Have I met them?"

He looks away. "She's not with us anymore."

"Oh." I swallow, unsure what to say. *I hope it wasn't one of my people who did it.* "I'm sorry. It sounds like mates are a big deal."

He nods. "Mating bonds are the core of every pack. But I don't think it's wise for me to discuss Were customs with you." He gives me a look that manages to be chiding and soft all at once. "Especially if you're chatting with your brother in a language no one else speaks."

Oh, *shit.* "It's not . . . I just missed home. Wanted to hear something familiar."

"Did you?" We come to a halt in front of my door. Mick opens it, and gestures for me to step inside. "How curious. You don't strike me as the type who ever had a home."

I let his words churn around me for several minutes after he leaves, wondering whether he's right. When they grind to a stop, I know he isn't: I did have a home, and her name was Serena.

I change my top into one less smeared with Max's DNA and silently slip out of my room. With everyone distracted by the commotion, breaking into Lowe's office is almost suspiciously easy. There are plenty of ways to hack into a computer, few of which are at my disposal. Fortunately, I have enough experience with brute-force techniques to be optimistic.

The sun is setting, but I don't turn on the lights. Lowe's desk is given away by Ana's grinning picture. I tiptoe there, kneel in front of the keyboard, and start messing around.

This is not my bread and butter, but it's relatively simple and not too time-consuming. It's clear that the Weres don't expect intrusions from within, and the machine is mostly unprotected. It only takes me a few minutes to force my way into their database, and a handful more to set up three parallel searches: *Serena Paris*, the date she disappeared, and *The Herald*, in case my suspicions are right, and Lowe was part of some story she meant to cover. It's just a start, but I hope that if she was mentioned on any communication device that's automatically backed up on—

Something soft rubs against my calf.

"Not now," I murmur, distractedly swatting Serena's damn fucking cat away. The terminal starts to populate with hits. I stroke a few keys to maximize. So far, not too promising.

The cat's wet nose presses against my thigh. "I'm busy, Sparkles or whatever. Go play with Ana."

He starts purring. No, growling. Frankly, it's a level of entitlement that pisses me off. "I told you to—" I glance down and instantly scramble back, nearly falling on my ass.

In the dim light of dusk, the yellow eyes of a gray wolf stare angrily at me.

CHAPTER 9

Ana interrupts her bedtime story to communicate to him important, time-sensitive information: "Miresy is so so soooo pretty. I loooove her ears."

He presses his lips together before resuming his reading.

AMONG THE VAMPYRES, FANGS ARE NOT JUST *TEETH*—THEY are status.

Take muscles in Humans: Was there a time, a bunch of millennia ago, in which having a mate with inflated, bouncy biceps meant more protection from . . . the dinosaurs? I'm no history buff; I thrived in math and zero other subjects. The point is, athletic prowess provided an evolutionary advantage that's now, in an era in which atomic bombs exist, fairly obsolete. And yet, Humans still find it attractive.

Canines are much the same for Vampyres: they're considered a symbol of strength and power, because in the olden days we'd hunt our prey and sink our teeth into their flesh to feast on their blood. The longer, the sharper, the bigger—the better.

And this wolf's . . . This wolf's fangs could win contests. Rule civilizations. Get their owner engaged, married, and very much laid at any Vampyre party. *And* they could shred me into M&M's.

"Are you an actual wolf?" I ask, fighting to keep my voice steady. "Or are you a Were who part-times?"

The only reply is a deep, long, panties-shitting *growl*.

"Would it make things better or worse if I growled back?"

"Wouldn't change it either way," a voice says from the entrance.

Lowe. Leaning against the frame, relaxed like a loungewear model during a photoshoot.

"Thank you, Cal," he says, coming my way. "That will be all."

And magically, with one last half-hearted snarl in my direction, the wolf shakes its beautiful gray fur and trots away. It stops by Lowe and butts its head against his thigh.

"Cal? As in . . ." He turns to me and I stare at his face, looking for similarities. I'd have expected consistency between Weres' shifted and human forms, but Cal's a redhead. I crane my neck to get a better look at the wolf, but Lowe steps in front of me, blocking my view.

"What the fuck are you doing, *wife*?" He sounds like a volatile mix of tired and irritated. Any thought of Were phenotypes instantly departs.

I just got caught. Doing something very bad. And I'm in real danger.

"Just looking for . . ." What? "Sticky notes."

"Do Vampyres keep sticky notes inside their computers?"

Fuck. "I was trying to check my email." I swallow. "Get in touch with friends."

"You don't have friends, Misery."

I'm not sure why this hurts when it's true.

"And I'm very much not an IT person, but that"—he points at my code, which is still crunching along—"does not look like Yahoo."

"Yahoo? Lowe, you're *really* dating yourself here."

"Come in," he orders, and I cannot comprehend how I didn't notice Alex idling by the door. Too busy contemplating my imminent demise, probably. "Can you figure out what she was doing?"

"On it."

I scrunch my eyes shut, running possible scenarios in my head. I could knee Lowe in the groin and try to run away, but I don't know if the crotch area is as sensitive to them as it is to us, and anyway . . . there are *wolves* prowling around. "You set me up," I say. It comes out whiny, which is exactly how I feel. "You asked Mick to leave right in front of me because you knew I'd take advantage of it."

"Misery." He clucks his tongue, chiding, and moves closer, like he knows I'm considering darting away. His heartbeat envelops me, steady, determined. "You set yourself up, because you're bad at this."

"At what?"

"Snooping around."

"I wasn't—"

"Why did you go to my room? Why did you look through my closet and my drawers?" He leans forward. His voice drops to a half whisper, meant only for my ears. There's something tortured to it, like he's in physical pain. "Why did my bed smell like you slept in it?"

It hadn't even occurred to me that I'd leave my scent behind. That Lowe would find my smell stuck to every surface of his room.

Fuck.

"Sorry," I breathe out.

"You should be," he says to the air between our lips. I wonder if my heart has ever beaten this loud before. This close to the surface of my skin.

"She—very astutely, I must say, and with only very primitive tools at her disposal—hacked into our servers," Alex announces. A little admiringly, which is flattering.

"Are you the one who built the Weres' firewall?" I ask.

"Yup. I'm the leader of our security team." He sounds distracted as he combs through my code. Whatever fear he had when we were alone doesn't hold if his Alpha's present.

"Nice job." Weird, how I'm having a conversation with Alex but staring up into Lowe's eyes. About an inch from mine. "It's pretty impenetrable."

"Thank you. Are you, by any chance, the same person who tried to smash it down a few weeks ago?"

I swallow. Lowe's eyes drift down to my throat. Linger there. "Can't remember."

"Alpha, she was running a search of our databases . . . three searches, to be precise. One for a date a little over two months ago, one for *The Herald*—a local human newspaper, I believe—and one for someone called Serena. Serena Paris."

A wave of dread sweeps over me. There is no air in the world left for my lungs.

"And who would that be?" Lowe murmurs, licking his lips. He inhales me deeply, purposefully. "How interesting. In the past week I've witnessed two attempts on your life, and you've never smelled as scared as you do just now. Why, Vampyre?" His stark face is all sharp lines, sculpted by the glowing lights of the monitor. His lips move, full and ruthless. I cannot look away. "Who is Serena Paris, Misery?"

He sounds sincerely curious, and I wonder if maybe he has nothing to do with her disappearance. But maybe he does. Maybe

he's pretending. Maybe he didn't know her name but hurt her anyway.

I push against his chest. It's like trying to move an army of mountains. "Let me go."

"Misery." His eyes bore into mine. "You know I'm not going to do that. Alex," he says, louder this time, still looking only at me. "Bring back Cal. It looks like we're going to have to extract Gabi and break the armistice with the Vampyres."

I overhear a hushed "Yes, Alpha." Boots leave the room as I sputter:

"What?"

"I have to consider this as an act of aggression on behalf of your father and the rest of the Vampyre council. They sent a plant into Were territory under the guise of Collateral." His jaw hardens. "And your scent—they tampered with it, didn't they? They knew it would distract me—"

"*No.*" I'm crowded. Breathless. "This has nothing to do with my father."

"Who were you planning to send this information to?"

"No one! Ask Alex to check. I didn't set up any transmissions."

He shifts closer. I can almost taste his blood on my tongue. "Alex isn't here anymore."

I knew we were alone, but now I *feel* it, just as I feel his warmth seeping through me. The heat has a predictable effect: my stomach twists and tightens. Hunger. Cravings. "I told you, I was just messing around."

"This is not a *game*, Misery." They vibrate through my bones, his words. "This alliance is new and frail, and—"

"Stop it. Just *stop* it." I press my hands against his chest, begging for some space, because I'm—my head is spinning, full of warm, heated, odd thoughts, thoughts that involve veins and necks and *taste*. "Please. *Please*, don't do anything. This has *nothing* to do with the alliance."

"Okay." He moves a step back, palms still leaning against the wall on each side of my head, and it's a relief. His blood was starting to smell really good, and—

Nothing like that has ever happened to me. I must have forgotten to feed.

"Okay," he repeats, "here are your options. First, you tell me who Serena Paris is and give me a reasonable explanation for this *very* poorly executed cloak-and-dagger quest. What happens to you next is *my* choice. Second, I proceed with the assumption you are a spy gathering intel on the Weres and use your corpse to send a clear message to your father."

"Serena was my friend," I blurt out. "My *sister*."

Lowe's entire body tenses. Like he had some guesses, but my answer was not among them. "A Vampyre, then."

I shake my head. "Human. But we grew up together. In my first few months as the Collateral, I was disruptive. And sad. I tried to run away, put myself in dangerous situations, once I even . . . It was just me and the Human caregivers, and they hated me. So the Humans decided that the company of another child might make me more well-behaved. They found an orphan my age and brought her in to live with me."

He huffs, bitter, and I'm afraid he might not believe me. But then he says, calm and yet not: "Fucking Humans."

I swallow. "They did their best. At least they tried."

"Not enough." It's a definite kind of judgment. Which I don't care to argue with.

"Serena is gone. She vanished a few weeks ago, and—"

"You think a Were took her?"

I nod.

"Who?"

I have no choice but to tell him the truth. And if he has anything to do with her disappearance . . . He'll have something to do with mine, too. "You."

He seems unsurprised. "Why me?"

"You tell me." I lift my chin. "Your name was in her planner, on the day she disappeared. Maybe she made plans to meet you. Maybe you were part of a story she was writing. I don't know."

"A story? Ah, that's why *The Herald*. She was a journalist." It's not a question, but I nod.

Finally, Lowe pulls back. He remains between me and the door, but he rubs his hands across the stubble on his jaw, frowning somewhere in the distance, instantly preoccupied. Trying to recall. If he's faking the confusion, he's a good actor. And I cannot begin to guess why he'd lie to me. I'm stuck here for the next year, with limited and highly supervised ways to communicate with the outside world. He could admit to running five drug cartels and hijacking Air Force One, and I'd have no way to warn anyone.

"It's a huge gamble." He searches my face, pensive. A little like he's seeing me for the first time. "Giving yourself as Collateral. Marrying me. All because someone wrote my name in her planner."

I bite my lower lip. My stomach sinks at the idea that he might really not know anything. My only trail, leading to a ravine. "My best friend, my *sister*, is gone. And no one will look for her if I don't. And the only thing she left behind, the only clue I have is a name, *your* name, L. E. Moreland—"

"Lowe!" The door bursts open. I expect Alex, or Cal, or an entire pack of rabid wolves coming to butcher me. Not a plaintive, "Where *were* you?" followed by the soft shuffle of socked steps on the hardwood floor.

I'm instantly forgotten. Lowe drops to his knees to greet Ana, and when she wraps her slim arms around his neck, his large hand comes up to cradle her head. "I was talking to Misery."

She waves up at me. "Hi, Miresy."

My throat feels full. "My name is not *that* hard to pronounce," I mumble, but she seems to revel in my glare. And to be in high spirits, despite her attempted kidnapping. I applaud her resilience, but wow, children. They're truly unfathomable.

"Will you read me a story before bed?" she asks Lowe.

"Of course, love." He pushes a strand of still-wet hair behind her ear. "Go brush your teeth, I'll—"

"Ana, where did you go?" Juno's voice drifts in from the hallway, harried, out of breath. "Ana!"

"Did you run away from Juno?" Lowe whispers.

Ana nods, mischievous.

"Then you better hurry back to her."

She pouts. "But I want to—"

"Liliana Esther Moreland! Come here at once, it's an order!"

Ana stamps a kiss on Lowe's cheek, mutters something delighted about how prickly it is, and then slips out in a flurry of blue and pink fabric. My eyes stay with her, and then on the ajar door, long after she disappears.

Dizzy.

I feel dizzy.

"Misery?"

I turn to Lowe. "Ana . . . ?" I swallow. Because, no. That's not the right question. Instead: "Liliana?"

He nods.

"Esther." *L. E. Moreland.* "I didn't . . . I had no idea."

Lowe nods again, eyes somber. "Misery. You and I need to talk."

CHAPTER 10

He is not reckless, or negligent, or quick to trust. But he recognizes a formidable ally when he sees one.

MANY ROOMS IN THE HOUSE WOULD BE PERFECTLY AD-equate for a discreet conversation, but we find ourselves sitting at the kitchen table, a mug of black coffee in front of Lowe, steadily steaming as the sun outside struggles to rise.

My night was sleepless, like most. His, too, going by the dark shadows under his eyes. His face is etched, as carvingly beautiful as usual. He hasn't shaved in a while, and it's clear that he could use some rest and a two-week stretch without a coup.

I have the sneaking suspicion he's not going to get either.

"I couldn't figure out why you'd accepted," he tells me between sips, almost conversationally. Every other interaction we've had has been fraught with tension, on the heels of him catching me in compromising situations. Now . . . We're not fast friends, but I wonder if this is Lowe when his energies are not fully focused on trying to protect his pack. A steady, reassuring, bulky presence. His mouth even twitched into an almost smile when he saw me make my way down the stairs, as he gestured for me to take a seat across from him. "Why you'd do it *again*."

"You thought I had a martyrdom complex?" I hug my legs to my chest, watching his lips as they close around the rim of his mug. "I have no allegiance to the Vampyres. Or the Humans, with a single exception. And I'm going to find her."

He sets the mug on the table, and asks, bluntly: "You're sure she is alive?"

"I hope she is." My heart twists. "If she isn't, I still need to know what happened to her." If I don't, no one else will think of her again. No one else will even know her name aside from a handful of orphans who bullied her for being cross-eyed, colleagues who never got her sense of humor, people she dated but felt tepid about. It's not acceptable. "She'd do the same for me."

Lowe nods without hesitation. Loyalty, I suspect, is a painfully familiar concept to him. "Do you know what article she was writing? What prompted her interest in Ana?"

"No. She usually talked about the stories she was working on, at least in passing. And she covered financial stuff."

"Crimes?"

"Sometimes. Mostly market analysis. Her degree was in economics."

Lowe taps his finger on the edge of the table, mulling. "Anything on Were-Human, or Vampyre-Human relationships?"

"She'd grown up as the Collateral's baby companion. She wasn't touching that shit with a ten-foot pole."

"Smart." He stands, goes to the no-blood fridge. His broad shoulders shrink the kitchen as he gathers a few items that he carries back to the table. A jar of peanut butter that has my most nefarious interests perk up. Sliced bread. Some kind of berry jelly that just stumps me.

Serena loved berries, and I tried memorizing their names, but they're so counterintuitive. Blueberries? Not blue. Blackberries? Not black. Strawberries? Straw free. Raspberries? Do not rasp, or make any noise at all. I could go on.

"I want to have a look at her communications prior to disappearing. You still have access to them?"

"I do. And have inspected them—no clues."

He takes out two slices of bread. His forearms are strong, large muscles interrupted by the occasional white scar. "If Were business is involved, you might not know what you're looking for. I'll have you talk with Alex and hand them over to—"

"Hey." I shift and tuck my legs under me. "I'm not turning over anything until you tell me what *you* would be looking for."

His eyebrow lifts. "You're not in a negotiating position, Misery."

"Neither are you."

The eyebrow lifts higher.

"Okay, maybe more than I am. But if we're doing this, I need to know what's in it for you, because I highly doubt you suddenly care about my random Human friend enough to help me find her."

He's good at staring, staring with those arctic eyes without saying anything, and I squirm in my chair, heated. How does this guy make someone with a basal temperature of ninety-four degrees and next to no sweat glands feel clammy?

"It's about Ana, right? You think Serena was looking for Ana."

More staring. Mistral, with a hint of assessment.

"Listen, it's obvious that you want to figure out why a Human knew of your sister's existence. And I'm not asking you to *trust* me—"

"I think I will, though," he finally says, decisive. And then starts spreading peanut butter on the bread, like he's settled an important matter and now needs a snack.

"You will . . . ?"

"Trust you."

"I don't get it."

"No." His expression is not tender, but approaching. Kind. Amused, for sure. "I reckon you wouldn't."

"I was just proposing we trade information."

"And you could do many horrible things with the information I'm about to give you. But you've been in Ana's shoes before. And you're hurt because you ran to help her when the sun hadn't set yet." Lowe points at the reddened skin of my right arm and hands me an ice pack.

He must have retrieved it earlier from the freezer. And it feels really, *really* good.

"Misguided as you were, I doubt you'd throw Ana under the bus."

"No more misguided than using her as *bait*. Nice parenting there, by the way," I add, a bit archly.

"There were eight Weres monitoring the situation," he says, unoffended. "And a tracker in her suit. Max had no vehicle at his disposal, so we knew he was going to attempt to hand off Ana to someone else. She was never in any real danger."

"Sure." I shrug, pretending I don't care. "And children are soft and adaptable and make for perfect pawns in the power plays of great leaders, right?"

"I can only protect Ana if I know where the threats against her are coming from." He leans forward across the table. The scent of his blood is like a wave lapping at my skin. "I'm not like your father, Misery."

My throat is suddenly dry. "Well, you're wrong. I *would* throw Ana under the bus, if I had to choose between her and Serena." I have priorities, very little heart, and find no pleasure in being deceitful when others are being honest with me. Ana might be growing on me, but she wasn't the one who slept next to me for a whole week when I was fourteen and gave myself seizures by trying to file off my fangs for the first time. With a cheese grater.

"Yeah?" He doesn't sound like he believes me. "Hopefully it won't come to that."

"I don't think it will," I agree. "And it makes sense for us to collaborate. As Ana's brother and Serena's sister."

His eyes meet mine, serious and unsettling. "Not as husband and wife?"

Because we're that, too, even if it's disturbingly easy to forget. I glance away, landing on a dollop of peanut butter on the rim of the jar. It's the variety without the crunchy bits, which . . . yeah.

I set down my ice pack and lean back in my chair, as far away from it as possible.

"She'll be seven next month, by the way," he tells me. "She's just better at lying with words than with her fingers."

"Are her parents . . . Where are they?"

There is an infinitesimal stutter in his movement, and he sets down the jelly jar. "Mother's dead. Father's somewhere in Human territory."

"There are Weres in Human territory?"

Lowe's jaw tenses. "This, Misery, is where I'm taking a leap of faith."

My heart goes wooden. A memory flashes: my first day alone among the Humans, after Father and Vania and the rest of the Vampyre convoy had left. The terrifying smell of their blood, their odd sounds, the weird *beings* crowding around me. Knowing I was the only member of my species for miles and miles. I don't want it for her. I don't want it for *anyone*. "Is Ana Human? A Collateral?"

He shakes his head. I'm flooded with relief. "Okay. She's Were. Then why—" I stop.

Because Lowe shakes his head again.

I know what Vampyres smell like, what their needs and limitations are. And Ana is *not* one of us. Which leaves one single other possibility.

"No," I say.

Lowe says nothing. His knife clinks against the side of the plate, and he crosses his arms on his chest. His expression remains anchored in a way that makes me utterly unhinged.

"It's not possible. They . . . No. Not *both*." Why is he silent? Why is he not *correcting* me? "Genetically, it's not . . . Is it?"

"Apparently."

"How?" There are so many levels of impossibility here. That a Human and a Were would even want to *engage* in what's necessary to produce a child. That it would work, physically. That it would have consequences. Weres may not struggle as much as Vampyres, but their reproductive rates are still lower than Humans'.

I shoot to my feet in a spurt of nervous, incredulous energy. Immediately sit down again when my abused soles protest. "But she's related to you, isn't she? The eyes . . ."

"My mother's eyes." He nods. "She was one of Roscoe's seconds. Overseeing the woods between Were and Human territories. Officially, under Roscoe's rule there were no diplomatic relationships. In practice, very limited agreements with Humans were constantly being negotiated, especially in high-conflict areas. I believe that's how she first met Ana's father, but I wasn't around at the time." He sounds regretful, and I remember the pretty house drawings. The only locked space in his room.

"He's not your father, is he?"

"My father was a Were, and he died when I was a child."

I'm not going to ask if my people were involved in that, because I'm sure I know the answer. "Why are you telling *me* this?"

He is silent for a while, eyes downcast. It's not until I follow his gaze that I realize he's staring at our wedding band on his ring finger. "You know what makes Alphas good leaders?" he asks without looking up.

"No clue."

He huffs out a laugh. "Neither do I. But at times, there are decisions that feel right, deep in the marrow of my bones." He wets his lips. "You are one of them."

Blood rushes to my cheeks, hot. There's no way Lowe misses it, which is mortifying. I'm just grateful that he chooses to continue without mentioning it.

"I was living in Europe when my mother was injured, but immediately flew back. When it became obvious that she might not make a recovery, she told me about Ana's biological father."

"Her *Human* biological father." Inconceivable.

"I thought she was delirious because of the drugs. Or just mistaken."

I tilt my head. "What changed?"

"There are things about Ana. Things that had me taking what my mother said as more than some morphine-induced delusion."

"Like what?"

"For one, Ana doesn't shift."

"Oh. Should she, already?"

"A Were child would. In fact, during the full moon, they'd have trouble *not* shifting. Her blood is a deep red instead of green. At the same time, she has Were traits. She's more agile, stronger than a Human. Her vitals are all over the place. After my mother passed, and very discreetly, I had her DNA tested. Juno is a geneticist, and she was able to help." He picks up the knife again, slathers more jelly. The peanut butter jar is still there. Open. "At the time, Roscoe was the Alpha; it was easy to predict what he'd do if he found out that he had a half Human in his pack."

"Roscoe was not a fan, huh?"

He gives me an understatement-of-the-decade look.

"And, she was the sister of the dude who smelled like he was gonna steal his job," I murmur without thinking. I notice Lowe's surprise. "What? I know things."

"Roscoe was never a peaceful Alpha, but in the past few years, his positions gradually escalated to extreme aggression. He demanded control of certain demilitarized zones, and began enforcing zero-tolerance policies. We killed more Humans and Vampyres in the last decade than we did in the previous five—and they killed more of us. That's when several of his seconds began to openly disagree with him. Their dissent was met with another ramp-up of violence. This time last year, more Weres were dying at the hands of other Weres than any other species. My mother was one of them." His lips press together. "I came home, challenged Roscoe, and won. His four most loyal seconds challenged me, and I won again. There were others, weaker and weaker, and it felt so wasteful to . . ." He rubs his jaw with his palm. His thinking gesture, I'm starting to realize. "It was my mistake. I shouldn't have let them live."

I study him, wondering if he ever *wanted* to be Alpha in the first place. Wondering how I'd feel, leading thousands of people without feeling a true calling to it. At least Father thrives on the high-stakes life of politics, and subterfuge, and petty pissing matches against the other councilmen.

"Let me guess: the ones you defeated but left alive rebranded themselves as the Loyals and have been radicalizing young Maxes like it's their birthday."

He nods. "It's a small group, but they're willing to stoop much lower than I can afford to. And they have the blessing and leadership of Emery, Roscoe's mate. She denies it, of course, and she's a smart-enough player to avoid having the recent attacks traced back to her, but we have intel."

"If it were me, I'd borrow a page from their beloved Roscoe and deal with dissent his way."

His mouth curves infinitesimally, like he's tempted to do just that, and I smile, too. Our eyes hold for a beat before he continues: "Ana doesn't know who her real father is."

"Who does she think . . . ?"

"Vincent. He was another of Roscoe's seconds, and he and my mother were in an on-and-off relationship for years. He was attacked in Vampyre territory, when Ana was about one year old. The rest of the pack are also under the impression, heavily encouraged by my mother, that Ana is Vincent's kid."

"How are you explaining away the not shifting bit?"

"It's not widely known, and there are other conditions that could cause it, including a psychological block. They are rare, but . . ."

"Not as rare as a half-Human Were. Who else knows?"

"Juno and Cal, because we grew up together and they're family. Mick, too. He was one of Roscoe's seconds, the only person my mother could rely on when I was gone. Aside from that, my mother told no one. But I'm starting to question that. I can only imagine Serena being interested in Ana . . ."

". . . because she's half Human. And if Serena knows . . ."

". . . there's no telling who else does," he finishes.

I drum my fingers on the table, thinking this through. "Max didn't say anything useful about the Loyals?"

"He doesn't know much, aside from the names of a few low-level members. The Loyals recruited him because he has ties to some of my seconds and easy access to Ana, but they didn't trust him enough to reveal anything. He didn't know who he was going to hand Ana to."

"Do you think the Loyals know about Ana?"

A thoughtful pause. "It's a possibility. But it's more likely that they're using my only living relative to force me to listen to their demands. They know I'm the rightful Alpha, and that no one could take me in the challenge." He sounds more resigned than proud. "It's not a well-thought-out plan on their part, but they are desperate. And damn annoying." He massages the bridge of his nose.

"Can't they just secede and form their own pack?"

"They're very welcome to do so, and they'd make my fucking life much easier. But they don't have the resources or the necessary leadership to do it. What they want is control of the financial assets of the Southwest pack. Emery comes from a long line of powerful Weres, and she sees it as her due. But for the past few months, the Loyals have been sabotaging construction projects, destroying infrastructure, assaulting my seconds. No one who'd resort to that should be in control of the largest pack in the country."

"Or of a chicken coop, if you ask me." I bite my lower lip, mulling it over. "Who is Ana's father?"

"My mother never told me. My impression is that he already

had a family, and that when she attempted to mention Ana to him, he . . ."

"Didn't believe her?"

"Yeah."

"Can't blame him. So, going back to Serena. Aside from you, only Juno, Cal, and Mick know about Ana. Could any of them . . . ?" I give him a long, pregnant look that will hopefully tell him what I'm not planning to voice.

He shakes his head and starts cutting the sandwich out of its crusts. I follow the rhythm, mesmerized by his graceful hands, and recall that this is something Serena used to prefer for her food when we were . . . younger than Lowe, for sure. I would *not* have thought a big bad wolf would be this picky.

"Not to be a discord sower, and I promise this is only marginally related to Juno's hankering for carving my organs out, but maybe you should investigate the possibility that one of them tattled you out."

"I did. Despite them having risked their lives for me a dozen times over." He says it angrily, like it was sour and painful, something he's ashamed of, and a thought hits me: that maybe Lowe is the kind of leader who measures his strength not by the battles he wins, but by the trust he is able to accord to others. There is something about him, about the way he commands, that manages to be at once pragmatic and idealistic.

He sets the crusts aside and leans his palms on the table once more, leveling with me. "I asked. They're not involved, and they haven't told anyone."

"Okay, yes, *but.* There is this thing people sometimes do, which you guys may not have a term for. The Vampyres call it *lying.*"

His look is withering. "I'd be able to tell if they were betraying me."

"Is this the smell-a-lie thing? Does it really work?"

This time he's less impressed by my knowledge of Were secrets. Perhaps because they aren't secrets at all. "Not always. But scent changes with feelings. And feelings change with behavior."

I scowl. "I still can't believe you knew Max was lying all along and still put a guard on *me*."

"I put a guard on you for *your* safety."

"Oh." He did? I had not considered that. It takes a long second for my assessment of the last five days to adjust, and . . . *Oh*, indeed. "I can take care of myself."

"Against a young Were with no combat training, yes. Against someone like me, doubtful."

I could scoff and be offended, but I like to think that I know my limits. "Does it build up?"

"What?"

"The odor. Just wondering if that's why I smell like fish soup to you. Have I lied too much in my life?"

It's a genuine question, but Lowe sighs deeply and leaves me hanging. He puts the food back in the fridge, with one glaring exception: the peanut butter. My gluttonous brain must be strained by the biological possibility of Were-Humans, because it dispatches my hand to scoop up a little glob from the rim, right to my lips, and it's been so long, it's so *fucking* good—

"What the hell?"

I open my eyes. Lowe stares curiously at the way I'm suckling on my index finger.

"Did you just *eat*?"

"No." I flush, mortified. "No," I repeat, but the peanut butter sticks to the roof of my mouth, garbling the syllable.

"I was told Vampyres don't eat food."

I can't remember the last time I felt this degree of embarrassment. "Serena made me," I blurt out.

Lowe glances around, to the zero number of Serenas in sight.

"Not *now*. But she made me try it for the first time." I wipe my finger off on my shirt. *Humiliating.* "The ensuing addiction was all mine," I concede with a mumble.

"Interesting." His gaze is sharp, and he seems more than interested. He seems intrigued.

"Please kill me now."

"So you *can* digest food."

"Some of it. Our molars are mostly vestigial, so no chewing, but peanut butter is smooth and creamy and I *know* it's wrong, but . . ." I shiver with how amazing it tastes. And with how shameful and self-indulgent food eating is considered among Vampyres. Not even living among the Humans has beaten the belief out of me. Not even watching Serena scarf down three cups of instant udon noodles at two a.m. because she felt "a bit peckish." "This is so undignified. Can you please not tell anyone and throw my corpse in the lake after I run myself through the garbage disposal, which I'm going to do right now?"

His lips twitch into the ghost of a smile. "You're embarrassed."

"*Of course.*"

"Because you're eating something you don't need to survive?"

"Yes."

"I eat for pleasure all the time." He shrugs, as though his broad shoulders want to agree with him. *We have a healthy appetite. We require nourishment.* "Just pretend it's blood."

"It's not the same. Vampyres don't drink blood for pleasure. We scarf it down when we need to and then don't think about it. It's a bodily function. Like, I don't know, peeing."

He takes a seat across from me and—*fuck* him. I hate him so much for the way he pushes the jar in my direction, holding my eyes the entire time.

He is *daring* me.

And it says something about how far gone I am for this stupid, addictive *nut paste* that I'm considering having a little more.

And then I just do.

"What *do* Vampyres do for pleasure?" he asks, voice a little hoarse. I don't want to flash my fangs at him, but it's hard when I'm licking peanut butter off my fingers.

"Not sure." My time among them was exclusively as a child, when rules abounded, and indulgences were in short supply. Owen, the only adult Vampyre with whom I have regular exchanges, enjoys gossiping and making caustic remarks. Father has his strategic maneuvers and soft-core coups d'état. How the others amuse themselves in their spare time, I have no idea. "Fucking, probably? Please, take this away from me."

He doesn't. Instead he stares too long and too intensely, rejoicing in my lack of control. When he lowers his eyes, it seems to require some effort.

"What could Serena be investigating?" His voice is gravelly. And sobering.

"She never mentioned the Weres to me, not even in passing. But she didn't love her colleagues in the financial division. Maybe she was angling for a better job and exploring nonfinancial stories. Though she would have told me." *Would she? She was clearly hiding stuff from you*, a nagging voice offers. I shush it. "I do know that she wouldn't have gone public with a story that had the potential to endanger a child."

I'm not sure Lowe believes me, but he strokes his jaw, carefully gathering his thoughts. "Either way, our priorities match."

"We both want to find out who told Serena about Ana." For the first time since this sham marriage—no, for the first time since that hag Serena didn't show up to help me change my sheets, I feel a real, genuine burst of hope. *L. E. Moreland* is not just a stray breadcrumb, but a thread to hold on to and tug at.

"I'm going to give you access to whatever technology you need—not that you ever asked for my permission," he adds with a drawl. "You should look into Serena's communications in the weeks before her disappearance. I know you already tried, but you should cross-reference it with our data. I'll give you information about Ana's whereabouts that might help bring more insight. And Alex will help and monitor you." I make a face, which has him adding sternly, "You are still a Vampyre living in our territory."

"And here I was, thinking we were firmly in the reluctant alliance stage of our marriage." I don't mind the supervision. It's more that Alex appears to be as good a hacker as I am—the one area in which I allow myself to be competitive. "Okay. Thanks," I add, a bit sullen.

He nods once. The conversation comes to a bit of a lull, which then stretches into something of an awkward silence, which means that Lowe is done with me.

I'm being dismissed.

I give one last half-loathing, half-longing glance at the peanut butter jar and stand, pushing my hands down into the pockets in my shorts. "I'll start tonight."

"I'll have Mick bring you something to put on them."

I'm confused. Then notice that his eyes are slowly traveling down my bare legs. "Ah. My feet?" I shiver, but it's not cold. Now that I think about it, this place hasn't been cold in days.

"And your shoulders. And your side."

I frown. "How do you know my side hurts?"

"Professional hazard." I tilt my head. Doesn't he have an architecture degree? Do I look like the Leaning Tower of Pisa? "We teach young Weres to study potential enemies for weaknesses. You've been rubbing your rib cage."

"Ah." *That* profession.

"Do you need medical attention?"

"Nah, it's just more burns." I lift my shirt and let it pool right under my bra, angling slightly to show him. "My tank top was askew, and the sun managed to get . . ."

All of a sudden, his pupils are as large as the irises. Lowe abruptly turns his head in the opposite direction. The tendons of his neck stretch, and his Adam's apple bobs. "You should leave," he says. Gruff. Cutting.

"Oh."

His shoulders relax. "Go take another one of your baths, Misery." His voice is husky, but kinder.

"Right. The smell. Sorry about that."

I'm at the bottom of the stairs when Ana comes racing down the steps, almost crashing into me. Her eyes are full of tears, and my heart clenches. "Are you okay?" I ask, but she runs past me, straight toward her brother. She's babbling something about bad dreams and waking up scared.

"Come here, love," he tells her, and I turn to study them. Watch him lift her into his lap, push her hair back to kiss her forehead. "It was just a nightmare, okay? Like the others."

Ana hiccups. "Okay."

"You still don't remember what it was about?"

A few sniffles. "Just that Mama was there."

Their voices lower to soft whispers, and I turn to climb the stairs. The last thing I hear is a phlegmy, "Okay, but did you cut the crusts off?" and a deep, hushed response that sounds a lot like, "Of course, love."

CHAPTER 11

Some nights, when he's walking past her door, he has to whisper to himself: "Keep going."

TWO THINGS CAN BE TRUE AT ONCE.

For instance: I like Alex, because he's an intelligent, pleasant young man.

And: spending time together and watching him be terrified of me sparks joy.

Just for fun, I'm tempted to contact a therapist and ask them to quantify how bad a person I am. But by the time Alex and I have been working side by side for five nights, I've accepted that reassuring him that I don't plan to feast on his plasma is futile. Nothing will convince him that I'm not going to exsanguinate him. And I really shouldn't enjoy it, but there's something genuinely fun about watching him move around the room like a contortionist to avoid giving me his back, or about running my tongue over my fangs and feeling the clatter of the keyboard stammer to a halt. It's usually followed by eyes scrunched shut, and low whimpers he thinks I cannot hear, and . . . The Were children who bike all the way to my bedroom window just to point at it are right. I *am* a monster.

And yet, I carry on. Even after overhearing Alex say, "Please, *please*, don't let me die until I turn twenty-five or I get to visit the the Spy Museum, whatever comes first." Yeah. He prays a lot.

He has no idea why his Alpha tasked him with helping me in a *Where in the World Is Carmen Sandiego?* errand, and to his credit, doesn't question it. Most of our work consists of reexamining Serena's correspondence, cross-referencing the people she had contact with in the last few months for Were connections. We gather info I couldn't have found on my own, like that one of the CEOs she interviewed last year for a story on speculative construction owns property near the Were-Human border through a shell company. Even if most stuff leads to dead ends, I still feel closer to Serena than I have since she disappeared.

Lowe checks in for updates once a day, briefly. Father's response to our lack of progress would be a mix of opaque threats and jabs at our intelligence, but Lowe manages to never sound pushy or disappointed, even as worry lines bracket his mouth and his shoulders strain under his shirt. Impressive, really, how civil he keeps it. Maybe it's part of that innate pull to leadership he has. Maybe they taught him patience at Alpha school.

When I wake up on the sixth evening, Mick informs me that the Alpha has been called away on urgent pack business and brought Alex along. Without unsupervised access to technology, I once again have nothing to do. I feed. Wander around the house until the sun fully sets. Then move to the porch.

The sky is prettier here, more expansive than in either Human or Vampyre land, but I can't put my finger on why. I've been chin up, studying it, for a quarter hour or so, when I hear a noise coming from the thicket.

A wolf, I think, instantly ready to retreat inside the house. But no. It's a woman—Juno. She emerges from the trees, looking beautiful, and powerful, and naked.

Newborn-just-slithered-out-of-the-birth-canal naked.

She waves, and then unhurriedly comes to sit on the chair next to mine. "Misery." She nods once, courteously.

"Hey." This is fucking weird. "Just checking: You know you're naked, right?"

"I was on a run." The moon will fill tomorrow, and the light gleams off her glossy hair. "Does it bother you?"

Does it? "No. Does it bother *you*?"

She looks at me like I'm one of those Humans who think premarital sex is a ticket to hell. "I've been meaning to talk to you."

"You have?" *Talk to* might be Were-speak for *severely injure*.

"To apologize."

I tilt my head.

"You helped Ana last week. With Max."

"Sounds like you guys were on it already."

"True. But you . . . cared. And Ana has been through enough that she could use more people who do that." Her full lips press together. "Lowe said you've been using your tech skills to help her, too."

"Kind of." I'd hate for her to think I'm selfless when I'm obviously not.

"I'm sorry I was so harsh with you when we first met. But Lowe is like a brother to Cal and me, which makes Ana family, too, and I was . . ."

"Worried?" I shrug. "I wouldn't be a fan of me, either. I assumed you were being protective."

She still looks apologetic. "She had a hard time. And it will likely only get harder as she grows up. Did Lowe tell you about Maria?"

"Maria?"

"Their mother. She was attacked by Roscoe when she criticized him over pack affairs. I don't think he wanted to kill her, but Weres can get carried away, especially in wolf form."

"He didn't say, no." But I'd gathered as much.

"I cannot begin to imagine how traumatizing it must have been for Ana, seeing her only parent be hurt by the single Were whose authority she'd been raised to never question."

My chest is heavy. "What a piece of shit."

Juno laughs softly. "You have no idea. He had some good years, but . . . Did Lowe tell you Roscoe felt so threatened, he sent him away?"

"Alex mentioned something like that. Where did he go?"

"To the Northwest pack, with Koen. And maybe it was for the best—Lowe got to observe one of the best Alphas in North America, and perhaps he wouldn't be nearly as good a leader if it weren't for Koen. But Lowe was twelve. He was forced to leave his home without knowing if he'd ever be allowed to come back, and he did it. He was angry and frustrated, I felt it, but he never said. And when he came of age, he still wasn't allowed to come back, so he moved to Europe, went to school, started a career. He built a life— and then Roscoe became deranged. Many challenged him, but no one won. We asked Lowe to come back, and he let all of it go. Everything he'd worked for had to come after the pack. Lowe never had a choice on the matter."

I think of flipping through pages.

The pretty buildings in the drawer.

My face.

"He hasn't had anything for himself, Misery. Not one thing. And I've never heard him complain about it, not once. Not that he had to leave, not that he had to take control of the largest pack in North America, not that he had to do it all alone. His life has been duty." She scans my face curiously, like I could right this injustice. I don't know what to say.

"I promise I'm not trying to make his life more difficult. And I feel so shitty about the mate thing."

Juno's eyes widen. "He told you about that?"

"No. I'm not supposed to know, but a friend of my father's mentioned at the wedding that she was who I swapped with. I know his mate is the Were Collateral. Gabrielle."

"Gabrielle?" Juno's look shifts from confused, to blank, to understanding. "Yes. Gabi. His mate."

"I'm not trying to interfere with Lowe's happiness. Our marriage is not real, and he's free to . . . find his happiness wherever he can." I bite into my lower lip. Honesty for honesty. "There is a reason I agreed to this, and I've come clean to him about it."

Her dark eyes linger on me, inquisitive. And after a long time, she says, "It might be cruel of me. But I think that, deep down, I always hoped that Lowe would never find his mate."

I'm still not wholly certain what that means. "Why?"

"Because being an Alpha means always putting your pack first." I'm about to ask why the two things are incompatible, but she stands. I try not to stare at her nipples as she offers her hand. "I'm sorry for the way I acted. And I'd love for you to accept my peace offering."

Her words make me chuckle. When I notice her scowl, I hasten to add, "Sorry—it's not about you. I just remembered that when we were around thirteen, my sister and I used to have this really weird caregiver, and whenever we had a fight he would force us to cut each other's toenails."

"What?"

"I think he got it from a TV show. For each nail, we had to say something nice about each other. And the habit kind of stuck, and it became the way we fixed all our fights?"

"That is . . ."

"Gross?"

Juno might be too polite to agree. "Would you like to do that now?"

"Oh, no. A handshake is so much better." I take her offered hand and grip it firmly.

"I don't know if you and I can ever be friends," she says. "But I can be better."

I smile at her, closemouthed and fangless. "Hell, I can *only* be better."

———— ›∕‹ ————

TURNS OUT, I WAS WRONG ABOUT THE FULL MOON.

It's further ahead than I thought, three whole nights, and the day before, Mick orders me not to leave my room—ideally—or the house, under any circumstances. He still looks out for me, but I haven't had a guard camped outside my door since my conversation with Lowe.

"How come?" I ask curiously. "I mean, I'll do as you say. But what's so different about the full moon?"

"It takes a really powerful Were to shift when the moon is small—and a really powerful Were to *not* shift when it's big. All Weres will be in their most dangerous form, including many youths who have little self-control. Better not test them with unusual scents." I laugh at his old-man-yells-at-a-cloud eye roll, but later that night the persistent howling that seems to be all over the lakeshore gets to me. When my door opens without warning, I'm much jumpier than usual.

"Ana." I exhale and set aside my book. It's about a nosy elderly Were lady who solves murder mysteries in the Northeast pack. I absolutely loathe her, but somehow I'm already at number seven in the series. "Why aren't you wolfing with . . ." Oh.

Right.

Because she *can't* do that.

"Can I come into the closet with you?"

She has been visiting a lot, but usually doesn't ask for permission—just climbs next to me and plays the little games I code for her on the fly. Tonight seems different. "Fine, but no cover hogging."

"Okay," she says. Two minutes later, not only has she stolen my duvet, but she also appropriated my pillow. Pest. "Why don't you sleep in a bed?"

"'Cause I'm a Vampyre." She accepts the explanation. Probably because she accepts *me*. Like Serena used to, and no one else ever. I turn the page, and we're silent for three more minutes, her breath hot and humid against my cheek.

"Usually Lowe stays human and hangs out with me when they're all gone," she says eventually. Her voice is small, and I know why. Alex returned yesterday, but Lowe is still out of town. That's why Ana sounds like something she rarely is: sad.

I put down the book and turn to her. "Are you saying I'm not as good company as Lowe?"

"You're not." I glare, but soften when she asks, "When will I be able to shift, too?"

Shit. "I don't know."

"Misha can do it already."

"I'm sure there are things you can do that Misha can't."

She ponders the matter. "I'm really good at braids."

"There you go." Pretty trivial skill, but.

"Can I braid your hair?"

"Absolutely fucking no."

A couple of hours later, half a dozen braids pull at my scalp, and Ana is snoring softly with her head in my lap. Her heartbeat is sweet, delicate, a butterfly finding a good landing flower, and *fuck* children for being little assholes who manipulate people into wanting to protect them. I hate that I curve my body around hers when I hear heavy, hurried steps through the walls. And I hate that when my bedroom door opens, I reach for the knife I stole from the kitchen and stashed under my pillow.

I'm ready to kill to defend her. This is Ana's fault. Ana is forcing me to fucking *kill*—

Lowe crouches at the entrance of my closet, his pale green eyes furious in the semidarkness.

"Did you know, my dear *wife*, that when I came home during a full moon and could not locate my sister, I was ready to destroy my entire pack and torture all the Weres guarding this house for their negligence?" His whisper is pure, ominous threat.

I shrug. "No."

"I have been looking for her."

"And this is my fault, why?" I make a show of blinking at him, and he closes his eyes, clearly gathering the strength to not butcher me, and clearly only because his sister is currently on me.

"Is she okay?" he asks.

"Yes. *I* am the victim here," I hiss, pointing at the mess on my head.

His eyes travel over the braids, abruptly stopping on the visible tips of my ears. I usually hide them, just to avoid upsetting people with my *otherness*, and the way Lowe stares at them—first with hypnosis-like intensity, then abruptly glancing away—only reinforces that resolution.

"I think Ana might want to become a hairdresser. You should encourage that."

"A better job than mine, for sure."

No arguing that. Especially when I notice the wound on his forearm—four parallel claw marks. It doesn't seem fresh, but there's still some green blood encrusted on it, and it smells . . .

Whatever.

"Was it the Loyals? You were gone for a while." I don't even mind admitting that I noticed. I'm sure he's aware I don't have a particularly fulfilling routine.

"Regular internal pack business. Then a meeting with Maddie, the Human governor-elect. And several Vampyre councilmembers— your father included."

"Yikes."

His lips nearly curl into a smile, but his expression remains grim. Maybe he went to Vampyre territory and managed to see his mate. Maybe he's angry that *I'm* what he comes home to these days. Can't blame him.

"Do you think . . ." After having been an instrument of politics for a decade, I've done my best to pretend it doesn't exist. But I find myself wanting to know. "Will they stick? These alliances?"

He doesn't reply, not even to say that he doesn't, cannot know.

Instead he looks at me for many, many moments, as though the answer might be written on my face, as though I am the key to unlock this.

"If Humans knew of Ana's existence," I say, thinking out loud. "That Humans and Weres can . . ." I let the thought dangle. She could be a powerful symbol of unity after centuries of strife. Or, people could decide she's an abomination.

"Too unpredictable," he says, reading my mind and bending to take his sleeping sister from my lap. Lowe's hands brush mine in the exchange. When he stands, Ana instantly snuggles in his arms, recognizing him by scent even in her slumber. Babbling something that sounds too heartbreakingly close to *Mama* for comfort.

I want to ask him why I found a jar of creamy peanut butter in my fridge. If he's the reason the house is now three degrees warmer than when I arrived. But I somehow can't bring myself to, and then he's the one to speak.

"By the way, Misery."

I look up at him. "Yeah?"

"We have sharper knives." He points at mine with his chin. "That one isn't going to do shit to someone like me."

"It's not?"

"Third drawer from the fridge." I listen to his heavy steps, and once the door to my room clicks closed, I pick up my book and start reading again.

Thanks for the tip, I guess.

CHAPTER 12

*The burden has been feeling lighter, but he lies to himself
about the reason, attributing it to habit, and the fact that
he's growing into his role.*

IT REMINDS ME OF A SKETCH IN A COMEDY SHOW, SO ABSURD
that I lean against the doorframe of Lowe's office and observe it
in silence for a few minutes, amused by the visual.

It's the big man. And the way he handles small gadgets, frowning down at them like they're poisonous spiders. The way he types
at the keyboard with one single finger. And the way he doesn't seem
to be able to follow simple instructions, even though Alex is explaining stuff to him in the tone of someone who's ready to bungee
jump out of his own life.

"—won't be activated until you enter this line of code."

"I entered it," Lowe rumbles.

"Exactly the way I wrote it here, on this piece of paper."

"I did."

"It's case-sensitive. *Alpha*," he tacks on. Reminding himself that
Lowe's his boss. His very *stubborn* boss.

"The problem is this fucking machine."

Lowe lifts his hand, ready to hit what has to be an expensive piece of technology. Which leads to Alex chanting with a Dostoyevskian level of dread, "Oh my God, oh my *God*." Which, in turn, leads to Lowe promising, "It's stuck. I'll punch it once and it'll fix itself." Which, of course, leads to Alex, whom Lowe does *not* pay enough, suddenly being on the verge of tears.

That's when I take pity on both of them and say, "I don't think percussive maintenance is the answer to a coding error."

They both turn to me, saucer-eyed and vaguely embarrassed. As they should be.

"Alex, are you really teaching Lowe how to code?"

"I am *attempting* to." Alex gives both of us a look. He's usually more at ease with me when Lowe's around, but he must know he's momentarily on his Alpha's shit list.

"How many times have you guys been over this?"

"A handful," Lowe mutters, just as Alex says, "Sixteen."

I whistle. "Big hands." My eyes flick to Lowe's.

"It's fine. I'll figure this coding thing out when I'm there. I can improvise." He stands, and Alex and I exchange an incredulous look, the words *digital illiterate* floating in the air between us in Papyrus. Lowe's incompetence might be healing the rift between us.

"I'll call you. You'll guide me on the phone," he tells Alex, this time with more gravity.

"I'm concerned for your safety. There could be traps."

"I'll deal with them." Lowe puts his hand on Alex's shoulder, reassuring. I'm about to break my none-of-my-business rule and ask what this is about when Mick appears.

"Dinner is ready. Ana . . . cooked." He says the last word with a small wince. "And requested everyone's presence." He looks at me. "Yours included."

I frown. "Me?"

"She asked specifically for Miresy."

"Is she aware that I don't eat?"

Lowe folds his arms on his chest. "You do, in fact—"

"Shhhh." I gesture frantically at him to shut his yapping mouth and turn to Mick. "I'm coming. We're coming. Let's go!" Lowe's smirk can only be described as evil.

Ana is delighted to see me. She runs to me, a blur of sparkly pink cotton and unicorn ears, and wraps her little arms around my waist.

"We don't *always* have to hug," I tell her.

She squeezes harder.

I sigh. "Fine. Sure."

It's been nearly a week since the full moon, and the cumulative time I've spent with my husband since then wouldn't be enough to bring a kettle to boil. But Juno came to visit one night and brought a deck of cards, and came back two nights later and brought a movie and Gemma and Flor and Arden, and both evenings felt similar: odd, but fun. I'm with Alex all the time, and Cal's daughter Misha asked to meet me to see "a real-life leech," and a couple other seconds stopped by because they were in the area, just to introduce themselves, and . . .

It's unexpected, especially after my rocky start. I should be a pariah, I *am* one, but I don't think I fit in this place anymore poorly than I did among the Humans, or the Vampyres. In the past seven days, I've had more social interactions than ever before. No: more *positive* social interactions than ever before. The Weres are being surprisingly amicable, even though they know I'm a Vampyre. And I'm being surprisingly relaxed with them, perhaps *because* they know I am a Vampyre. It's a new experience, being treated as what I am.

And now I'm sitting at a table with Lowe, Mick, and Alex, while Sparkles watches us from the windowsill and Ana serves goldfish crackers, heavily implying they are seafood. I hear their heartbeats mix together like an out of tune symphony, and the stray thought hits me that Lowe is my husband, and Ana is my sister-in-law. Technically, I'm having the first family dinner of my life. Like those human sitcoms, the ones with twenty minutes of banter about snap peas that only sounds funny because of the laugh track.

I let out a befuddled snort and everyone turns to me curiously. "Sorry. Carry on, please."

I'm proud of the way I cut my meatloaf and move the crackers around the plate to mimic a half-eaten meal. But I'm not very good at using cutlery, and the context—a meal, *shared*—is as foreign to me as crocodile wrestling. Ana, of course, notices.

"Why is she acting like that?" she whispers theatrically from the head of the table, pointing at my ramrod straight spine, the way I lift and lower my fork like an animatronic puppet.

"She's just not very good at this. Be kind," Lowe murmurs back from next to me.

Ana nods owl-eyed, and moves the conversation to the important matter of whether she'll get a new pair of roller skates before her birthday, what color they might be, will they have glitter, and, more important, will Juno take her to the rink to practice. I get to observe Lowe when he's relaxed. He pretends not to know what roller skates are to irk Ana just a little bit, or that her birthday is coming up to irk her a whole lot. When he's not leading a pack against a group of violent dissidents, he smiles quite a bit. There is something soothing about his teasing humor and his innate self-confidence.

"When is *your* birthday?" Ana asks me, after Mick reveals an unexpected expertise in astrology and informs Ana that she's a Virgo. Alex is an Aquarius—a fact that, like everything else under the sun, violently alarms him.

"I don't have one," I tell her, still reeling from the mental image of middle-aged, rugged Mick perching rimmed glasses on his nose and settling in bed with a copy of *The Zodiac for Dummies*. "My mate used to dabble," he whispers at me, picking up on my befuddlement.

Peas sputter out of Ana's mouth. "How can you *not have a birthday*?"

"I don't know what day I was born." I could find out from council records, since it was the day Mother died. I doubt Father would know. "It might have been spring?"

"How do you keep track of your age?" Alex asks.

"I count one up on Vampyre New Year's Day."

"And you have a party?"

I shake my head at Ana. "We don't do parties."

"No . . . gatherings? Soirees? Board game nights? Communal blood drinking?" Alex is shocked. Maybe relieved. I wonder what stories he was told as a child when he resisted cleaning his bedroom.

"We don't commune. We don't meet in large groups, unless it's to set up war strategies, or business strategies, or other kinds of strategies. Our social life is all strategizing." For the next Father's Day, I should get him a mug that says *All I care about is machinating and like, three people*. Except we don't celebrate Father's Day, either. "But if we *did* have communal blood drinking, we'd feast on promising young computer engineers," I add, and then smack my lips as though I'm thinking of a scrumptious meal, just to watch Alex pale.

"Regarding blood," Mick warns while Ana spills several gallons of water on the table under the guise of pouring us "cocktails," "Misery, the blood bank messaged us that this week's delivery will be delayed a couple of days."

"D-delayed?" Alex chokes out.

Mick's eyebrow lifts. "You seem very invested, Alex. I didn't know you've been partaking."

"No, but . . . what will she eat?"

"I guess I'll have to find another source of blood. Hmm, who could it be? Let's see . . ." I drum my fingers against the edge of the table to create suspense. It sure works on Ana, who's looking at me gape-mouthed. "Who smells good around—"

Lowe's hand closes around mine. Our wedding bands clink together as he lifts it from the table and sets it in my lap, his grip lingering for a second.

I feel hot.

I shiver.

Lowe clicks his tongue. "Stop playing with your food, *wife*," he murmurs, and it feels almost intimate, smiling at him and catching the amused gleam in his eyes while Alex crumples into himself. "She has several bags left," he informs Alex, who's trying to camouflage with the wallpaper.

"Let's make up a birthday for you," Ana proposes, bright-eyed. "And have a biiiig party."

"Yikes." I scrunch my nose. "Let's not."

"Let's yes! Your birthday is this weekend, and you're going to have a bouncy castle!"

"I'm not a very bouncy person."

"And this weekend your brother will be gone, Ana," Mick says. Alex's fork clicks against his plate. Something shifts, and the silence in the room is suddenly tense as Lowe chews his meatloaf.

"Feel free to have the party without me," he says once he's swallowed, with the calm, effortless tone of someone who knows that every word of his is law. Then, with a conspiratorial wink at Ana: "Take pictures of Miresy bouncing."

She nods enthusiastically as Mick offers, "Or you could cancel."

Lowe sips on his water and doesn't reply, but it's clear that this conversation has been ongoing for a while.

"At least take Cal with you—"

"Cal wasn't invited. And anyway, I'm not bringing a father of two into *that*."

"But *you* are going." Mick's usually mellow tone hardens. "It's too dangerous for your most trusted second, but for the Alpha of the pack—"

"For the Alpha, it's duty," Lowe interrupts, conclusive.

"I've been in this pack for over fifty years, and I can promise you that no other Alpha would have agreed to those conditions. You're going above and beyond and have no self-preservation."

I have no idea what the context is, but Mick is probably right. There is something selfless about Lowe, as though when he became Alpha he left behind any trace of himself.

Or, more accurately, locked it into a drawer.

"Were those Alphas dealing with internal sedition?" Lowe responds, calm and harsh at once. Mick looks away, more sad than chastised. Ana picks up on it.

"Lowe?" Her voice is small. "Where are you going this weekend?"

He smiles at her warmly, his tone instantly softer. "To California."

"What's in California?" I'm glad she asked. Because I was about to, and I'm not entitled to this piece of information.

"It's pack territory. An old friend lives there. Uncle Koen will be there, too."

"Emery's no friend, Lowe," Mick interjects.

"And that's precisely why I cannot pass up the opportunity to have access to her house."

"It's not an opportunity. If you could bring Alex or someone else who's tech-savvy to help you with your plan, yes. But not on your own."

"Hang on." I'm too curious to shut up. "Isn't Emery Roscoe's former . . ." I don't need a reply, not going by the men's faces. "Oh, shit."

Ana chortles.

"You're almost disappointingly easy," I tell her, and she chortles harder, then sneaks around Lowe's chair to sit on my legs and steal my goldfish. I don't know what it is about me that says *Please make yourself at home on my lap*, but I'll have to fix that. "Lowe, are you really going to meet with this lady?"

Mick gives me a validated smile. Alex is, as usual, terrified. Lowe's withering look says: *Not you, too, and by the way, who the fuck gave you the right?*

Which, fair.

"You know Emery is behind everything that is happening," Mick says.

"But I have no proof. And until I have indisputable evidence, I will *not* act against her."

"You could. It would be a show of strength."

"Not the kind of strength I'm interested in showing."

"Max already told you—"

"A mumbled confession about who he believed sent him when he was under thrall by a Vampyre is unlikely to hold up in a tribunal." Lowe's striking face is stony, but I see the fatigue around the edges. It must be tiresome, being a decent person, and I can't relate. I revel in my moral flexibility. "Meeting Emery on her turf is how I get that evidence."

"Or how you get yourself . . ." Mick's eyes dart to Ana and he doesn't continue, but the word *killed* bounces between the adults at the table.

"Do you really think I cannot hold my own against her guards?" Lowe asks, leaning back in his chair. His lips curve into a smile. He looks less like a diplomatic leader, and more like the cocky, invincible twentysomething young man he is. "Come on, Mick. You've seen me fight."

Mick sighs. "Just because we haven't found your limit yet doesn't mean there isn't one."

"Doesn't mean there is, either."

Ana turns on my lap and climbs up my torso like a squirrel, hugging my neck and nuzzling my hair. It's the most direct physical contact I've experienced, *ever*—to my surprise, not excessively unpleasant. I ask, "Are you sure Emery would agree to meet you, after you . . ." *Slaughtered her husband?*

"She extended the invitation," Mick says, resigned.

"No way."

"As is customary for the mate of the previous Alpha. To guarantee a peaceful succession."

"Wow." Ana starts fidgeting and reaches out for Lowe, but he's exchanging a long stare with Mick and doesn't notice. I pat his arm to get his attention and he gives me a wide-eyed, disturbed look, like I tried to scorch him with a cattle iron. Does he think my smell is going to rub off? He's way more skunk adjacent than I'll ever be.

"I think it's a trap," Mick decrees.

Lowe shrugs. The movement delights Ana, so he repeats it. "I'm willing to risk it."

"But—"

"My mind is made up." He smiles at Ana and shifts register. "I'll have someone look into bouncy castles," he adds, and the rest of the dinner conversation is just that—Ana planning the cake she'll buy for my "birthday," Alex concerned that my fangs will pierce the inflatables, Lowe looking at us with an amused expression. We stay longer than the time it takes to finish the meal—a common occurrence, apparently, spending time chatting about nothing of particular importance. Weres' social customs are different, and they have me wondering how Lowe's mate is faring among my people. She left friends behind, family, a partner. Who is she having around-the-table conversations with? I picture her trying to chat with Owen—and Owen excusing himself to go capture a mountain lion to set after her.

I shake my head and tune back in to the conversation. Ana laughs, Lowe grins, Alex smiles. And then there's Mick, who stares at me with a worried expression on his weathered face.

CHAPTER 13

He tries to avoid thinking about what he'd do to her father if only it wouldn't cause the worst diplomatic incident of the current century.

ANA WAS RIGHT: IT ISN'T THAT DIFFICULT, CLIMBING UP TO THE roof, even for someone with the hand-eye coordination of a platypus.

I.e., me.

It takes me less than fifteen seconds to get there, and it's vaguely empowering, the way I never even feel like my brains will end up splattered in the plumbago flower bed. Once I'm sitting on the tiles, vaguely uncomfortable but not willing to admit it, I close my eyes and breathe in, then out, then in, letting the breeze play with my hair, welcoming the tickle of the night sky. The waves wash gently over the shore. Every once in a while, something splashes on the lake. *I don't even mind the bugs*, I tell myself. If I persevere, I'll believe it. That's what I'm failing at when Lowe arrives.

He doesn't notice me right away, and I get to observe him as he gracefully lifts himself up the eave. He stands on an edge that should be terrifying, lifting a hand to his eyes and pressing thumb and index fingers into them, so hard he must see stars. Then he lets his arm drop to his side and he exhales once, slowly.

This, I think, is *Lowe*. Not Lowe the Alpha, Lowe the brother, Lowe the friend, or the son, or the unfortunate husband of the equally unfortunate wife. Just: Lowe. Tired, I think. Lonely, I assume. Angry, I bet. And I don't want to disturb his rare moment alone, but the breeze lifts, blowing in his direction and carrying my scent.

He instantly spins around. To me. And when his eyes become all pupils, I lift my hand and awkwardly wave.

"Ana told me about the roof," I say, apologetic. I'm intruding on a cherished private moment. "I can leave . . ."

He shakes his head stoically. I swallow a laugh.

"If you sit here"—I point to my right—"you'll be between me and the wind. No bouillabaisse smell."

His lips twitch, but he makes his way to the spot I was pointing at, his large body folding next to mine, far enough to avoid accidental touches. "What do *you* even know about bouillabaisse?"

"As it's not hemoglobin or peanut based, nothing. So." I clap my hands. The cicadas quiet, then resume their singing after a disoriented pause. "Tell me if I got it right: You'll use your meeting with Emery as an excuse to plant some spyware or interceptor that will allow you to monitor her communications and gain proof that she's leading the Loyals. But you are going into enemy territory alone, and have the computer skills of an octogenarian Luddite, which puts you at great risk. Actually, no need to tell me if I'm right, I already know. When are you plunging to your imminent death? Tomorrow or Friday?"

He studies me like he's not sure whether I'm a bench or a

postmodern sculpture. A muscle twitches in his jaw. "I truly don't get it," he muses.

"Get what?"

"How you managed to stay alive despite your reckless outbursts."

"I must be very smart."

"Or incredibly stupid."

Our eyes clash for a few seconds, full of something that feels more confusing than antagonism. I glance away first.

And just say it, without thinking it through. "Take me with you. Let me help with the tech part."

He huffs out a tired, noiseless snort. "Just go to bed, Misery, before you get yourself killed."

"I'm nocturnal," I mutter. "Little offensive, that my *husband* doesn't think I can take care of myself."

"A lot offensive, that my *wife* thinks that I'd take her with me into a highly volatile situation where I might not be able to protect her."

"Okay. Fine." I glance back at him—his earnest, stubborn, uncompromising face. In the fading moonlight, the lines of his cheekbones are ready to slice me. "You can't do it on your own, though."

He gives me an incredulous look. "Are you telling me what I can and cannot do?"

"Oh, I would never, *Alpha*," I say with a mocking tone that I only half regret when he glares back. "But you can't even start a computer."

"I can start a fucking computer."

"Lowe. My friend. My spouse. You're clearly a competent Were with many talents, but I've seen your phone. I've seen you *use* your phone. Half of your gallery is blurry pictures of Ana with your finger blocking the camera. You type 'Google' in the Google bar to start a new search."

He opens this mouth. Then snaps it closed.

"You were about to ask me why that's the wrong way."

"You're not coming." His tone is definitive. And when he makes to stand, driven away by my insistence, I feel a stab of guilt and reach out for the leg of his jeans, pulling him back down. His eyes fix on the place where I'm gripping him, but he relents.

"Sorry, I'll let the matter go." For now. "Please, don't leave. I'm sure you came here to . . . What *do* you do here, anyway? Scratch your claws? Howl at the moon?"

"Deflea myself."

"See? I wouldn't want to be in your way. Do go on." I wait for him to pick critters out of his hair. "Shouldn't you be sleeping, anyway? *You* are not nocturnal." It's past midnight. Prime awake time for me, the cicadas, and no one else for miles.

"I don't sleep much."

Right. Ana said that. When she mentioned that he had . . . "Insomnia!"

His eyebrow quirks. "You seem overjoyed by my inability to get decent rest."

"Yes. *No*. But Ana mentioned you had pneumonia, and . . ."

He smiles. "She mixes up words often."

"Yup."

"According to Google, which I apparently don't know how to use"—his side look is blistering—"it's normal for her age." He looks pensive for a long moment as his smile sobers.

"I can't imagine how difficult it must be."

"Learning to talk?"

"That, too. But also, raising a young child. Out of the blue."

"Not as difficult as being raised by some asshole who doesn't know to buy a car seat for you, or gives you Skittles before bed because you're hungry, or lets you watch *The Exorcist* because he's never seen it, but the protagonist is a young girl, and he figures that you'll identify with her."

"Wow. Serena and I watched that at fifteen and slept with the lights on for months."

"Ana watched it at six and will need expensive therapy well into her forties."

I wince. "I'm sorry. For Ana, mostly, but also for you. People usually ease into parenthood. We're not born knowing how to change diapers."

"Ana's potty-trained. Not by me, obviously—I'd have somehow managed to teach her to piss out of her nose." He runs a hand over his short hair and then rubs his neck. "I was unprepared for her. Still am. And she's so fucking *forgiving*."

I rest my temple on my knees, studying the way he stares into the distance, wondering how many nights he's comes up here in the witching hour. To make decisions for thousands. To beat himself up for not being perfect. Despite how competent, self-denying, and assured he appears to be, Lowe might not like himself very much.

"You used to live in Europe? Where?"

He seems surprised by my question. "Zurich."

"Studying?"

His shoulders heave with a sigh. "At first. Then working."

"Architecture, right? I don't fully get it. Buildings are kind of boring. I'm grateful they don't fall on top of my head, though."

"I don't get how one can type stuff into a machine all day and not be terrified of a robot uprising. I'm grateful for *Mario Kart*, though."

"Fair enough." I smile at his tone, because it's the poutiest I've ever heard. I must have found his touchy spot. "I do like the style of this home," I volunteer magnanimously.

"It's called biomorphic."

"How do you know? You learned it in school?"

"That, and I designed it as a present for my mother."

"Oh." Wow. I guess he's not just an architect—he's a *good* architect. "When you studied, did you do the Human thing?" Their school system is often the only option, simply because there's more of them, and they invest in education infrastructure. In Vampyre society, and I assume among Weres, too, formal degrees are not worth the paper they're printed on. The skills that come with them, however, are priceless. If we want to acquire them, we create fake IDs and use them to enroll at Human universities. Vampyres tend to take online classes (because of the fangs, and the whole third-degree burns in the sunlight thing). Weres are undetectable to Humans' naked eye, and could come and go from their society more easily, but Humans have installed technology that singles out faster-than-normal heartbeats and higher body temperatures in plenty of places. Honestly, I'm just lucky they never expected Vampyres would go to the trouble of filing their own fangs and never developed the same degree of paranoia about us.

"Zurich was different, actually."

"Different?"

"Weres and Humans were attending openly. A few Vampyres, too. All living in the city."

"Wow." I know there are places like that around the world, where the local history between the species is not so fraught, and living side by side, if not together, is considered normal. It's still hard to imagine, though. "Did you have a Vampyre girlfriend?" I point at my ring finger. "Once you go Vamp, you can never go back, huh?"

He gives me a long-suffering look. "You'll be astonished to hear the Vampyres didn't hang out with us."

"How snobby." I fold my hand back in my lap, but start playing with my wedding band. "Why all the way to Zurich? Were you on the run from Roscoe?"

"On the run?" His cheeks stretch into an amused grin. "Roscoe was never a threat. Not to me."

"That's brave of you. Or narcissistic."

"Both, maybe," he acknowledges. Then quickly turns serious. "It's hard to explain dominance to someone who doesn't have the hardware to understand it."

"Lowe, was that a *computer* metaphor?" I get another of those don't-sass-me looks, and laugh. "Come on. At least *try* to explain it."

He shakes his head. "If you met someone without a nose and had to explain to them what a smell feels like, what would *you* tell them?" He looks at me expectantly. And I open my mouth half a dozen times—only to close it just as many, frustrated. "Yup." He doesn't even sound too told-you-so-y. "It was like that with Roscoe. He was a grown adult, I was barely past puberty, but I always knew that he was never going to win a fight against me, and he always knew it, and everyone in the pack knew it, too. As much as I despise him now, I'm thankful that he gave me long enough without a reason to challenge him."

Without becoming a despotic leader, he means. "What changed him?"

"Hard to say. His views escalated very suddenly." He licks his full lips, looking faraway, in the grip of a memory. "I got the phone call and didn't even have the time to stop by my apartment on the way to the airport. My mother had vocally opposed a raid. She was wounded, and Ana was defenseless."

"Shit."

"It was eleven hours and forty minutes from the moment I got the phone call until I pulled up Cal's driveway and found Ana sobbing in Misha's room." His tone is emotionless, almost disturbingly so. "I was terrified."

I can't imagine. Or can I? Those first few days after Serena was gone, and I was so frantically preoccupied with looking for her that it didn't occur to me to bathe or feed until my head pounded and my body was feverish.

"Did you ever get to go back to Zurich? To pick up your stuff? To . . ." *Get closure. Say goodbye to the life you'd built. Maybe you had friends, a girlfriend, a favorite takeout place. Maybe you used to sleep in in the morning, or take long weekend trips to travel around Europe and check out . . . buildings, or something. Maybe you had dreams. Did you go back to retrieve those?*

He shakes his head. "My landlord mailed a couple of things. Threw out the rest." He scratches his jaw. "Feel kinda bad for leaving my dirty breakfast dishes in the sink."

I chuckle. "It's kind of your thing, isn't it?"

"What?" He turns to me.

"Blaming yourself for being anything less than perfect."

"If you want to wash my dishes, by all means."

"Shush." I lightly bump my shoulder into his, like I do with Serena when she's being obtuse. He stiffens, stills in a breathless sort of tension for a moment, then slowly relaxes as I pull away. "So, this *dominance* thing. Is Cal the second most *dominant* Were in the pack?" This sounds foreign, like picking words at random. Magnetic fridge poetry.

"We're not a military organization. There's no strict hierarchy within the pack. Cal just happens to be someone I trust."

Can't be more dysfunctional than arbitrary councils whose membership is established through primogeniture. And Humans elect leaders like Governor Davenport. Clearly, there's no perfect solution here. "Did he also have to challenge someone to become a second? Maybe Ken Doll?"

"It's fucked up that I know who you're referring to."

I chuckle. "Hey, he has never introduced himself."

"Ludwig. His name is Ludwig. And our pack has over a dozen seconds, who are chosen within their huddle through a caucus system."

"Huddle?"

"It's a web of interconnected families. Usually geographically close. Each second reports to the Alpha. After Roscoe, new seconds were elected, which means that most of them are as new to this as I am. Mick is the only one who kept his position."

"You mean, the only one who didn't try to kill you?"

"Yup." His laugh could be bitter, but it isn't. "He and his mate were close friends of my mother's. Shannon used to be a second, too."

"Did you kill her?" I ask, conversationally, and he's so gonna push me off the roof.

"Misery."

"It's a fair question, given your precedents."

"No, I did not kill the mate of the man who used to change my diapers." He massages his temple. "Hell, they both did. They taught me how to ride bikes and track prey."

"What happened to her?"

"She died two years ago, during a confrontation at the eastern border. With Humans, we think." He swallows. "So did Mick's son. He was sixteen."

Not something my people would be above, but I still flinch. "That explains why he always seems so melancholic."

"He smells like grief. All the time."

"Well, he's my favorite Were." I hug my knees. "He's always so nice to me."

"That's because he has a weakness for beautiful women."

"What does that have to do with me?"

"You know what you look like."

I laugh softly, surprised by the backhanded compliment.

"Why do you always do that?" he asks.

"Do what?"

"When you laugh, you cover your lips with your hand. Or you do it with your mouth closed."

I shrug. I wasn't aware, but I'm not surprised. "Isn't it obvious?" It's not, judging by his puzzled look. "Okay. I'm going to be super vulnerable with you." I take a deep, theatrical breath. Steeple my hands. "You may not know this about me, but I'm not like you. I'm actually another species, called—"

"Misery." His hand comes up to snatch my wrist. My breath catches in my throat. "Why do you hide your fangs?"

"You're the one who told me to."

"I asked you not to respond to an act of aggression with another act of aggression, to avoid coming home and finding my *wife* torn to pieces—and someone torn in even smaller pieces next to her." His hand is still around my wrist. Warm. A bit tighter. His touch flusters me. "This is different."

Is it? Would you *not tear me into pieces?*

"Come on, Lowe." I free my arm and cradle it to my chest. "You know what my teeth are like."

"Come on, Misery," he mocks. "I do know, and that's why I don't get why you hide them."

We stare at each other like we're playing a game and trying to make the other lose. "Want me to show you?" I'm trying to provoke him, but he just nods solemnly.

"I'd like to know what we're dealing with, yeah."

"Now?"

"Unless you need specific tools, or have a previous engagement. Is it bath time?"

"You want to see my fangs. Now."

His look is vaguely pitying.

"It's just . . ." I'm not sure what's so concerning about the idea of him seeing them. Maybe I'm just remembering being nine, and the way my Human caregivers always stopped smiling the second I began. A driver, making the sign of the cross. A million other incidents through the years. Only Serena never minded. "Is this a trap? Are you looking for an excuse to watch my entrails fertilize the plumbago?"

"Would be highly inefficient, since I could just push you and no one in my pack would question me."

"What a beautiful flex."

He makes a show of hiding his hands behind his back. "I'm harmless."

He's as harmless as a land mine. He could destroy entire galaxies with a stern look and a growl. "Fine, but if your wolfy sensibilities are repulsed by my vampyric tusks, remember you asked for it."

I'm unsure how to initiate it. Snarling, pulling my upper lip back with my fingers like Human dentists do in toothbrush com-mercials, biting into his hand for an applied demonstration—all seem impractical. So I simply smile. When the cold air hits my ca-nines, my lizard brain screams at me that I'm caught. I'm found out. I'm . . .

Fine, actually.

Lowe's pupils splay out. He studies my canines with his usual unalloyed attention, without recoiling or trying to eat me. Little by little, my smile shifts into something sincere. Meanwhile, he looks.

And looks.

And: looks.

"Are you okay?" My voice snaps him back into his body. His grunt is vague, not quite affirmative.

"And you don't . . ." He clears his throat. "Use them?"

"What? Oh, my fangs." I run my tongue over my right one, and Lowe closes his eyes and then turns away. Either too gross, or he's scared. Poor little Alpha. "We all feed from blood bags, with very few exceptions."

"What exceptions?"

I shrug. "Feeding from a living source is kind of outdated, mostly because it's a huge hassle. I do think that mutual blood drinking is sometimes incorporated into sex, but remember how I was cast out as a child and am universally known for being a ter-rible Vampyre?" I should force Owen to explain the nuances of it to me, but . . . ugh. It's not like I plan to get that close to another Vampyre, ever. "I'm not going to bite you, Lowe. Don't worry."

"I'm not worried." He sounds hoarse.

"Good. So now that I've shown you my fearsome weapons, you'll take me to Emery's with you? It is, after all, the honeymoon you owe your bride. Pleasure doing business with you. I'll go pack, and—" I make to stand, but his hand snatches me back down.

"Nice try."

I sigh and lean backward, wincing when the tiles press into my spine. The stars crowd the sky, drift us into a moment of silence. "Want to know a secret?" I ask, weary. "Something I thought I'd never admit to anyone."

One arm brushes against my thigh as he twists to look at me. "I'm surprised you'd want to tell *me*."

I am, too. But I've carried it so tirelessly, and the night feels so soft. "Serena and I had a huge fight a few days before she disappeared. The biggest ever." Lowe remains quiet. Which is exactly what I need from him. "We fought plenty, mostly about trivial shit, sometimes over stuff that took us a bit to cool down. We grew up together and were at our most annoying with each other—you know, sisters? She spat into the pockets of the caretakers who were mean to me, and I read smutty books to her while she was so sick she needed IV drips. But also I hated that sometimes she just wouldn't pick up her phone for days, and she hated that I could be a stone-hearted bitch, I guess. That last fight we had, we were both fuming, after. And then she never showed up to help me put on the duvet cover, despite knowing that it's the single hardest thing in the universe. And now the things she said keep circling in my head. Like sharks that haven't been fed in months."

I can't see Lowe's expression from down here. Which is ideal. "And what do the sharks say?"

"She got a recruiter from this really cool company interested in me. It was a good job—something challenging. Something only a dozen people in the country could do. And she kept telling me how perfect I'd be for it, what an opportunity it was, and I just couldn't see the point, you know? Yes, it was a more interesting job, with more money, but I kept wondering, why? Why would I bother? What's the end goal? And I asked her, and she . . ." I take a deep breath. "Said that I was aimless. That I didn't care about anything or anyone, including myself. That I was static, headed nowhere, wasting my life. And I told her that it wasn't true, that I did care about stuff. But I just . . . I couldn't name anything. Except for her."

. . . this apathetic spiral of yours, Misery. I mean, I get it, you spent the first two decades of your life expecting to die, but you didn't. You're here now. You can start living!

Dude, you're not my mother or my therapist, so I'm not sure what gives you the right to—

I am out there, trying. I had a fucked-up life, too, but I'm dating, trying to get a better job, having interests—you're just waiting for time to pass. You are a husk. And I need you to care about one single fucking thing, Misery, one thing that's not me.

The sharks gnaw at the inner walls of my skull, and I won't be able to make them stop until I find Serena, but in the meantime, I can distract them. "Anyway." I sit up with a smile. "Since I so selflessly opened my heart to you, will you tell me something?"

"That's not how—"

"What the hell is a mate, precisely?"

Lowe's face doesn't move a millimeter, but I know that I could fill a Babel tower of notebooks with how little he wants to have this conversation. "No way."

"Why?"

"No."

"Come on."

His jaw works. "It's a Were thing."

"Hence, me asking you to explain." Because I suspect that it's not just the Were equivalent of marriage, or a civil union, or the steady commitment that comes with sharing monthly payments to multiple overpriced streaming services one forgot to discontinue.

"No."

"Lowe. Come on. You've trusted me with far bigger secrets."

"Ah, fuck." He grimaces and rubs his eyes, and I think I won.

"Is it another thing I don't have the hardware for?"

He nods, and almost seems sad about it.

"I understood the whole dominance thing." We really made some strides in the past fifteen minutes. "Give me a chance."

He turns to me. Suddenly he feels a little too close. "Give you a chance," he repeats, unreadable.

"Yeah. The whole rival-species-bound-by-centuries-of-hostility-until-the-bloody-demise-of-the-weakest-will-put-an-end-to-the-senseless-suffering thing might seem discouraging, but."

"But?"

"No buts. Just tell me."

His lips quirk into a smile. "A mate is . . ." The cicadas quiet. We can only hear the waves, gently lapping into the night. "Who you are meant for. Who is meant for you."

"And this is a uniquely Were experience that differs from Human high schoolers writing lyrics on each other's yearbooks before heading to separate colleges . . . how?"

I might be culturally offensive, but his shrug is good-natured. "I've never been a Human high schooler, and the experience of it might be similar. The biology, of course, is another matter."

"The biology?"

"There are . . . physiological changes involved with meeting one's mate." He's choosing his words with circumspection. Hiding something, maybe.

"Love at first sight?"

He shakes his head, even as he says, "In a way, maybe. But it's a multisensory experience. I've never heard of someone recognizing their mate just by sight." He wets his lips. "Scent is a big part of it, and touch, but there's more. It triggers changes inside the brain. Chemical ones. Science articles have been written about it, but I doubt I'd understand them."

I'd love to get my hands on Were academic journals. "Every Were has one?"

"A mate? No. It's fairly rare. Most Weres don't expect to find one, and it's by no means the only way to have a fulfilling romantic relationship. Cal, for example, is very happy. He met his wife on a dating app, and they went through years of push and pull before getting married."

"So he settled?"

"He wouldn't consider it that. Being mates is not a superior kind of love. It's not intrinsically more valuable than spending your life with your best friend and getting to love their quirks. It's just different."

"If they are so happy, could his wife be his mate? Could he have overlooked the signals when he met her?"

"No." He stares at the moonlit water. "When we were young, I was there when Koen's sister met her mate. We were on a run. She smelled her, suddenly went real still in the middle of the field. I thought she was having a stroke." He smiles. "She said that it felt like discovering new colors. Like the rainbow had gained a few stripes."

I scratch my temple. "It sounds like a good thing."

"It's . . . really good. Not always the same, though," he murmurs, as if he's talking to himself. Processing things through his explanations. "Sometimes it's just a gut feeling. Something that grabs you by the stomach and doesn't let go, not ever. World-shaking, yes, but also just . . . *there*. New, but timeless."

"That's how you felt? With your mate?"

This time he turns to look at me. I don't know why it takes him so long to produce that simple:

"Yeah."

God. This is just total, utter shit.

Lowe has a mate, which is apparently amazing. But his mate is stuck among *my* people while he's married to *me*.

"I'm so sorry," I blurt out.

His gaze is calm. Too calm. "You shouldn't be sorry."

"I can be sorry if I want to. I can apologize. I can prostrate myself and—"

"Why are you apologizing?"

"Because. In a year at the most I'm going to peace out." His well-being is not my responsibility, but already so much has been taken from him—and swiftly exchanged with bricks of duty. "You'll be able to be with your mate, and you'll live bitingly ever after. There's biting involved, right?"

"Yeah. The bite is . ." His gaze flickers down to my neck. Lingers. "Important."

"It looks painful. Mick's, I mean."

"No," he husks, eyes on me. My pulse flickers. "Not if it's done right."

He must have one on his body. A secret buried into his skin, under the soft cotton of his T-shirt. And he must have left one on his mate, a raised scar to guide him home, to be traced in the middle of the night.

And then something occurs to me. A petrifying possibility.

"It's always reciprocal, right?"

"The bite?"

"The mate thing. If you meet someone, and you feel that they are your mate, and your *biology* changes . . . theirs will change, too, right?" I don't need a verbal answer, because I see in his stoic, forbearing expression that *no. Nope.* "Oh, shit."

I'm no romantic, but the prospect is appalling. The idea that one might be destined to someone who just . . . won't. Can't. Doesn't. All the feelings in the world, but one-sided. Uncomprehended and unbound. A bridge built of chemistry and physics that stops halfway, never to pick up again.

The fall would break every last bone.

"It sounds fucking horrible."

He nods thoughtfully. "Does it?"

"It's a life sentence." No parole. Just you and a cellmate who'll never know you exist.

"Maybe." Lowe's shoulders tense and relax. "Maybe there is something devastating about the incompleteness of it. But maybe, just knowing that the other person is there . . ." His throat bobs. "There might be pleasure in that, too. The satisfaction of knowing that something beautiful exists." His lips open and close a few times, as though he can only find the right words by shaping them first to himself. "Maybe some things transcend reciprocity. Maybe not everything is about *having*."

I let out a disbelieving laugh. "Such wisdom, from someone whose mating is clearly reciprocated."

"Yeah?" He's amused—and something else.

"No one who has ever dealt with unrequited love would say that."

His smile is secretive. "Is that how your love has been? Unrequited?"

"There has been no love at all." I rest my chin over my knees. It's my turn now to stare at the shimmery lake. "I am a Vampyre."

"Vampyres don't love?"

"Not like that. We definitely don't talk about this stuff."

"Relationships?"

"Feelings. We're not raised to put a whole lot of value in that. We're taught that what matters is the good of the many. The continuation of the species. The rest comes after. At least, that's how I understood it—I grasp my people's customs very little. Serena would ask me what's normal in Vampyre society, and I couldn't tell her. When I tried to go back after being the Collateral, it was . . ." I flinch. "I didn't know how to behave. The way I spoke the Tongue was choppy. I didn't get what was going on, you know?" Yes, he does. I can tell.

"Is that why you went back to the Humans?"

"It hurt less," I say instead of yes. "Feeling alone among people who were never supposed to be my own."

He sighs and draws up his knees, hands clasped between them. A thought vibrates through me: right here, right now, I don't feel particularly alone.

"You're right, Lowe. I don't have the hardware to understand what a mate is, and I can't imagine meeting someone and feeling the sense of kinship you're talking about. But . . ." I close my eyes and think back fifteen years. A caregiver knocked on my door and introduced me to a dark-haired girl with dimples and black eyes.

The breath I draw is stymied. "I was able to install the software. Because Serena gave it to me. And maybe I disappointed her at times, maybe she was angry at me, but that means nothing in the big picture. I understand that you're willing to face Emery on your own, or to sacrifice everything for your pack. I understand because I feel the same about Serena. And for reasons I cannot fully articulate, because feelings are fucking *hard* for me, I'd like to come with you. To help you find whoever is trying to hurt Ana. And I think that Serena would be proud of me, because I've finally managed to care about something. Even just a little bit."

He studies me in the moonlit air for far too long. "That was a badass speech, Misery."

"Badass is my middle name."

"Your middle name is Lyn."

Shit. "Stop reading my file."

"Never." He inhales. Tips back his head. Stares at the same stars I've been mapping all night. "If we do it—if I take you with me, it will have to be my way. To make sure that you're safe."

My heart flutters with hope. "What's your way? Architecturally? With a Corinthian pilaster?"

I'm not funny. But neither is he.

"If you come with me, Misery, you'll have to be marked."

CHAPTER 14

She tastes the way she smells.

I EXPECTED A TWENTY-HOUR ROAD TRIP IN THE HYBRID PARKED in Lowe's garage, or maybe a shorter plane ride in economy class with cotton discreetly stuffed in my nose to avoid being bombarded with the smell of Human blood.

I did *not* expect a Cessna.

"Honey," I ask, lowering my sunglasses to the tip of my nose, "are we rich?"

His glance is only mildly blistering. "We're just banned from most Human-owned airlines, *darling*."

"Oh, right. That's why I've never flown before. It's all coming back to me."

It's hard to overstate how little Mick, Cal, and Ken Doll Ludwig like Lowe's decision to take his Vampyre bride to Emery's home. In the waning light of dusk, they practically throb with tense concern and unspoken objections.

Or spoken, maybe. I slept most of the day, and it's entirely possible that while I was stuffed in the closet for my midday coma, they went through several rounds of screaming matches. I'm glad to have missed them, and just as glad that my time awake has been spent organizing tech stuff with Alex.

"If someone tries to kill Lowe," he told me, showing me a USB Rubber Ducky, "it's your duty to give your life for your Alpha."

"I'm not full-body diving between him and a silver bullet." I held the GSM interceptor against the light to study it. Nifty. "Or whatever it takes for you guys to be killed."

"Just a regular bullet. And if you marry into a pack, the pack's Alpha becomes your Alpha. You marry an Alpha, he *most definitely* becomes your Alpha."

"Uh-huh, sure. Can I see that microcontroller over there?"

I'm not sad Alex didn't come see us off at the little executive airport, because the others exude enough existential angst. Tight-lipped, bouncer-posed, frowny. Mick repeatedly shakes his head while holding Sparkles like a burping child—because, yes: Sparkles is, according to someone who's been scolded multiple times in the past two hours for stuffing Play-Doh into outlets, "a valued family member" who "really loves to watch planes go whooosh." Juno is the least opposed to the op, which is nice of her. The real happy camper, however, is Ana, and only because of the promises she extracted from Lowe: presents, candy, and, in a required logistical effort that far overestimates his abilities, stealing an *L* from the Hollywood Sign.

"*L* for Liliana," she whispers at me conspiratorially, because her faith in my alphabet skills is shaky at best. Then she skips away to subject Sparkles to unspeakable cuddly things that have him purring his heart out, but would earn *me* permanent disfigurement.

"Let's go," Lowe tells me after bending down to kiss her

forehead. I follow him up the steps, waving back at Ana before disappearing inside. It looks less like a one percenter's luxury jet, and more like a cross between a nice living room and first class on an Amtrak train.

"Is the pilot Were?" I ask, following Lowe to the front of the plane. It's not a particularly cramped space, but we're both tall, and it's a tight fit.

"Yup." He opens the door to the cockpit.

"Who—"

I shut up when he lowers himself into the pilot seat. He presses buttons with quick, practiced movements, puts on a large pair of headphones, and talks to air traffic control in hushed tones.

"Oh, for fuck's sake." I roll my eyes. I'm tempted to ask when, between leading a pack and becoming an architect, he got a small aircraft license. But I suspect he wants me to, and I'm too petty to oblige. "Show-off," I mutter, bumping my right hip into half a dozen protuberances on my way to the copilot chair.

His smile is lopsided. "Strap in."

Like everything else, Lowe makes flying look effortless. Being in a giant metallic bird in the sky should be terrifying, but I press my nose against the cold window and gaze at the night sky, the sprawling lights interrupted by long stretches of desert. I only re-emerge when we get permission to land.

"Misery," he says, softly.

"Mmm?" From up high, the ocean is unmoving.

"When we land," he starts, then takes a long pause.

So long, I pry myself from the cold glass. "Ouch." I'm stiff from not moving for hours, so I stretch my neck in the narrow cabin, trying to avoid accidentally pressing an ejector seat button. "Everything hurts." When I straighten after arching my spine, the way he's staring at me is too intense to not be judgmental. "What?" I ask, defensive.

"Nothing." He turns back to the control board. Too fast.

"You said, 'when we land'?"

"Yeah."

"You realize that's not a sentence, right? Just a temporal subordinate clause."

His eyebrow lifts. "You're a linguist now?"

"Just a helpful critic. What happens when we land?"

He roams the inside of his cheek with his tongue.

"Are you going to tell me?"

He nods. "I need to send Emery and her people the message that you're part of my pack and no violence against you will be tolerated. Not just the *verbal* message."

"You said you'd do that by marking me, right?" Whatever that is. The blinking lights in the landing strip are approaching, and the turbulence is making me nauseous. I shift my focus to Lowe. "I don't need to speed-read *Architecture for Dummies* and pretend I can tell Gothic and art deco apart?"

He turns to me, stone-faced. "You're joking."

"Please look ahead."

"You can, right? You *are* able to tell apart—"

"Husband, darling, deep inside you know the answer to that, and please look at the road when you're *landing a plane*."

He turns back. "It's about scents," he says, clearly forcing himself to change the topic.

"Of course. What isn't?" He's been a champ. He doesn't seem to react to my scent anymore. Maybe it's all the baths. Maybe he's getting used to me, like Serena when she lived by the fish market.

By the time her lease was ending, she found the eggyness almost comforting.

"If we smell the same, it'll send that message."

"Does it mean you should be smelling like dog breath?" I joke.

"I'm going to do that." His voice is raspy.

"To do what?"

"Make you smell like"—the plane touches down with a graceful bump—"me."

My hands tighten around the armrests as we race down the runway. I'm horror-stricken, scenarios of us splattered against the building at the end of the strip blooming in my brain. Little by little, we slow down—and little by little, Lowe's words settle like dust.

"Like you?"

He nods, busy with some final maneuvers. I notice a small group of people gathered by the hangar. Emery's welcoming committee, ready to slaughter us.

"That's fine. Do what you want with my body," I say absently, trying to guess which one of them is more likely to throw a clove of garlic at me. "Fair warning, Serena often bitches about how gross and cold I feel. Those three degrees make all the difference."

"Misery."

"Seriously, I don't care. Do whatever."

The maneuvering is over. He unbuckles and assesses the Weres waiting for us. There's five of them, and they look tall. Then again: so am I. And so is Lowe.

"If they attack us—"

"They won't," he interrupts me. "Not now."

"But if they do, I can help—"

"I know, but I can take them on my own. Come on, we don't

have much time." He takes me by the wrist, pulling me into the main sitting area, which is larger than the cabin, but too small for the way we're standing in front of each other. "I'm going to—"

"Do whatever." I crane my neck past him to catch a glimpse of the Weres through the portholes. Some are actually in wolf form.

"Misery."

"Just hurry and—"

"*Misery.*" I jolt back to him at the command in his voice. There's an angry V between his brows. "I need your explicit consent."

"For what?"

"I'm going to scent you the traditional Were way. It entails rubbing my skin against yours. My tongue, too."

Oh. *Oh.*

Something electric, liquid, pools inside my body. I deal with it the only way I can: by laughing. "Seriously?"

He nods, as serious as quicksand.

"Like a wet willy?"

His hand lifts to my neck.

Stops.

"May I touch you?" He's asking for permission, but there's nothing insecure or tentative about it. I nod. "Weres have scent glands—here." He brushes the pad of his thumb against the hollow on the left side of my throat. "Here." The right side. "And here." His hand wraps around my neck, palm flush against my nape. "Your wrists, too."

"Ah." I clear my throat. And resist the urge to squirm, because I'm feeling . . . I have no idea. It's the way he looks at me. His pale, piercing eyes. "This is a, um, fascinating anatomy lecture, but— Oh, *shit.* The green markings, at our wedding! But I—"

"You don't have scent glands," he says, like I'm more predictable than taxes, "but you do have pulse points, where your blood pumps closer to the surface, and the heat—"

"—will augment the scent. I'm familiar with the whole blood thing."

He nods and holds my eyes expectantly, until he understands that I have no clue what he's waiting for. "Misery. Do I have your permission?"

I could say no. I *know* that I could say no and he'd probably just find another way to protect me—or die trying, because he's *that* kind of guy. And maybe that's exactly why I nod and close my eyes, thinking that it won't be a big deal.

Which, I soon realize, might not be the case.

It starts with heat, drifting over me as he shifts closer. The faint, pleasant scent of his blood climbing into my nostrils. After that, his touch. First his hand on my jaw, holding me still, angling my head to the right, and then . . . his nose, I think. Nuzzling down the column of my throat, moving back and forth over the place where my blood flows the strongest. He inhales once. Again, deeper. Then travels back up, the scratch of his jaw tickling my flesh.

"Okay?" he asks in a low rumble.

I nod. Yes. It's okay. More than okay, though I wouldn't be able to qualify how, or why. An "I'm sorry" stumbles out of my mouth.

"Sorry?" The word vibrates through my skin.

"Because." My knees are buckling, so I lock them. I still feel like I might lose my bearings, so I blindly reach up. Find Lowe's shoulder. Grasp it for dear life. "I know you don't like my scent."

"I fucking *love* your scent."

"So the baths *did* work— *Oh*."

When he said *tongue*, I expected . . . *Not* that his lips would part at the base of my throat, and then a soft, drawn-out lick. Because this feels like a kiss. Like Lowe Moreland is kissing my neck, slowly. Grazing it with his teeth and finishing off with a light nibble.

I nearly moan. But at the last moment, I manage to swallow back inside my body the whimpery, throaty sound, and . . .

God. Why does what he's doing feel so phenomenally *good*?

"Is this as weird for you as it is for me?" I ask, trying to make light of the flutters of pleasure in my stomach. Because this thing spreading like spilled water below my navel, it's *arousal*, and it could explode into wildfire *very* fast. It makes me think of blood and touching and maybe fucking, and as things are happening to my body, I'm terrified that he'll be able to smell them.

Smell *me*.

"No," he growls.

"But—"

"It's not weird." Lowe lifts his head from my neck. I'm *so* close to begging him to come back and do it some more, but he's just switching sides, and I almost yelp in relief. This time, his palm cradles the entire back of my head, and for a few moments he thumbs the tip of my ear, exhaling slowly, reverently, like my body is a precious, beautiful thing. "It's perfect," he says, and then his mouth lowers again.

First a delicate bite on my earlobe. Then the swipe of his tongue at the base of my jaw. Last, right as I'm thinking that this is different from what I thought scenting would be, he moves to the bottom of my throat and *sucks*.

He grunts.

I gasp.

We both let out staggered breaths as my hand creeps up to press his face deeper into me. He pulls gently at my skin, open-mouthed, and the stimulation is like electricity, flooding me with warmth.

Weres' body temperature is much higher than Vampyres', and his body is a scant inch of air and possibilities away, and the *heat* of him . . .

My breasts ache, nipples hard as gems, and I want to arch into him. I want contact and flesh and skin. Lowe is solid, and I feel so soft, and his thundering heartbeat—*his delicious beating heart*—is a hazy, indescribable wonder pulling me to him. I squirm in his arms, trying to press against him, rub just a little, but no.

Because Lowe pulls back. His hand closes on my shoulder, spinning me around until I'm facing away from him. My breath catches as I clasp a headrest for balance.

"Okay?" he asks, wrapping his fingers around the base of my throat. I say yes as fast as I can, well before the word is fully out of his mouth, and he doesn't waste time, either: he lifts away the heavy mass of my hair. Clutches my hips in his palm. Presses my body against his.

And once he has me how he wants me, he bends down.

His teeth close around the back of my neck, *hard* this time, and I am flooded with a filthy, instant kind of pleasure. The cry that I managed to leash earlier burns out of my throat. There's pressure inside me, heady, scalding, and I can't bear for it to grow. Lowe's hand travels down to my stomach, settling me more tightly against him. The curve of my ass finds his groin, and he lets out a satisfied, guttural sound that jolts my nerve endings.

My blood sings. My ears roar. I'm melting.

"Fuck," he mouths. He runs his tongue over the knob at the top of my spine one last time, as if to soothe the sting of his bite, and suddenly I'm cold. Shivering. When I turn, he's standing several feet away from me, eyes pitch-black.

The roar in my ears is getting louder—because it wasn't in my ears at all. A car is driving across the tarmac, toward our plane.

Emery.

"I'm sorry." Lowe sounds like a rake has run through his vocal box. His fingers twitch at his side, a reflex. Like my hand lingering on the damp spot at the base of my throat.

"I . . ." My hand shifts to massage my nape. I can still feel his touch. "That was . . ."

"I'm sorry," he repeats.

My fangs ache, itch, *want* like never before. I trace them with my tongue to ensure they aren't on fire, and Lowe watches me do it, every second of it, lips parting. He takes a small, involuntary step toward me, then retreats again, appalled at his lack of control.

This might be new to me, and I may not be a Were, but whatever just happened between us went beyond *let me disguise you real quick* and straight into something different.

Something sexual.

And if *I* know it, there is no way *he* doesn't.

"Lowe." We should talk about this. Or never mention it again.

The way he's looking, he's opting for the latter. "I'm done," he says to himself, eyes glassy. "It's done."

"Is it better?"

His lips press together. As though there is a flavor he wants to hold in his mouth a moment longer. "Better?"

"My smell. Do I smell like . . . ?"

"Mine." It's a rumble in his throat. "You smell like you're mine, Misery."

Something charged shimmers through my body.

It is, after all, exactly what we were going for.

CHAPTER 15

She's not like he imagined. He won't admit to picturing how she'd be while he was growing up, but there was always something in the back of his head, a faint hope that maybe, one day.

She's not like he imagined. She's more, in every possible way.

EMERY MESSNER IS PETRIFYING. MOSTLY BECAUSE SHE LOOKS really nice.

I expected unhinged, rabid-looking, bloodthirsty greetings. Unpredictability. Threats of violence. What I find is a sweet woman in her fifties, wearing a *Hope Love Courage* pin on her cardigan. I'm no great judge of character, but she seems kind, and friendly, and sincerely personable. Her heartbeat is faint, almost reticent. I could picture her baking peanut-free treats to pass around after her children's soccer practice, but *not* abducting and murdering people.

"Lowe." She stops a few feet away from us, hanging her head in salute. When she looks up, her nostrils twitch, undoubtedly smelling what happened between me and Lowe on the plane.

I want to disappear into the ether.

"Welcome to you and your Vampyre bride." She faces my husband. Who killed her mate. This is so messed up. "Congratulations on your alliance."

"Emery." He does *not* smile. "Thank you for welcoming us to your home."

"Nonsense. This is your territory, Alpha." She waves a hand like a gal at brunch. Her eyes flicker back to me, and for a fraction of a second the polite facade crumbles, and I see myself reflected in her eyes.

I'm a Vampyre.

I'm the enemy.

In the current century, my people have been among the top five causes of death for *her* people. I'm as welcome as a piece of gum stuck under the sole of her pumps.

However, I'm *Lowe's* gum, and he's making it abundantly clear: his hand lingers possessively on the curve of my lower back, and I know enough about self-defense to understand that he positioned himself strategically, and that he plans to shove me behind himself at the slightest sign of intimidation. There's no way Emery's guards—all eight of them, evenly split between wolf and Human form—cannot see that. Judging from their tense expressions, they seem to believe that Lowe offers a considerable threat, even this starkly outnumbered.

As his fake wife, I find it flattering.

But Lowe was right, and Emery doesn't want a fight, at least not now. She forces a strained smile just for me. "Misery Lark." Her voice oozes civility. "I haven't seen any of your people in my territory in decades."

Not alive, for sure. "Thank you for having me."

"Perhaps it's time to bury the hatchet. Perhaps new alliances can be formed, now that the old ones are burning to ashes."

"Perhaps." I bite the *Seems unlikely, though*, off my tongue.

"Very well." Her eyes flicker to my hand. Because, I abruptly realize, Lowe wrapped his own around it. "Follow me, if you please." She turns her back to us with one last smile. Her guard trickles behind her, flanking her like an armor made of flesh.

Lowe's fingers squeeze mine. "That was civil of you," he says under his breath. "Thank you for not causing a diplomatic incident."

"As if."

His eyebrows quirk.

"Come on. I wouldn't."

The look he gives me telegraphs: *You absolutely would.*

"I'm not going to piss off the lady who tried to kidnap Ana," I say, outraged. Then clarify, "I might stab her. But I'm not going to *sass* her."

His mouth twitches. "There you are."

He tugs me toward a black sedan, his hand still holding on to mine.

—◦◦◦—

DINNER IS A WEIRD AFFAIR, NOT IN THE LEAST BECAUSE I'M SERVED a plate of cavatelli and a glass of red wine that looks enticingly like blood.

It's standard for the mate and children of the former Alpha to maintain formal relationships with the current leadership, and several Weres have been invited for the weekend. Tonight, though, it's just the three of us at the table, and I'm too clueless regarding Were affairs to participate in the conversation. I try to follow as they talk about borders, alliances, other packs, but it's like starting a triple-timeline TV show from season four. Too many plot points, characters, world-building details. What I *can* do is appreciate the complex dynamics at play during the meal, and the expert way

Lowe navigates them. No one mentions that he killed Roscoe, and I'm grateful for that.

We're escorted to our room early in the morning. There is one bed, which will luckily not lead to any weird sharing situation, because I'll disappear into the closet the second the sun is up. I gesture at Lowe to sit and lift a finger to my lips. He gives me a confused look but complies without argument, even as I reach for his jeans pocket and take out his phone. For an Alpha, he's surprisingly good at doing as I say.

I spend several minutes sweeping the place for bugs and cameras, and checking for strong Wi-Fi networks under Lowe's increasingly amused gaze. When I find none, I catch his pitiful must-be-hard-to-live-subsumed-by-this-level-of-paranoia look, and I'm tempted to scrape a lint ball from my pocket and tell him that it's state-of-the-art spyware, just to be *right* for once.

He probably wouldn't know better.

"Can I speak? Or would you like to espionage more?"

I glare. "Your golden boy Alex told me to do this."

He shakes his head with a small smile. "Emery knows better."

"So we're not going to entertain the possibility that she's going to slit our throats in our sleep?"

"For the time being."

"Hmm." I go through his phone to make sure it's not being tracked. It's an interesting, vaguely wistful window into Lowe's life. Not that I expected to find it chock-full of MILF porn, but his most visited websites are European sports news and fancy architectural magazines that look as entertaining as a traffic jam.

"Sorry your baseball team is doing so poorly," I offer.

"It's doing fine," he mutters, offended.

"Uh-huh, sure."

"And it's rugby." He stands to retrieve my blood cooler.

"Anyway. Emery doesn't seem *that* bad."

"No, she doesn't." Lowe opens the cooler, and then the secret compartment where we stowed the tools Alex gave me. "Mick has been collecting intel on the attacks and sabotages in Were territory, and it overwhelmingly suggests that she's behind them. But she also knows that if she were to openly challenge me, she wouldn't stand a chance. And it's possible that several of the Loyals aren't even aware of the kidnapping attempt. They might not know they're on the bad side of this war."

I stand by him, checking that all the equipment is accounted for. "Father used to say that there are no good or bad sides in a war."

Lowe chews on his lower lip, pensively staring at the bags of blood. "Maybe. But there are sides I want to be part of, and others that I do not." He looks up, pale eyes just inches from mine. "Do you need to feed?"

"I can do it in the bathroom, since we're sharing this"—I glance around at the flowery wallpaper, canopy bed, landscape-based art—"marriage chamber."

"Why would you use the bathroom?"

"I'm assuming you'll find it gross?" Serena always said that there's something repulsive about hearing blood being swallowed, though she eventually got used to it. I get it: I might be a (shame-fully enthusiastic) peanut butter consumer, but I find most human foods gag-worthy. Anything that requires chewing should be launched into space via a self-destroying capsule.

"I doubt I'll care," Lowe says, and I shrug. I won't babyproof his environment. He's a big boy who knows what he can take.

"Okay."

I grab the bag and make quick work of it. Blood is too

expensive—and too hard to clean up—to risk spillage, which is why I use straws. The process takes less than two minutes, and by the time I'm done, I'm smiling to myself, thinking of the three-hour dinner I've just been subjected to and feeling superior.

Weres and Humans are *weird*.

"Misery."

Lowe's voice is gravelly. I dispose of the bag, and when I glance at him, he's sitting on the bed again. I have the impression that his eyes have been on me for the entire time. "Yes?"

"You look different."

"Oh, yeah." I turn to the mirror, but I know what he's seeing. Rosy cheeks. Blown-up pupils with a thin lilac rim. Lips stained with red. "It's a thing."

"A thing."

"Heat and blood, you know?"

"I don't."

I shrug. "We get blood-hungry when we're hot, and we get hot after we feed. It won't last long."

He clears his throat. "What else does it entail?"

I'm not sure what to make of this line of questioning on Vampyre physiology, but he was forthcoming when I asked the same about the Weres. "Mostly just that. Some senses are heightened, too." The scent of Lowe's blood, but also everything else that makes him *him*, is sharper in my nostrils. It has me wondering if *I* still smell like him.

Which has me thinking of what happened earlier.

Not that it was ever far from my mind. "In the plane. When you were marking me." I expect him to act embarrassed, or dismissive. He just holds my gaze. "Not to make a weird situation even weirder, but it seemed like it was . . ."

"It was." He briefly closes his eyes. "I'm sorry. I didn't mean to take advantage."

"I— Me neither." I was as much into it as he was. More, probably.

"It's the act of it. It's something that usually happens between mates, or in serious romantic relationships. It's intrinsically sexually charged."

Oh. "Right." I'm a bit mortified to have assumed he was attracted to *me*. Not because I don't think I'm attractive—I'm hot, and fuck you, Mr. Lumiere, for saying that I looked like a spider— but because Lowe has Gabi. Someone he's biologically hardwired to focus the entirety of his attraction on.

"I'd never done it before," he says. "I didn't know it would be like that."

Hold up. "You'd never done it? You'd never marked anyone before?"

He shakes his head and starts taking off his boots.

"But you have a mate. You said so."

He moves to the other shoe. Without looking up. "I also said it's not always reciprocated."

"But yours—yours *is*, right? You said so." Gabrielle. She's the Collateral now, but before, they were together. They probably met in Zurich. Ate that cheese with the holes together, all the time.

"Did I?"

I cover my mouth with my palm. "Shit. No." I stalk across the room to the bed, but once I'm sitting next to Lowe, I have no idea what to do.

What did the governor say at the wedding? That the Were Collateral was his mate. But he never said that they were together. As a matter of fact, no one in the pack ever acted as though Lowe was in a relationship with her. Ana never mentioned Gabi, not even in passing. There were no signs of her in Lowe's bedroom.

His mate, the governor said, and it makes sense that Lowe would share that, to guarantee that he was handing off a valuable Collateral. But no one ever said that Lowe was *her mate*.

"Does she know? That she's your mate, I mean."

A micropause, and then he shakes his head. As though reaffirming a decision. "She doesn't. And she won't."

"Why won't you tell her?"

"I won't burden her with the knowledge."

"Burden? She'd be into that! You're basically swearing eternal love to her—and you're kind of a catch. I used to vet all of Serena's dating app matches; I've seen what's out there. The pool is *shallow*. As far as I know, you have zero criminal convictions, a house, a car, a *pack*, and . . . okay, a wife, but I'm happy to help you clear that out." I wonder why I'm being so proactive about this. I'm not the kind to want to meddle with other people's love lives, but . . . maybe it has to do with this heavy feeling deep in my stomach. Maybe I'm just overcompensating my irrational disappointment with enthusiasm. "Honestly, she'll be *stoked*." She's the current Collateral, she's probably as perfectly self-immolating as he is, and—something occurs to me. "Is it about your sister? You think she won't accept Ana?"

He exhales a laugh and goes to put his shoes away. "The opposite. Ana would be delighted, too." He checks that the door is locked and comes back to bed. "Scooch over," he orders, pointing at the side of the bed that's farthest from the entrance.

I obey without hesitating. "What if she feels the same about you?"

"She can't."

The mattress dips with his weight. He lies back, still wearing his jeans and shirt. The back of his head sinks into the pillow as he crosses his arms on his chest. The bed is king-size and still a little too short for him, but he doesn't complain.

"Maybe she doesn't have the hardware. Maybe she doesn't feel the same biological pull toward you that you feel toward her. But she could still develop feelings." I toe my shoes off and kneel next to him. Is he going to *sleep*? "You could still date her."

"We're *still* talking about this," he drawls without opening his eyes.

"Yes."

"What about now?"

"Yup." No, I'm not going to examine my interest in the topic. "Frankly, it's a bit childish, this all-or-nothing attitude of yours. You could still have a—"

He props up on his elbow. One second I'm staring at his handsome, relaxed face, the next his eyes burn bright into mine and I can feel his breath, warm over my lips. They still taste faintly like blood.

Something charges between us. Something *ready*.

"You think that the reason I won't tell her is that a small part of her wouldn't be enough?" he growls. "You think that I would care, if she were to love me less than I love her? That this is a matter of pride for me? Of greed? Is that why you think I'm *childish*?"

I open my mouth. A wave of heat—embarrassment, confusion, something else—slams over my body. "I . . ."

"You *think*, but you don't *know*. You don't know anything about what it's like to find your other half," he continues, voice low and sharp. "I would take anything she chose to give me—the tiniest fraction or her entire world. I would take her for a single night knowing that I'll lose her by morning, and I would hold on to her and never let go. I would take her healthy, or sick, or tired, or angry, or strong, and it would be my fucking *privilege*. I would take her problems, her gifts, her moods, her passions, her jokes, her body— I would take every last thing, if she chose to give it to me."

My heart pounds in my chest, my cheeks, my fingertips. I've forgotten how to breathe.

"But I won't take *from* her." His eyes leave mine and steadily trail down my face. They stop at the neckline of my dress. Tonight I'm wearing our wedding band as a necklace, and he studies the way it disappears into the curve of my breasts. His gaze lingers, leisurely, for what feels like hours but is probably a brief moment. Then it moves back up. "Above all, I won't take her freedom. Not when so many others have already done so."

That aggressive energy between us dissipates as quickly as it formed, melting like salt in water. Slowly, comfortably, with one last glance at my lips, Lowe settles back on the bed. His arms come up to lace behind his skull.

"She wouldn't admit it—she might not even realize it herself, but she's the kind of person who would feel beholden to me. She would think I need her. When what I *really* need is for her to be happy, whether it's with me, or alone, or with someone else."

His eyes flutter closed again. I manage to gulp in some air, and I watch his body relax from a tense, angry line, back to soft strength.

I'm utterly ashamed. And other things that I'm unlikely to be able to articulate. My hands are trembling, so I curl my fists into the cotton coverlet. "I'm sorry. I went too far."

"My feelings are mine to deal with. Not hers."

I cannot help myself. I lick my lips and say, "It's just—"

"Misery."

It's that tone again. The Alpha one. The one that makes me want to say yes to him, over and over again.

"I'm sorry," I repeat, but I think I'm forgiven. I think Lowe is simply too big a person to hold grudges. I think Lowe is too fucking principled for his own good, and doesn't deserve to have his heart broken, or his life only half full. "Shall I retreat into the closet in shame? So you don't have to see me?"

His mouth twitches. *Definitely* forgiven. "I can just turn the other way."

"Right. Will you have to . . . scent me again? Tomorrow?"

His smile disappears. "No. The message came across. They think you're important to me now."

"Okay." I scratch my temple and do *not* ruminate over the fact that he said "they think" instead of "they know." I should get ready for bed. The sun will be up soon. But it's such a rare opportunity to study Lowe at will. He's just—so, *so* handsome, even to me, someone who's so different, so chronically weird, that I'm rarely afforded the privilege of noticing these things in others. And yet, the more I know him, the more I find him magnetic. Unique. Genuinely decent, in a world where no one seems to be.

And I'm convinced that his mate would agree with me, but I'm not going to belabor the point. Even if I can't imagine anyone refusing him. Even if *I* have developed an attraction toward him, and I'm not even his species.

"You can get changed before sleeping. I'm going to keep my hands off you, even if your pj's have cute little drops of blood on them."

"I'm not going to sleep," he murmurs.

I frown. "Is it a Were thing? You only sleep every third day?"

"It's a me thing."

I tear my eyes away from his full lips. "Right. The insomnia. When we were teens, Serena was the same."

"Yeah?"

He hasn't moved a muscle, but he sounds genuinely interested, so I continue. "She had horrible nightmares she could never remember. Probably something that happened in the first few years of her life—she had no memories of that period at all."

"And what would she do?"

"She wouldn't sleep. Would always look exhausted. We were concerned—me and Mrs. Michaels, who was our caregiver at the time, and a nice one at that. We tried white noise machines. Pills. Those red lights that should have facilitated melatonin production but just made the room look like a brothel. Nothing worked. And then we found the solution by chance, and it was the simplest trick."

"What was it?"

"Me." Lowe's body tightens. "What she needed was someone she trusted, next to her. So I'd hang out in her room. And scratch her."

"Scratch her." He sounds skeptical.

"No— Yes, but not what you think. It's just what we called it. Here—" I lift my hand to his forehead, and after a small hesitation, I press my palm to his hair. It's at once bristly and soft, not long enough to run my fingers through. I caress it a couple of times, letting my nails brush softly against his scalp, just enough to give him an idea of what Serena used to enjoy, and then pull back to—

His hands dart up, lightning fast.

He doesn't open his eyes, but his fingers close around my wrist with deadly precision. My heart slams into my chest—shit, I've overstepped—until he brings the hand back to his head, as though he wants me to . . .

Oh.

Oh.

He doesn't let go until I resume the scratching. A ball of *something* swells in my throat. "You're so much luckier," I say, hoping a joke will deflate it.

"Why?" he rasps.

"I just fed. It reduces the clammy, mollusk feel Serena had to deal with."

He doesn't smile, but his amusement is thick around us. His dark hair is short, so short, and I wonder if he cuts it like that because the upkeep is easier—no need to style it, ever. I think about how much research I put into the best cuts to hide my ears, about the way Serena enjoyed shopping for clothes and makeup that suited her moods. And then imagine Lowe having no time to do any of that. Having no time for himself.

Like Juno said, his entire life is sacrifice. He was asked for so much, and always said *yes, yes, yes.*

Oh, Lowe. No wonder you can't sleep.

"You're not as terrible a husband as you could be," I say for no particular reason, continuing to caress him. "I'm sorry you had to give up your entire life for your pack."

This time he's definitely smiling. "You did the same."

"What?" I tilt my head. "No."

"You spent years among the Humans, knowing that if a very flimsy truce was broken, you'd be the first to be killed. Then you spent more years building a life among the Humans—and now here you are, having given that up. Doing stuff for your people, whom you claim to care so little about."

"Not for *them*, for Serena."

"Yeah? Then what's your plan, after you find her? Run away

together? Disappear? Send the alliance between the Vampyres and Weres into chaos?"

It's not that I haven't thought that far. I just don't like to dwell on the answer. "This marriage is just for one year," I punt.

"Yeah? Misery, I think you should ask yourself something." He sounds more tired than I've ever heard him.

"What is that?"

"If Serena hadn't disappeared, would you have been able to say no to your father? Or would you have ended up in this marriage anyway?"

I think about it for a long, long time, watching my fingers trace patterns in Lowe's hair. And when I think I have an answer—a frustrating, depressing answer—I don't say it out loud.

Because Lowe, who suffers from something that's definitely not pneumonia, is breathing softly, and has sunk into a tranquil sleep.

CHAPTER 16

He's been picturing her during her baths. He's been having
filthy, unspeakable thoughts. He's too tired to keep them at bay.

THE FOLLOWING DAY, LOWE DISAPPEARS TO DO WERE THINGS.
I wake up in the late afternoon with only vague memories of
having crawled into the built-in closet, and find a note tucked under
the doors. It's a piece of white paper, folded once and then again.

On a run, it says.

And, on a new line: *Be good.*

Followed by: *L. J. Moreland.*

I snort. For unclear reasons, I don't toss it in the trash bin, but
slip it in the external pocket of my suitcase.

I draw a bath and lower myself into the tepid water. Holding on
to garbage is dumb, but I come by it honestly: it's what Serena used
to do with wrappers of rare import candy bars. A maniac-worthy
move, in my humble opinion, the way she'd pin them to the wall. A
surefire method to spot a future serial murderer, together with
pyromania and torturing small animals. *When I look at the wrappers,*
I remember the taste, she told me when we were thirteen and I tried
to throw them away. It led to me rolling my eyes, which led to us

not talking for two days, which led to me passive-aggressively littering our shared spaces with used blood bags, which led to flies, which led to an explosive showdown in which she couldn't decide whether to call me a leech or a bitch and blurted out "Bleetch," which led to us cracking up and remembering that we *liked* each other.

"Misery?" Lowe's voice pulls me back. I'm staring vacantly at the stained windows, a faint smile on my lips. "Where are you?"

"Bathroom!"

"Are you dressed?"

I look down and shift the foam around strategically. "Yup." The door opens a moment later.

Lowe and I regard each other from across the room—him blinking, me staring—with similarly dumbfounded expressions. He clears his throat, twice. Then remembers that looking away is an option. "You said you were dressed."

"I'm wearing my modesty froth. *You*, on the other hand."

He frowns. "I'm wearing jeans."

Plus a healthy layer of sweat, and nothing else. The curtains are pulled, but sheer. The incoming light is warm, and tints Lowe's skin a pretty gold—his wide shoulders, his broad, heavily muscled chest. He's still glowing with the flush of being outside, in nature, and he looks healthy, even with more scars than anyone his age should have—narrow, thin stripes and knotty twists. *So I like looking at my husband who's a different species and fated to be someone else's mate. Whatever. Take me to court. Impound my nonexistent assets.*

"I'll overlook your nudity if you overlook mine," I offer.

Lowe's hand comes up to rub his nape. "I took off my shirt before shifting and lost it. Lemme find a clean one."

"I don't care. Plus, you're sweaty and gross."

His eyebrow cocks. "Gross?"

I shrug, which maybe misplaces the foam. I'm not sure, nor am I going to check, as the answer could be mortifying. "So, you went frolicking in the mud with Emery?"

He snorts. "With Koen. He arrived early this morning."

"That sounds fun." He got to hang out for a couple of hours with someone he clearly loves and trusts. Let his guard down.

"It was."

It must be why his eyes are dancing, at once boyish and animated. Why he seems younger than last night. Why, when he walks inside and sits by my feet, on the edge of the tub, he looks like he's been smiling.

"You know," I muse, relaxing into the water, "I think I want to see you."

He looks down at his body. "You want to see me."

"No, not *naked*."

His head tilts in confusion.

"As a *wolf*."

His "Ah" is soft and amused.

"Can you quickly shift? Right now? But keep your distance, please. Animals tend to hate me."

"Nope."

"Why?" I sit upright, covering my breasts with my arms. "Oh my God, does it hurt, shifting?"

"No." He seems offended.

"Phew. How long does it take?"

"Depends."

"How long does it take for you, on average?"

"A few seconds."

"Is it another Alpha thing? And your motor proteins are *suuuu-per* dominant?"

His glare tells me I'm on the right track. "Shifting is not a party trick, Misery."

"Clearly it's not a supersecret deal, either, because I've seen Cal as a—" I gasp. "I got it."

"Got what?"

I smile. Fangs out. "You don't want to show me because your wolfy coat is hot pink."

"Not *wolfy* coat, just coat."

I splash him with my foot. "Is it purple?"

He flinches and screws his eyes shut.

"Is it glittery?" I splash some more. "You have to tell me if it's glittery—"

His fingers close around my ankle, vise tight. "You done?" He wipes his eyes with the back of his free hand, and it comes away wet.

My calf is pale against Lowe's skin, slick with water and soap suds. When his grip slips, he turns his wrist to adjust it, and it transitions into something that's more in the realm of a caress.

Okay.

So.

We've been touching a lot, since yesterday.

We *are* touching a lot.

"About tonight," he starts. New topic, but his hand stays firmly in place. "I talked to Koen. He'll buy us some time. Distract Emery."

"How?"

"We'll see. Koen's a creative thinker."

"Does he know what we're planning?"

"Not yet." He lowers my trapped foot under the water but

doesn't let go of my ankle, as though he doesn't trust me to behave. Or as though he doesn't want to. "He might suspect, but he knows better than to ask. Plausible deniability."

"Wise. Hey, why *is* Koen here?"

"Emery is his mother's sister."

"His *aunt*?"

"Correct. She was originally in the Northwest pack, then moved when she met Roscoe. That's why I was sent to him."

"Wow. And he's still going to help you?"

"He is no fan of Roscoe. Or his own family."

So relatable. "After dinner, then."

"You're going to say you need to feed."

"And you'll come with me because you're my worried and possessively protective Alpha husband, and I have terrible orientation skills. All we need to do is get to the office, plant the devices, and get out." I bite into my lower lip. "I could also do it on my own."

"I'm not sending you out there on your own."

I think—I'm not positive, because of the water, and the foam, and the sheer improbability of it—but I think Lowe might be brushing his fingertips against the arch of my sole.

A tactile hallucination.

"You're a Vampyre. If Emery's guards find you, they'll attack first, ask questions later." He presses his lips together. "Stick close, okay?"

"I can fight," I say. To give him an out. To avoid thinking about what's going on underwater.

"I don't care. I'm not taking the chance, not with you."

I'm not sure whether to be flattered or indignant. So I opt for a flat "Okay."

He nods and finally lets go of me. I watch the play of his shoulder blades as he walks away and savor the glow his skin left on mine for a long time after he's gone.

———— ◥◤ ————

KOEN IS AN ASSHOLE, IN THE MOST DELICIOUS AND ENTERTAINING of ways. He seems to have distinct preferences, strong opinions, and little interest in keeping either to himself.

"Let's all thank Lowe for the opportunity to *not* have to tune out one of Roscoe's deranged rants tonight," he proclaims loudly while taking a seat at the dinner table. I nearly choke on my spit, but no one else appears concerned that a brawl might be on the verge of erupting, not even Emery.

I'm relieved that he doesn't hate me. The opposite, actually: when we meet, he clasps my shoulder and pulls me in for a bear hug that has me wondering whether he's aware that I'm a Vampyre, or that Lowe and I are not *actually* married. He must be around ten years older than us, somewhere between a big brother and a father figure for Lowe. But before dinner, when I watched them talk—two tall men wearing identical button-downs and exchanging hushed, comfortable words—the mutual affection and respect was obvious.

And yet, they're as different as night and day. Lowe might be aloof at times, but there is something fundamentally kind about him, selfless and patient. Koen is brash. Cocksure. A little vicious. He's indeed no fan of Emery's, and willing to declare it as forcefully as possible.

Other guests are more relatives, and a few former seconds of Roscoe's who decided to stay neutral during the change in leadership. Most seem to have realized that Lowe is their best bet, or maybe they're simply beguiled by whatever his Alpha magic is, and act deferentially, but one of them—John—is wearing a necklace with a vial of something purple that looks a lot like Vampyre blood. Lowe stares at him for a long time when he notices, long enough that I'm certain a fight will break out, and I find myself reaching for one of the meat knives, just in case. After a beat, John lowers his eyes—a show of submissiveness if I've ever seen one—and the tension in the room seems to deflate.

When I next see him, the necklace is gone.

The topic of new alliances with the Vampyres and the Humans comes up at the table, and the only person to bring up objections is Emery. "I hear you and that new Human governor-elect have been . . . meeting," she tells Lowe.

"Maddie Garcia, yes."

"Do you really mean to establish an alliance with—"

"It's done," he says, eyes holding hers. "There are details to iron out, but the Weres and the Humans are going to be allies as soon as her term begins."

Emery composes herself. "Of course. But is it not offensive to the memory of the Weres who fought and died in the wars against the other species?" she asks, with the tone of someone who's merely asking an innocent question.

Amanda, a young woman who came with Koen and is sitting across from me, theatrically rolls her dark eyes. When she smiles at me, I smile back.

"That's not my intention, but if it were, it still seems preferable to more of my pack dying." Lowe stresses the word *my*, a not-so-subtle reminder.

"I understand the push for a ceasefire, I suppose." Her eyes flicker to me. "Are you not worried about what this might mean for your pack, Koen? The Humans border your territory."

"No." Koen takes a bite of his steak. He and Lowe bickered like an old married couple over who'd get to eat mine, so I decided to give it to Amanda. *Look, Serena, I'm making friends.* "Not all of us live to stir up shit with other species, Emery."

"Indeed. Some of you even have Vampyre spouses." Her tone is chilly. Here I was, thinking she approved of our love.

"Some of us are lucky," Lowe says, sincere-sounding, like our marriage is one of his proudest accomplishments, the culmination of years of deeply harbored love. Good actor. "Do you need to feed?" he asks, turning to me, voice instantly more intimate, and yep.

Great actor, great timing.

"Please." I smile adoringly at my nurturing partner, pretending not to notice the gagging looks around us.

He holds my eyes and murmurs, "Let's go, then." We step out of the dining room just as Koen calls John a *fuckwaffle*.

"Does he like to make enemies? Start fights? Watch the world burn?"

"Koen's big on . . ." Lowe searches for the right words. "Unfiltered honesty."

No shit. "Who did he challenge? To become Alpha, I mean."

"No one. His mother was Alpha before him. When she passed, Koen just ascended."

"How delightfully monarchic. And the pack was just okay with it?"

"Not all of them."

"And?"

His hand presses on my lower back, wordlessly asking me to take a right. "There were challengers."

"And?"

"He's been Alpha for well over a decade, has he not?"

"Mmm. True. Are he and Amanda doing it?"

"She's his second."

"Well, are they?"

A brief pause. "Traditionally, the Alpha of the Northwest pack takes a vow of celibacy."

Oh, God. "Did you?"

Lowe shakes his head. "Feels like it, though," he murmurs, just as we reach the office. I immediately unhook a pin from my nape and drop on my knees in front of the lock, letting my dress bunch up my thighs. A few seconds later I open the door with a butler-like flourish.

"What?" I whisper, noticing the upturned corner of Lowe's mouth.

He slips in first, scans the room, then gestures me inside. "Just picturing you doing the same . . ." He closes the door behind him and turns on the light. I see a fireplace so large it could comfortably sleep a midsize family—and a suspicious amount of antlered wall decor. "To break into *my* room."

"Ah. Right." I flinch. "About that, I *am* sorry that . . ."

"You went through my underwear?"

"Yeah, that."

He points at the computer on the desk with a small smile, and I dart there, giving the antlers a wide berth, glad to have something else to focus on. "I'll hide your scent, but make sure you touch as little as possible," he reminds me.

We don't have much time, so I nod and hurry. Lowe already bugged several spots in the house, but what I'm doing will allow us to track and rifle through any communication from all of Emery's devices. And since she doesn't have an Alex, she'll never realize.

"Need anything from me?" Lowe asks while I slip into the network, voice pitched low.

I nod between keystrokes. "Set up the Ubertooth and hand me the LAN Turtle." I snort at his wide-eyed I-didn't-know-the-essay-was-due-today-and-my-dog-ate-it-anyway expression. "I was kidding. Just keep guard."

"Thank fuck." His relief could jump-start a truck's battery. "How long do you need?"

"Six minutes, tops. Too long?"

"No. I doubt they know how little time it takes you to feed."

I beam up at him. "Why, thank you."

"Was that a compliment?" His head tilts in confusion.

"Wasn't it?"

"Not intentionally."

"Weren't you trying to say how low-maintenance I am?"

"No."

"Bummer." I bend my head and quickly type the code. "Well, I rescind my warm acceptance of your non-compliment."

"If you think that's what it was, you need better ones."

"Better what?"

"Compliments."

I look up once more. He's staring, his eyes halfway between unreadable and indecipherable. "What do you mean?"

"You need to be told the right things." He shrugs casually, but the movement feels the opposite of casual. "That you're intelligent, and incredibly skilled at what you do, and brave. That despite your weird belief that you're heartless, you're more genuinely caring than anyone I've ever met. That you're so resilient, I can't quite wrap my head around it. That you're very . . ." He pauses. Wets his lips. My heartbeat skips. "Very beautiful to look at. Always so beautiful. And that—"

He pauses abruptly, lifting his palm. His shoulders tense, shifting to acute vigilance.

"Someone is coming," he whispers.

"Emery?" I mouth. I can't make out any noises, but Were hearing is better than mine.

Lowe shakes his head, and two seconds later I hear them, too. Voices. *Two* voices. Two men, coming down the stairs.

"Emery's guards," he says, barely audible.

The possibility of being caught freezes me. Then the image of Ana pops into my head—the way Emery tried to take her, how terribly she might have hurt her, and fear, *real* fear drives through me like a spear. We can't go back home empty-handed.

"Don't," I whisper when Lowe is about to turn off the computer. The steps sound terrifyingly closer. "It just needs a couple more minutes."

"If they come in and find us—"

"They won't." I turn off the monitor. "And we'll—"

I have an idea, but it's easier shown than explained, so I grasp Lowe's hand and tug him closer, walking backward until I hit one of the square columns on the sides of the fireplace. The cliché almost makes my teeth hurt, and if Emery's guards are media literate even just at a third-grade level, they're not going to fall for it. But it might buy us a couple of minutes, and that's all that matters.

"Kiss me," I order, pulling him farther into me. He needs to be inside my space, towering over me.

"What?" Lowe's brow is one deep furrow.

"Let's just pretend we got—we're newly married and got, I don't know, horny, and—" And ended up in a random office. Maybe we're kinky. Maybe we're idiots. Maybe we're pathetic.

Shit, the guards are *never* gonna fall for it. And they're *coming*.

"They think you're feeding," Lowe hisses from above me. If I could devote any brain cells to not panicking, I would roll my eyes.

"I know, but since we're here, and *they* are basically here—"

"Feed. From me." He looks dead serious.

"*What?*"

"Pretend that's what we came here for."

"No! It's—"

Actually, a pretty good idea. A *really* good idea, even. Still doesn't explain why we're in here. We could say we got lost and it was the first unlocked door we found.

"Okay." I nod. The steps are getting closer. "Tilt your neck, I'll pretend I'm drinking from your vein."

"Misery." His eyes drill into mine. "You have to bite me."

"Why?"

"They're Weres. They're going to be able to smell it if you're not really drinking."

"What? *What?* I've *never*—"

"Misery," Lowe orders, or maybe it's a plea, or maybe my name is just a word he likes to say, a word he likes to think of.

A second later, my fangs sink into the vein at the base of his neck.

Two seconds later, the door to the office opens.

CHAPTER 17

The past year notwithstanding, he was always comfortable
with sex and everything that came with it. He knew what he
liked, and he knew how to get it. He was content.
Now he can't remember what satisfaction felt like.

IT'S SURPRISING HOW SMOOTHLY IT ALL GOES, ESPECIALLY CON-
sidering how new we both are at this.

There's Lowe, who cannot possibly have a clue of what to expect. There's me, a notoriously bad Vampyre. And then there are
some very shitty circumstances. Like how mauled we're about
to get.

And yet, even without knowing what to do, I know *exactly* what
to do. I know to draw the tip of my nose across the base of his
throat to find the perfect spot. I know to stop where his blood
smells the sweetest and his skin forms the thinnest veil. I know to
press my lips to his flesh in a brief, indulgent moment of silent gratitude. Above all, I know without any trace of doubt, or hesitation,
or fear, to bite. My canines might be unused, but they are plenty
sharp, guided by instinct if not experience. And after a brief, suspended moment of screaming disorientation, Lowe's blood fills my
mouth.

It's unlike anything I've ever tasted. And not because I've only ever fed from chilly, refrigerated bags, and in comparison, this feels scorching as fire. I think it has to do with the fact that . . .

The fact that this is Lowe. And his blood tastes like blood, yes, but it's also spicy, coppery, a thrill on the back of my tongue. His blood tastes like his scent, and his smiles, and his hands lingering on my skin. Like the serious way he stares into the distance and rubs his jaw when he's worrying about Ana. His blood is everything that he is, and I'm drinking of it. It's the most delicious, the most earth-shattering, the most inside-out moment of my entire life.

And then the first few drops hit my stomach, and everything changes.

Mere feet from us, things are happening. I hear them distantly, dreamily: gasps; a frantic, hushed conversation that includes words like *Lowe*, and *wife*, and *feeding*; a rushed, panicked apology; a door slamming closed. But all I can think of is . . .

"Misery," Lowe grunts.

Warmth. I'm feverishly, beautifully warm. And empty. And bursting. And dizzy. Liquefying. And I feel like I need, need, *need*.

I need more. I need Lowe to be closer.

"Misery," he breathes.

I don't know when, but my hands have hiked up to his shoulders. I moan into his neck, unable to stop myself. I want to climb under his skin. I want him to slide under mine. I want to give him every last thing he asks for.

"Fuck." His breath is shallow against my temple. I think he gets it, though, because he does exactly what I'm unable to beg for: his hand travels down my spine to cup my ass, and he holds me to himself while my legs wrap around him. My breasts are achy and tender, my core throbs, and there's an alarm in my head telling me that I should stop, that I'm drinking too much. It's killed into silence the moment Lowe winds his fingers into the thick hair at my nape and orders: "Take more."

I moan a blissful hum into his skin. Something wet and eager bursts inside me, spills into my stomach.

"Misery. *Misery*." He scoops my head deeper into his neck. Bucks against me in a way that feels not wholly voluntary. "Take all you need."

I cling to him like I'd die if he let go, desperate for friction. My hips grind against his abs, seeking relief, and when the contact feels good, I need *more*. More blood, more Lowe, more of the stretching, rocking, taut feeling coasting inside me.

"I'm going to—fuck." His voice is a thick, urgent rumble against my ear. "Misery, let me—" A stifled, filthy sound comes out of his throat. He's rock-hard, and when he lifts me higher, fingertips pressed into my ass, trying to thrust against the perfect spot in me, I almost lose contact with his vein. *Almost*. I let out a plaintive, needy whimper, even as I writhe against his cock.

"I know," he murmurs, soothing, commanding. "I know. Be good, I'm going to—"

The first twitches of pleasure hit me so hard, so sudden, I cannot process them. My back arches, my shoulders shake, my core spasms, and for a long second I'm just there—stretched, untethered—until something clicks and my orgasm explodes inside me, leaving me without breath. The pleasure is sharp, loud, all-consumingly bright. It bursts to *everything*, and then it doubles, and then it swells again until everything else is gone, and I come, and come, and come, sinking into its tide for seconds, minutes, centuries. Then, slowly, it shrinks to aftershocks pulsing through my body and licking down my spine.

I'm glad Lowe is pinning me to the fireplace, because I've lost control of my limbs. My breath is stymied, and I pant into his still-open vein. I'm—

His vein. His precious, beautiful vein.

I'm not capable of rational thought at the moment, but I lean forward and suck at the wounds I opened, then lick at them like a kitten, rescuing every last green drop. It's an automatism, something written in my genes, and Lowe seems to enjoy it, too. Intense satisfaction radiates from him. His big hands clutch at my hips. Soft, pleased praises are muttered against my cheekbones.

The blood stops seeping through, his skin sealing shut. I pull back feeling supremely smug, brimming with pride for a job well done. I'm full. Satiated. Happy. I'm strong and warm all over, comfortable in a way I haven't really experienced before, and it's all thanks to Lowe, and his powerful blood, the way his heavy breath rolls against my skin—

Oh, God.

Lowe.

"I—" I push against his shoulders, and he doesn't immediately react. "Let go of me."

It's all it takes. He gently lowers me until my feet are on the ground, then tries to take a step back, but I don't—*can't*—let him. I cling to his shirt, following his retreat.

"Misery."

I'm physically unable to give him up.

"Misery."

His hoarse voice jerks me out of my trancelike state. I put some air between us, which feels like a supremely bad idea, cold and invasive and all wrong. My hair is wild and the fabric of my dress caught at my waist, but I'm too busy staring at Lowe to do anything about it. His pupils have swallowed the irises. They travel down my legs, mesmerized.

With the distance, the awareness of what just happened slowly trickles into me—then *drowns* me like a water flood.

Shit. It's not that I fed from him, even though I did, but also . . . I had no clue that . . . "I am *so* sorry," I gasp out, straightening my clothes.

He shakes his head, chest heaving rhythmically up and down. His eyes are different. Not *his* anymore.

"I'd never . . . from someone. I had no idea it would be . . . Did I hurt you?"

There's something raptorial about the way he shakes his head. Slow, careful. I take a step back, feeling like I'm being tracked by a much stronger, faster predator.

"Okay." I lick the corner of my lip. This aftertaste in my mouth is his *blood*, and there is something deliciously erotic about it—he is alive, breathing in front of me, warm and strong. This living being, this man, this Were, produced plasma and green blood cells and chose to provide me with them.

Life and sustenance.

It's so *intimate*. Sexual, but more than that. Not something I could imagine sharing with just anyone, except for . . .

Lowe. Of course.

I look down at my crumpled dress, feeling like a child who just found out that she didn't really come from the cabbage patch.

"Misery." I peel my eyes from my feet. Lowe looks disheveled. A little shell-shocked. Confused. Obviously horny. He strokes his erection once over the tented fabric of his pants, staring at my face in that spellbound way. "Are you okay?"

"I don't know." I lick my lips, finding more traces of him. "I don't think so."

That's when I hear the steps and remember *why* I was sucking on his blood a second ago. "They're coming," I hiss, hurrying to the computer to disconnect the hardware. In the first lucky break of the evening, the code is done. I unplug everything, making sure to leave nothing behind. Lowe is still standing still, following my every gesture like a wolf about to pounce on a rabbit. When my fingers disappear into my cleavage to hide the USB, his breath hitches.

"Lowe? You know someone's coming, right?"

"Yeah," he says simply, and for a moment I think he might be broken. Then I realize—what should we even do? Run? We've already been caught. Now it's all about committing to the show.

"Are *you* okay?" I ask. Because I didn't think to, before.

He murmurs, "Come back," a hand outstretched in my direction. I don't think he's okay, but neither am I, so I cross the room.

He hugs me, both arms enveloping my shoulders, my head nestled under his chin. It's not like before—not in that sexual, feverish way that's all about heat and shared skin and contact. This hug is all about closeness, and Lowe burying his nose in my hair, and my heartbeat seeking his. We should probably discuss what to do when the next person barges in, come up with an action plan, but all I want is to be here. Cling to him.

"I could fuck you very nicely right now," he says into my ear. He sounds honest, and a bit resigned. "I almost did."

"I'm sorry. I never imagined it would lead to . . ."

"I know. I'm just really . . ." His lips move against my forehead, soft and warm. "I've never felt like this."

"Like what?"

"Turned on. Smitten. And . . . and other things."

I feel the exact same. "I'm sorry," I repeat. "It must be—I'm going to talk to my brother. It might be something I've done." *It's not. It's just right.*

Lowe's stubble drags against my temple. "Have you had enough?"

"Enough?"

"Blood."

"Oh. Yes."

But, *I'd like more.*

But, *May I have more?*

I want it. So bad. I'm about to say fuck it and ask for it assertively, like a big girl, when the door opens again. This time, Lowe and I manage to break apart. He steps protectively in front of me, the tenderness between us dissolving.

"I thought my guards were having hallucinations," Emery says, eyeing us suspiciously. "I must have forgotten to lock this room." Her gaze lingers on Lowe's neck—woundless, but faintly bluish-green. As if someone latched on to it and didn't let go for a long while. "When you mentioned feeding, Lowe, I assumed . . ." Her lips twist into something that resembles disgust.

"You should never. Assume, that is." Lowe's voice is cutting.

And then Koen appears behind Emery, leaning against the doorjamb with a shit-eating grin. "I, for one, am glad the kids are having fun."

"Yeah, *well*. When you're done, please come back to the table. We're waiting for you for dessert."

"Aunt Emery, they already had dessert."

Emery makes a revulsed face and brushes past Koen. Lowe doesn't relax even when she's gone: his broad shoulders remain tense, gaze fixed on Koen as if he were a threat, someone I should be shielded from, instead of Lowe's most trusted and valuable ally.

Which, going by his amused smile, Koen knows. "And to think that you're the most sensible Were I've ever met. Look how finding her made you," he says cryptically. He gives Lowe a fond glance, and then his expression shifts. "I got a phone call. Cal tried to reach you with something important but wasn't able to. It's urgent."

"I left my phone back in my room."

Koen's eyebrow lifts. "Yeah. Not sure it would have made a difference if it had been in your pocket."

Lowe rolls his eyes but eases up a fraction. "What's going on?"

"He mentioned the possibility of you heading home tonight instead of tomorrow morning. Something about Ana, I think."

CHAPTER 18

Her presence soothes him more than a full-moon run.

I TRY TO USE THE TIME ON THE PLANE TO MAKE SURE THAT THE tracker is in place and working remotely, but the Wi-Fi signal is too spotty, and I end up tossing my Raspberry Pi to the side with an angry grunt. Lowe and I don't exchange more than a couple of perfunctory words on the flight. He pilots in a focused, self-assured way, his thoughts clearly full of concern for Ana.

My heart aches for him.

"It started when you left," Mick explains grimly when he picks us up. "I know, I know," he immediately adds when he sees Lowe's expression, "I should have told you, but it was a low fever. I assumed she'd eaten something funny. But then she started shivering and said that her bones hurt. And started to vomit."

Lowe, whose Alpha nature manifests through having to drive every single means of transport he boards, pulls up to the house. "Can she keep liquids down?"

"Not much. Juno's upstairs with her." He looks about five years older than when we left. And so do Juno and Cal, who are pacing outside of Lowe's room, where Ana chose to make her sickbed. I wonder if her brother's smell is thicker in there, reassuring her that everything is going to be all right.

I have no doubt Lowe is terrified, but he never shows it. Even earlier tonight, when we were about to be discovered, he never panicked. Maybe it's an Alpha trait, the making of a good leader: the ability to back-burner emotions and focus on what needs to be done. I think Father would agree.

"Is this—being sick. Is it not something that happens to full Weres?" I ask.

Cal and Mick seem taken aback. Juno just asks Lowe, calmly, "You told her about Ana?" and seems unsurprised when he nods. "We're not really susceptible to viruses," she explains to me, "or bacteria, or whatever this is. There are select poisons that affect us, but not this way."

It occurs to me that because of Ana's physiology, a Were doctor would be useless. And because of Ana's physiology, a Human doctor would put her at risk of being discovered. "Is it the first time this has happened?"

Lowe nods. "She's had a runny nose and some sneezing in the past. We passed them off as allergies."

"We still have that Tyler medicine," Cal offers. "The one we got months ago."

"Tylenol?" I ask.

He gives me an admiring look. "How do you know?"

I smile. "Just guessing. That might help with the fever and the pain, but . . ." I shrug, and while the others try to decide how to proceed, I go check on Ana directly. She looks small and fragile in the middle of Lowe's king bed, and her forehead burns under my hand. I'm convinced she's asleep, but her "Can you keep it there?" when I'm about to leave tells me otherwise. "You feel so cool."

"Who do you think I am?" For her pleasure, I produce a deep frown. "Your personal ice pack?"

Her giggle squeezes my chest.

"How do you feel?" I ask.

"Like I'm about to puke on you."

"Could you please puke on Sparkles first?"

She gives it a long thought before formally declaring, "As you wish."

Lowe joins us a few minutes later. He presses his lips to Ana's temple and gives her what he announces to be the first of her California presents—a large pink giraffe that I cannot figure out where or when he acquired.

"Were there giraffes in California?"

"Not in the wild, love."

She purses her lips. "I'd like a more aunenthic present next time."

"Noted."

"Lowe?"

"Yes."

"I miss Mama."

Lowe's eyes briefly flutter shut, like he can't bear to keep them open. "I know, love."

"Why does Misha get to have two parents and I get none? It's not fair."

"No." He gently smooths down her hair, and I feel it deep inside my bones that he'd burn the entire world for her. "It's not."

He holds her head when, just a couple of minutes later, a new wave of nausea has her dry-retching into a bucket. We stay with her until she falls asleep, clutching both our hands with her little fingers.

When we step out of the room, there are deep grooves around Lowe's mouth. "I'm going to take her to Human territory," he says to the others, in that Alpha decree tone of his that doesn't allow pushback. "I'll find a doctor who won't ask too many questions or perform any unnecessary exams. It's not ideal, but we simply don't know enough about her Human half, even at baseline, to interpret—"

"I do," I interrupt. Everyone turns to gawk at me. "At least, I have more experience with Humans than you guys."

"Actually," Cal starts.

"Experience with Humans that doesn't involve *murdering* them," I tell him with a pointed look. He concedes that I'm right with a sheepish nod.

But Mick, who's usually my ally, scratches his neck and says in a pained tone, "Misery, it's a really kind offer, but you're not a Human, you're a Vampyre."

"I lived among Humans for one and a half decades. With a Human sister."

"You're saying you know what's wrong with her?" Lowe asks me.

"No, but I'm fairly sure it's either bacterial or viral, and I know what meds Serena used for each." They're all still looking at me skeptically. "Listen, I'm not saying this is foolproof, and I'm no physician, but it's probably better than moving her while she's already so weak, or exposing her to someone who might figure out her . . . situation."

"It seems risky. And there's no telling what could go wrong." Mick sighs and shakes his head. "We should take her to Human territory, Lowe. I can do it myself. I'll be quick about it, and have her back—"

"Do you have the names of the drugs?" Lowe interrupts, looking at *me*.

"I can write them down for you. You'll need to go to a Human pharmacy, most of which will be closed by now, and you'd normally need a prescription, but—"

"I don't need that."

I grin. "I figured." I have no doubt that someone like Lowe can slip in and out of other territories undetected.

"Lowe. Misery's friend was fully Human." Mick is protesting a lot, which is probably related to how invested he is. Lowe said that he lost his son, and I wonder if that has anything to do with the attachment he's formed to Ana.

"True," I say gently, "but any doctor will evaluate her as a fully Human child, too. There is simply no one like Ana. We might as well use Serena as a template."

"I agree," Juno intervenes. "We should trust Misery."

Mick looks on the verge of complaining again, so Lowe clasps his hand around his shoulder. "If this doesn't work, we will take her to a doctor. Tomorrow."

He's back in less than an hour. We're all waiting for him with Ana, but his eyes meet mine first when he steps inside. His knuckles are dusted with green blood as he hands me the meds, and I'm relieved to find no traces of red.

I make quick work of smashing the pills for Ana, like I used to for Serena before she learned how to gulp them down—an embarrassingly recent development.

"Why so many?" Ana whines.

"Because we don't know exactly what you have," I explain. "These will help whether it's a virus or bacteria, and this other one will lower your fever. Now quit bitching."

She says the pills taste like poison, which earns me several nasty looks from the peanut gallery. I decide to make myself scarce and go look for Alex, hoping he's still awake. I'm in luck, because I find him in Lowe's office. I walk up behind him, curious about what has him so engrossed that he didn't hear me coming.

"Playing smuggled Human games, and *GTA* no less, at your boss's desk. The sheer gall of today's workforce."

"Shit a brick!" He almost falls off his chair. "Where are you— You're so *close* all of a sudden. I had garlic for lunch and my blood is probably poisonous to you!"

I give him my best disappointed pout. "I missed you, too. We're intercepting, right?"

He nods, still clutching his chest. "Yes. I'm getting great signal. Emery can't book a chiropractor appointment without us knowing."

"Lovely. Anything yet?"

He shakes his head. His nostrils twitch. "You smell different. That's why I didn't notice you coming in."

Uh-oh. "Maybe my vampyric stench is growing on you?"

"No. No, you smell like—"

"By the way, Lowe asked us to work on a project," I interrupt. It's a lie. But I don't think Lowe will mind.

"What?"

It's something that just occurred to me because of what Ana said. *Misha gets to have two parents and I get none.* When trying to figure out who told Serena about Ana, we assumed that it couldn't be her father, because he never believed Maria when she said she was pregnant. But what if that's not the whole story? "He wants us to get a list of Humans who were part of the Human-Were Bureau, say, ten to five years ago?" It is safer than saying eight. Alex is not stupid. "Lowe is looking for people who would have interacted with Weres in our"—*Our?*—"in his pack."

He blinks curiously. "Why?"

"I don't know. Something came up when we were at Emery's and he said he'd need to know." Maybe I'm a better actor than I gave myself credit for.

"Any person who worked for the Bureau? No other criteria?"

I run a hand through my hair, thinking. "Men. Just men."

"Okay. Yeah, sure."

"Do you have time to start now?" I smile as fanglessly as I can. "Or are you too busy playing pretend street gangster?"

He flushes a cute shade of green, clears his throat, and we spend the next hour finding very little because of the disorganized mess of the Human archives. We give up when Alex starts yawning.

"Oh my God," he says after I stand to leave.

"What?"

His eyes are moon-wide. "I got it."

"Got what?"

"What you smell like."

Fuck. "Good night, Alex."

"Why do you smell like my Alpha *marked* you?" is the last thing I hear as I head back to Ana's room.

Mick and Cal have left, but Lowe and Juno are standing outside of his room, talking in hushed tones. They fall silent when I arrive, and turn to me with heavy eyes.

I freeze. "Shit. Is she okay?"

Juno's response only lags about a second, but my stomach's weight doubles. "Her fever broke, and she's been able to keep liquids down. She said your 'gross stuff,' direct quote, made her feel much better."

I smile. "Really?"

"Yup." She gives her Alpha an appraising look. Her eyes bounce between the two of us, and then she adds, "You guys make a surprisingly good team."

"It was mostly me." I dust off the dress I put on for dinner and am somehow still wearing.

Juno's mouth twitches. "Just take the compliment."

"Fine," I concede, watching her wave at Lowe and leave. This friendship, or lack of enmity, appears to be highly rewarding to my dopaminergic system.

I expect to find Lowe smiling. Instead he's staring at me with a grave, almost haunted expression.

"Is Ana asleep?"

He nods.

"Do you want to sleep in my bed?" His throat bobs before it occurs to me to clarify. "I sleep in the closet, anyway. And you could keep the door open, in case Ana wakes up, and . . . I'm not coming on to you while your sister is still sick because of what happened between us earlier," I finish, considerably less strongly than I began.

But I don't think he cares. Honestly, I doubt he's listening. He nods robotically, and once he follows me inside my room, his gaze fixes on the night outside the window. On something that might not even be there.

There is an unpleasant twist in my throat. I sit on the bare mattress and softly call, "Lowe?"

He doesn't respond. His eyes, pale and otherworldly, stick to the darkness.

"Is there . . . Are you okay?"

I'm afraid he'll ignore this question, too. But a few minutes later, he shakes his head. Slowly, he turns and comes to stand in front of me. "What if you hadn't been here?" he murmurs.

"I . . . What?"

"If you hadn't been here, with your knowledge of Human anatomy." His jaw works. "I'd have had to choose between her health and her safety."

"Ah." I see now where all of this is coming from. I see it, and I feel it, deep in the pit of my stomach, a stone sinking heavily. "It'll be okay. She'll be okay. It's probably just the flu."

"What if next time it's something more serious? Something she needs extensive Human medical care for?"

"It won't. Like I said, she'll be okay—"

"Will she?" he asks, in a tone that makes it impossible for me to lie.

The truth is, I don't know. I have no idea whether Ana will be okay. I have no idea whether Lowe and I will be okay. I have no idea whether Serena is alive. I have no fucking idea whether a war is inevitable, whether my people care enough about me not to leave me here as its first casualty, whether every single choice I've made since the day I turned eighteen was a mistake.

I have no idea what *will* happen, I have no idea what *has* happened, and it's terrifying. I respect Lowe, this man who feels so similar to me, this man I've known less than a handful of weeks and yet cannot quite make myself not trust. I respect him too much to lie to him, or to lie to myself in his presence.

So I say, "I'm not sure," and it's barely a whisper, but he hears me. He nods, and I nod, and when he sinks to his knees, when he buries his face in my lap, I welcome him. Let my hands run over his soft hair. Feel his deep inhale. His shoulders, so broad and strong, rise and fall. I slide my hand down the back of his neck, inside his shirt, hoping my cool skin will be as soothing as his heat is to me.

"Misery," he sighs, and his breath warms the skin of my belly through the fabric of the dress, and I'm still alone, still different, still mostly on my own, but maybe a little less than usual. His fingers close softly around my ankle, the metal of his wedding band hot against skin and bones, and for the first time in more than I can remember, I feel held.

I'm here, I say, only in my head. *With you.*

We stay like that for longer than I can keep track of.

CHAPTER 19

She is fearless, and the thought terrifies him.

"THIS QUESTION YOU JUST ASKED ME . . . I DON'T LIKE IT."

Not rolling my eyes at Owen requires a degree of control over my ocular muscles I didn't know I had. Normally I wouldn't bother with civility, but I need my brother to get me some answers.

On the plus side, Ludwig is not paying attention to my call. Earlier today, when I found him in the sunroom trimming a rose plant and asked whether I could chat with my brother, he looked at me like I was asking for permission to get a liger tattoo. "I don't care. Lowe said your movements are not to be restricted. Call whoever you like." A pause. "Maybe avoid phone sex, but really, it's up to you."

"Is phone sex even a thing anymore?"

"Pretty sure all kinds of sex are a thing, and will be till the sun swallows the Earth." He went back to pruning, then added, "If you're ordering pizza, get extra large."

I'm not sure why a Vampyre would order pizza, but I'd love to be on the phone with some bored teenager trying to upsell me some garlic knots. And not at the mercy of a less-than-loving brother's judgment.

"Your dislike breaks my heart," I tell him in the Tongue, straight-faced. *"Please answer anyway."*

"Who have you fed from?"

I straighten my face. Even more. *"I didn't say I fed from someone."*

"No. You asked whether there can be any negative consequences if a live source is fed upon, and I brilliantly deduced it. Because you've never exhibited any curiosity on the topic before, and—I'm not a damn idiot. Who?"

I let out a deep breath. *"Who do you think?"*

He face-palms. *"Your husband. Your Were husband. Your Alpha Were husband."*

"Please."

"Did you force him?"

"What? No."

His curse is not soft. *"Do not tell Father this happened."*

"Why?"

"He'd try to exploit it."

"How is— In what way is there anything to exploit about this?"

He pinches the bridge of his nose. *"Misery, do you know nothing?"*

"What should I know?"

"How did you not just pick up stuff growing up?"

The noise that comes out of my throat has Ludwig checking in on me. *"From whom? From my Human caregivers?"*

"Okay." His hands lift, a silent order for me to stay quiet while he collects himself. I consider hanging up on him and asking Father out of spite. *"It's not normal for him to let you feed. For any Were to let a Vampyre feed."*

"Maybe Lowe doesn't know that."

"Our species have been enemies for centuries. Do you think they didn't grow up thinking that being sucked on by a leech is the highest level of defilement? Do you think using his blood to keep alive the people who killed his ancestors is something his pack will be okay with?"

I remember Emery's disgusted expression. Her seconds' gasps. Even Koen had to suppress his initial shock at seeing my marks on Lowe's neck.

And Lowe, pulling me to himself after I said I wasn't okay.

"Lowe is different."

"Clearly. And clearly this is something you should bring to your grave. It's obvious that there is some . . . friendship here."

I think about it for a minute, then nod.

"So he took a liking to you." He rubs his forehead. *"This is weird. I'm glad you're alive and maybe going to stay that way, but—"*

"It's weirder than that. When I fed from him . . ."

"Misery." He gives me a blistering look. *"I went through puberty in Vampyre territory. I know exactly what happened when you fed from him. Please, do not continue. People who shared a placenta for nine months should not talk about this stuff."*

Am I flushing? I am. *"We're dizygotic twins, which means that we never shared a placenta or an umbilical cord. A womb at best, really."*

"Still, do not subject me to a retelling." Owen tips his head back and looks at the ceiling.

"Can you just tell me if there will be any negative consequences for Lowe? I want to be sure I didn't harm him."

Owen sighs. *"As long as you didn't take too much, he'll be fine. And you'll probably be fine, too? Honestly, there aren't that many case studies of Vampyres feeding from Weres."*

"Okay." Phew. *"Thank you for letting me know. Have a good life. I'm hanging up now—"*

"Misery, listen carefully. There is a reason our species decided to transition from live feeding as soon as the technology to safely draw and store blood became available. Drinking from a live source is not just something that's hard to tease apart from sex. It has hormonal and biological consequences that are trivial in the moment but might build up in the long run. That's why it's been discouraged among Vampyres for centuries—we need to fuck as many people as we can and reproduce, not form bonds. *Repeat feedings create complex dynamics that . . ."* He stops abruptly, shaking his head. His expression has softened, and I wonder if *he* has done it before. If it's something he'd *want* to do with someone else. *"Don't do it again, Misery. Be his friend. Build a chicken coop with him. Fuck him, if you want. But do not feed from Lowe Moreland again."*

The irritation of being told what to do by my useless brother sticks with me the entire night. I'm still miffed hours later, when I wander into the kitchen after reading a story to Ana, about an annoying llama who's being deservedly bullied by a goat.

The place is dark and deserted, so I open my fridge and take out the jar of peanut butter. It's not like I planned to feed from Lowe ever again. Nor do I think he'd appreciate it, given the questionable side effects. I'm here to find Serena, and I've not forgotten. But Owen has no right to—

"The man you and Alex are looking for. He's Ana's father, isn't he?"

"Yeah." I shrug mechanically, dipping the tip of a spoon in the peanut butter. "I figured it'd be the most likely way Serena—" I turn around, abruptly realizing that I'm not having a conversation with myself anymore. Lowe stands by the table, arms crossed. Eyes veiled with something. "When did you get here?"

"Just now."

"Oh." We haven't really talked since two nights ago, when we awkwardly untangled from each other after Ana woke up and called for a glass of water. He stood in front of me, as earnest and shaken as I felt, and then left to take care of her. I slipped into my closet, under the mound of pillows and blankets, smiling a little when I overheard them talking about the pink giraffe in hushed tones. They—okay, *Ana*—named her Sparkles 2.

Yesterday was some sort of hearing day, with lots of Weres coming over to bring concerns, advice, requests to their Alpha. I remained *very* out of the way for that, but most of the meetings happened in the pier area, and from my window it was fascinating, witnessing the span of Lowe's responsibilities. I couldn't help overhearing how warmly and easily he interacted with pack members, and how many of them lingered just to exchange a joke or to mention how relieved they are that Roscoe is gone.

I guess I felt envious. Maybe I, too, wanted a minute with the Alpha. Maybe during our trip I got used to having him nearby.

"Ana's father. Why?" He talks like we're past preambles, and I think we might be.

"Why not?"

He lifts one eyebrow.

"What if he did know? What if he did believe your mother eventually? What if he told someone else?"

He tilts his head, curious and wolflike, and hums for me to continue.

"Serena was a lot of things, but computer savvy wasn't one of them. Nothing as tragic as you"—I power through Lowe's glare—"but if *I* wasn't able to find traces of Ana while snooping around, it's very unlikely she came across it on her own. Which means that someone must have told her, and we need to figure out who." I shake my head, marveling for the millionth time at Ana's existence. She's here. She's perfect. She's like nothing I've ever conceived of before. How the fuck did Serena get embroiled with her? The theory I keep coming back to is someone pitching Ana's story to a hungry young journalist. But the Serena I know would never, *never* go public with Ana's identity. "Lowe, if it makes you uncomfortable, if you feel like this is intruding on your mother's privacy, I'm okay with pursuing this one on my own."

"It doesn't. What you're saying makes sense, and I wish I'd thought of it sooner."

"Okay. Well, glad to have you on board. Juno did say that we make a good team."

"And you replied that—"

"Who even remembers?" I gesture breezily, and feel my face slowly widen into a smug grin, one with fangs. He smiles back, small and warm. And then we seem to reach an impasse: I'm not sure what to say, neither is he, and the events of the last time, no, *two times* we were together finally catch up with us.

I'm no coward, but I don't think I can bear it.

I've been wanting to be in his presence, but now I'm not sure what to do with him. So I dip my spoon in the peanut butter jar once more, just to keep busy, and stuff it in my mouth. "Well, I think I'm overdue for my nightly bath, just to avoid smelling like phlegm. After that I have a hot date with Alex, so—"

"Does phlegm smell?" he asks.

"I . . . Does it?"

"No clue. Weres don't get colds."

"Stop bragging."

"Do *you* get colds?"

"Nope, but I'm classy about it."

"You'd be classier if you didn't have peanut butter on your nose."

"Damn. Where?"

He doesn't say, but comes forward to show me, walking into me until I'm nestled between him and the counter, and . . . am I cornered, here? By a Were? A wolf, the stuff of bogeyman tales?

Yes.

Yes, I'm cornered, and no, I'm not scared.

"Here." His hand swipes the tip of my nose. He holds his fingertip up to show me the small clump of peanut butter. I should be wondering how it got there to begin with. What I do, instead, is lean forward and lick it off Lowe's thumb.

I regret it instantly.

I don't regret it at all.

I contain every pair of opposing feelings as his eyes, pupils expanding in a way mine could never, fix on my mouth in an entranced, absent way.

I should not have done it. My stomach twists in what feels like pain and something else, something sweet and hot. "Ana's feeling much better," I say, hoping that it'll defuse this thick tension between us.

We're a seesaw, Lowe and I. Constantly pushing and pulling for a precarious balance on the brink of this . . . whatever *this* is that we are always about to fall into. Alternating in chaos.

"She's completely healed," he agrees. We're too close to be having this conversation. We're just—really close.

"Back to her pestering self."

He takes a small step back, barely an inch, and I almost cry with relief, or disappointment, or both. "Yeah," he says, even though there's no question to answer. It's punctuation—he's leaving. He's about to.

"Wait," I blurt out.

He stops. Doesn't even ask me why I'm keeping him here, tethered to me. He knows. The atmosphere between us is too awkward and rich and lush for him not to know.

"Do you—" he starts, with a small, abortive, uncharacteristically insecure gesture of his hand, just as I say, "When did—"

We fall silent at once, letting the sentences swing between us. The silence swells, triples, and when it reaches critical mass, it bursts inside my head.

This time I'm the one moving closer. My head swims deliciously. "What's happening? What is—this thing between us?"

"I don't know," he says. And then. "That was a lie. I do know."

I know, too. My stomach is an empty, open ache. "You have a mate."

He nods slowly. "It's never far from my mind."

"And I'm a Vampyre." I have to lick my fangs to make sure that I really am one. Because my people don't itch to touch his. It's simply not how things go.

"You are." His eyes are on my teeth, and yeah. He doesn't mind them at all.

"This can't be real, can it?"

He is silent. Like I have to work through the answer on my own, and he cannot do it for me.

"It just *feels* real," I tell him. I'm heated. Glowing. I didn't think my body was capable of these temperatures. "I'm afraid I'm misinterpreting, maybe."

One of his hands, large and warm, curves around my waist, tentative at first, then firm, like a single touch is enough to double his greed. "It's okay, Misery." His thumb climbs to the back of my neck, rubbing over the fine hairs at my nape, and I shiver in his arms. "It can just be us," he whispers.

Suddenly, I'm not sure that there's something wrong about the fact that we're about to kiss. It *feels* right, for sure. I've never kissed anyone before, and I like the idea of my first being special. And Lowe—Lowe is that and more.

I'm unsteady. Muddled. Off-balance. But it's normal. Who wouldn't be, next to someone like him, someone who'd carry them through? So I stretch on the tips of my toes, leaning into his touch, and I feel shaky.

I feel ready.

I feel happy.

I feel light-headed, as though I'm made of glass, about to shatter into pieces. My limbs have never been this heavy, and I wish I could just drop to the ground.

Yes, I think. *I'll just let myself do that.*

"Misery." The mix of worry and fear in his voice is unexpected. "Why are you so—"

Searing pain stabs throughout my body, and that's when the world turns pitch-dark.

CHAPTER 20

Whoever did this will pay.
Slowly.
Painfully.

THE NEXT FEW HOURS ARE SHEER, CONCENTRATED AGONY.
The mere act of breathing is an ordeal. My stomach hurts like it's about to digest itself, bruised from the inside out by a thousand wild creatures who are having way too much fun carving their name in its lining with a rusty knife. There are several moments—and then a single one, long, protracted—when I'm sure, just sure, that this is the end. No living being can sustain this level of torment, and I'm going to die.

Which is just fine. Nothing can be worse than what I'm experiencing. I welcome the blissful release of nothingness and all that good shit, but just when I'm about to tip into the void, *something* pulls me back.

First there's someone—okay, Lowe, yes, *Lowe*—giving orders. Barking orders. Growling orders. Or perhaps *not* Lowe, because I've never seen him any way but in control. He sounds desperate, which makes me want to crawl out of my corner of pain and reassure him that it'll be okay—maybe not *me*, but everything else.

And yet, I'm unable to speak for eons. Many, many times I drift right up to the edge of consciousness, only to sink back into sweaty, suffocating darkness. And when I finally manage to drag my eyes open . . .

"There she is."

Dr. Averill? I try to say, but my tongue is glued to the roof of my mouth.

I know him. The Collateral's official physician. With diplomatic passage into Human territory, where he'd give me annual checkups to ensure that I remained healthy enough to . . . be killed if the alliance dissolved, I guess? His duties must have expanded, which is a shame, because he looks as ancient now as he did when I was ten. Except that there's something weird about him. Is he experimenting with facial hair?

"Little Misery Lark. It's been a while."

"Not the mustache," I slur, delirious, unable to keep my eyelids up.

He clucks his tongue. *"If you have the energy to question my appearance, maybe you don't need this painkiller,"* he mutters in the Tongue, ornery as always. I would beg my apologies, claw that syringe out of his hands and into my body, but the needle is already pushing into my arm.

The burning quiets. There are voices, from inside the room or several miles away.

"—her organism deals with the poison. She'll gradually slip into a healing trance. She'll look very still, and you'll be worried that she's dead. But it's simply the Vampyre way."

"How long?" Lowe asks.

"Several hours. Days, maybe. Don't look at me like that, young man."

A few muttered curses. "What do I do?"

"There's nothing to do. It's her body's job to combat the infection now."

"But what do I *do*? For her?"

Dr. Averill sighs. "Make her comfortable. At some point after she wakes up, she'll need to feed—more than usual, in quantity and in frequency. Make sure that you have blood at her disposal, the fresher the better."

A long pause. I picture Lowe running a hand over his jaw. His worried gesture.

"And of course, there's the matter of her father. I'll have to inform Councilman Lark about what happened. He might see this as an act of aggression, even a war declaration against the Vampyres . . ."

Dr. Averill's voice fades, and I fall back inside myself.

—◦◦◦—

". . . NEED TO REST."

"No."

"Come on, Lowe. You need to sleep. I'll watch over her while you—"

"*No.*"

—◦◦◦—

"—TAKE ANA AWAY."

"We cannot be sure that Ana was the real target," Mick protests. "The intended victim could have been Misery."

"But what if Ana was?" Juno points out. "We shouldn't risk it."

"Agreed," Cal says. "Let's move Ana to a safe place until we find out who did this."

"We all know it was Emery." Mick.

"I know no such thing, and I'm done assuming." Lowe is icily, murderously angry. "My wife was on the brink of death until hours ago. I'm going to move Ana to a safe place. This is not up for discussion."

"Where will you move her?" Mick asks.

"That's for me to know."

———— ⟶◆⟵ ————

COOL LIPS PRESS A SOFT KISS INTO MY FEVERISH PALM.

"Misery, I . . ."

———— ⟶◆⟵ ————

I COME OUT OF THE HEALING TRANCE ALL AT ONCE, LIKE A SALMON bursting from a stream.

I sit up in bed, clammy and breathless and utterly disoriented, and wait for the pain to make itself known. I expect it to follow its usual roads: start from my stomach, irradiate out to my limbs, rake through my nerves like an army of knives. When nothing happens, I look down at my body in bafflement, wondering where it's gone. But there it is: colder than usual, perhaps; paler, definitely; intact, ultimately.

Healed? I pull back the covers to test that theory. The large white T-shirt I'm wearing doesn't belong to me, but the pretty lace underwear is mine—courtesy of the wedding stylist. I haven't worn it since the ceremony, and I refuse to wonder how it ended up on me. Instead I stand. Even though I'm wobblier than a newborn calf, my legs are functional. I push through the exhaustion and force myself to walk.

The clock on the wall says one thirty in the morning, and the house is dead silent, but I'm fairly sure that more than a few hours have passed since I first lost consciousness. Did I skip a day? I have no phone to check, so I do the pre-technology thing: head outside to ask someone.

Hopefully not the person who poisoned my peanut butter.

I open the door to a dimly lit hallway and almost stumble on the pile of clothes right outside—Ana giving her dolls another make-over, I bet. I hold on to the wall and weakly step around it, but the pile *moves*.

It uncurls. Then gets up. Then stretches, very much like a cat would. Then it opens its eyes, which happen to be a very beautiful, very pale, very familiar green.

Because it's not a pile at all. It's a wolf. Curled outside my room. Guarding my door.

A huge white wolf.

A fucking *gigantic* white wolf.

"Lowe?" My voice is unused and rusty. I may have been out more than just one day. "Is that you?"

The wolf blinks at me, still enjoying his stretch. I blink back, hopefully stumbling on the Morse code for *pls pls pls don't eat me.*

"I don't want to assume, but the eyes look like yours, and . . ."

He trots to me, and I scurry back in a blast of panic, plastering myself to the wall. Oh, shit. Oh, *shit.* He's just so much larger than Cal, so much larger than I thought wolves could be. I squeeze my eyes shut, not wanting a high-def view of my duodenum getting ripped out of my abdominal cavity and then eaten.

And then something soft and damp pokes me in the hip. I crack one eyelid open, and there it is: a muzzle, pressing against my skin. Pushing gently, but firmly. Like he's herding me. Back inside the room.

"You want me to . . . ?" He doesn't reply, but he radiates satisfaction when I take a few steps back, and when I stop, he nudges me again, even more insistent. "Okay. I'm going."

I march back where I came from. The wolf follows at my heels, and once we're both in the room, angles his body and closes the door with more ease than anyone without opposable thumbs should display.

"Lowe?" I just want to be sure. The eyes seem proof enough, but . . . God, I'm exhausted. "It *is* you, right?"

He pads to me.

"You're not Juno? Or Mick. Please, tell me you're not Ken Doll."

A soft, rumbly noise rises from the back of his throat.

"I guess I expected your fur would be dark. Because your hair is." I let him prod me toward the bed. "Yes, I'm going back to sleep. I feel like total shit, but not the bed, please. The closet."

He understands, because he closes his very impressive jaws around a pillow and carries it to the closet. And then does the same with a blanket, under my bemused stare.

"God, you're just so fluffy. And . . . sorry, but you're kinda cute. I know you could murder me in less time than it takes to stick a straw in a blood bag. But you're *soft*. And your coat is not even sparkly pink. I don't know what you were embarrassed about, you majestic fluffball—yes, fine, I'm going."

He all but drags me to the closet, and doesn't stop bossing me around until I'm lying down in my favorite spot. I wonder how he managed to find it. Might be a scent thing.

"FYI, your Alpha tendencies are even worse in this form."

His tongue darts out and licks at my neck.

"Ew, gross," I giggle. His teeth close around my arm. A joking, playful warning that could shatter my ulna. But won't.

"Can I pet you?"

His head turns to butt under my hand. *Yes, please.*

"Well, then," I half laugh, half yawn, scratching him behind the ears, luxuriating in the beautiful, comforting feeling of his coat. It's not hard to ask, not when he's in this form, a fierce hunter who loves a cuddle: "Do you want to stay? Sleep with me?"

Apparently, it's not hard to say yes, either. Lowe doesn't hesitate before curling right next to me.

And when I inhale deeply, the smell of his heartbeat is all it's always been: familiar, spicy, rich.

I fall asleep twined with him, feeling safer than ever before.

CHAPTER 21

She told him Vampyres do not dream. And yet, once her mid-day rest is over and the evening approaches, her sleep becomes fitful, agitated. His touch seems to comfort her, and the thought fills him with pride and purpose.

SERENA ARRIVED AT THE COLLATERAL RESIDENCE AT THE END of a pleasantly mild January, many months after I first moved in, and came of age at the beginning of an unpleasantly wet April, spent crunching numbers to see how long the transitional sum of money allotted to her by the Human-Vampyre Bureau would stretch in the real world. The rain ticked and ticked, incessant against the windowpanes. We packed our bags and tried to decide what pieces of the past decade to bring into our new lives, sifting through memories, splitting apart the ones we hated from the ones we still hated but could not bear to let go.

That's when he arrived: a child of eight, the new Collateral, sent from the Vampyres for his official vesting ceremony. He was escorted by Dr. Averill and several other councilors I recalled meeting at various diplomatic relations. A sea of lilac eyes. Conspicuously, not the boy's parents'.

It was a sign that we were taking too long to vacate the premises, but we didn't speed up. Instead, Serena stared at the child roaming the spotless hallways in which we'd skinned our knees, fought over hide-and-seek rules, practiced less-than-video-worthy choreographies, ranted about the casual cruelty of our caregivers, wondered if we'd ever fit in somewhere, panicked over how to keep in touch after the end of our time together.

"Why are they *always* children?" she asked me.

"He must be related to someone important." I shrugged. "That's how you make the Collateral a deterrent, by taking the heir to a prominent family. Someone who's valued by a person in power."

She snorted. "They haven't met your father."

"Ouch," I said with a laugh.

The child heard it and wandered our way, eyes lingering on my mouth, as though he suspected I might be like him. When he approached us, Serena dropped to her knees to level with him. "If you don't want to be here," she said, "if you'd rather come with us, just say the word."

I don't think she had a plan—not even a contrived, improbable one only for show. And I don't know how we would have rescued— abducted?—the child if he'd asked us to whisk him away. Where would we have kept him? How would we have protected him?

But it's who Serena was. Badass. Caring. Committed to doing the right thing.

The child said, "This is an honor." He sounded rehearsed, too formal for his years. Not at all like I did when I was nine and begged Father to let me go back to Vampyre territory over, and over, and over again. "I am to be the Collateral, and that is a privilege." He turned around and left.

I was of age, and finally free, and chose not to attend his ceremony.

This is not a core memory for me. I barely ever recall it, but I'm thinking about it now, awake just before sundown. Perhaps because of what came after the child left us: Serena, furiously determined to burn down the entire world—the Vampyres, the Humans, and whoever else made themselves an accomplice of the Collateral system.

I listened to her rant without quite understanding her, because the most I could feel was resignation. There was little fight left in me, and I simply couldn't afford to spend it on something hopeless and unchangeable when waking up every morning in a hostile world was already so exhausting. Her anger was admirable, but I didn't get it then.

I get it *now*, though. In the fuzzy, yellow light filtering into my closet and splattering over the walls, in the worn-out ache that has nested in my bones—I get her anger now. Something within me must have changed, but I still feel like a fairly accurate version of myself: exhausted, but *furious*. Above all, glad to be alive. Because I have something to do. Something I care for. People I want to keep safe.

And I need you to care about one single fucking thing, Misery, one thing that's not me.

Well, Serena, you're still part of this, whether you want it or not. But there's Ana, too. And Lowe, who really needs someone to take care of him. In fact, I should go to him.

Standing takes me several tries. He's not in his room, so I wrap a blanket around my shoulders and make my way downstairs. The trip feels five times longer than usual, but when I walk into the living room, he's there, surrounded by over a dozen people.

His seconds, all of them. A few of them I know, but most I'm seeing for the first time. It must be a meeting, because everyone looks pinch-eyed and serious. A handsome Were with cornrows is saying something about supplies, and I catch the tail end of his explanation, see several people nod, and then lose track when a familiar voice asks a follow-up question.

Because it's Lowe's.

The rest of the room fades. I sink into the doorframe and stare at his familiar face, the dark shadows under his clear eyes and the stubble he hasn't bothered shaving. He speaks with patience and authority, and I find myself lingering, listening to the rhythm of his deep voice if not to the content, my marrow-deep exhaustion soothed at last.

Then he stops. His body tenses as he turns, at once intensely focused on me. Everyone else stares, too, not quite with the thinly veiled distrust I'd expect from them.

"You should go," Lowe commands somberly. "I'll see you later."

"Oh, yeah." I flush. I'm acutely aware that I'm half naked and crashing an important pack meeting that's probably about how to handle their never-ending conflict with *my* people. "I didn't mean to interrupt." But he's crossing to me, and when the seconds stand, I realize that I'm not the one being dismissed.

Lowe is in his usual human form, and I wonder whether I hallucinated my encounter with the white wolf. His seconds walk past us, some nodding at me on their way out, a few patting my back, all wishing me well. I'm unsure what to say until Lowe and I are finally alone. "So." I gesture at myself with a flourish. "It appears that I survived."

He nods gravely. "My felicitations."

"Why, thank you. How long was I out?"

"Five days."

I close my eyes. "Wow."

"Yeah." There is a microcosm in the way he says the word. I want to explore it, but I'm distracted by the slight twitch in his fingers. Like he's actively stopping himself from reaching out.

"Are we—you . . . at war? With the Vampyres?"

He shakes his head. "It came close. The council was not happy."

"Aw. I bet Father was heartbroken." Not.

Lowe's set jaw tells me how perfectly fine Father was. "Once we were sure that you'd pull through, Averill pointed out to the council that the poison is toxic to Weres, too, and that since you ingested it through Were food, it's unlikely that it was meant for you to begin with."

"Oh, God." I hide my face into the doorjamb. "Does Father know about the peanut butter?"

"Is that what worries you?"

"Not sure what it says about me, but yeah." I sigh. "Was it meant for Ana?"

"No way to be sure. But she's the only one in the house who eats it regularly, aside from you."

I squeeze my eyes, too worn out to deal with the anger sweeping over me. "How is she?"

"Safe. Away from here."

"Where?" It occurs to me that it might be a secret. "Actually, you don't have to tell me. It's probably confidential."

He doesn't hesitate. "She's with Koen. And yes, it's confidential. No one else knows."

"Oh." I massage the curve of my neck. It's a level of trust I cannot fathom. Not because I'd ever tell anyone, but because he's aware that I wouldn't, not even if my life depended on it. I *care*, and he *knows*.

"Was it Emery? The Loyals?"

"I don't know," he says carefully. "I can't think of anyone else having a motive, let alone the resources for this."

". . . but?"

"All of Emery's communications are monitored. We have found evidence that she and her people are behind the arson that happened in the spring at one of the schools in the East. But if she's behind Ana's kidnapping attempt, I see no proof of it." He presses his lips together. "I'm going to move you, too."

"Move me?"

"To the Vampyres. Or the Humans, if you prefer. Koen is also an option. He'd keep you safe, and Ana would love to have you there, and I'd feel better knowing you two are together."

"Lowe." I take a step closer and shake my head. Which, apparently, now makes me dizzy. "This is very much not the first time someone has tried to off me, and I'm not going to— I don't want to go away." Why would I? I thought we . . . "We're a team, right? And what would even happen with the armistice if I left?"

"It doesn't matter. Your father doesn't need to know. I can take care of everything and make sure that you're as free—"

"*No.*"

I don't realize how loudly I spoke until the word echoes through the room. For a split second, I see the guilt and agony Lowe's wrestling with on his face. He sighs and bends his head.

"I almost got you killed, Misery."

"*You* didn't. Someone else did, and we should figure out who. Together."

"My job is to protect you, and I failed. It happened under my watch, when I was standing inches away from you."

"There you go." My cheeks heat up. "A good reason for me not to leave. In fact, you should keep me even *closer.*" I say it a little flirtatiously, and it messes with his head as much as with mine. He steps into me, inhaling sharply. His words are a heated, barely audible hiss.

"Do you have no fucking fear?"

"No."

"I have enough for both of us, then." His jaw works, the intensity of his fury thick in the space between us. "How are you?" he asks after a while, voice once again calm. The change of topic is so brusque, I'm even dizzier.

"Kinda gross?" I shrug. "Like there should be flies buzzing around me. But maybe not, because they'd stick to my skin."

"You sweated through your sheets multiple times."

A feat, since Vampyres barely have sweat glands. "Did Dr. Averill change them?"

"I did."

"Oh."

"Juno helped. Sometimes. When I was able to let her. Once I calmed down." He wipes his palm down his face. "It's hard for me."

"What is?"

"To see you like that. To let anyone else touch you when you're hurt or sick or just . . . I didn't need that qualifier, actually. To let anyone else touch you is . . ." He rubs the back of his hand against his mouth. I can't quite follow—and then I can, when he says, "I'm not sure who I can trust anymore."

"Ah."

"I won't let you . . ."

I reach out to clasp his shoulders. "Lowe, there's no *letting.* And you can trust *me.*" I smile up at him. "Please. I'm going to stay, and I'm going to help, and I'm going to . . ." I take a deep breath.

No. *God, no.*

"Shower. I'm going to shower. I had *not* realized how bad I stink. I am *offending* myself."

He studies me, undoubtedly preparing more rebuttals, lining up arguments, all ready to drive me away. But they never come. Instead, the corner of his mouth lifts into a soft smile, and he abruptly picks me up, arms under my back and knees. "What are you— What is happening?"

"You do need washing," he agrees, carrying me out of the room.

"Are you going to hose me off in the garden?"

"We'll see." But he brings me to my bathroom, deposits me on the marble counter, and draws a bath. I'm not so weak that I couldn't do this on my own, but I enjoy watching his graceful movements, the hypnotic play of muscles under his T-shirt as he bends to fill the tub. The water level slowly rises, and he tests the temperature with his fingers. I think about Owen—the only person who may have been remotely upset by me being on the brink of death. I should contact him. I should ask after Lowe's mate. As the Were Collateral, she must have been terrified, because *my* death would lead to *hers*. I bet Lowe was acutely aware, and feared for his mate.

But I also believe that he cares for me. Deeply.

He chooses a lavender bottle from the shelf. I can't smell its scent, but as steam fills the room, I pack my lungs with warm air. I may not be who Lowe was meant for, but that doesn't mean that there isn't *something* here. And I've had so little throughout my life, I know better than to demand all or nothing. I'm good at making do.

"It's ready," he says with his deep, mundane voice.

It's a dreamlike sequence, but we're on the same page: I slide to my feet and untie my hair, running a hand through it until it falls limp around my shoulders. I take everything else off and stand naked, skin pale and cool and tacky.

Should I be nervous? Because I'm not. Lowe . . . I'm not sure how he feels. He certainly doesn't pretend to be uninterested, and looks his fill, following each curve of mine more than once, betraying little but hiding nothing. I'm not made like a Were woman. I'm not toned, and have no defined muscles. Either Lowe knew to expect it, or he doesn't mind. His eyes glaze over as I step forward, and I take his hand when he offers it. I'm drowsy, wobbly-kneed. He lowers me into the tub.

"This feels nice." I sigh once I'm submerged. I lean forward, forehead against my knees, letting my hair float around me.

"It does." He's not in the bath, but perhaps he's referring to the shaky warmth of this unspoken agreement. This moment we're sharing. He takes a washcloth from the shelf and dips it into the water.

His first pass is delicate over my bent neck. "So you're one of them," I say, instantly relaxed under his touch.

"Of who?"

"People who use washcloths."

I hear his smile in his voice. "If you have a sponge . . ."

"I don't use anything," I offer.

Because it's very much an offer. A request, even. But he says nothing and continues with my arms, starting from the ball of my shoulder. His hands are firm but lightly trembling. He might be more tense about this than I am. "It seemed too forward," he admits at last. His cheekbones are dusted with an olive tone, his voice husky. He patiently works his way to my ankle, then slowly up my leg.

I decide to be forward. I take his hand into mine and stroke each knuckle with my thumb, one by one, and once his guard is relaxed, I steal the cloth from him and let it float away. I *know* he wants to touch me. I *know* he won't ask. I *know* he needs me to do this—put his hand back on my knee, this time without barriers.

His breath hitches, then comes faster. His jaw shifts, like he's biting the inside of his mouth. The skin of my thigh glistens under his eyes, and his fingers tighten around my flesh, on the verge of something wonderful, something we both want.

But Lowe talks himself out of it. He squeezes his eyes and stands to take care of my back.

I swallow a whimper. "Coward," I whisper good-naturedly.

In retaliation, he leans in to kiss my nape like he did on the plane—sucking and licking and some gentle biting. A subtle reminder that he's different from me, a whole other species. If we do this, we'll have to work things out.

"Do you . . . How do Weres have sex?"

He laughs softly against my skin, but I sense an edge. "Are you worried?"

I tip my head back. "Should I be?"

He massages my sternum. "I'm not going to hurt you. Not ever."

"I know. I'm not sure why I asked." I close my eyes, and he takes the invitation as what it is.

I lose myself in his touch, wondering how something that requires so little can feel so good. He lingers on my breasts, around my hips, but also everywhere else. All the curves and angles, all the soft, vulnerable places. My skin tingles, simmering with an unknown sort of pleasure. Lowe is painstaking: he finds spots he wants to explore, slows down, and his breath grows heavy in my ears, broken by soft hums of approval. He takes his time, delays moving on until he's satisfied that his task has been completed.

There is something patently sexual about this, no question, but it goes beyond. I'm being discovered. Mapped. Soothed and ignited at once.

"You are so beautiful," he whispers, an absentminded thought more than a declaration, and suddenly I can't stand it anymore. Eyes closed, my hand searches for his under the water. I braid our fingers together and guide them to my inner thigh. It's a silent plea.

"I'm just so tired." I sigh. "And I really want it."

"God, Misery." His heartbeat smells like he'd die for this. And yet he's about to ask me if I'm really sure, and I'm going to laugh at him. Or snarl.

"Lowe. Will you help? Please?"

His "Fuck" is soft and awestruck, but his fingers shift to where I need them. Barely a brush of knuckles against my labia, but I hiss right as he inhales. Our breaths catch together, balancing in the room. "Okay." A rumble from deep in his chest. "Okay."

The pad of his thumb finds my clit in warm, rhythmic circles. Lowe licks his lips and half asks, half growls, "Like this?"

I nod. It's not what I'd do for myself, but it works, somehow even better. There is some clumsiness on both our ends, but he figures out where to touch me. How long. How hard. "Yes." I bite into my lower lip, fangs exposed, and press into him.

"The night we met, when you came down the mezzanine stairs," he groans against my shoulder, "I thought about doing this."

There must be something dramatically, massively compatible between us, because I feel every stroke of his fingers deep inside this soul that I'm not supposed to have. "Yeah?" The hot, mounting sensation in my lower belly knots into a tangle of heat. I squirm, arch my back. Cool air sweeps over my wet nipples.

"You looked cold in your jumpsuit." He sucks at the same spot on my neck that he fixated on back at Emery's, on the tarmac. "You looked so lovely, and so determined, and so fucking lonely."

I grind against his hand, shamelessly whimpering at the empty, swollen feeling inside me, clutching blindly at his muscled arm with both hands.

"I thought about taking you away. I thought about getting you a blanket." His index finger slips inside me, and with a brief adjustment, I push against it. "I thought about making you come with my mouth until you couldn't take it anymore."

The pleasure snaps inside me like fireworks, a glow of heat and relief. I clench around Lowe's hand, curling into his arm, shaking all over it. A scream burns in my throat, but I swallow it down into a small moan, and then it's a mess, cobbled together with fluttering heartbeats and gasping breaths. Lowe is staring at me, mouth parted, throat bobbing. His icy eyes flare into mine, and I . . .

I *laugh*, throaty and raspy.

"What?" he sounds winded. Just a hairbreadth from an unspecified turning point. I'm still pulsating around his hand, and he stares at the water sloshing around my hard nipples while licking his lips.

"Just . . ." I clear my throat, still laughing. "Could we kiss?"

"What?"

"We haven't yet. It'd be nice, if we did. At some point."

"At some point," he repeats in a haze. His hand cups the slick inside of my thigh, vibrating with restraint.

"Now, if you want. Though I'm worried."

He scowls. "Worried?"

"About my fangs. What if I cut you? Or bite your lips accidentally?"

"You've bitten me before. I didn't mind then." He leans forward, eager. "I won't mind now."

It doesn't immediately work. My nose bumps against his, I cock my head a little too quickly, my hands glide off the slippery edge of the tub. "Misery," he murmurs against the corner of my mouth, when his lips somehow end up there, sounding more delighted than dismayed by my lack of skills.

But then we get the hang of it, and oh.

It's a messy kiss. Instantly, stunningly *good*. I'm cautious, afraid I'll hurt him, but Lowe's the unrestrained one. Feral. He's the one who moves everything along, who nibbles and sucks and bruises. He uses his thumb to tilt my jaw upward, gripping my neck with his large palm once he's satisfied with my position. It's very deep, very quickly, and I give myself to it, to the filthy way he angles me as though he wants to know my taste from every side.

I pull back to breathe, but he only gives me a second before asking for more. He licks my fangs, and I feel it deep in my core. His desire bursts between us, longing, frustrated. I want to do something about it.

For him.

"Lowe," I mumble against his mouth, forcing myself to stand. Warm water sluices over my skin, and he follows the journey of every single drop. He leans forward to press his lips to the soft skin underneath my belly button, then rises to towel me dry.

The front of his shirt is wet. My lashes are clumpy, beaded with water, and he kisses the drops out of my eyes. "I was scared." It comes out like a confession. "You went limp in my arms, and I was so fucking scared."

I nod. "I was, too."

His eyes are paler than ever. "Come here."

He picks me up again, and I want to remind him that I'm not defenseless, but this might be more for him than me. So I bury my face into his neck, and instinctively dart my tongue to lick the glands he told me about.

His entire body shudders, and then we're in my room. I expect us to tumble onto my mattress, but he lowers me inside the closet, on the mound of blankets and pillows I've assembled. Then instantly pulls back.

"Lowe?"

The timbre of his voice is rough and low. "You smell like you just came."

I stare back, speechless at his directness. I did just come.

"And I need to eat you out."

He *needs* to. "Okay?"

"It's a Were thing," he says, almost apologetic.

I nod, and when he bends to nip at my hipbone, I close my eyes and welcome it: the stretch of my thighs as they are spread out, the hitch of his breath as he looks and looks and looks some more, his raspy groan, and then the contact with his mouth.

There is something beseeching about the way he licks and sucks, something not quite in control, and when the pleasure begins fizzing in my stomach again, I writhe against his lips and give him what he wants. I comb my fingers in his short hair, but he takes my hands, both wrists locked in his large fingers, and pins them to my side. "Be still," he orders, and the sight of me restrained must do something for him, because his other arm disappears down his body, the rhythmic flex of his corded shoulder a mesmerizing sight. He's touching himself because what he's doing to me makes him want to, and the idea is like fire in my belly.

"I can't," I hiss out, arching into him even more.

"Hush." My brain cannot unravel how much he seems to be enjoying this, the sounds he produces, the consuming way he kisses my clit and my opening, the sweet scrape of his stubble against the crease of my thighs. I'm mindless, completely unraveled. And I'm dragging him with me.

"You are fucking *unreal*," he says, and when a knuckle slides inside me, I feel myself clench around it. I don't think Lowe is inexperienced, but there is an edge to his movements, something more enthusiastic than skilled, something just *perfect*. He gently bites my swollen lips, making me jolt, and then chases the sting with his tongue. When the heat rises in my chest, when the pressure coils and I thrash around, he anchors me with an arm over my hipbone. That's what has my legs quivering and my nipples aching and me coming hard: Lowe's presence surrounding me, taking up every molecule of air.

Once I'm a shaking mess, he groans against my pussy and lets out a low "I'm going to—" His grip on my thighs becomes nearly painful. His hips jerk, and my heels dig into his shoulder as the pleasure crests violently inside me once again.

I probably black out a little. Because when everything recedes, I find Lowe crowding my body, still hard against my hip. His jeans are warm and sticky. His heartbeat pounds on the back of my tongue as he guides my head to his neck. "I think," he says, winded, hoarse, "I'm going to lock you in this closet forever."

I nuzzle closer. "I think I'd love that." My fangs graze against his vein until he growls. I reach for the button of his jeans, fumble with it, and I almost have it open when his phone rings.

I whimper, disappointed. Lowe clutches my hip once, forcefully, then again before letting go. He vibrates with frustrated tension as he disentangles us. He sighs heavily after checking the caller ID, and hands the phone to me with shaky hands.

I reach for my discarded towel to cover myself and try not to pay attention to the way Lowe is breathing deeply, trying to calm himself down.

Owen's formal "Congratulations on evading your first assassination attempt" is so factually incorrect, I almost hang up on him.

"My *first*? Excuse me?"

He rolls his eyes. "I meant in this round of Collateral duties. My apologies. Allow me to restate: I fucking told you this would happen, and you need to come back home immediately."

"Home." I drum my fingers against my chin. "You mean, to the people who sent me twice into enemy territory?"

"They technically sent you into *ally* territory, and you almost got killed, so get your ass back here."

I open my mouth to ask him if Father has died and made him councilman, then close it when Lowe enters the screen. "Her safety is my priority," he tells Owen in a stately manner.

My brother studies my bare shoulders, the wet-T-shirt-contest condition Lowe's chest appears to be in, the flush on both our cheeks, and says, "You two really *are* fucking, huh."

It's not a question. I turn to look at Lowe, who turns to look at me. And we both get a little lost in the exchange.

Not yet, I think.

I wish we were, he seems to say.

Maybe we could—

"Stop eye-fucking each other in front of *me*—this is incest. Bestiality, at the very least. Misery." Owen switches to the Tongue, *"There is something I need to tell you. About your friend—"*

"In English," I interrupt.

He gives me an incredulous look, eyes darting between me and Lowe.

"He's helping me search for Serena," I explain.

"He's *helping* you."

"Yup."

He rolls his eyes again. "Your friend's apartment was broken into three days ago."

"What?" I shift forward. "By whom?"

"Not sure, because whoever did it also messed with the cameras in the apartment complex. But I'm having some friends look into alternative sources."

"Like what?"

"Footage from security cameras in the surrounding buildings."

"Did they take anything?" Lowe asks.

"Very difficult to tell, considering the state they left the place in."

I massage my temple, wondering for a millionth time what Serena got herself involved in.

"And there's more," Owen adds. "Something important. But I can't talk about it on the phone, so we'll need to meet in person."

I glance at Lowe. "Could we arrange it?"

"Yes. Give me a few hours."

"Very well." He nods at Lowe, then switches back to the Tongue. *"I am glad you're still with me."* His eyes meet mine, and I almost believe he means it. When I notice the brackets on each side of his mouth, it occurs to me that there's an air about my usually carefree, glib brother that mirrors Lowe's: Tired. Worried. Heavy.

"I'm glad to still be with you," I reply. It might be the most vulnerable we've been with each other. Marriage is making a sap out of me.

"And whatever is happening between you two, fuck it out of

your system before people find out." He hangs up, and I instantly turn to Lowe.

"Will we really?" I ask.

His eyes are instantly hooded. His lips move unintelligibly for a few moments. "The things I want to—"

"I mean, will we be meeting him in person?"

"Ah." He clears his throat. "As soon as I can arrange it."

I nod gratefully. "Thank you. Um, the other thing, too, I would—"

His phone rings again. He picks up with a curt "Lowe," peeling his eyes from mine with great effort.

"Yeah. Of course. I'll take care of it."

He slips the phone in his pocket and then lingers here, on the floor of my closet, more than is necessary. "I have to go—pack business. And I should get changed first. But I'll be back soon."

"Okay. I'll be here, I guess." I'm not sure what to say. All that happened in the past hour is slowly solidifying. Becoming concrete and awkward between us.

I think he wants to stay.

I think I want *him* to stay.

"Be good," he says, getting up.

And then immediately crouches down again, just to kiss my forehead.

CHAPTER 22

She makes him want to draw again.

I MUST HAVE FALLEN ASLEEP AGAIN, BECAUSE WHEN I OPEN MY eyes it's a little before midnight. Dragging a T-shirt and leggings on is a feat worthy of a thousand armies, and I barely manage. I haven't fed in a week, and my body must be well enough to demand sustenance, because my stomach cramps painfully.

I stagger downstairs, trying to recall if I've ever gone without blood this long before. The closest was when I first moved back to Human territory, before Serena found me an under-the-table seller I could afford. By the time I got my hands on a small bag it had been three days, and I felt as though my internal organs were feasting on themselves.

Maybe it's because my body is shutting down, but I stumble into the kitchen without noticing Lowe and Alex. I stop like a deer in the headlights, wondering why they're huddled in front of a computer. It's a bit late for a meeting.

"Is Ana okay?" I ask, and they both look up at me in surprise.

"Ana's fine."

I relax. Then tense again. "Did Owen find that footage?"

Lowe shakes his head.

"You both look really serious, so— Wait, Alex, what are you—"

Alex has stood from his chair and is currently *hugging* me.

This is a nightmare. Maybe Vampyres do dream, after all.

"Thank you," he says. "For what you did for Ana."

"What did I— Oh." This is *weird*. "You know that I didn't ingest that poison voluntarily to protect her, right? I just happen to be disgracefully into peanuts."

"You would have, though," he mumbles against my hair.

"What?"

"Protected her."

I gently push him away, too hungry to argue over whether I'm a good person. I might like him better when he's terrified of me. "Listen, I'm going to feed before I'm tempted to bite one of Ana's stuffies or—" I gasp. "Fuck."

"What?"

"Fuck, fuck, fuck. Sparkles. Serena's damn fucking cat. I forgot about him! Did someone feed him? Is he *dead*?" How long can cats go without eating? An hour? A month?

"He's safe with Ana," Lowe informs me.

"Oh." I press my palm to my chest. "I'll need him back if—when I find Serena. Though at this point he's been with Ana longer." I take a bag out of the fridge. "Maybe they can work out some joint custody—"

"Misery, I found it," Alex tells me excitedly. "Serena Paris!"

"You found *Serena*?"

"No, but I found the connection." He leads me back to the table and we both take a seat next to Lowe. "That search we were working on before you . . ." He gestures at me.

"Almost croaked?"

"Yes. I continued it while you were . . ."

"Almost croaking?"

"And it was surprisingly difficult. So difficult, I figured we were onto something."

"How so?"

"The identities of the Human-Were Bureau workers were nowhere to be found, which is odd for that kind of government employee." I glance at Lowe, who stares back calmly. He's already been briefed. "So I looked . . . harder, let's say. And stumbled on a list with a very familiar name."

"What name?"

"Thomas Jalakas. He was the Human—"

"—comptroller of public accounts." I nod slowly. I'm not sure what that even means, but I do know that it has to do with finance and the economy, because: "Serena emailed with his office. For an article that she was writing. And then she met him in person."

"Yup. She interviewed him, though the article was never published."

"But I background checked him. I checked everyone she talked to—I found nothing about him being in the Human-Were Bureau."

"*Precisely*. His CV is all over the place, but there are no mentions anywhere that he was at the Bureau for eleven months, eight years ago."

My head spins. I cover my mouth.

"Now," Alex adds, "you've both been very withholding, and I don't fully understand the significance of any of this, but if you tell me *why* I'm looking into this guy, I could—"

"Alex," Lowe interrupts gently. "It's getting late. You should go home."

Alex turns to him, wide-eyed.

"You did a great job. Have a good night."

Alex's hesitation is negligible. He stands, bows his head once, and clasps my shoulder on his way out. Lowe's eyes hold mine the entire time, but I wait until the kitchen door locks in the frame to say, "Thomas Jalakas must be Ana's father. I mean, could this be a coincidence?"

"Yes."

I scoff, skeptical. "Fine. But is it?"

He shakes his head. "I don't believe so, no." He navigates through the browser tabs and shows me a picture. "This is Thomas."

"Holy shit." I study his wide mouth. The square jaw. The dimples. The resemblance to Ana is undeniable. "This means that Serena met with Ana's father—and I never realized it, because I assumed it was for her financial stuff."

Lowe nods.

"He has to be the person who told her about Ana. We have to talk to him."

"We can't."

"Why? I can get answers from him. If you help me, I might be able to thrall him and—"

"He's dead, Misery."

Dread crawls up my spine. "When?"

"Two weeks after Serena disappeared. A car accident."

The implications sink into me instantly. Serena, that fucking idiot, got herself involved in something incredibly dangerous. And the other person who was involved in it is now dead, which—

"Misery." Lowe's hand blankets mine, large and warm. "I don't think it means she's dead."

It's what I needed to hear. I silently beg him to continue.

"I don't believe for a second that this is a coincidence, but who-ever got rid of him had the resources to make it look like an acci-dent. They would have done the same for Serena to avoid loose ends."

I stare at his strong fingers and think it through. Maybe. Yes. It makes *some* sense. At the very least, it's something to hope for.

"If not with him, we should still talk with his aides, his col-leagues, his predecessor, someone who—"

"Governor Davenport."

I look up. Lowe's eyes are calm. Direct. "What?"

"Thomas Jalakas was appointed by Governor Davenport, Misery. Both his Bureau position and his latest one."

"I . . . Is it even a normal career path? Going from an interspe-cies bureau to some huge financial office?"

"Excellent question." Lowe removes his hand. The cool night air hits me like a slap. "You should ask Governor Davenport to-morrow, while we're having dinner at his place."

My jaw drops. "When did you get us a dinner invitation?"

"When Alex told me about this. Three hours ago."

"That was quick."

"I am the Alpha of the Southwest pack," he reminds me, a little archly. "I do have *some* power."

"I guess." I let out a single, incredulous laugh. I could kiss him. I *want* to kiss him. "What did you tell him?"

"That we have a gift for him. To thank him for hosting our wed-ding ceremony in his territory."

"He believed that?"

"He's an idiot, and Humans are apparently big on thank-you gifts." He shrugs. "I read it online."

"Wow. You were able to fire up a browser all on your ow—"

He shushes me with his thumb on my lips. "I know you can fight. I know you've been taking care of yourself since you were a kid. I know you're not part of my pack, or my real wife, or my . . . But there isn't a single part of me that wants to take you into enemy territory. Especially days after you were almost killed in mine. For my peace of mind, please be careful tomorrow."

I nod, trying not to think about whether anyone else has cared about my safety as much as he does. The answer would be too depressing. "Lowe, thank you. This is the first lead on Serena in a long time, and—" My stomach growls, and I remember why I came downstairs.

My organism, slowly self-cannibalizing.

"Sorry." I get to my feet and reach for the bag I left on the counter. "I know we were having a moment of gratitude and rainbows, but I really need to feed. I'll just need a—"

Lowe is suddenly behind me. His hand closes around mine, stopping me.

"What—?"

"I don't want you to drink that."

I look at my bag. "It's sealed. It cannot be contaminated. Plus, I can smell crappy blood."

"That's not the reason."

I tilt my head, confused.

"Use me."

I don't get it. And then I *do* get it, and my entire body melts into lava. Stiffens into lead.

"Oh, no." I feel hot. Hotter than after a feeding. Hotter than while gorging myself on blood. "You don't have to—"

"I want to." He is so earnest. And young. And the boldest I've ever seen him—when his baseline is pretty bold. "I want to," he repeats, even more determined.

Jesus. "I talked with Owen. Before the poison."

Lowe nods. His gaze is eager.

"I think I shouldn't have fed from you."

"Why?"

"He said that it's not something people should do unless they are . . ."

Lowe nods as though he understands. But then he licks his lips. "And you and I aren't?" He's so genuinely eager to know, it's like electricity injected straight into my nerve endings.

I think about the last few days. The escalating intimacy between us. Yes, Lowe and I *are*. But. "It goes beyond just sex. Long-term feedings create bonds and tangle lives together. It's something that is strictly done by people who have deep feelings for each other, or the will to develop them."

Lowe listens intently, eyes never wavering. When he asks, "And you and I don't?" it's like a knife skewering my heart.

"We . . ." My stomach is an empty, open ache. "Do we?"

He's silent. Like he has his answer, but he's willing to wait for me to find mine.

"It's just, it would be different from what we've done before. It's not just sex, or fun. If we get into the habit of this, in the long term, there could be . . . consequences."

"Misery." His voice is soft. Faintly amused. There is a solemn shine in his eyes. "We *are* the consequences."

The problem is: this cannot possibly end well. I'm not sure I'm even *ready* to demand someone's unconditional love and devotion, but Lowe's heart is occupied. And it's reckless to see what's

happening between us as something more than the forced proximity of two people thrown together by a flurry of political machi-
nations.

I've come after something, after *someone*, my entire life—always
the means, never the end—and I've made my peace with it. I don't
resent Father for putting my safety after the well-being of the
Vampyres, Owen for being chosen as his successor, Serena for valu-
ing her freedom more than my company. I may never have been
anyone's main preoccupation, but I know better than to spend my
time on this Earth simply *begrudging*.

But when I'm with Lowe I feel different, because *he* is different.
He never treats me like I'm the runner-up, even though I know I
am. I could see myself becoming jealous, envious. Greedy for what
he cannot give. It could quickly become unbearable, the pain of
being just an afterthought to him. Not to mention that if—when,
dammit, *when*—I find Serena, I'm going to have to make some important choices.

"Misery," he says, patient. Always patient, but also urgent. I
realize that he's offering me his hand. It's outstretched, waiting for
me, and . . . This cannot possibly end well. And yet, I think Lowe
might be right. The two of us, we're well past avoiding what's between us.

I smile. His warmth is tinged with intense melancholia. This
won't end well, but so few things do. Why deny ourselves?

"Yeah?" I take his hand, registering his mild surprise when my
fingers slide past his knuckles, then close around his wrist. I hold
his palm in both of mine, upturn it. The meat of it is fun to trace,
full of calluses, scars littering the rough skin.

A large, capable, fearless hand.

I bring it to my lips. Kiss it lightly. Scrape it gently with my teeth, which has his eyes fluttering closed. He mumbles a few hushed words, but I cannot make them out.

"If I really do this," I say against his flesh, "I should avoid your neck."

"Why?"

"It might leave a trace. People would notice."

His eyes shoot open. "You think I'd mind?"

"I don't know," I lie. I doubt Lowe cares about what others think of him.

"You can do what you want with me," he says, and it feels like he means more than just his blood.

My fangs graze his wrist. I'm teasing myself as much as him. "Are you sure?" I hover, afraid that it won't be as good as the first time. Maybe I embellished it in my head, and he'll taste like every bag I've ever had—satisfactory, unremarkable.

"Please," he says, soft, hungry, and I sink my teeth into his vein. The wait for his blood to hit my tongue lasts long enough for thousands of civilizations to collapse. Then his flavor floods my mouth, and I forget about everything that is not *us*.

My body blooms with new life.

"Fuck," he slurs. I take more with a strong pull, cradling his arm to myself, and he presses me against the fridge. His teeth come to my neck and bite, hard enough to leave a mark. He seems to have descended into a trancelike state, to be moved by instinct. "Sorry," he gasps, and then resumes sucking on my neck, licking my pulse. Marking me. "Of all the good things." He grasps my hips as I roll them into his. "Of all the good things I've felt in my fucking life, you are the best."

I take one last gulp and seal the wound with my tongue. His eyes are stark, wide. A wolf's eyes. They stare at my fangs like he's desperate to have them in his body once again. "Am I?"

He nods. "I'm going to—" He kisses me, eager, immediately deep, tasting the rich flavor of his blood on my tongue. "Can I . . ." He picks me up and carries me upstairs. I bury my face into his neck, and every time I nibble at his glands, his arms tense with pleasure.

Lowe's room is dark, but light filters from the hallway. He deposits me in the middle of the unmade bed, pulling back instantly to take off his shirt. I sit up and look around, processing that this is really happening.

"I didn't change them for the longest time," Lowe says.

I admire his beautiful form, the corded strength of his body. I could bite him anywhere and would find nourishment. Sip from his round biceps, the V on his stomach, the hill of his lats.

"What?" I'm losing track. Skipping words. "Didn't change what?"

"The sheets."

"Why?"

"They smelled like you."

"When— Oh." My break-in. "Sorry."

"The scent was so sweet. I got myself off to the filthiest fantasies, Misery." He gently flips me around, belly against the mattress. My leggings are pulled down to my thighs, my shirt in the opposite direction. "And then the smell faded." He climbs over me, on each side of my legs. His hands close on the round globes of my ass, half stroking, half gripping. Through the rough cloth of his jeans, his erection drags against my thighs. When I twist my head back, he's tracing the shallow dimples in my lower back with a pleased expression. "Not the fantasies, though." He descends over me, his heat an iron blanket. "I can't be anything but what I am about this," he whispers against the arch of my ear. There's a hint of apology there.

"What you are?"

"Were." His hand wraps around my rib cage, but halts right underneath my breast. A silent reminder that we can always stop. "Alpha."

Ah. "I wouldn't want you to be not you."

"Can I . . ." His teeth close gently around the ball of my shoulder. "I'm not going to draw blood, or hurt you. But can I . . . ?"

I nod into the mattress. "It seems only fair."

He grunts, grateful, and licks a long stripe up my spine and into my nape. He's vocal in his pleasure, vocal in his praise, and even though I don't fully understand it, this is a *thing* for him, something important and consuming and maybe even necessary. His hand pins my wrists again, above my head, as though he needs to know that I'm here to stay. I struggle against his hold, just to test it.

"Be good." Lowe clicks his tongue. "You're all right. Aren't you, Misery?"

"Yeah," I breathe.

"Nice. Very. I am profoundly obsessed with these." I feel hot air against my skin, and realize he's talking about my ears. "Are they sensitive?"

"I don't think—"

His teeth close around the tip, and it's like a current passing through me.

"I see that they are," he drawls. His cock presses harder against my ass, and his lips drift back to my nape over and over again, like he cannot help himself, like it's the center of gravity in my body. I remember the plane, how close he got to losing control when he first touched me there. "Do Weres have a gland there?" I ask, words muffled into the sheets. I'm more wet than I can remember being. If this is the hottest thing I'll ever experience, I'd love to know why.

"It's complicated." He sucks a mark into the knob at the top of my spine and I make a guttural sound. Then *he* does. There's some fumbling behind me—his belt, unbuckled, the zipper of his jeans, lowered—and after a few seconds of rustling, his cock splits the cheeks of my ass, pushing between them. It's wet and hot, rubbing up and down for the right amount of friction.

Lowe makes a stupefied sound.

"Condom," I gasp. Not something Vampyres ever use, but maybe Weres do? "Do you have one?"

He goes back for one last nibble before turning me around. "No." His eyes glow with determined, reflected light as he takes off my leggings. He stares down at me with a transfixed look that strikes me as the culmination of many things I'll never hear about, and when he bends down to lick my collarbone, I feel how hard he is, leaking against my stomach. The heat of him feeds my hunger for blood in a confusing, beautiful buildup.

"But do you want to use something?" I ask.

"We don't need to," he says, pushing up my shirt. This time his bite is on the side of my breast. His tongue circles around my nipple before pressing flat against it. Then he sucks, mouth wet and elec-trifying.

"Stop," I force myself to say.

He instantly pulls back, holding himself up on his palms, peeling his gaze from my chest with some difficulty. "We don't have to," he pants. "If you—"

"I do, but." I prop myself up on my elbows. My shirt slips to cover the upper curve of my breasts. Lowe's eyes wander down again, until he tears them toward the window. "Why don't you want to use contraceptives?" If Weres and Humans can reproduce, nothing is off the table.

"I don't— We can, if you'd like. But we can't have sex."

"We can't?"

"Not like that."

I sit up, pulling down my shirt, and he shifts back, sitting on his knees. We stare at each other, breathing heavily, like we're in the middle of a Regency-era duel. "Maybe we should discuss this."

His throat bobs. "We're not compatible like that, Misery." He says it like he knows this to be a fact. One he's given a lot of thought to.

My eyebrow lifts. "If Ana exists . . ." It must be feasible.

"It's different."

"Why? Because I'm a Vampyre?" I look down at the way I'm clutching the hem of my oversize shirt like it's a life raft. What we need here is some humor. To defuse. "I swear I don't have teeth down there."

He doesn't smile. "*You* are not the problem."

"Ah." I wait for him to continue. He doesn't. "What's the problem?"

"I don't want to hurt you."

I glance at his groin. He pulled his underwear back up. It's tented, and the room is dark, and my view is not exhaustive by any means, but he looks normal. Good. Big, sure. But normal.

I remember what he told me about Switzerland. The way different species lived together. He said he didn't hang out much with Vampyres, but . . . "Have you ever . . . with a Human?"

He nods.

"And you hurt them."

"No."

"Then—"

"It will be different."

We're discussing sex, right? Penetrative intercourse? This insurmountable obstacle he's talking about must be located somewhere between his and my hardware. Except that he seems structurally standard. "I grew up with a Human. My reproductive organs don't significantly differ from Humans who are assigned female at birth."

"It's not because you're a Vampyre, Misery." He swallows. "It's because you're *you*. Because of what that does to me."

"I don't understa—" He interrupts me with a kiss, bruising in a delicious, unhinged way. He cups my face, teeth pulling at my lower lip, and I lose track of our conversation.

"You're going to smell like this," he murmurs against my lips. "It's happened already, and you weren't even in the fucking room." It? "And I'm not going to be able to stop myself from wanting to finish."

"That's fine." I laugh. My forehead settles against his. "I want you to finish, I—"

"Misery, we are different species."

I close my fingers around his wrists. "You said you'd . . . You said we would. In Emery's office." I'm blushing, embarrassed to admit that I've been thinking about those words for days.

"I said I *could* fuck you." His throat works. "Not that I would."

I lower my eyes. "Were you ever planning to tell me? That we couldn't have sex?"

"Misery." His eyes capture mine, and I suspect he can see everything. The very inside of me. "It's sex, what we've done. What we're going to do. It's all sex. And it's all going to feel really good."

I believe him, I really do. And yet: "Are you sure? That you and I can't . . . ?"

"I can show you. Would you like me to?"

I nod. He kisses me again, tenderly, clearly trying to take things slowly. I'm the one to wriggle away to take off my shirt.

"Have you done any of this before?" he asks against the crook of my neck, and I shake my head. He'd never judge me for it, but I want to explain. "It felt weird. Doing this with a Human when I was already lying to them about everything." And Vampyres were never an option. I was always alone, at the border between those two worlds. The fact that I feel more at home than ever before with a Were, with someone whose proximity I should have never been in . . . There's something wrong about it. Or painfully right.

"Feed more," he orders, pushing me down on the bed. We end up on our sides, facing each other. Not a position I'd associate with wild and uninhibited sexual activities.

"If I feed, we can't—"

With a hand on the back of my head, he guides my face into his neck. "We can." He kicks his jeans away, and it's just his skin, hot against mine, the rough hairs on his arms and legs subtly foreign. I slip my shin between his knees and let my hand roam, curious, eager to explore. He is gloriously different, and while I'm not one to admire beauty, I cannot stop thinking that I *like* him: the way he looks, the way he feels, the way *he* likes *me*. The slight tremble in his fingers as they settle on my waist, the muscles of his body tightening with patient anticipation.

"You are so beautiful," he murmurs into my temple. "I thought so since they gave me that first picture of you. You came walking down the aisle, and I was afraid to look. I hadn't even smelled you yet, and I already couldn't stop myself from staring."

A stray notion crosses my mind, sweet and terrifying and utterly unlike me: *I wish I was your mate.* I know better than to say it. I know better than to *think* it. Instead I feel his large hand close around my nape. "I really want you to feed, Misery."

Sinking my teeth into him is becoming second nature, his flavor lovely and familiar. I don't let myself wonder how I'll go back to chilly bags. I just take deep, blissful gulps, and when I hear his drawn out, vibrating moan, when his hand drags my wrist to his cock and closes my fingers around it, I'm happy and pliant and eager to please.

He is hard, but also soft, and doesn't want much. He guides my hand up and down once, once more, and beyond that, he has no instructions for me. My touch appears to be enough, just like the rest of me.

"I'm going to come really fast," he puffs out.

I let go of his vein with a wet pop. "You don't have to."

He laughs, rocking into my fist. "Not much of a choice." He tightens my grip, giving himself the pressure he's craving. "And then I'll show you what you do to me."

Whatever he needs, I want the same. One of his thighs wedges between mine, and I rub myself against it, vaguely embarrassed at the lewd, rhythmic sounds the contact makes, at the mess I'm making on him. But it feels good, too good to stop and good enough to forget, and then even better when his hand kneads my breasts, moves to the small of my back to cant my hips, positioning me so that yes—there, "There." I hum the word into his neck, around mouthfuls of blood. I'm shameless and dizzy and briefly happy, grinding and searching for pleasure like it's something he has in store for me—not if, just *when*. I take one last drag, and swallow, and then ask, "Is this good?"

Lowe's eyes stare unseeing into mine, and the fact that he seems too awestruck to be able to speak, the choppy, uncoordinated way he tries to nod his pleasure, that's what pushes me over.

I let out a low, resonant whimper, and my orgasm spreads like a wave of heat. My breaths shorten, my vision narrows, and then I'm shuddering all over Lowe's thigh, rolling against him like a wild creature. I forget about what I was doing for him, the rhythm I was keeping, the twisty, lingering touch he enjoys. But even then, just seeing and hearing my pleasure seems to do it for him.

His arms tighten around me. His cock becomes harder. His mouth against mine chants a string of obscene, pleading things about how much he wanted this, how beautiful I am, how he'll always think of me when he does this from now on, till the day he dies. His semen is hot on my fingers, on my belly. The sounds in his throat belong to something that lives in the underbrush of the forest, someone lost to rational thought.

It's beautiful, I think. Not just the pleasure, but sharing it with someone else, someone I care about and maybe love a little bit, as much as I'm able.

And then the things he's saying change. Unlike my orgasm, which bloomed and exploded and ebbed, his lasts. Crests. And Lowe shivers and pants and groans through it before he asks me, "You want to know?"

I nod, still out of breath. His hand comes down to guide mine lower on his cock, until we reach the base.

"Shit."

His cheeks are flushed, head tilted back. I don't immediately understand, not until his soft skin changes. Something inflates under my palm. Lowe's hand closes around mine, pressing it there, circling the swelling protuberance like all he wants is for it to be enclosed, held within something. It grows larger, and Lowe's stifled groans grow louder, and—

"Misery."

He's saying my name like a prayer. Like I'm the one thing standing between him and heaven on Earth. And that's when I understand what he meant.

Sexually, he and I might not be fully compatible.

CHAPTER 23

She makes him laugh. It's no small gift.

THE PROBLEM OF USING A GIFT AS AN EXCUSE TO VISIT GOVernor Davenport is that we cannot show up empty-handed. It takes one hour in Human territory, three different antiques stores, and a whole lot of bickering before Lowe and I find a present we both consider appropriate. He nixes my choice of a vintage bicycle pump ("That's a hookah, Misery."). I veto his ceramic vase ("Someone's grandpa's in there, Lowe."). We insult each other's taste, first covertly, then passive-aggressively, then with unabashed contempt. When I'm about to suggest that we fight it out in the parking lot and see how well his claws hold up against my fangs, he has a momentous realization and asks, "Do you even like the governor?"

"Nope."

"Is it possible that we're putting too much thought into this?"

My eyes widen. "Yes."

We slip back inside the last store and buy a mysterious ashtray shaped like a polar bear. It's simultaneously the ugliest thing we can find *and* well over three hundred dollars.

"Where does the money come from, anyway?" I ask.

"What money?"

"Your money. Your seconds' money. Your pack's money." I glare at him on our way back to the car, making sure no one is around. I'm wearing brown contacts, but haven't shaved my canines in a while. Opening my mouth in public would probably get animal control called on me. "Do you work in insurance while I'm passed out during the day?"

"We rob banks."

"You—" I stop him with a hand on his arm. "You *rob banks.*"

"Not *blood* banks, don't get too excited."

I pinch his left side, miffed.

"Ouch. My . . ." An elderly Human couple walks past, giving us an indulgent *Young love* look. "Liver?"

"Wrong side," I whisper.

"Appendix."

"Still wrong."

"Gallbladder?"

"Nope."

"Fucking Human anatomy," he mutters. He laces his fingers with mine, pulling me in his direction.

"You're not serious, right? About robbing?"

"No." He opens the door for me. "A lot of Weres have jobs. Most Weres. I had a job, before . . . Before."

Before his life became something his pack owned. "Right."

"Most Were packs have highly organized investment portfolios. That's where the expenses for infrastructure and the leadership roles who don't have the time to hold other jobs come from." He watches me slip into the passenger seat and then leans forward, one hand on the door and the other on the roof of the car. "It's different from the financial framework of Vampyres."

"Because our leadership positions are hereditary."

"I'm sure that families like yours rely on estates passed on over generations, but generally, Vampyres are not as centralized. There's fewer of you, less community culture."

I purse my lips. "Kind of annoying, that you know more about my people than me and that you're such a show-off about it."

"Is it?" he drawls. He leans forward and presses a kiss against my nose. "I'll have to do it more often."

It's the most fun I've had with someone who's not Serena. Even *more*, at times. Although that might be due to the way I find him glancing at me between bouts of perusing stained glass lamps, and the fact that he silently hands me his sweater when I shiver in the AC of the store, and how when we're alone in the car he steals a kiss that has me forgetting how to breathe, his tongue soft across my fangs until I taste a drop of blood, and then *he* is the one groaning, pressing his hand around my waist, telling me that he cannot wait to be home.

Home.

I try not to think about it—that the territory of his pack is most definitely *not* my home—but it's difficult. I'm relieved when Governor Davenport welcomes us at his door, making a show of explicitly inviting me in. I wonder if in all their years of political dealings, my father never dispelled that specific myth for him. It's the kind of mindfuck he'd indulge in.

"It's so refreshing to see a Were-Vampyre union that has not yet ended in bloodshed." Going by the smell of his blood, he's not fully drunk, but on his way there. His house is a mix of pretty and ostentatious, and his wife is definitely not his first. Probably not his second, either. When he tells me, half paternal and half salacious, "You must have been behaving, young lady," Lowe's glance at me clearly asks, *Would you like me to hold him down while you tear his jugular to shreds?*

I sigh and mouth a *Nah*.

Still, Lowe's "Thank you for having us" is accompanied by a more-than-firm handshake. The governor holds his fingers to his chest as he escorts us to a sitting room, and I tip my head down to hide my smile.

He appears to have a prurient interest in the workings of our marriage, and he's not shy about asking. "It must be challenging. Full of arguments, I bet."

"Not really," I say. Lowe takes a sip of his beer.

"Disagreements, at least."

I glance around the room. Lowe sighs.

"I cannot imagine that when topics such as the Aster come up you see eye to eye."

"The what?" Lowe looks at me blankly. It occurs to me that the Were might remember the event by another name. One less centered on Vampyres' blood.

"The last attempt at an arranged marriage before ours," I explain. "Where the Weres betrayed and massacred the Vampyres."

"Ah. The Sixth Wedding. It was an act of revenge. At least, that's what we are taught."

"Revenge?"

"For the Vampyre groom's violent treatment of his Were bride during the previous marriage."

"They don't tell us that," I snort. "Wonder why."

"Are you going to argue about it?" the governor asks, like we're his personal source of entertainment.

"No," we say at once, giving him harsh looks.

He clears his throat bashfully. "It's time for dinner, don't you think?"

Lowe doesn't have the Machiavellian, manipulative skills of Father, but he's nonetheless crafty at guiding the conversation where it needs to go without giving too much away. The governor's wife is mostly silent. So am I: I stare at my risotto with mushrooms, which according to Serena are different from the fungus she once got under her foot, though I can't really recall in what way. I lazily wonder why Humans and Weres keep throwing food at me, and listen as the governor informs us that he and my father are "great friends" who've been meeting in Human territory about once a month to discuss business for the past decade—despite the fact that Father visited me once per year when I was the Collateral; I'd love to be shocked, but I'd rather save the energy. The governor has never been in Were territory, but has heard beautiful things and would love an invitation (which Lowe doesn't extend). He's also going to transition to a lobbying position once Maddie Garcia fully takes over.

Then Lowe moves the conversation to his mother. "She used to be one of Roscoe's seconds," he says, switching our plates once he is done with his dinner and starting the meal over. "Worked closely with the Human-Were Bureau, as a matter of fact."

"Ah, yes. I met her once or twice."

"Did you?"

The governor reaches for a piece of bread. "A lovely woman. Jenna, right?"

"Maria." I hear the displeasure in Lowe's tone, but I doubt anyone else can. "I was under the impression that most of her dealings were with someone in charge of border affairs? Thomas . . . ?"

"Thomas Jalakas?"

"That sounds right." Lowe chews my risotto in silence. "I wonder if he remembers her."

I tense. Until the governor says, "Sadly, he passed a while ago."

"He did?" Lowe doesn't act surprised. Paradoxically, it makes his reaction more believable. "How old was he?"

"Young, still." The governor sips on his wine. Next to him, his wife plays with her napkin. "It was a terrible accident."

"An accident? I hope my people were not involved."

"Oh, no. No, it was a car accident, I believe." The governor shrugs. "Unfortunately, these things happen."

Lowe's stare is so intense, I suspect he's going to confront him. But after a moment, it relaxes, and the entire room breathes out in relief. "Too bad. My mother talked of him fondly."

"Ha." The governor downs the rest of his wine. "I just bet she did. I heard he got around." Of all the things he could have said, this one is the most wrong.

Lowe calmly dabs his mouth with his napkin and rises to his feet. He unhurriedly walks around the table, toward the governor, who must realize the error of his ways. His chair screeches against the floor as he stands and begins retreating.

"I meant no offense— *Ow.*"

Lowe slams him against the wall. The governor's wife screams, but stays put in her chair. I run to Lowe.

"Arthur, my friend," he murmurs in the governor's face. "You stink like you're made of lies."

"I'm not— I don't— Help! *Help!*"

"Why did you have Thomas Jalakas killed?"

"I didn't, I swear I didn't!"

Four Human agents storm inside the room, weapons already drawn. They instantly point them at Lowe, shouting at him to let the governor go and step back. Lowe gives no sign of noticing them.

"Tell me why you killed Thomas, and I'll let you live."

"I didn't, I swear I *didn't*—"

He leans in. "You know I can kill *you* faster than they can kill *me*, right?"

The governor whimpers. A drop of sweat trickles down his red face. "He— I didn't want to, but he was talking to journalists about some embezzling my administration was involved in. We had to! We *had to.*"

Lowe straightens. He dusts himself off, takes a step back, and turns to me as though we are the only two people in the room and four firearms are not still trained on him. His hand leisurely finds my elbow, and he smiles—first at me, then to the guards.

"Thank you, governor," he says, leading me away. "We will see ourselves out."

"I HAVE SEVERAL PEOPLE TAILING HIM," LOWE INFORMS ME ONCE we're in the car. "And Alex is working on monitoring his communications. He knows we're onto him, and we'll be alerted as soon as he makes the next move."

"I hope ten wolves are currently shitting in his backyard," I mutter, and Lowe half smiles and puts his hand on my thigh in an easy, absentminded way that would only make sense if we'd been driving places together for years.

"It just doesn't add up," I vent. "Say Serena really did just interview him for a financial crime story. Maybe she was the journalist he was talking to. Where does Ana's name on her planner come from?" I guess it could be unrelated. But. "There is no way she coincidentally met with Ana's father *and* found out about Ana through other channels. No fucking way. Did someone *plant* the name? But it was in our alphabet. No one else knew about it." We're silent while I churn on it, staring at the streetlights. Then Lowe speaks.

"Misery."

"Yeah."

"There is another possibility. Regarding Serena."

I look at him. "Yeah?"

He appears to painstakingly line up the words. When he speaks, his tone is measured. "Maybe it wasn't Thomas who told Serena about Ana, but the opposite."

"What do you mean?"

"Maybe Serena found out about Ana from another source, and then used the information to blackmail Thomas over his relationship with a Were and force him to tell her about financial crimes he might know about. Maybe she wanted to break the story, but changed her mind when she realized that she was in danger of being targeted by Governor Davenport. Unlike Thomas, she wasn't a public individual, and she had the option to disappear."

I shake my head, even as I realize that some of this is a distinct possibility. "She wouldn't have left without telling me, Lowe. She's my sister. And there are no digital traces. She wouldn't know how to avoid them. She's not *me*."

"She's not. But she did learn from you for years." He looks deeply sorry to have to say this.

I let out a laugh. "Not you, too, trying to convince me that

Serena didn't care about me as much as I cared about her. She wouldn't leave me here to picture the worst. She always told me everything—"

"Not everything." His jaw tenses. Like this conversation is painful for him, because it's painful for *me*. "You mentioned that you had a fight before she left. That sometimes she'd leave for days on her own."

"Never without saying."

"Maybe there was no time. Or she didn't want to put you in danger."

I wave it away. "This is ridiculous. What about Sparkles? She *abandoned* her cat."

"Tell me something," he asks. I hate how measured and rational he sounds. "Did she know you well enough to predict that you'd go looking for her and find the cat?"

I want to say no so bad, my lips almost hurt. But I can't, and instead I remember her last words to me:

I need to know that you care about something, Misery.

And she did leave *something* behind. Something that needed caring for. The damn fucking cat. God, what a wacky plan this would be.

A Serena plan.

"Maybe you're right, and she doesn't want to be found. But she wouldn't put the life of a child at risk, not even in exchange for the biggest, juiciest story of her career. I know Serena, Lowe."

And that's the problem with Lowe's theory: it would mean that Serena is safely tucked somewhere, but also that she wasn't the person I believed her to be, and I can't accept it. Not for a minute.

Lowe knows this, because he opens his mouth to say something else, something that undoubtedly will make impeccable sense and feel like a punch in the solar plexus. So I stop him by asking the first thing that comes to mind:

"Where are we going?" We're headed south, toward downtown. Toward Vampyre territory.

"To meet your brother. We're nearly there."

"Owen?"

"You have others?"

I frown. "I thought he'd come to us."

"Were territory is more tightly patrolled and harder to infiltrate. Since we don't want to attract attention and turn this into a formal summit, it's safer to meet with him at the Vampyre-Human border."

I'm well familiar with this road. I took it for the first time at eight years old, on my way to the Collateral residence, and I still remember that drowning, sticky feeling low in my throat, the fear that I'd never get to go home again. I squeeze my eyes shut, trying to redirect my thoughts to the *last* time. Shortly before the wedding, I imagine. Maybe when I was asked to choose between flowers that all looked the same, white and pretty and ready to wither. A handful of days and a million lifetimes ago.

"Are you okay?" Lowe asks softly.

"Yeah. Just . . ." I'm not usually sentimental, but something about being with him softens me. My guard is down.

"Feels weird, huh?"

I nod.

"We can always turn around," he offers quietly. "I'll figure out a way to have Owen come south."

"No. I'm fine."

"Okay." He turns into a small side street. When I glance at the

GPS it's not on the map, but we come to a stop at the edge of a cultivated field.

Lowe's expression is bemused. "I'm actually curious about this."

I glance around. All I can see is darkness. "About the wholesome experience of picking your own tomatoes?"

"About meeting your brother."

He gets out of the car, and I immediately follow him. I thought we were alone, but I hear another car door clicking, and—there he is.

Owen, sneering at the soil sticking to his loafers, swatting away bugs. It's shocking how happy I am to see him. That jerk, climbing up my good graces uninvited. I'm tempted to yell some insults at him, just to make up for it, until I hear another click.

Owen didn't come alone. There's a woman with him. A woman I've never met. A woman whose blood smells a lot like a Were's.

Lowe's mate.

CHAPTER 24

He feels like the entire world is in the palm of his hand. She seems happy, too. And mystified by her own happiness, as though the feeling is something new and foreign. It has him wondering whether he could make this work. She's not Were, and her lack of familiarity could be a blessing. She wouldn't need to know the full truth, which in turn would ensure her freedom.

LOWE LEANS BACK AGAINST THE TRUNK OF HIS CAR IN WHAT seems to be the official position of performative harmlessness—crossed ankles, relaxed shoulders, his best I-may-be-one-powerful-Were-but-I-have-no-intention-of-brawling-with-you air.

I settle next to him as Owen and Gabi make their way to us, trying to ignore my heart pounding in my chest. I nearly startle when Lowe laces his hand with mine.

"You're trembling," he says. "Are you okay?"

"I don't know why." Except that I do. "I'm cold, I think."

He pulls me closer—the best he can do, since I'm already wearing his sweater. I'm immediately enveloped in that toasty warmth his body always welcomes me with, and the scent of his heartbeat is delicious in my nostrils. Lowe peers at me like he knows something's off.

I brace myself for . . . I don't know. Seeing Lowe reunited with his *mate* is something that requires preparation from me. I've sunk way too deep into this thing between us.

"I asked you to fuck it out." Owen's voice is flat and annoyed, but no more than usual. "And yet, here you are. Subjecting me to this."

"Owen," Lowe warns. His eyes linger on me for another instant, concerned, then flicker to my brother's. "A pleasure."

"Learn from Gabrielle and me," Owen continues. "We live together at the Nest, but haven't developed unnecessary feelings for each other or any kind of sexual attraction. We cultivate a relationship of mild collaboration at best, severe indifference on average."

"Gabi." Lowe's nod is warm, cordial, surprisingly neutral.

She's a beautiful woman, with glossy dark hair and the patient expression that people forced to deal with Owen for any length of time tend to acquire. She briefly dips her head, like all of Lowe's seconds do when they see him. "Nice to see you, Alpha. Everything okay at home?" There's affection and respect in the words. I read nothing else.

"For the most part."

"Good to hear." She gives me a curious look. Her eyes briefly dart down, and I don't have to follow them to know they're on Lowe's and my joined hands.

A thought strikes me like a bolt—he might be using me to make her jealous. I let it poison my brain for a moment, then dismiss it. Lowe would never stoop to those kinds of plays.

"How lovely," Owen says drily. "In significantly less wholesome news, no luck on the security footage outside Serena's place yet. We were hoping to get a good view from the apartment complex in front of hers, but the cameras were tampered with."

Lowe frowns. "Only for the date of the break-in?"

"Correct."

I frown. "How?"

Owen shrugs. "What do you mean?"

"How did the tampering occur? Was it software? Hardware? Did they paintball the lens or trip the circuit breaker or cut the data cable?"

"I'm not certain. My guy did mention, but . . ." Owen waves his hand. "Technical witchcraft that nobody could understand aside, it's clear that—"

"Jammers," Gabi says, and smiles when I give her a surprised look.

"They disrupted the signal?"

"Likely used a radio frequency detector to figure out the broadcast."

It's the sophisticated way. The one someone with resources would use. Someone who works for powerful people and is looking for clues on the whereabouts of a journalist on the run. It would fit with Lowe's theory, for sure. "Crafty," I say.

"Right?" She grins. Owen and Lowe exchange a commiserating look. "I know this has nothing to do with me," Gabi continues, "but Owen is the only person who'll talk to me at the Nest. He told me about your friend, and I'm sorry that happened to you. I can't imagine how hard it must be, the uncertainty."

Her words are disorienting, because no one else has said them to me before. In my quest to find Serena, people have helped me, mocked me, dismissed me, nudged me, but no one has stopped to tell me they were sorry. A thick feeling rises to my throat. "Thank you."

Owen makes a gagging sound. "How *touching*. Moving on to more entertaining topics and the reason for this meeting." His lilac eyes settle into mine. "I'm going to take over Father's seat on the council."

I must have misheard. "What?"

"I'm going to take over Father's seat on the council."

Nope, I heard correctly. "Did Father . . . die?"

Owen tilts his head. "Do you think I would neglect to inform you if Father died? Actually, I could see myself doing that. No, Father is alive. But I am in disagreement with many of his decisions of late. *Many*. I think I could do better, and I decided to make a bid for his seat. I'd love your support."

"My *support*?" I push away from the car and disentangle from Lowe, facing my brother. My *cuckoo-bananas brother*. "Making a *bid*? That's not a thing people do."

He shrugs. "It's a thing I'm doing."

"*How?*"

"I'm happy to share my plan in detail. In two weeks, at the annual meeting, I plan to—"

"Do *not* share." I look between Lowe and Gabi, who seem engrossed in our exchange. "You know what the punishment for high treason is?" He must, because I do, and I never know shit. But I do remember what happened when I was seven and Councilwoman Selamio's brother tried to steal her birthright from her, or when Councilman Khatri died suddenly, without naming which one of his two sons would inherit the position.

Slaughter, that's what happened. Lots of purple spatter. Father would never react to having his seat usurped with anything but bloodshed. And by his lazy, hedonistic son? "He's not just a member, Owen. He's the leader of the council."

"Unofficial."

"Bullshit."

"And anyway," he continues like he didn't hear me, "his prominent position could be in my favor. Lots of councilmembers are dissatisfied with the way he's been seizing power."

Wild. Buck wild. "Who knows about this?"

"I have been slowly spinning a web of allies. Establishing tactical collaborations."

He's dead. My only sibling left is as good as dead. "Why?"

"It seemed prudent."

I pinch my nose, because—fuck. *Fuck.* "Do you even *want* to be a councilman?"

He shrugs nonchalantly. "Why not? Could be fun."

"Owen. Just . . ." I bury my face in my hands and Lowe stands from the hood of the car, coming to massage my shoulders in this moment of desperate need. I suppose he's trying to be comforting, but I feel his amusement in my bones.

Maybe I could punch him *and* Owen. Just a little bit. Wouldn't that make me feel better?

Yes. Yes, it would.

"Misery. My sister." He shifts to the Tongue. "*You are displaying more feelings than usual. Are you not well?*"

I straighten and take a deep breath. Even though Owen and I were born three minutes apart, clearly I'm the adult. "Listen, I'm *really* trying to find that bitch Serena, and I've grown *really* fond of Lowe's annoying little shit of a sister. Unfortunately, they're both *really* good at getting themselves in trouble. So if you could avoid making my life even harder because of some half-assed plan you put together two hours ago out of spit and shoelaces—"

"Three months ago."

"—it would be really . . . What?"

Owen's eyes harden. "Three months ago, Misery. I've been

working on this plan since I discovered that my father was considering sending my sister into enemy territory. Again." He bares his fangs, and his tone is uncharacteristically earnest. "*I could do nothing when we were children. I could do nothing when you returned, because I was too much of a coward to take a stand. I cannot do anything now, but I am determined to try.*" His gaze fixes mine for a long moment, and he picks up in English again. "I want to be the one negotiating the next set of alliances. I want all Collateral systems gone. I want to stop enforcing artificial border lines, or holding on to disputed territories out of spite. I want to turn this place into something that's not a powder keg."

I study him, astonished. Realizing that in all the years we spent apart, as I grew and changed and built my own life, my idiot brother did, too, and turned into . . .

Not an idiot, clearly.

"Father is going to kill you," I repeat. This time not with the intent of dissuading him.

"Maybe." He turns to a spot high above my shoulder. Lowe. "Any advice on how to successfully carry out a coup, Alpha?"

"I was going to recommend a hearty breakfast, but . . ."

"How unfortunate."

Lowe's hand slides to my waist, pulling me into his larger body. "I'm no fan of your father. And as the Weres and the Vampyres form alliances, I would love to see someone whose priorities align with mine." My brother and my husband look at me, then at each other. Something I cannot decipher passes between them. An agreement. A shared port of call.

Owen spends the next minutes updating me on the complex network of his supporters, allies, and coconspirators. He assures me that no one knows about his plan, and surprisingly, I find that

I believe him. He may seem ostentatiously careless, but he's been nothing but careful and circumspect about this. Still, he quickly shifts to inane gossip I'm not interested in, and I find myself tuning him out when I overhear Lowe asking Gabi, ". . . anything you need?"

"Not really. There have been no signs of danger so far. Owen is surprisingly decent company and gave me access to his gaming consoles. Everyone else has been treating me coldly and leaving me alone, which is fantastic—they're real pros at this Collateral exchange thing. They've had to deal with Human children for decades, and I'm much lower maintenance than that. They're monitoring my internet usage, of course, but I have plenty of time to work on my master's. I'm taking five classes this semester."

"Finance, was it?"

"Electrical engineering. I should be done at the end of the year."

"Congratulations."

"Thanks. And you? You seem happy with your . . ." I think Gabi is pointing at me, but I cannot turn to verify. Just like I cannot be sure that Lowe nods and smiles faintly, even though it nearly resonates through me, the fact that he *is*. Happy. With me.

"Let's go, Gabi," Owen calls, spinning on his heels. "I'm boring my sister with trivial details about who's fucking whomst among our people."

I roll my eyes, then brace myself again. Lowe and Gabi didn't greet each other warmly, but now it's sure to happen: a hug, a tender moment, a wistful goodbye. She may not know that she's his mate, but he feels for her.

I would take anything she chose to give me—the tiniest fraction or her entire world.

He'll take what he can now, and even though I told myself I'd be able to deal with this when it happened, the jealous heartache is too much. I cannot watch. I wave goodbye at Owen and Gabi and step around Lowe's car.

But I'm just a couple of feet away when I hear, "Let me know if the situation changes," followed by a short, "Yes, Alpha." There are two sets of steps: Gabi walking after Owen, Lowe heading for the driver's seat, and nothing else.

Nothing more than a friendly wave.

When I glance at Lowe, he's not looking back in her direction. Not tracking her with his eyes. Not rubbing his jaw with his palm like he does when he is worried, or nervous, or pensive. His mate is heading back to enemy territory, and he might never see her again, and he is . . .

Smiling, actually.

I sit in the passenger seat, staring at my knees, thinking about what Lowe told me. *A mate grabs you by the stomach*, he said, and he was so sure of it, I felt it in *my* stomach, too. He made it sound like a thought that won't quit, a spectacle impossible to tear one's eyes from. But with Gabi . . .

Maybe I cannot read him. But he doesn't seem to gravitate toward her. He was by my side for the whole conversation. He couldn't remember what she *studied*.

I look up from my lap. Lowe is staring at me with a tender, amused expression. The keys are in the ignition, but he hasn't turned them. He's motionless, like he forgot what he was about to do.

"What?" I ask, a little defensive.

"Nothing." His smile is soft. Like a boy who got caught. "You okay?" He clearly has no idea what I'm thinking.

I nod, keeping my eyes on the darkness outside as he starts the car. My cheeks are hot. I'm on the verge of something.

It's possible that I understand next to nothing about Weres. About love. About Lowe and Gabi. It's possible that I'm an idiot who reads too much into too little. But I feel something deep in my belly, and I know it to be right.

Lowe may have a mate, but she's not Gabi.

CHAPTER 25

He should never have told her. He made a mistake—several, in fact.

SOMETHING ELUSIVE DANGLES IN FRONT OF MY NOSE, BUT I can't focus on it. It's a tip-of-the-tongue state, a sneeze that won't start and teeters there, waiting.

Lowe's mate is not Gabi. I fiddle with the memories of past conversations, trying to recall what I know, what Lowe openly acknowledged, and what gaps I filled on my own. There's a nagging spark of *something* in my chest, something fizzy and not unhappy. I try to rationalize it into nothing, and when that fails, I force my attention away by saying, "I live five minutes from here." I wet my lips, studying the familiar contours of my old neighborhood. "Lived." I bite my lower lip. "I guess I still do. The council took over my rent."

"Want to stop by?"

"Why?"

"I'd like to see it."

I snort. "It's not a very architecturally pleasing building."

"It's not about the building, Misery."

It takes more like ten minutes to get there, but Lowe follows my directions without complaints. I punch in the code at the main entrance, but didn't bring any keys with me, so once we're in front of my door, I pluck a hairpin off.

"You're . . ." He lets out a low, affectionate laugh, shaking his head.

I push the door open and lift an eyebrow. "I'm?"

"Amazing."

My chest is too tight for my heart.

"How long did you live here?" he asks, following me inside and glancing around.

I calculate it in my head. "Four years, more or less."

The Collateral is entitled to a small trust fund, and I used pretty much all of my money on my fake Human IDs, and then to put myself and Serena through college. We were on a tight budget for a few years, sharing cramped spaces and constantly compromising on the decor. The result was a mix of minimalism and shabby chic that we both looked back on with equal fondness and horror.

This place, though, is where I moved after graduating. I had my first salary and could splurge a little. I was pleased with the clean, no-fuss spaces. I rescued most of the furniture from flea markets Serena and I visited on cloudy days, early in the morning, and loved how uncluttered and roomy the final result was. I listened to synthwave music without anyone judgmentally asking me what trauma had led to me to enjoy "that shit," and could even display my lava lamp in all its cringe glory.

And yet, when I glance around the living room, trying to see the place from Lowe's perspective, it only seems empty. Lifeless. Like a museum.

Picturing myself in it has my stomach in twists. It's only been a few weeks—my tastes can't have changed so *much* in so *little*, can they?

I turn to Lowe and find him white-knuckling the doorframe. "Are you okay?"

"It smells a lot like you," he says. His voice is hushed, eyes glassy and unfocused. "More than your room in my house. More . . . layers." He wets his lips. "Give me a second to get used to it."

I don't ask him if my scent bothers him, because it's clear by now that it doesn't. He used to hate it, though. Or did he? He sure didn't deny it, and I thought he only recently changed his mind, but maybe . . .

"Are you and Gabi close?" I ask. Not what we were discussing, but Lowe appears to welcome the distraction.

"I don't know her well." He takes a deep breath, slowly getting himself under control. "She's a couple of years older, and grew up in another huddle. I've only met her a handful of times."

"Why was *she* chosen to be the Were Collateral?"

"She offered to." He takes a few steps inside, fingers lightly tracing the empty surfaces, as though he wants to leave little snippets of his scent in this home. Braid it with my own. I see no dust, which means that Owen must have arranged for a cleaning service. He really is a better brother than I gave him credit for. "She was a second. She wanted a truce with the Vampyres. She lost relatives in the war, I believe."

"I see. Did you ask for volunteers?"

He shakes his head. "Your father's proposal was discussed during one of our round tables. I wasn't going to ask anyone to put themselves in danger, and was very clear that if us providing a

Collateral was nonnegotiable, I wouldn't go through with the marriage. After the meeting, Gabi took me aside and asked to be sent in."

"Right." I wander into the kitchenette and idly open the fridge. Inside there's a forgotten bag of blood. What a waste. "She asked. Lowe?"

He leans against the wall, already more relaxed. "Yeah?"

"What did I study in college?"

He gives me a puzzled look. "You?"

"Me."

"Why?" He shrugs when I don't reply. "You majored in software engineering and minored in forensic sciences."

Okay, okay.

Okay.

"It was never her."

His stare is perfectly blank.

"Gabi. She is not your mate."

"She—no. Did you think she was?" He blinks, uncomprehendingly.

"Governor Davenport said so. Back at the ceremony."

His eyes widen with understanding, and I watch the realization hit him. "No. The traditional contract between Vampyres and Weres requires the Collateral to be two things: in good health, and related to the Alpha of the pack."

I knew that. But for the first time, I actually *think* about it. "Do you have any living relatives aside from Ana?"

He shakes his head.

"I see. And you weren't about to let her go."

"It was also nonnegotiable."

"So . . . ?"

"We made the case that a mate is equivalent to a blood relative within a Were pack. It's not quite as straightforward as that, but . . ."

"The council bought it."

Lowe nods. "I asked your father not to publicize that she was my mate to avoid issues for Gabi once she returned home. I didn't think . . ." I watch understanding fully sink into him. That I'd been assuming it was her. That I thought he'd brought *me* to meet his mate, even as we . . . "No. No, Misery." He seems distressed on my behalf. "She isn't. I'm sorry."

"It's okay." It's not his fault if I assumed, and it has nothing to do with me, anyway.

But it *has*. We study each other across several feet, and there's a question bubbling deep in my belly, and an answer simmering inside him, a tentative certainty that warms the air between us.

My feet drag me to Lowe of their own accord. They push me up on my toes, and I'm kissing him as intensely as I can, too much pressure too fast, my arms looped tight around his neck like a noose. He doesn't immediately respond, but it's confusion more than hesitation. After a beat his hands close around my waist, trapping me between him and the wall, deepening the contact. "Misery." The words come out jumbled between our lips. His erection brushes against my stomach and we both gasp.

"We shouldn't," he says, pulling back.

But when I ask him "Why?" his lips find mine again. The kiss started high, but still manages to escalate. "I know. I *know*, I think—" My hands travel down, pulling up his shirt and exposing a strip of warm skin. "I want to—" I cannot say it out loud, because I don't know what I need. It has to do with the truth, and him admitting it, but it's a confused, painful thorn tangled in my head. "Can we—"

"Yeah. Yeah, we can." He's at once urgent and soothing. "We can."

There is a couch right behind us, but Lowe flips me around until my front is pressed to the wall, forehead and forearm flush against it. "Slow down," he commands, mouth sucking on my neck, a large hand splaying over the center of my back. My heart flutters. In the slipperiness of this moment, it's exactly what I need to hear.

"You're just so good." He's being Were, or Alpha, or *Lowe* again. Pressing open-mouthed bites into my neck. I moan, and he pushes harder into me. "You need to tell me. This place smells like you and your scent is shooting up my brain and I cannot think about anything but fucking you. So if you want me to stop, I need you to tell me."

I press my forehead harder against the wall. "Please, don't stop."

He swears softly, sounding *ruined*. He makes quick work of pulling up my shirt and unfastening my jeans. I arch against him— his mouth, his chest, his cock. One of his large palms comes up to the wall, right beside mine, and I extend my little finger to brush against his thumb. I'm requesting *more*, and he gets it. But instead of giving it to me, he nuzzles the crook of my throat. "We should slow down." He laughs, rueful, hot into my skin.

"The opposite."

"Misery—" he starts.

"I want to have sex."

A yearning, guttural noise vibrates into my skin. "Misery."

"It's fine. It's going to work out."

"It's not."

"Why?"

"You know why." His arms cross on my belly and pull me to him, possessive, a little frustrated. "We can't." We're both shaking with . . . This deep, bottomless need inside me, is it *desire*? Is this why people do impulsive, mindless, hotheaded things?

"I just— It must have happened before. A male Were and a female Vampyre." Our species have existed for thousands of years, and we didn't always hate each other. "We could try. I'm not afraid of your. . ."

He laughs unsteadily against my throat. "You don't even know what it's called."

"What does it matter?"

"Am I wrong?" I let out a bitter hum, and he shushes me with a nip on the valley behind my ear. "You don't know what you're asking for, do you?"

"Just tell me, then. Then I'll know, and—"

"A knot. It's called a knot." I savor the word in my head, marveling at how well it fits. "Say it," Lowe orders. And when I hesitate, he adds, "Please."

"Knot. A knot."

His grip tightens. His breath grows shallow. "Shit."

"W-what?"

"I think I'd like to hear you say it again."

I do, just because he asked. He clutches my hip as though he likes the encore even more.

"You know what its purpose is?"

I may know nothing about Were biology, but I'm not stupid, or naive. "Yes."

"Say it."

This is simultaneously mortifying and the most erotic experience of my entire life. "To keep it inside."

His hand slides underneath my shirt, gently stroking the underside of my breast. "Keep what inside, sweetheart?"

I close my eyes. My heart beats a pounding, sluggish rhythm into every inch of my skin. "Your come."

His big body shudders for a moment. Then rewards me with a nibble on the tip of my ear. "You'd be okay with that?"

I nod. He groans.

"I'm not sure *I'd* be willing to risk hurting you."

I wish I could see his face. "You can stop. If it hurts, if it doesn't work."

"What if I can't?"

"You will. I know you will."

"Or I won't be able to. Because I want it too much." His fingers move back down, skimming my underwear, knuckles white against the damp blue cotton. He murmurs something about how slick I am, and when the heel of his palm starts massaging my clit in a slow rhythm I sigh in pleasure and relief.

"I—I *really* want to."

"Fuck," he exhales, and then he shifts behind me. His palm fully covers my hand on the wall.

I'm here. Okay. I've got you.

"Let me just— I can't just fuck you like this." He pulls my jeans around my knees and crowds me tighter into the wall. "Let me get you there."

I don't fully understand what he means, until one of his hands grips my hip bone and the other slips inside my panties, stretching the cotton in a way that feels obscene. He parts me with two of his fingers, and lets out a hushed, reverential groan as he stares at himself touching me under the soft fabric. His heartbeat punches into my back, and when his teeth find my throat and start scraping, then nibbling, then biting just hard enough, when his finger circles my clit just right, that's when I come.

It's unexpected, too fast. Barely a climb and I'm already dropping down, gasping for air. But it feels like an interrupted, half thing, and I don't let myself catch my breath. I reach back, frantically grasping to undo his jeans.

"Quiet," he orders, pinning my hands to the small of my back. "You need to give me a minute. I'm figuring this out."

I force myself to relax. It's obvious that, on average, the sex *his* people have and the sex of *my* people are different flavors. Just as it's obvious that he and I inhabit some overlapping space. I would expect nothing less.

"This would be easier if you smelled a little less fuckable," he says raggedly, but I hear the clinking sound of his belt and then I *feel* it, the head of his cock pressing against the soaked panties that stick to my pussy. I free myself to reach down, stroke his length, and he makes a choked sound. It's hot and large, but the thing at the base—his *knot*—hasn't swelled yet. Last time it inflated when he came. I want to know if that's the norm, but asking will send Lowe into another spin of concern, and I don't need him to worry about me.

"Please," I beg. "Please, put it in."

He nods against my temple, breath shallow and quick. He hooks my underwear to the side and pushes his cock inside me, the burning stretch deepening until it cannot go any farther, and whatever it was that I expected from having a man—having Lowe—inside me, this is different.

I inhale abruptly.

He exhales in the same way.

There's no need for negotiation, no pain, and no struggle. I'm pliant and he's hard. I'm wet and he's groaning. We *fit*. The biological compatibility Lowe told me about, the one between mates . . . I don't presume to know what that would be like. All I know is that we feel pretty fucking—

"Perfect," he murmurs, bottoming out, gripping my waist like he's trying to collect himself. I know why: this feels exquisite in a sharp, cruel way. Vampyres don't read minds, but I know what he's thinking: how easy it would be to live in this forever. To just *never* stop. "Don't move, or I'll come." He licks a stripe up the back of my neck. "Shit, I might come anyway. Just from your scent and your little bent neck."

I might, too. Very soon. Especially as he moves with experimental, shallow thrusts that hit *everywhere* inside me. I feel myself tighten in little flutters around him, and he stops. Then he bends over to whisper against my ear: "If you're about to come, tell me. Because that will make *me* come, and I need to pull out or I might hurt you. Okay?" He sounds calm, even when his control is about to snap.

I nod, trying to stave off the surge of pleasure.

"Okay." He presses another gentle, chaste kiss against my nape, and then draws out. The friction is delicious, and I arch back, making plaintive sounds as only the tip is left inside. When he pushes in again, a little deeper, I whimper. "Too much?"

The only answer I can manage is a squeeze around his cock. His palm slaps against the wall with a curse.

"I've been thinking about this," I tell him, barely a whisper.

His "Yeah" is apologetic. "I tried not to."

I turn my head. He's hulking, wrapped around me. His cheek is there, stubbly and flushed olive and perfect for me to kiss. "Me, too." Then I add, smiling, "Not too hard, though."

I lose track of time when he starts thrusting, and so does he. We move together, sweaty and winded. He stops after a few minutes, to take off the edge, and then again a couple of minutes after that. He pulls out when he needs a break from the stimulation, and I feel empty, shaking with frustrated pleasure, so he slides his fingers inside me, keeping me full as he winds down, hot and hard against my hip. The lights from the street pour in through the windows, and our breathing grows choppy. When I can't stop myself, when I'm sensitive and swollen and about to shatter so hard that a single thrust is okay to bring me off, I can barely remember to warn him.

"I'm about to—"

I come again, the pleasure curling tight inside me. What happens to Lowe is fuzzy, eclipsed by my own pleasure, but I make out some of it: a sharp grunt; a sudden feeling of emptiness; that part of him swelling hotter and harder against the globes of my ass; then his come, warm and wet, pooling onto the small of my back.

And then we stay like that, breathing together, wiped of thought. He presses his forehead against my shoulder, one hand splayed on my abdomen as if to contain me, and maybe it's whatever chemicals flood Vampyre brains after sex, but I cannot accept that this is not destined. That we are not meant to be.

"Do Weres . . ." My voice is raspy from swallowing my moans. I clear my throat and hear myself ask, "Do Weres always knot?"

He lets out a shuddering breath. "Don't move." He presses a kiss against my cheekbone. "I'm going to clean you up. Where do you keep—"

"Don't leave." I turn around to look at him, and he looks— ravaged. Vulnerable. Happy. My shirt slips down, but this is my apartment. I have nothing but changes of clothes. "Can you answer my question first?"

He shakes his head. "We don't." But then adds: "It's complicated."

I don't think it's complicated. In fact, I suspect it might be very simple. "Explain it to me, please."

"It's a sign of . . . It only happens between certain people." My shirt is completely askew, and he trails kisses on the jutting bone of my shoulder, getting lost in the act before straightening my neckline. He inhales deeply. "On second thought, I'm not going to clean you up. I'll just leave you like this." His hand snakes around my waist. To my lower back, where I'm sticky and wet. "Send a clear message to anyone who smells you. Who you belong to."

"Had it ever happened to you before?"

He's smearing his come into my skin with his thumb, and why am I okay with this? "Before?"

"Before me. Knotting. Did it ever happen with anyone else?"

His eyes darken. "Misery—"

"I'm just starting to put things together, you know?" We're still buzzing from the pleasure, and it's unfair of me to press him right now, when our defenses are lowered and we're full of the wrong kind of hormones, but . . . Just *but*. "I think it was there for me to see all along. But you threw me off on purpose, didn't you? There was your reaction to my scent when we first met, and it was so extreme, I assumed that you didn't like it. How adamant you were about not having me around." I swallow. "I would have realized it sooner, if I hadn't taken for granted that it had to be another Were. It made so much sense that Gabi would be the one. In the end, though, it was all about getting to know you. Because now that I understand what kind of person you are, I cannot help but wonder: If Lowe were in love with someone else, would he be like this with me? And I can't picture a reality, or even a damn simulation, in which that would be the case." I let out a short laugh.

Lowe says nothing. He stares, impenetrable. His pale, decent, kind eyes retreat into something that offers no clarity.

"It happens between mates, right? Knotting, I mean." Biologically, it makes sense in so many ways. Honestly, nothing else does. "It's me, isn't it?" I attempt a wobbly smile. *It's okay. I know it. I feel it, too.* "I'm your mate. That's why . . ."

"Misery." He's not looking at me, but at some spot around my feet. And his tone is like I've never heard it before: Unreadable. Empty.

"That's why, right?"

He's silent for heavy seconds. "Misery." My name, again, but this time there's a world of hurt behind the word, like I'm torturing him.

"I'm not . . . I feel the same way you do," I add quickly, not wanting him to think that I'm accusing him of something beyond his control. "Or maybe not—maybe I don't have the hardware. Maybe only another Were could feel the same. But I really do like you. More than that. I haven't quite figured it all out, because I don't have much experience with feelings. But maybe you think that this frightens the shit out of me, and . . ." My voice weakens, because Lowe has lifted his gaze, and I can see the way he's looking at me.

He understands, I think. *He knows. He feels exactly the way I do.*

But then his expression shutters. And his tone can only be described as compassionate. "I'm sorry if I've ever given you the wrong impression about what is happening between us."

My assurance wobbles, when I was secure in his feelings for me till a moment ago. I shake my head. "Lowe, come on. I know Gabi isn't your mate."

"She isn't." He presses his lips together. "But I'm afraid you reached the wrong conclusions."

"Lowe."

He shakes his head slowly. "I'm sorry, Misery."

"Lowe, it's fine. You can—"

"We should stop discussing this now."

"No." I let out a laugh. "I'm right. I know that I'm right."

There is something about the way he stares at me. Like he knows he's about to hurt me, and himself in the process, and the thought is simply unacceptable. Like I'm leaving him no choice.

"You said that a mate grabs you by the stomach, and—"

"Misery." He speaks harshly this time, like he's scolding a child. "You should stop filling your mouth with Were words you cannot understand."

My throat falls into my stomach. "Lowe."

"It was a mistake, telling you about the concept of mates." His voice is detached, like he's reading from a script and sucking every emotion out of his performance. "It's not something any non-Were can fully comprehend, let alone a Vampyre. But I understand how appealing it might be, for someone who struggles with belonging."

"What?"

"Misery." He sighs again. "You have been abandoned and mistreated your entire life. By your family, by your people, by your only friend. You are fascinated with the idea of eternal love and companionship, but that just doesn't reflect what I feel for you."

My heart cracks. The ground beneath my feet undulates as I come to terms with this version of Lowe. Who, apparently, would take things I told him about my past and use them against me. "You . . ." I shake my head, stupefied by how much his words hurt. Even when they cannot be true. "You're just trying to push me away. Tell me," I order, stubborn all of a sudden. I feel like a bumbling mess. Not myself. Every instinct screams at me to retreat, but this is an unacceptable, obvious lie. "Tell me that you're not in love with me," I challenge. "That you don't *want* to be with me."

He doesn't miss a beat. "I'm sorry," he says, dispassionate, with a hint of condescension. Some pity. Sorrow. "I think you're very attractive. And I enjoy spending time with you. I enjoyed——" His voice almost breaks. "I enjoyed fucking you. And I wish you the best, but. . . ." He shakes his head.

I open my mouth, hoping for a good comeback, only to find that I cannot breathe. And then the worst of it happens: Lowe wipes the back of his hand where, if I could cry, a tear would streak my cheek.

The pain of his rejection is a fist around my heart.

"I see that this was a mistake," he continues. "But it's for the best. You don't want to be tied to someone like me. You should be free." He almost stumbles on the last word, but recovers quickly. "And from now on, you and I should probably be apart."

"Apart?"

"I can find another place for you to live." His eyes are trained on a spot behind my shoulders. "You're getting the wrong ideas, and I frankly don't *want* you to——"

A phone rings.

His eyes dart away, annoyed, but when he steps back from me, it's a reprieve. I stare down at my feet, tuning out the soft conversation that ensues, trying to breathe through the crushing cold lodged behind my sternum.

I was wrong.

I misunderstood.

I was mistaken, and he *isn't*—he *doesn't* . . .

"I'll be right there."

Lowe hangs up. When he addresses me, it's with his usual calm, as though our conversation never took place. As though *nothing* between us ever took place.

"I need to leave." He adjusts his jeans.

I nod. With difficulty. "Okay. I—"

"I'm going to have someone come pick you up and take you back into Were territory."

"It's fine. I can just—"

"It's dangerous," he interrupts flatly. "So *no*, you can't. You may persist in not caring about your safety, but I . . ." He doesn't continue. Just looks and looks and looks at me, and the silence between us grows intolerable.

"Okay. You can let yourself out. I'm going to shower and get changed." I head blindly toward my bedroom, but barely manage two feet before a strong grip around my fingers stops me in my tracks.

I don't want to turn to him, but I do. And tremble when he leans in to kiss my forehead. He inhales once, hard. I feel his lips move against my skin into what feels like three short words, but probably isn't. For a second I wonder if maybe I was right after all, and my heart soars.

Then he pulls back, and it collapses on itself once again.

"Go," he orders, and I do. I've had enough of this careless, cruel brand of honesty for tonight.

I walk into my room and don't wait for him to leave before I close the door behind me.

CHAPTER 26

He is being kinder to her than to himself, and hopes she can never realize it.

THERE WAS NEVER A BED IN THIS APARTMENT. I WAS HAPPY IN the closet, and whenever Serena stayed over, she made do on the couch. For the first time in my life, though, I wish I'd done the Human thing and bought something soft to fall on.

As it is, I settle for sliding to the floor and spending way too long with my forehead on my knees, trying to regain my bearings.

Baby's first heartbreak, I guess.

Whatever this pitiful, soul-rending feeling inside me is, it seems too dense to be borne. Because Lowe is right: I've spent years being at home nowhere, and my best friend disappeared after the worst argument of our lives—yes, probably voluntarily, and probably because she doesn't give a fuck about me, not nearly as much as I do about her. I'm no stranger to pain, to loneliness, to disappointment, but *this*. This pressure inside me, it's not *solvable*. The weight of it, how does one bear it?

I find no answer by pressing my fingers to my eyes until I see stars.

My shower takes five minutes. I valiantly try to scrape the rejection and humiliation off my skin, but fail. I barely have time to find a change of clothes before the buzzer rings, and Mick's voice informs me that Lowe asked him to come get me. A heartbeat later I'm sliding into the passenger seat of his car. "How are you, Misery?"

"Good." I try for a small smile. "You?"

"I've been better."

"I'm sorry." I give him a cursory look. Then another. Maybe taking care of someone else's distress will alleviate mine. "Is there anything I can do?"

"No."

I go back to focusing on the streetlights and wait impatiently for Mick to finish puttering around and start the car, but I don't know why. I have no reason to be impatient, because I have nowhere to be. No place to call mine.

"Have you talked with Ana recently?" I ask. If Lowe sends me elsewhere, I likely won't see her again. I guess I've grown overly attached to her, too, because my heart squeezes even tighter.

"No," Mick says. "But I think it's for the best."

I lean my temple against the window. My head pounds with a dull kind of ache. "Why is that?"

"It's complicated."

I huff out a sour laugh, and my breath mists the glass. The same fucking words as Lowe's. What a cunning way to get out of telling the truth. "You Weres sure love to say—" A bug prickles my skin, and I swat it away. But when I turn around, what I find is not something I can make sense of.

Mick.

Holding a small syringe.

Injecting it in my arm.

I look up at his face, trying to parse what is happening. "I'm sorry, Misery," he says. His voice is soft and his eyes are sad, down-tilted in a way that makes my battered chest hurt even more.

Why? I ask.

Or I don't. The word doesn't make it out, because I'm tired, and my limbs are heavy, and my eyelids so laden with iron that the darkness behind them feels too sweet to—

CHAPTER 27

There is very little he wouldn't do, very few people he wouldn't kill, just to ensure her well-being.

WHEN WE WERE YOUNG, ELEVEN OR MAYBE EVEN TWELVE, BEfore Serena managed to grasp the difference in our physiologies, she would sometimes get bored of spending her afternoons all alone doing homework or watching TV, and slink into my room to shake me awake when the sun was still too high in the sky. She'd be surprisingly ruthless, more forceful than her little body looked capable of. She'd grasp my shoulder and waggle it hard, with the force of a pack of rottweilers chewing their favorite toy into a slimy chunk of plastic.

That's how I know that she's here, with me. Even before I open my eyes. Vampyres do not dream. Therefore, this commotion must be happening for real. And there is simply no other being in The City, on this Earth, who could be this fucking—

"*Annoying,*" I say.

Or slur. My tongue is still asleep, far too cumbersome for my mouth and made of papier-mâché. I should open my eyes, at the very least one of them, but I suspect that someone embroidered my eyelids to my cheeks and then soaked them in superglue. Upon consideration, the best choice would be to ignore all of this and go back to my nap.

"Misery. Misery? *Misery.*"

I groan. "Don't—yelling."

"Then don't—going back to sleep, Bleetch."

The word tears my eyes open. I'm once again on a damn bed, where I once again don't remember lying down. My internal clock is shot, and I have no clue whether it's day or night. I instinctively move my neck—*ouch*—checking for sunlight pouring in, and find . . .

No windows. I'm in a wooden attic, large and climate-controlled, with ceiling-high shelves full of books on every wall. There is a plate on the coffee table nearby with leftover pasta smeared all over it, and a small pile of soda cans and plastic water bottles.

I take an achy breath, feeling the drugs fade at a snail's pace. It's not day, not yet. Not even close to sunrise. I must have been out an hour, two tops, which means that Mick didn't carry me that far. Mick—Mick, *what the fuck, Mick?*—must have decided to stash me with—

Serena.

I'm with *Serena.*

"Holy shit," I mumble, trying to sit up straighter. It takes two attempts and substantive help from her to manage a still mostly prone position. "Holy *shit.*"

"Why, hello. How lovely of my oldest and most treasured friend to join me in my humble abode."

"I'm your only friend," I cough out, wondering whether my brain is making shit up. Vampyres do not dream, but they do hallucinate.

"Correct. And rude."

"I . . ." I smack my lips. This dry-mouth situation needs to be addressed. Is this why Humans and Weres drink water all the time? "What the *fuck*?"

"Did they knock you out? I couldn't find a bump on your head."

"Drugged me. Mick did."

"Mick being the older Were who deposited your lifeless body here like a sack of potatoes and brought me SpaghettiOs?"

"Not *lifeless*."

"The thing about Vampyres is, you tend to look pretty lifeless."

"Shit—Serena, you know how long I've been looking for you?"

Her smile is commiserating. "No. But if I may hazard a guess, I would say . . ." She taps her chin several times. "Three months, two weeks, and four days?"

"How—?"

She points behind her. She's been carving lines on the side of the bookshelf, tallying time in groups of five days.

"Shit," I whisper. There are so *many*. The physical manifestation of how long Serena has been gone and—

Without thinking, I half roll, half push off the bed to hug her close. I can barely hold my arms up, and it cannot be a good experience for her, but she valiantly squeezes me back. "Did you just initiate physical touch? What is happening? Did you start therapy while I was gone?"

"I missed you," I say into her hair. "I didn't know where you were. I looked for you everywhere, and—"

"I was here." She pats my back. Squeezes me harder.

"Where the fuck is *here*?" I pull back to study her. She's wearing a pair of too-large jeans and a long-sleeved shirt I've never seen on her. She's soft and curvy as always, but the last time I saw her she had bangs and a bob that made it just past her chin, and her hair has now grown into a completely different cut. "You look good."

Her eyebrow lifts. "That's a weird thing to say in the let's-exchange-vital-info stage of a joint abduction."

"It was a damn compliment!"

"Fine. Thanks. I was always very self-conscious of my forehead, as you know, but maybe unnecessarily? Maybe I'll spare myself the whole monthly trim—"

"Okay, now shut up. Where are we?"

She rolls her eyes. "I have no clue. And believe me, I've tried to figure it out, but there are no openings and the place is really well acoustically insulated. There must be at least four or five stories underneath us, just based on listening to the pipes in the bathroom. The guards who feed me are very careful not to show themselves or come near enough for me to guess their species, but now that your friend Mick is in the picture, I'd guess we're in Were territory. That doesn't narrow it down by much, though."

Emery. She has to be part of this. And Mick must have been helping her all along. He was one of Roscoe's seconds, after all.

I pinch my forehead. "Why did you get yourself involved with the Weres?"

"Excellent question! Would you like the long or the short answer? I've had plenty of time to workshop both versions in the last months."

"Did they hurt you? Are they torturing you, or interrogating you, or—"

She shakes her head. "They treat me well, if you discount the perpetual infringement of my Human rights. But they've never brought me out of this room, and I've tried. I've pretended to be sick, I've gotten aggressive—no dice. The guards are assholes of unspeakable proportions and refuse to talk to me."

"How did they take you?"

"The last thing I remember was walking down the sidewalk on my way to your apartment from work—then bam, I was here."

I glance around the attic. "What do you even do all the time?"

"I've been catching up on sleep. Reviewing my life choices. Stewing in regret. Mostly, I read." She gestures at the shelves. "But the selection here is limited to the classics. I've read, like, three Dickens novels."

"Appalling."

"*The Catcher in the Rye*, too."

"God."

"And an entire mystery series I don't even like." She shrugs. "Now, would you like to hear my theory on why someone even bothered to kidnap little old me, so you can say I told you so, or something?"

Irritation fuels me enough to finally sit up straight. "No, because I *didn't* tell you so."

"Oh." She nods, bemused. "Well, this is a pleasant surpr—"

"I couldn't tell you so, because you hid the *story* you were working on and the shit you were doing from me."

She frowns. "Okay. Well, at least let me explain—"

"I already know."

"Whatever you're thinking, that's not it. I was actually—"

"You were looking into the Weres, or Thomas Jalakas, or financial crimes or something. You found out that Liliana Moreland is a Human-Were hybrid, possibly one of a kind, and then got kidnapped for your efforts."

Serena recoils. "How do you . . . ?"

"Your cat was . . . There was that butterfly alphabet thing on your planner, and . . ." I massage my temple. "Just trust me when I say that I know, frankly, way more than I ever wanted about anything. Lowe said that—"

"Who's Lowe?"

My heart pangs. I swat the memory and the pain away in one big swipe. "The Were Alpha. My husband."

"You know what, it doesn't matter. Tell me how they—" She stops abruptly. Does a double take. Blinks at me multiple times. "Did you just say . . . ?"

I sigh. "Yeah."

"Misery."

"I know."

"Seriously."

"I know."

"I'm gone for three months, and after a lifetime of having literally no news, now you are *married to a Were Alpha*?"

"Yes."

"Oh my *God.*"

"Technically, it's your fault."

"*Excuse me?*"

"You think I got married because I found sweet Were love on a dating app? I was looking for *you*. The entire time you were gone. In whatever way I could. That's how I ended up married to the brother of the *very* young, *very* innocent half-Were girl you were willing to exploit, and now we're here, and I'd bet my entire collection of hacking tools that it's Emery who took us, and that Mick has been working with her behind Lowe's back the whole time—I bet . . . You know what? I bet Emery *knows* that Ana is a hybrid, and wants to make sure that Ana can never serve as a symbol of unity between the Weres and the Humans, and the way you were snooping around put you on Emery's radar, and Serena, *it was so fucking hard for me to find you.*" It all comes out so quickly, I barely have time to keep my tone in check. But I regret it instantly when Serena's hand comes up to press against her chapped lips. Her nails are bitten to the quick—a habit she grew out of years ago.

"It's just . . ." She swallows. "I wasn't sure."

"Sure of what?"

"That you'd be looking. We had that fight, and . . ." Her voice breaks a little. "I kind of said things I didn't mean, and I figured that maybe you were done with me."

I stare at her, momentarily speechless. Maybe the larder beetles have eaten her brain? "Dude. I didn't know that was an option."

She lets out a small laugh, a little shakier than her usual. "I just had a lot of time in here to think about what I said."

I nod. Poke my tongue around my very dry, very sour mouth. "I had lots of time out there, too."

We regard each other. If we were better people, less screwed up, we'd probably be able to say something like *I love you*, or *So glad to be together again*, or a slightly more macabre *Thank fuck you're not dead*. But we both stay silent, because that's what we do.

We both know the unsaid, because that's who we are.

Serena clears her throat first. "Shall we consider the matter archived for the moment?" she asks. "We can clip each other's nails when we're out of here, or something."

"Excellent suggestion. Let's focus on what to do."

She takes a fortifying breath. "I've actually been working on a plan."

"Let's hear it."

BRIDE

"It involves staying here. Building a life. Growing old. Developing cataracts."

I smile. "You always had the worst fucking plans."

She laughs. And I laugh. And then we laugh some more, until the whole thing sounds less like laughter and more like slight hysteria, and *God, I missed this.*

"Another plan," she says, wiping her eyes and lowering her voice, "that I've hatched in the past three minutes, is to lure the guard at the door, and use your Vampy magic to thrall them into letting us go."

I scowl. "You know I can't do that without touching people."

"Misery. Babe."

"What?"

"I doubt there's another way."

"We could fight. There's two of us, and we know self-defense—"

"They won't come inside. Everything is handed to me through that opening." She points at the square panel in the door. "But now that you're here, we might be able to trick them. I could distract the guard long enough for you to get a hook in him."

I shake my head. Fully aware that I'm not saying no. "This could go so badly."

"They wouldn't take it out on you," she points out. "You're the daughter of a Vampyre councilman and I guess *the wife of a Were Alpha?*" She pinches her nose. "Unlike me, you're a valuable hostage to use in negotiations, and this Emery person must know that. If anything, they'd take it out on me, which is—"

"Also unacceptable."

She bites the inside of her cheek. "I really would love to get out of here. Spend more time with Sylvester."

"Sylvester?"

"My cat."

"Ah." I glance away guiltily. "About that."

"I swear to God, if you tell me that you let my cat starve or choke to death on my yarn or get eaten by a raccoon—"

"I did not, even though he'd deserve it. However, his name is now Sparkles. And he's grown very attached to Liliana Moreland, or vice versa." I ignore her withering look. "There's nothing but cats in the world, and Sparkles is mediocre among them, so I'll get you another one if we ever—"

A knock at the door, and we both startle.

"Yeah?" Serena calls. She pushes me out of sight, even when the door and the food slot stay closed.

"I have a . . . bag of blood. For the Vampyre."

"Who's that?" I whisper.

"Bob."

I tilt my head. "Who the hell is Bob?"

"It's a name I made up for the guards. They're all Bob." And then, louder. "Misery's not feeling well," she yells. Which is true— I feel like total shit. "I think the drugs might be about to kill her or something!"

What the hell? I mouth. I cannot deal with a Serena plan right now.

"Well, that's above my pay grade. I can't do anything for a leech, anyway—"

"She is Vampyre *royalty*. Whoever your boss is, do you think they'll be pleased with you if she dies under your watch?"

There are a couple of muttered curses I can barely make out. Then the slot opens. "What's going on?"

I look at Serena, stumped. All she does is gesture vaguely at me, probably trying to telepathically transmit her plan. I scrunch my face into a raisin, hoping to cringe myself out of this world. When that doesn't work, I reluctantly make my way to the door.

The opening is at head height, but because of the way the attic is built, Bob's view of the inside is limited. "There is something wrong. With my . . . eye," I tell him once we're face-to-face. He's a Were, and looks younger than I expected. Too young to be doing this shit, just like Max.

Fuck you, Emery, and fuck you, Mick.

He mutters something about leeches whining and asks, "What's wrong?"

"This." I sniffle and make an assortment of dramatic noises. On my right, hidden from Bob's eyes, Serena gives me the thumbs-up. The most useless enabler in the world. "You see?"

"I can't see anything." He leans forward a little, but he's smart enough not to tilt his head into the door. Pity, as I'd have loved to punch him. Then again, that would leave me satisfied, but still locked in here. "It's just a regular purple eye. What am I supposed to notice?"

"It must be a reaction to the drugs. You have to tell a physician," I say. Maybe too flatly, because Serena is miming something that can only mean *Up the histrionics.* "I could *die.*"

"Die of what?"

"Of *this*, you see?" I point under my right eye, and he focuses on it, trying to find some abomination within. When my intraocular muscles start twitching to initiate the thrall, I put everything I can into the movement, hoping to get a quick hook.

For a moment, it does work. I anchor myself just below the surface, Bob's confusion obvious in his slack mouth and empty eyes. *I have him*, I think. *I have him, I have him, I have him.*

Then he frowns and pulls back, and I realize that I failed.

Abysmally.

"Did you . . ." He blinks at me, twice, and the realization dawns on him. "Did you just try to thrall me? You fucking *leech*!"

He is furious—so furious, he thrusts his hand through the opening and comes for my throat. And that's when Serena reminds me of something.

How fucking *badass* she's always been.

Moving faster than I thought possible for a Human, she snatches Bob's wrist, bending it at an unnatural angle. Bob yelps and immediately tries to pull back, but my half-assed thrall must have affected him somehow, because despite his Were strength, he seems too weak to escape Serena's grip.

"Open the door," Serena orders.

"Fuck *no*."

She bends the wrist farther. Bob squeals.

"Open the door or I'll do this—" She snaps his thumb. I hear it pop out of its socket, and it's *disgusting*. "—to *all* your fingers."

It takes two more, but Bob unlocks the door. Despite his Were strength, it's clear that he's not a trained fighter, and it takes us little effort to switch places with him. We're both winded and a little bruised, but once he's bolted inside, I turn to Serena to make sure that she's okay, and find her slapping her hand to her mouth and jumping in place.

Maybe she's badass, but she's also incredibly dorky. My heart skips a beat at how relieved—how fucking relieved and happy I am. She is here. She is fine. She is being unashamedly herself, even after I spent so long without her.

"Told you I couldn't do it without contact," I say. Bob screams at us to let him out, and Serena gives the security door a guilty look.

"Seriously?"

"On the one hand, he's a dick. On the other, he did sneak me extra vanilla pudding once."

"I cannot wait to hear *everything* about this retirement home life of yours."

She winces. "Let's go. I don't think he had a phone with him, but I might have missed it."

We run to the end of the hallway, only to find another locked door. "This one looks pretty light. If we both throw our weight at it, we should be able to break through. At my three, okay?"

Serena gives me a puzzled look. Then takes a step forward, grabs the handle, and turns it.

The door opens.

"How did you know—?"

"I didn't. I did this thing—it's called checking. You should try it sometime."

I clear my throat and brush past her on my way out, my chest squeezing at how much I've missed her.

"Not that watching you hammering your way through the whole thing wouldn't have been peak entertainment, but . . ." She falls silent and stops in her tracks. And so do I. We're both stunned into immobility, because . . .

I had it right when I said Serena's cell was in an attic, but the building is much taller than we'd expected. There are at least twenty floors underneath us. This is a high-rise, one that's very familiar.

Because I grew up in it.

"Is this the Nest?" Serena murmurs. She's been here only once, but the place is too distinctive to forget.

I nod slowly. When I look behind me, I see that the door we just exited is painted the same color as the wall. Near perfect camouflage. "I don't get it."

"Bob was a Were, right? I didn't get it wrong, did I?"

I shake my head. Bob's blood pumped much faster than a Human's, and he definitely wasn't a Vampyre.

"So we had Were guards, and the Mick guy brought you here, but we're in Vampyre territory. How?"

"I don't know."

Serena shakes herself. "We can figure it out later. We need to get the hell out of here before someone catches us."

I nod and start down the stairs. About halfway through the first flight, Serena takes my hand. When we reach the end, I lace my fingers with hers. I have no clue what's going on, but Serena is here, and everything will be all right if—

"Stop," a voice says from behind us. A very memorable one.

Fear creeps up the back of my neck. I spin on my heels to find Vania smiling at me.

"I'm going to need you to come with me. One last time, Misery."

CHAPTER 28

He didn't think he could love her more, but she is a constant surprise.

SERENA AND I ARE FAIRLY WELL-TRAINED IN SELF-DEFENSE, BUT Vania is my father's most skilled enforcer. She's holding not one, but two knives, and is flanked by two guards—the same who escorted me into Vampyre territory all those weeks ago. Attempting to take them would be severely idiotic, and Serena and I are not quite *that* bad. So we march in front of her, hands raised over our heads, and follow her directions. Aware that should one of us decide to run, the other would end up with a knife in her back.

Let's be real: *Serena* would end up with a knife in her back. I would probably just get dragged by the ear in front of my father.

Because we're at the Nest. And Vania answers to him and no one else.

"If they murder me, avenge me," Serena whispers.

It's nice, all this faith she seems to have in me. "Any preferences on how?"

"Be creative."

Father is waiting in his office, once again sitting in the high-back leather chair behind his massive wooden desk, surrounded by four more guards. His smile doesn't reach his eyes, and he doesn't stand, nor does he offer us a seat. Instead he leans his elbows on the dark mahogany and joins his fingertips in front of his face, waiting for me to say something.

So I don't.

I'm hurt, betrayed, shocked at my father's involvement in something *this* egregious, but I'm also . . . not. No point in being surprised by a notoriously ruthless, selfish assassin when they stick a knife in your back—even if they are a relative. It's a totally different story when the stabbing is done by someone you consider to be a kind, decent person. Someone you consider a *friend*.

My gaze lands on Mick, who stands by Father's desk like one of his enforcers would. It lingers for as long as it takes for Mick to lower his own eyes. He looks ashamed, and I'm okay with that.

"Why?" I ask him flatly. When he says nothing, I add, "It was you, wasn't it?"

The grooves at the sides of his mouth deepen.

"Is Emery even in on this? Or did you just talk everyone around you into believing that she was targeting Ana because the Loyals were a convenient scapegoat?"

He looks away in what can only be confirmation, and my fists curl with fear and anger. *You're despicable*, I want to say, *I hate you*. But he seems to be already filled with self-disgust.

"Why?" I ask again.

"He has my son," he whispers, looking at Father. Who has the self-satisfied expression of someone who checkmated everyone in the game.

"Then you should have told Lowe."

Mick shakes his head. "Lowe couldn't—"

"Lowe would have done *anything* for you," I hiss, nauseous with rage. "Lowe would die himself before he let anything happen to a pack member. You've known him since he was a child—he's your Alpha, and yet you don't understand him at all." Anger bubbles. I can't remember the last time I spoke this harshly to someone. "The poison, it was *you*, wasn't it? Did you also send Max after Ana?"

"Misery," Father interrupts. "You are a never-ending source of disappointment."

My head whips in his direction. "Yeah? Since you've been taking people hostage and blackmailing them, I could say the same, but the bar was already so fucking *low*."

His eyes harden. "This is what you miss, Misery. Why you could never become a leader."

I snort. "Because I don't go around kidnapping people."

"Because you have always been selfish and close-minded. Stubbornly unable to understand that the ends justify the means, and that things like fairness and peace and happiness are bigger than one specific person—or than a handful of them. The good of the most, Misery." His shoulders rise and fall. "When you and your brother were little and the need for a Collateral arose, I had to decide which one of you would have the grit to take my place on the council. And I'm glad I chose Owen over you."

I roll my eyes. There's a good chance I won't be alive when Owen's coup goes down, but boy, do I wish I could witness Father shitting himself.

"Why do you think Vampyres still hold power, Misery? All over the world, our communities have been splintering. Many of them don't hold their own territories, and are forced to live among the Humans. And yet, despite our dwindling numbers, here in North America we still have our home. Why do you think that is?"

"Because you *so selflessly* kill everyone who stands in your way?"

"Like I said: a source of disappointment."

"Because of your strategic alliances within this geographical region," Serena answers evenly in my place. Everyone turns to her in surprise, as though her presence was a forgotten thing.

Not by my father, though. "Miss Paris." He nods courteously. "You are, of course, correct."

"In the past hundred years, Humans and Weres have alternated between ignoring each other and being on the brink of war because of border disputes. They both have advantages over Vampyres, physical and numerical, but they've never even considered leveraging them. Because the Vampyres have somehow managed . . . well, not *somehow*," Serena explains, a trace of that bitterness in her tone. "Through the Collateral system, you cultivated a very beneficial political alliance with the Humans. And the Weres knew this, just like they knew that any overt attack on Vampyre territory would unleash Human military power on them. That's how you kept yourselves safe through the decades, despite being the most vulnerable of the three species."

"Very thorough." Father nods, satisfied.

"I imagine there's more. For instance, I'm certain that if we were to look closely at the border skirmishes between Weres and Humans in the past few decades, we'd find that they were facilitated by Vampyre action. Just like I'm certain that considerable bribes were involved. Governor Davenport is undoubtedly not above accepting them."

Father doesn't deny it. "I see the weeks you spent reading improved your reasoning skills, Miss Paris."

Her chin lifts. "My reasoning skills have always been on point, fuckwaffle."

Must be the first time Father has been called *that*. It's the only explanation for the mildly outraged, mostly baffled hesitation that fills the room: no one knows how to respond to an overt insult, because unlike subtle jabs and assassination attempts, in Father's world they are not a thing. Eventually, after several awkward seconds, Vania steps forward and raises her hand to hit Serena.

I angle myself between the two of them, which in turn has Serena wanting to protect *me*. But Father puts a stop to that by ordering, "Let them be. We want them both intact, for now."

Vania glares at Serena. At a flick of Father's wrist, two of the guards come to stand next to us. The implied threat is crystal clear.

"I could have killed your friend, Misery. So many times. You know why I didn't?" he asks me.

"To spare my feelings?" I answer, skeptical.

"That was a nice bonus, I agree. Because no matter what you may think, I do not enjoy hurting you, or taking things away from you. I was not happy to send my child off, although I doubt you'll ever believe that. But ultimately, no, that was not the reason. I can only assume that Miss Paris neglected to tell you why I was forced to take her, then."

"She didn't have to tell me shit. I already know what happened." But when I glance at Serena, her eyes dart away. And that's when my stomach tightens. "She was working on an article," I add, even though she won't return my look. "And found out something she shouldn't have."

"So you really have no idea." That complacent, self-congratulatory smirk, I want to punch it off Father's face. "Let me enlighten you: several years ago, my dear friend Governor Davenport told me something he thought I might be interested in."

"Of course the governor is in on it," I sneer.

"Oh, you give him too much credit." Father waves his hand. "He is in on it . . . sometimes. Over the years, I've gotten well acquainted with his mind. Thralling him, planting hooks in his brain, has become easier and easier. Practically traceless. He's been giving me much useful information, some of particular intrigue. For instance, when he told me about a young child who had been born of Were and Human parents."

Ana. Of course. The governor must have found out, perhaps from Thomas, or maybe from . . . I turn to Mick again. "Did you tell the governor?"

"Oh, no," Father interrupts. "You are mistaken, Misery. Mick wasn't part of this until very recently, and it was I who sought him out. I will take credit where it's due, even if you'll accuse me of being a heartless monster. It was *my* idea to use his son once we realized that the boy we had taken during a raid had ties to a prominent Were. It was easy enough for me to thrall him. He even helped with guarding Miss Paris."

"What a thing to brag about, Father."

"Indeed. But it was quite a while ago that the governor told me about the half-Were, half-Human child. Over two decades, in fact."

I stiffen. A wave of dread sweeps over me.

"There had been stories before. Rumors of reproductive compatibility. If there's something Humans are good for, it's breeding." Father stands, lips curled in mild disgust, and leisurely steps around his desk. "But the stories came from other countries, and there was never any proof. Here, Weres are insular, and Humans are cowards. Like Miss Paris said, they simply don't interact enough. But this child was very young. They were not being raised by their biological parents for several reasons. They didn't know about their origins or their questionable genetic makeup, but they appeared to have taken after their father. They presented as Human, fully, which I must admit, made them less interesting to me—the implication of their existence was much less concerning. And yet, the occurrence was unique, and I decided to monitor the situation. It felt like the wise thing to do." He leans against his desk, drumming his fingers along the wooden edge. Something close to terror is beginning to stuff the inside of my throat. "Where could a Vampyre stow a half-Were child who presented as Human? Human territory appeared to be the best option. But how? It seemed like an impossible predicament. And that's where I remembered that I, myself, had a child stashed away in Human territory. And that she might enjoy some companionship."

My heart thumps loudly against the confines of my rib cage. I tear my eyes from Father's and slowly turn to my right. I find Serena already looking at me. Her eyes are welling with tears.

"Did you know?" I ask.

She doesn't answer. The tears, though, start falling.

"She did not." It's Father who responds, even though I'm rapidly losing interest in what he has to say. "I would know otherwise. Like I said, I monitored her for years. Even when your tenure as the Collateral ended, nothing that she did set off any alarms. In fact, she seemed to have no interest in Weres at all. Did you, Miss Paris?" He smiles at Serena, and the hatred in her glare could burn him as viciously as the sunlight. He ignores her and turns to me. "She was all about financial journalism, or something or other. I must say, our vigilance lapsed for a few years. The girl had grown into a promising, if *very* Human, young woman. Sometimes she'd disappear for a few days without warning, but that's the youths. Carefree. Adventurous. I never suspected that it might have something to do with her genes. Until . . ."

"I despise you," Serena hisses.

"I would expect no less. Human-Were hybrid that you are, you are well predisposed to, and I do not blame you. But the sloppy way you went about it when your Were half began emerging and you decided to research your parents, that certainly *is* your fault. You went around asking questions, stuck your nose into every nook and cranny of the Human-Were Bureau. You made it outrageously clear that something was changing in you, and that you were looking for guidance." His tone is scolding. More than anything Father has ever said to *me*, it makes me want to punch him. "In hindsight, it all made sense. The fact that most of your trips and disappearances were timed with the full moon. You needed to be outside, didn't you? The urge to be in nature became so irresistibly strong, you—"

"You know *nothing*," Serena spits out.

"But I do, Miss Paris. I know your bloodwork was all over the place. I know your senses became almost unbearably acute, so acute that they exceeded your Human doctor's ability to measure them. I know that you underwent genetic testing and the results came back as though the sample was contaminated—three times. I know that every full moon you felt like you needed to crawl out of your skin, and that one day you cut through the flesh of your forearm, just to see if your blood had turned green overnight. You were that far gone, suspecting that something inside you was very, very different."

Serena's jaw clenches. "How do you even—"

"Some of it I discovered once we started surveilling you assiduously. Most of it, you told me."

"No. I would never."

"But you did. When I thralled you, on the first day you got here."

Serena's mouth drops open, and the weight at the bottom of my stomach sinks heavier.

"I made sure you wouldn't remember. You may have been thralled before by Misery, but like everything else about her culture, my daughter was never properly taught." He appears amused by Serena's horrified expression. "And you know what else you told me? You were, tragically, unable to find out who your own parents were, and to ascertain whether one of them was a Were. However, once you started digging and using your considerable investigative skills, you heard about Thomas Jalakas.

"Thomas was an interesting man. He'd been working for the Bureau some years earlier, had struck up a relationship with one of Roscoe's seconds, and . . . I believe we all know how the story goes. Or maybe you don't, Misery." His eyes laser onto mine. "The Were woman became pregnant. Thomas, understandably, didn't believe her when she told him that the child was his. The relationship ended, and career politician that he was, I doubt he thought about his former lover much in the following years. Instead, he steadily rose through the ranks. Then, about a year ago, he went back to the Human-Were Bureau, this time as director. The security clearance that came with it gave him access to several intelligence reports, and he grew curious about the fate of his former paramour. He searched for her name, and came across a very interesting picture."

The most infinitesimal movement of Father's finger, and one of the guards activates the monitor on his desk. She swipes the touch screen a few times, then turns it in my direction.

I recognize Maria Moreland from the picture in Lowe's room. And Ana, who's holding her hand, from some of the best moments in the last month of my life. They are sitting on the lakeshore, feet submerged in the water. It's a candid photo taken from a distance, similar to something the Human paparazzo would produce. "The child piqued his interest. Earlier tonight you confronted Arthur Davenport, so I assume you already know how much the child resembles her biological father. Thomas now had very strong suspicions that hybrids were possible. So he decided to bring the knowledge to Governor Davenport."

"And the governor had Ana's father killed," I conclude.

"Ana? Ah, Liliana Moreland. As a matter of fact, he did not. But he did recognize that the allegations could prove very dangerous. His solution, admittedly a poor one, was to remove Thomas from his position as the head of the Bureau and give him a far more prestigious one. Thomas should have been pleased. Instead, he became obsessed with finding out more about his daughter. He brought attention to himself, and several months later, word reached Miss Paris that someone else had been asking the very same questions she had been. When they set up a meeting, I finally knew I had to intervene.

"So, no, Misery. It wasn't the governor who eliminated Thomas Jalakas. Or it was, but only in the sense that I thralled him to think that if he didn't, his embezzlement peccadillos would be unearthed. Just like Emery and the Loyals were a convenient candidate for Lowe's suspicions when we were forced to attempt to take Liliana. Mick was very helpful with that."

"You weren't *forced* to take Ana, or Serena. You *chose* to do it."

He sighs, as ever let down by me. "Sometimes, we become more than who we are. Sometimes, we become symbols. And that's something you should be well aware of, Misery. After all, you spent most of your life as a symbol of peace."

"If anything, I symbolized the utter lack of trust between Humans and Vampyres," I retort.

"People like Miss Paris here, and Liliana Moreland," he goes on as if I never spoke, "are dangerous. All the more if they share the traits and talents of both their species. For now, neither of them is able to shift. But they might still transcend themselves and become important, powerful symbols of unity between two peoples who have been senselessly at odds for centuries."

"And that would leave you defenseless in the region, and drastically reduce your influence," Serena murmurs, icy cold. I wonder how she can be so calm. Perhaps I'm feeling both our angers. "Maddie Garcia won the Human elections, didn't she? She knows she holds all the power, and she's refusing to meet with you because of the way you've been puppeteering Governor Davenport for decades."

"Miss Paris, I wish some of your political acumen had rubbed off. Maybe my daughter would stop looking at me as though I am a villain for acting in the interest of my people."

"Oh, fuck *off.*" I glance around at his enforcers, hoping at least one of them is seeing the vileness of this. They remain statue-like and betray no emotions. "You didn't put this through a vote. You didn't inform anyone of your decision. Do you really think that most Vampyres, or even the damn council, would be okay with you going about killing and abducting people?"

"Our people are accustomed to a certain degree of comfort. Few of them bother wondering what goes into providing it."

"Why haven't you killed me?" Serena asks, as though our exchange is a pointless tangent. She's not wrong.

"A difficult decision," he concedes to her. "But as we know nothing about hybrids, you seemed of better use to me alive."

"And yet you tried to kill Ana," I snap.

The look he gives me is first puzzled—then half amused, half pitying. "Oh, Misery. Is that what you think? That it was Liliana who I tried to kill?"

I glance at Mick, confused by Father's words, and his expression has turned into something compassionate that I simply cannot—

The loud knock at the door startles me. With the exception of Serena, the rest of the room is unsurprised. "Just in time. Please, enter."

Another of Father's enforcers comes in first. Right behind him is Lowe, eyes deep set and hooded, face stony. My throat knots a million times over, then sinks into my stomach when Owen follows him inside. His lips are bent in a shallow, enigmatic smile, and the reason is instantly obvious.

He has Lowe in handcuffs. Because Lowe is *not* here of his own free will. He glances around the room, taking stock of my father, of all the enforcers, of Mick. He doesn't allow any feelings to seep through, not even when his oldest second, his father figure, bends his head in the customary salute. Then his eyes reach me, and for a split second I see every emotion in the observable universe pass through them.

After a heartbeat, we're back to nothing.

My brain frantically tries to catch up. Did Owen lie about wanting to take over Father's seat? Was his help with Serena a lie?

"Lowe." Father's voice is nearly welcoming. "I was waiting for you."

"I don't doubt it," Lowe replies. His deep voice reverberates in the large room, filling it in a way a dozen people hadn't managed. "It appears you had a plan all along, Councilman Lark."

"Not all along. You know, you are a very hard man to thrall. I tried during our only meeting alone, after the marriage ceremony.

Usually I'll be able to hook into a Were or a Human in a matter of seconds, but with you, it simply didn't work. How frustrating." He sighs and points to Mick. "I told myself that it didn't matter. I had infiltrated your inner circle anyway. And yet, I still was unable to get my hands on your sister. And now that you've hidden her, I have been unable to find out where. I simply never managed to get any real leverage on you. Until now." He smiles at Owen. "Thank you for bringing him to me, son. I certainly consider this proof of your loyalty."

Owen's eyes shine with pride. I clench my teeth. "Lowe is never going to give you Ana."

"A month ago, I would have agreed with you. But Mick explained a few things to me. Including what his reaction to you at the wedding meant. The concept of mates." Father comes to stand in front of me, one hand clasping my shoulder. "Your usefulness truly knows no bounds."

"You are *unbelievable*." I shake his touch away, disgusted.

"Am I?"

"Yes. And mistaken." I lean forward, taunting him, suddenly powerful in the heartbreaking knowledge that he's wrong. "I'm *not* Lowe's mate. Whatever leverage you think you have, it's not—"

"Is she not, Lowe?" Father asks, suddenly louder. He's still holding my eyes. "Your mate?"

I stare back, waiting for Lowe's answer, waiting to see the disappointment in my father's eyes. Hoping it'll make the one *I* experienced earlier tonight less bitter. But time ticks on by. And Lowe's reply just temporizes, hangs back, hesitates, and never comes.

When I turn to him, he's at once blank and profoundly, indelibly sad.

"Tell him," I order. But he still doesn't speak, and it feels like a slap to my face. My lungs seize, and suddenly I cannot breathe. "Tell him the truth," I whisper to him.

Lowe runs his tongue over the inside of his cheek, and then presses his lips together in a small, sad smile.

Something inside me trembles.

"Now that it's settled," Father says dryly. "Lowe, Mick informs me that no one but you knows where Liliana is hidden. I want her—don't worry, not to dispose of her. Just like I didn't dispose of Miss Paris when I had the opportunity." He stops to give Serena a small smile, as if expecting gratitude. I envision her spitting on him and being promptly murdered by three enforcers. "All I want is assurance that Humans and Weres won't join forces against the Vampyres. And that starts with not giving them a reason to believe they're more similar and compatible than they thought." Father turns to Lowe one last time. "Make arrangements to hand over your sister."

Lowe nods slowly. And then asks with a genuinely curious tone, "And I would do that, because . . . ?"

"Because your mate will request it."

Lowe exhales a silent laugh. "You know my mate very little, if you really think she would request anything like that."

Lowe doesn't get a verbal response. Instead Father reaches forward. He moves so fast, the air shifts with momentum, and the next instant something cold, shiny, and very sharp appears next to my neck.

He's holding one of Vania's knives. To my throat.

Lowe, Owen, Serena—even Mick, they all attempt to reach for me, but are restrained by Father's enforcers, and when the tip of the blade grazes my skin they stop at once, with equally terrified expressions on their faces. The silence that follows is overstrung, filled by loud heartbeats and heavy breathing.

"No," Father says calmly. The hand holding the knife is steady. "In normal conditions, she wouldn't ask. But what if she had to choose between her life or Liliana's future? What then?"

"He's bluffing. He's not going to kill me," I tell Lowe, hoping to reassure him.

He remains expressionless, and certainly doesn't seem relieved. The opposite, perhaps. I wonder if he already knows what's to come.

"Won't I? I did have you poisoned. Oh, don't make that face. Yes, the poison was for you. I was hoping that the pain of losing a mate would distract Lowe enough for me to take Liliana. But Mick mixed up the doses, didn't he? It made me angry enough to take it out on his son. And after that, Lowe was smarter than to trust anyone." He moves even closer, his eyes a dark purple that's nearly blue. Whatever was left inside me that bound me to my family, already cracked and battered, finally splinters. "I have sacrificed you before, and I will do it again," my father tells me. There is no remorse in him. No conflict. "For the good of the Vampyres, I will not hesitate."

I laugh, full off disdain. "What a fucking coward you are." I should feel cornered, but I'm just angry. Angry on behalf of Ana and Serena. Of *myself*. Angrier than I thought possible.

And then there's Lowe, and the way he's looking at me. His calm fear, like he knows that nothing about this could ever end well. Like he's not certain what he'll do with himself afterward.

I'm sorry, Lowe.

I wish we had more time.

"Watch your language," Father admonishes lazily. The blade nicks my skin. The single purple drop of blood sliding down my neck has Lowe thrashing to free himself, but the restraints Owen put on him hold.

"You love to purchase the good of the Vampyres by paying with the lives of others, don't you?" I taunt Father. "Only a coward would put others in front of himself."

"I will leverage what I can."

"Well, I won't. I'm not going to ask Lowe to choose me over his sister."

"But there is no need, is there?" Father turns to Lowe. "What do you think, Alpha? Should I murder her in front of your eyes? I hear that Weres who lose their mates can sometimes go insane. That there is no greater pain," he adds with relish.

Don't be in pain, I think, staring him in the eyes over the glint of the blade. *Whatever happens, don't be in pain over me. Just be with Ana, and draw, and go on your runs, and maybe think of me sometimes when you eat peanut butter, but don't be in—*

"Misery," Serena's voice interrupts my thoughts. And then she says something else, something garbled and nonsensical that my brain takes a second to untangle. The enforcers look at each other, equally confused. Father frowns. Owen tilts his head, curious.

But she's not speaking in tongues. There are real words.

"He's wrong." That's what Serena said. In our secret alphabet.

Without looking away from Lowe, I ask, *"About what?"*

"About whether I can shift."

I don't immediately understand. But the corner of my eye catches a burst of movement. Her hand. No—her fingers.

Suddenly, her nails are long.

Unnaturally long.

Newly long.

I take a deep breath, mind racing. "Very well, Father," I say. I hold Lowe's gaze, hoping he'll get this. "Since you're going to have to kill me, if I may have some last words with my mate."

I swallow. Lowe's several steps away from me, and his eyes are . . . It's impossible to describe them. Not with words.

"Lowe. You are the best thing that ever happened to me. And I would never ask you to put Ana before me." My voice is little more than a whisper. "And if you ever put someone else before her, I'd love you a little less. But when you see her next, since I probably won't, will you give her a message from me? Tell her that she's as annoying as Sparkles. And that . . . that *thing* she isn't able to do? She shouldn't be sad about it. Because she'll grow into it. And she'll *definitely* be able to do it by the time she's twenty-five or so."

Lowe stares at me, confused—until the meaning clicks for him. His eyes dart from mine to Serena's, and I wish I had time to savor how incredibly wrong, and fucked up, and just *odd* this is: the two people who make up my entire universe, meeting under these ridiculous circumstances.

I hope one day the three of us will be able to laugh about this moment. I hope this is not the end. I hope that even if I'm not around, the two of them will be there for each other. I hope, I hope, I *hope*.

Serena nods.

Lowe nods.

Understanding runs through them like a current.

"Now," Lowe whispers.

All of a sudden, Owen steps forward. In a lightning-quick moment, Lowe's restraints are undone, and his body begins to shift. Contort. Merge and turn and transform. I turn to look at Serena and find that she's doing the same—the perfect, blindsiding distraction that none of the guards saw coming. Nor Vania. Nor Father.

"What are you—" he only has the time to say.

Because two large, majestic white wolves fill the room. The noise of tearing flesh rises above the screams, and I watch the two people I love the most hold absolutely nothing back.

CHAPTER 29

There are many matters to settle, and his pack needs him more than ever, but he cannot concentrate on anything but her. He understands why some Alphas take vows of celibacy and renounce love.

She distracts him. His feelings for her, they distract him.

THERE IS SOMETHING I'LL NEVER, EVER LET MYSELF LIVE DOWN, not until the day I kick the bucket, not until the moment I vanish into the nothingness of matter: in my weeks of living with the Weres, it never occurred to me to wonder where their clothes went when they shifted to wolf form.

It's so, *so* stupid of me.

And in the aftermath of the scariest night of my life, sitting in the Nest's stairwell, with Gabi treating the puncture wound Father's knife cut into the flesh of my collarbone, I simply cannot let go of it.

"Did you think they'd transform with us? *Sartorially?*" Alex leans against the handrail. He's sticking around for no reason other than to mock me. Or maybe he's genuinely interested—I cannot tell. All I know is, I miss when he was terrified of me. "You thought that the end result would be a wolf in a little sweater vest and a bow tie? Just to be clear, is that what you expected?"

"I don't *know* what I expected. But Serena's top was all tattered and stuck around her neck, and I'm just saying that it was disturbing to watch a pink shirt dangle from her while her teeth sank into Vania's throat." I rub my face with my palms, hoping to unsee the past two hours. When I look up again, Ludwig and Cal and another handful of seconds are walking down the hallway to Father's office. They stop in front of us, and . . .

We all know they were interrogating Mick. I wonder if it still looks like the Aster in there: purple and green blood splattered all over the walls. The most gruesome of flowers, finger-painted by the world's creepiest child.

"Is she still talking about the clothes?" Ludwig asks.

Alex nods with a deep sigh. Gabi bites back a smile.

"I just want to know what the hell she was thinking would happen to them," Cal mutters.

"I *didn't* think," I say. Defensively.

"Obviously," Alex mutters.

"Shouldn't you be *intimidated* by me? Also, what are *you* doing here?" This must be the most Weres in Vampyre territory ever.

"It was determined that an IT expert might be of use, and frankly, you lost all of your intimidation points."

"I can still drink you dry, nerd."

Owen arrives to interrupt our bickering. "Are you done here, Misery? I need you with me for a moment."

I follow him down the staircase with one last glare at Alex, mostly in silence. Owen got a bit beaten up during the fight: his black eye is courtesy of Vania, or maybe that auburn-haired guard who escorted him in. From the way he carries himself, I suspect his entire right side is bruised, too. When we turn into a dark hallway and are out of earshot, I ask quietly, "Are you okay?"

"I should ask *you* that."

I mull it. "I'd feel better if I could speak to Serena."

"She's with the ginger. The girl, not the guy."

"Juno. I know."

"Apparently, she doesn't quite have the whole turning-into-a-beast-and-then-back-into-a-person thing down, and she's still working on controlling her . . . I don't fucking know, wolfy impulses. Red took her for a run to—"

"I know," I repeat. I'm still worried. "And it's not 'turn.'"

"What do you mean?"

"The Weres prefer the term 'shift.'"

He gives me an appalled glance, like I'm a first-row nerd yelling *Teacher, pick me!* and then stops in front of a closed door. "I saw your face when I stepped into the office. You thought I was going to screw you over, didn't you?"

I resist the temptation to avert my gaze. "You did come in holding my husband captive."

"That was *his* idea. I called him about an hour after you guys drove away—we were finally able to get footage of the break-in in Serena's apartment."

So that's why Lowe left after we . . . better not think about that. "Let me guess—it was Mick."

He nods. "I showed Lowe the recordings, and he immediately recognized him. Misery, he freaked the fuck out."

"Yeah, Mick and Lowe go way back—"

"No, he freaked out because he knew that *you* were with Mick. I thought your boy toy was a pretty even-tempered guy, but he's actually *bloodcurdling.*"

I don't bother to deny it. "And what did you do?"

"The Weres were still monitoring the governor to see what his next step would be, and he made a call to Father. At that point, it became clear that they were collaborating on something, and that Mick was aiding them. Lowe told me to call Father and lie—the story was that once you and Mick disappeared, Lowe contacted me to find you because he thought I might be willing to help, and instead I took him captive. You've seen the rest." He squints at me. "Again, it was *his* idea."

"I didn't say anything—"

"I'm not going to screw you over, Misery."

I nod, feeling almost close to my twin. It's long forgotten, but familiar. "Neither will I."

"Very well, then." He points at the door. "You ready?" He doesn't say what's inside, but I already know.

Lowe is wearing a pair of jeans he must have found somewhere, and nothing else. He turns our way when we come in, but remains leaning against the wall, patient. A few feet from him there is a chair and, cuffed to it, a Vampyre.

Father.

He's covered in blood, mostly purple, but then again—so am I. And so is Owen, and everyone else who was in that office during the carnage. When Alex arrived on the scene, his first question to me was whether all the blood was making me hungry. Once we're back in Were territory, I plan to smear a pancake on the inside of a toilet and ask him the same.

If I ever go back to the Weres.

My eyes meet Lowe's, briefly and for entirely too long. What passes between us is too combustible a moment not to glance away immediately.

"You okay?" he asks.

No. "Yeah. You?"

"Yeah." He means *no*, but for now it doesn't matter.

Father is blindfolded, I assume to save some moron from wandering in and getting themselves thralled within an inch of their life. The headphones they put on him must be noise canceling, but he knows exactly who's in the room, from heartbeats and blood scent alone. His enforcers are gone, and so is his power. For the first time in his adult life, he's defenseless. I close my eyes and wait for feelings of any kind to hit me.

None arrive.

"May I?" Owen asks cordially, pointing at Father. Lowe nods, observing him calmly as he rips off the blindfold and the headphones. Owen crouches down, sitting on his haunches. It's my first time witnessing an interaction like this one: my brother as the active, dynamic part, and Father restrained and unmoving. Weak. Losing.

They regard each other. It's Father who finally breaks the silence by saying: "I want you to know that I would do all of it again." His voice is too strong for my taste, almost obscenely calm. I wish I could watch him beg for mercy, see him doubt his ridiculous righteousness and the courage of his stupid convictions. I wish he could suffer even just an ounce, even just at the end of it. I wish there was some comeuppance for everything he has done.

And then I don't have to wish. Because after nodding pensively, Owen grins. Wide.

"Fair enough. What *I* want *you* to know," he promises, voice low and clear, "is that as I take over your place on the council, I will work hard to undo every shitty little thing you have built in the last few decades. I'm going to broker alliances with the Weres and with Humans that won't just benefit *us*. I'm going to do everything I can to facilitate truces between *them*. And when this area is at peace and the Vampyres' influence is reduced to near insignificance, I'm going to take your fucking ashes and scatter them where the borders and the entry points used to be, so that Weres, and Humans, and Vampyres can step over them without even realizing it. *Daddy.*" He smiles once more, ferocious, *scary*.

Wow. My brother is . . . wow.

"Misery, anything you'd like to say to this wretched piece of shit before he can no longer hear you?"

I open my mouth. Then think better of it and close it.

What could I tell him? Is there anything that would hurt him even a hundredth of how much he has hurt *me* and the people I love? Maybe only: "Nah."

Owen chuckles, and Lowe's expression is at once tender and amused. Father doesn't give us the satisfaction of thrashing around, or yelling insults, or relinquishing control in any way. But his eyes meet mine before disappearing behind the blindfold. There is a defeated tinge to them, and I tell myself that maybe he knows: I will think of him as little as possible, for as long as I can.

"What would you like me to do with him?" Lowe asks once Father can't hear us. The question should be directed at Owen, but he's very much looking at *me*. Perhaps this is not a leader working on behalf of his people, but a Were, asking a question to his . . .

I hang my head. No. I'm not even going to think about the word. It's been abused and dragged in the mud enough for tonight.

"What happens if he stays alive? Actually, what happens if he gets killed? Would there be repercussions?"

"There is no official body regulating Were-Vampyre relationships. Yet." Lowe adds. "I assume that it would be up to the Vampyre council to seek retribution, or punishment—on your father, or on whoever executed him. Whoever takes his seat is going to have some say in that."

"Owen, then."

They share a glance. And after a split-second hesitation, Lowe says, "Or you."

Shockingly, Owen nods. And then they both look at me expectantly.

"You guys think *I* want to be part of the council?"

Lowe says nothing. Owen shrugs. "I don't know. Do you?"

A laugh explodes out of me. "What *is* this?"

"Father decided I'd be his successor decades ago." Owen looks dead serious. "I think we should stop doing as he says."

"Are you saying that if I want that seat, you'll hand it to me?"

"I . . ." He rolls his lips over his fangs. "I wouldn't be happy about it. And I'll warn you—our people would not like it. But they'd have to acknowledge you've done far more for the Vampyres than any of them, and eventually they'd make peace with it."

I didn't know Owen could be this sensible. I find it so mystifying, I actually stop and allow myself to consider the idea of a world where I can truly be at home among the Vampyres, if only because I am their duty-bound leader. I wouldn't be alone, wouldn't be rejected, wouldn't be constantly out of place. The appeal of it is . . .

Low to nonexistent. Honestly: fuck the Vampyres.

"What you said earlier," I tell Owen. "About working with the Weres and the Humans. You meant it, right? You weren't just fucking with Father?"

"Of course." He scowls, indignant. "Lowe and I are basically best friends."

Lowe's puzzled frown doesn't quite broadcast best friendship.

Owen snorts. "Thank you for the vote of confidence. It's truly inspirational to know that the Were Alpha and his bride, who also happens to be my goddamn sister, think that I'd be a great leader. Truly the support system of champions. *Assholes.*"

I smile. Lowe's lips twitch up, too. Our eyes catch, and it feels even more menacing than before, a dangerous storm coming, like a current buzzing up my spine and water after a drought.

It's frightening, this thing between us. I need to interrupt it. "Can I . . . I have questions," I hurry to say. "Where is Mick's son?"

"Owen and I have several people looking for him," Lowe says. He rubs his hand across the back of his neck, looking pained.

"And Mick? What's going to happen to him?"

His face sets. "I'll let you know when I decide."

"And Ana? My father—"

"—never knew where she was. She's safe."

Relief floods through me. "I'm glad."

"She'll be back as soon as the situation is resolved. Anything else you need to know?"

I press my lips together, wishing this was the time and place for more questions. Wishing we were alone.

Am I your mate?

Is it okay if it doesn't matter? Is it okay if I want to be?

How much of what you said, what I said, what everyone said was real?

Some of it must be, right?

"No." I glance at Owen. He's either unaware of how much I'd love for him to leave us alone, or doesn't care. The latter, probably.

"You still haven't told me what you'd like me to do with your father," Lowe says softly.

I glance at the chair. Father's posture is as impeccable as always, but with his pointed ears hidden by headphones and his white hair slightly mussed, he could almost pass for Human. How the mighty have fallen.

Maybe I'm truly horrible. Maybe he deserves it. Maybe it's a little of both. Still, I say: "I don't care. I leave it to you two."

When I walk past Lowe, the back of my hand brushes against his, and a shiver of undistilled warmth travels up my arm.

I grip the door handle, still feeling his heat in my fingers. Without turning, I add: "Unless the need arises, feel free to never tell me what you settle on."

—— ⋅∖∕⋅ ——

I FALL ASLEEP IN MY CHILDHOOD BEDROOM, WHICH IS THE WEIRD cherry on top of the weirdest fucking night.

In the month leading up to my wedding I was often at the Nest, but never in here. In fact, I haven't been here since my brief stint back in Vampyre territory after graduating as the Collateral. The place is fairly clean, and I wonder who's been dusting the empty shelves or changing the light bulbs, and on whose orders. I open empty drawers and unused closets. About an hour after the sun has risen, I go to sleep.

My bed is Vampyre style, which consists of a thin mattress on the floor and a wooden platform about three feet above it, ideal for protection from the light. *A tipped-over coffin, basically*, Serena said the first time she saw it, and I still hate her a bit for it. But it's deliciously comfortable, and I bemoan the fact that I could never find anything like this in Human territory, let alone among the Weres. Then, before I doze off, I wonder whether that's even relevant. What will happen to me next? With Owen ascending, will there even be a need for marriages of convenience between our people?

No. So maybe I'll go back to my own apartment. And pen testing.

But I'd walk into the sun before working with whatshisface—Pierce, yeah—before working with Pierce again. So I should probably refresh my CV and . . .

I wake up forty minutes before sundown, with a body next to mine. It's warm, very soft, and everything about it screams familiarity.

"Get your own bed, bitch," I say groggily, turning to Serena.

"Never." She yawns, huge, with no consideration for her stinky breath or my poor nose. "So."

"So." I reach up to clean my eyes, and can still smell the Vampyre blood under my fingernails. I should take a shower.

"Let's just get this over with," she starts. "I know you're mad, but—"

"Hang on. I'm not mad."

She blinks at me. "Oh."

"I'm not going to . . . I'm not mad, I promise."

She searches my face. "But?"

"No buts."

"But?"

"Nothing."

"But?"

"For fuck's sake, I told you—"

"Misery. *But?*"

I press my fingers into my eyes until golden spots appear. God, I hate it when people *know* me. "Just . . . why?"

"Why, what?"

"Why didn't you tell me?"

She bites the inside of her cheek. "Right. So. I kind of kept an unhinged number of secrets from you in the past year or so, and I'm not sure which one you're referring to, so—"

"The big one." My tone is flat. "That you're actually, you know. Another fucking species?"

"Oh." She scrunches her nose. "Right. Well."

"I thought you trusted me. I assumed you felt you could tell me everything and our friendship was unconditional, but maybe——"

"I do. I do trust you. It's . . ." She flinches. Then massages her forehead with the palm of her hand. "I wasn't sure, you know? At the beginning, especially, my body was being so weird, and there were these odd sensations, and it seemed bonkers. I wasn't sure whether I was having delusions, and it felt like the precise type of thing that I should avoid thinking about and just pray would go away. And then, when I really started suspecting . . . Well, for one, you guys hate Weres."

I gasp, mortally offended. "*I* don't."

"You make jokes about them all the time."

"What jokes?"

"Come on. They run after mail carriers, are obsessed with squirrels. There was that night we met that wet dog that stank so bad——"

"It was a *joke*. I had never even *smelled* a Were at the time!"

"Yeah, *well*." She takes a deep breath. "My blood is red. And when your father took me, I still wasn't able to shift. I wasn't sure. At that point, all I knew was that something weird and terrible and amazing was happening, and I swear, Misery, all I kept thinking about in the past six months was—what if I die? What if this thing inside me kills me? What is Misery going to do then? Am I going to drag her with me, am I going to be the reason my sister, the person I care about the most—the *only* person I fucking care about—will die, because of this weird codependency of ours, and——"

I reach out, closing my hand around hers, like we used to when we were kids.

Serena slows down. Stops. Then, after a few moments, she continues, and her voice is much quieter. "In the last three months I had lots of time. Obviously. And there was a surveillance camera in the attic, but it had several blind spots. Before, I had felt like I needed information. I had researched the possibility that I might be a Were, or something else altogether, like I would normally research an article. But once I was alone, all I could do was research myself. Try to *feel* it. And I practiced. Shifting is like flexing a muscle, except that the muscle is also in the brain. And I still don't really understand what's up with me, and what about me is Were or Human, but . . ."

She takes a deep breath.

Another.

Another, and I squeeze her hand.

"So." She's not crying, but I can hear the tears in her voice. "Can you . . . Can you once again be my only good friend in the whole fucking world, Bleetch?"

I smile.

Then laugh.

Then she laughs.

"You talk like we ever stopped."

She *is* crying now, and I'd be, too, but I can't. Instead I scoot forward, bumping into a million different elbows, and hug her.

She hugs me back, tighter.

"You can be whatever you are, and you'll still be my friend. And I won't ever have any issues with you being a Were," I say into her hair, which is matted with soil and *God*, this baby wolf needs a bath just as bad as I do. "In fact, I think I might be in love with one."

CHAPTER 30

It could have been anyone who was sent to him. Any Vampyre.
And yet, it was her.
A roll of the dice.
The luck of the draw.

I DON'T SEE LOWE FOR THE FOLLOWING THREE DAYS.

Or: I do see Lowe. Several times. Constantly, even. But it's never Lowe, the guy who hung out with me on the roof and drew me baths and once pulled back my hair to stare at the tips of my ears and then mouthed *pretty* to himself. It's always Lowe the Alpha. Discussing urgent matters. Shuttling between Were and Vampyre territory with Cal and another gaggle of seconds in tow. Conferring with Owen and Maddie Garcia in closed-door meetings I don't care to be part of, but find myself wishing I were.

Serena and I are attached at the hip, surgically, like we're twelve again and figuring out trigonometry together. We go on long, comfortably silent walks at dusk. We make jokes about the fact that she can grow fur on her elbow at will. We hang out in my room, Serena reading up on everything that's happened while she was cut off from the world, me blinking sleepily at the black dots on the ceiling, trying to figure out whether they're tiny bugs or specks of dirt.

Somehow, I'm always wrong.

"We have good genetic testing registries," Juno tells us when she comes over to chat with Serena. "We can work on figuring out who your Were parent was. At the very least, what pack and huddle they came from."

Serena looks at me, searching, and my first instinct is to encourage her. Then I see her throat jerking fitfully, once and then again. "Maybe you should take some time to think it through," I say, and she nods in relief, like she needed my permission to even consider it.

It's not like her, the indecision. Then again, Serena is not like *her* anymore. Serena was held alone in a windowless attic for months, and that's *after* she started getting an inkling that maybe she was another species. Serena falls asleep at odd hours and then tosses and turns, and I've caught her weeping more times in the past week than in the previous decade of our acquaintance. Serena seems . . . not diminished, but distracted. Insubstantial. Transitioning.

Later that evening, while she absentmindedly braids her hair and stares out the window, she murmurs, "I wonder whether it'd be okay to spend some time with the Weres. Just to see how they are." It occurs to me that Juno is the first of Serena's people who hasn't abducted her, imprisoned her, or abandoned her.

"I need to ask Lowe something," I tell Owen the following day, when I catch him between council meetings. He's staring at the touch screen in Father's office with a deep frown. The bloodstains haven't been taken care of—or maybe they have, and the near black marks are permanent mementos. "Where is he?"

"In his home, I assume."

"When will he be back?"

"I don't know." He looks stressed, like he's been running a hand through his hair. Power does *not* become him—not yet, at least. "The negotiations are over for now, so not for a while."

"Oh." My eyes widen, and Owen finally looks up.

"What?"

"Nothing. I guess I thought I'd go back with him? Since I live there."

"Do you want to?"

"What do you mean?"

"You don't have to live there if you don't want to."

"What about the alliance?"

He shrugs. "Next week the council will take a formal vote on the parameters of our alliance with the Weres. In the meantime, Lowe and I see eye to eye, and neither of us is going to ask you or Gabi to serve as Collateral any longer."

"I doubt the council will approve of—"

"The council has enabled Father to do a bunch of very illegal things, which they are now scrambling to pretend they knew nothing about, and even if they weren't intent on covering their asses, I'm bringing them a conditional alliance with the Weres and the Humans. So yes, they'll approve whatever I tell them to." Okay, maybe I was wrong. Power *does* become him. "Gabi's already back in Were territory. You're free to live wherever you like, so let me ask you again: Do you want to live with Lowe?"

It's such a baring, direct question, I can only deflect with another. "Has he said anything?"

"Like what?"

"Like, does he want me to—does he expect me to . . . Has he said *anything*?"

He gives me a merciless look. "I am not an agony aunt."

I tilt my head. "You look like it, though."

"Get the fuck out of my office."

I step out to avoid the paperweight he's eyeing. Then I realize I never got what I came for. I make an executive decision: retrace my steps, steal Owen's car keys, and a few minutes later Serena and I are on the road, crossing the bridge as a pallid sun sets behind the oaks. I don't have any diplomatic paperwork on me, but when I declare my name the Were at the checkpoint puts me through the face scanner and lets me through.

I drop Serena off at Juno's and smile as I watch them prance into the woods in wolf form, the wind weaving ripples through their soft fur. Were company is what Serena needs right now, and I'm happy to facilitate that. Also, I'm staggeringly relieved that she's asking for help and not shutting me out.

"Text me when you're done chasing moles, or smelling each other's buttholes, or whatever," I yell after them. "I'm going to Lowe's!"

His home is unlocked, as usual, but uncharacteristically empty. I toe off my shoes and pad up the wooden stairs, wondering if blood bags are still being automatically delivered for me. When I'll get to see Ana again. Whether Serena and Sparkles/Sylvester will ever be reunited.

My stomach drops as I enter my room. The place looks un-inhabited, more than when I first moved in. My knickknacks, books, movies, and even some clothes have been put back inside boxes.

I'm not welcome here anymore. I am being evicted.

There's probably a reason. Lowe wouldn't just kick you out.

But I can't twist myself into not caring. There is a shrinking pull in my heart, and if I'm not being thrown out, I'm still being inched away. I have served my purpose, and—

"Misery?"

I turn around and my heart flips.

Lowe. Staring at me in the warm glow of the ceiling lights. Not smiling per se, but radiating happiness at seeing me. He's wearing a leather jacket and his hands are at his sides, a bit stiff. Like he's consciously keeping them there. "Hey."

"Hey." I smile. He smiles back. Then we're silent for long enough for me to remember our last conversation alone.

Too long.

"I wasn't sure if I could . . . I hope I'm not trespassing."

"Trespassing?" His delight at seeing me fades into confusion, which morphs into a stern sort of understanding. "You live here."

I don't ask, *Do I?* because that would sound insecure and whiny and maybe a little passive-aggressive, and I just remembered that I'm none of these things. Not with Lowe, at least.

"I dropped Serena off, and I think it would be great if she and Ana were able to meet. It could do Serena some good, and vice versa. I doubt they're the only two half Weres out there, but . . ."

"As far as we know."

I nod. "Would that be okay?"

He scratches his jaw. His beard is the longest it's ever been since I met him. What have the last few days been like for him? "I'm planning to tell Ana about her parents once Koen brings her back. I was going to save that conversation for later, but there are simply too many people who know, and I don't want her to find out from someone else. After that, I'd love for her to meet Serena. And of course, Serena is always welcome among us. She is part of our pack, if she wants to be. I tasked Juno with checking in with her while I was gone, but I'll arrange a meeting to explain everything now that I'm back."

"Back?"

"We were dealing with Emery."

My eyes widen. "Yikes?"

He lets out a soft chuckle and leans a shoulder against the door. "Indeed."

"We kinda suspected the wrong Were, didn't we?"

"When it came to Ana. We finally have enough evidence to hold Emery accountable for the activities of the Loyals, including an explosion at a school that happened three months ago. I went to inform her that there will be a tribunal. But when it comes to my sister . . ." His expression darkens. "It's not her fault if I chose to believe Mick."

"Did you find his son?"

"Yes. They're together, heavily guarded. I'm not sure yet what I'm going to do." He presses his lips together.

"I'm really sorry, Lowe," I say heavily. "I know how much you trusted him."

"Any other Were, I'd have realized that they were lying to me. But Mick . . . his scent had changed drastically. It was sour and bitter and overpowering, but I figured it was grief. That losing one's mate and son would do that to someone."

I take a step closer, wanting to comfort him, not quite sure how. Eventually I just repeat an utterly inadequate "I'm sorry." I try to continue, to unspool that ball of words that weighs on my stomach so densely, but the sound dies on my lips. I'm stunted, incapable of being coherent.

"It's not like you," he says with a slim smile.

"What isn't?"

"Not saying exactly what you think."

"Right. Yeah." A gust of irritation sweeps over me. I bounce my foot to stave it off. "It was easier, being honest with you, when I thought you were being honest with me."

He frowns. "You can speak honestly with me, Misery. Always."

I let out an impatient breath, then march to him, ready to attack. I only stop when I'm so close, he has to bend his neck to look me in the eye. "Why would I, though? So you can use my deepest wounds and what you know about my past to hurt me when you decide that you should push me away?"

He looks crestfallen at the memory of the things he told me, as though they hurt him as much as me. "I'm sorry," he whispers.

"You lied," I accuse. "You said all of that—and it was all a lie."

He doesn't deny it, which makes me angrier. Instead he inhales, deep and slow until his lungs are full.

"Why?" I prod. When no answers come, I lift my hand to his face. "I could force you to tell me the truth." The flat of my thumb presses between his brows. "I could thrall you."

His smile looks sad. "You already have, Misery."

I squeeze my eyes shut. Then open them to ask, "Am I your mate?"

"I meant what I said," he says calmly. "You should not use Were words you cannot comprehend."

"Right." I spin on my heels angrily and stalk away. Fuck this. If he didn't want me to use Were words, then he shouldn't have given them to me.

"Misery." Lowe's hand closes against my wrist, stopping me in my tracks. When I try to wriggle out, his arm wraps around my waist to haul me back into him.

His heat is scorching. The scratch of his cheek against the crook of my neck, deliciously coarse.

I hear him breathe in again, this time without restraint. "My feelings. My wishes. My desires . . . They're mine, Misery. Not yours to deal with."

I try to twist in his grip, furious. "Of course they are. What the hell does that even mean—"

"It means that I don't want you to make decisions based on *my* needs. I don't want you to be with me because you have to, because you're worried that otherwise I'll be miserable." I wish I could see his eyes. His voice is at once thick and rough and low, as if someone stuffed as much emotion in it as possible and then tried to erase it. "At the wedding, when you were near me for the first time, I was angry. I was furious that for some joke of fate I had found my mate, and they were someone I could never really love. I wanted you more than anything else, and yet I felt *trapped* by you. And then I began spending time with you. I began knowing you, and you made me happy. You made me better. You made me want to be every part of myself, even the ones I thought I'd left behind. And one day I woke up and realized that if you didn't smell like the best thing in the world, I still wouldn't want you any less."

"Lowe—"

"But I *can* survive without you, Misery. All I need to do is . . ." He exhales a warm, soundless laugh. "Be without you. All I need to do is bear it. And it won't be good. But I think it would still be better than watching you become unhappy. Than letting my love for you bind you to me when you would rather—"

"What about *my* love for you?" I turn around in his arms, and this time he lets me. "Can *that* bind me to you? Do I have your permission to reciprocate what you feel?"

His lips part.

"No. *No.* You don't get to be surprised about what I feel for you. Not when I've been nothing but honest about it, and you know what?" My hands are starting to shake, and I fist them against his chest. "No. If I want to be in love with my stupid Were husband, I'm going to be in love with my stupid Were husband, whether he wants to admit that he loves me back or not. And there's more—I'm going to be living here, so you can unpack those boxes right now. I'm going to be in Ana's life, because she likes me and I *somehow* like her, okay? And I'm going to stick around Were territory, because my best friend is one of you, and for once in my life people have actually been pretty fucking nice to me, and I like living on a lake, and I wouldn't mind being the bloodsucking weirdo of this pack, and—" I could sputter my way through more threats, but he interrupts me.

"The windows. I'm changing them."

"How does that even—"

"I saw the ones you have at the Nest. Owen explained how they work. I wasn't moving you out, I just didn't want your stuff to get damaged."

"Oh." It doesn't compute. "That's very, ah . . . thoughtful. And expensive?"

He doesn't seem to care. Instead his forehead comes down against mine, and his hand engulfs my cheek. His voice is a broken whisper. "I'm afraid, Misery. I'm terrified."

"Of what?"

"That there is no world, no scenario, no reality in which I'll gracefully allow you to leave me. That if I don't let you go now, five years, five months, five days down the line, I won't be able to. Every second, I want you too much, and every second, I'm on the verge of wanting you more. Every second is my last chance to do the decent thing. To let you live your life without taking up all of it—"

I tip my chin up to press my mouth to his. We've exchanged many kisses, and this is probably the most restrained of all of them. But there is something desperate and frantic about the way his lips cling to mine, something utterly lost.

I pull back. Smile. Say, "Shut up, Lowe."

He laughs, Adam's apple bobbing. "Not the appropriate way to speak to the Alpha of the pack you claim to want to join."

"Right. Shut up, Alpha." I kiss him again, lingering this time. He holds me tight, bruising, like I'll bolt the second he stops. "You've seen me with Serena," I murmur against his lips. "I'm not the type to change my mind."

"No. You're not."

"I get it, feeling pinned down by the mate thing." I take a hurried step back, suddenly wondering whether this conversation requires physical distance. "It has to be hard, to feel like you couldn't walk away even if you wanted to. Like someone is going to be your problem forever—"

He shakes his head, eyes burning into mine. "You're not a problem, Misery. You're a *privilege*."

My heart slows to a thud just as Lowe's picks up, three beats of his for every one of mine. Our bodies, screaming how different we are at the most basic, fundamental level.

I don't care, though. He doesn't, either. "We'll try, then. Isn't that what any relationship is, in the end? Meeting someone and wanting to be with that person more than with anyone else, and trying to make it work. And I . . . maybe I don't have the hardware, but the software is here, and I get to program it. Maybe you're not *meant* for me the way I'm meant for you, but I'm going to *choose* you anyway, over and over and over again. I don't need a special genetic permit to feel sure that you are my—"

I don't get to finish the sentence. Because he's kissing me ravenously, like he's never going to stop, and I'm kissing him back in the same way. The intensity, this time, is spiked with relief.

"You're here," he says against my neck, pushing me backward.

It's not a question, and not for me. His strong hands cup the back of my head and won't let me nod. "You're staying." I feel the matter settle inside him, the certainty of us.

A different part of Lowe takes over, and he pushes me back into the wall.

"Mate. My mate," he groans, like he hasn't allowed himself to think of the word in relation to himself before this moment. When he picks me up and carries me to the bed, the air rushes out of me. "My mate," he says again, voice deeper than usual, so rough that I tie my arms around his neck and pull him down, hoping it'll soothe the urgency in him, the frantic trembling in his hands. His breath is staggered in my hair, so I push against his broad shoulders until he flips us around. Then I'm the one setting the pace, with languid, savoring kisses, and that vibrant tension inside him slowly melts.

I inhale the scent of his blood, heady and potent. "I love this," I say. "I love *you*."

He sucks in an incredulous breath. Warmth crawls into my stomach, up my backbone. I pull off my shirt, and he follows me eagerly with his hands and his mouth. He nips at my collarbone, sucks at my nipples, nibbles at my breasts. With every touch I feel like we're slowly being welded together—until he stops.

His long fingers flex around my hips, impossibly tight, then go limp.

When he pulls back to look at me, his lips are dark red, eyes stark and clear.

"We might need to stop."

I laugh, already out of breath. "Is this another bout of Alpha Were guilt?"

"Misery." He stops. Licks his lips. "I'm *really* wound up. We've been apart, and you smell so damn good, and you said some . . .

intoxicating things, like that you're here to stay, and I'm closer to the edge than—"

I laugh against the edge of his jaw. "Okay. Before you devolve into more self-loathing, let me just say, I'm going to drink your blood again. Okay, Lowe?"

He hisses a low "Fuck," and nods eagerly.

"And we're going to have sex."

His hips press against mine. Our breaths hitch. "Okay. Okay," he repeats, suddenly determined. Gathering his self-control. "I can stop. I'm going to stop when—"

"You're not going to stop." I kiss his cheek, tighten my arms around his neck, and then whisper in his ear. "When your . . . knot happens, you're going to . . ." Tie? Hitch? *Bind*? I will need a better vocabulary. "Do that inside me."

Lowe squeezes me to his chest. "If I hurt you—"

"Then you'll hurt me a bit. Like *I* hurt you when I feed from you, since I'm ripping your skin. And then after a few minutes it gets really good for me, and I think it does for you, too."

His only answer is a deep grunt. It seems involuntary, and I kiss his lower lip to avoid laughing.

"It's going to be okay. If it's not, we'll talk about it. We are different species, but this is long-term, and we should be honest about our wants and needs, and it's clear that you *want* this, and probably even *need* it—"

He closes his eyes. Like he really does need it.

But most importantly: "And the thing is, I *want* you to. It's different, I won't deny that, and maybe it won't work great, but the idea of it is kind of . . ."

"Weird?"

"Actually, I was going to say . . ." My mouth is dry. "Hot."

I see his pupils widen, and then it's a done deal. Lowe's self-control snaps, and I'm underneath him. My clothes come off with frenzied tugs, then his follow, and I remember the first time we did anything that approached this. His restrained hesitation in the bathtub. I can barely recognize it in the way he touches me, the way his hand shapes my lower back to arch my body into his like an offering.

We both mean to ease into this, but he's harder than I thought and I'm wetter than he expected. It takes very little, just a few thrusts through my folds, but we're on the brink. The blunt head of his cock is bumping against my clit, and when he pulls back, it's caught against my entrance, ready to slide in.

"You're so warm inside. So wet, just for my knot." He presses a kiss at my temple and whispers something that could be *soft*. Then he pushes deep inside me. He's big in a stretching, satisfying way that rings faint alarm bells in my head. I squirm, feeling pinned, impaled, and it's the readjustment we both need.

He slides in to the hilt.

I arch up, slapping my palms against the mattress.

Our hearts stop at the same time, and then resume. Mine with lagging thuds. His, a beating drum.

"Misery. I want to live inside you."

He gathers me in his arms. I lift my chin to kiss the corner of his mouth, and we don't ease into the sex. Lowe pulls all the way out and then thrusts back inside in an uneven, pounding rhythm, without pacing himself. Last time, he tried to make it last. This time he's hurtling headfirst into what's coming, and my body might not understand, but it responds enthusiastically. His gaze holds mine as he fucks me, the pressure of his hips spreads me open, and when my eyes flutter closed I surrender to the pleasure. He pants into my ear, things like *good* and *okay*, garbled talk that doesn't make sense, because he's well beyond thought. My internal muscles tighten to keep him inside longer, squeezing around his cock, and that liquid heat I'm now familiar with climbs within me.

And then something changes. Lowe pumps once, twice, so hard that my hands slip over his sweaty shoulders. The crescendo of heavy breathing stops abruptly, and my eyes open.

I expect to find him worried again, to have to reassure him, but his control has unraveled past that. He commands, "Eyes on mine," and there is no uncertainty in his voice, just the knowledge that this is how it's supposed to be. I cannot speak, so I nod. He nods back and rasps, "It's starting."

A moment later I feel an impression of immense pressure. He fills me slowly, thrusting languidly once, twice, until the swelling at the base of his cock is too big to slide back out. Then he's shaking, grunting from deep inside him. I run my teeth down his neck, and he moans, cradling my face to his throat and my hips to his groin. The bulge of his knot grows larger and larger.

I feel strange. Full. Nice. I might even feel . . .

"I'm going to do it, Misery. I'm going to come where I'm supposed to." His voice is barely comprehensible. "I'm going to pop a knot in your tight little—" A sudden shift, and the pressure increases. Lowe is coming, his orgasm a powerful thing that neither of us is ready for. He tries to get deeper, even when there's nowhere to go, even past the moment where I think his pleasure should have ended. I make myself pliant and welcoming, until he seems to recover enough presence of mind to say, "My beautiful mate. Taking it so well." Another wave of pleasure crashes over him as he spurts inside me, and his neck strains back, eyes glazed.

I circle my hips, testing, tugging, and find that he's lodged into me, and we're tethered together, and yes, it feels . . .

"Good," I say. Just on the edge of pain. But also, I'm a being made of heat and sensation. My muscles twitch, and he exhales, still shuddering inside me. The spasms of his climax contracting his big body. "This is so *good*. I just . . ."

It feels so nice, I need more contact. More friction. I need him to move even if he can't. I try to fuck myself over his knot, but there is no give. I try to squeeze around him, and Lowe lets out a breathless laugh. He seems to recover himself from the daze of his orgasm, just enough to shush me and reach between us.

It takes so little, just a brush of his thumb, and then I'm coming, too. My eyes roll in the back of my head, and I've never felt anything so violently, madly, painfully *good*—

"*Lowe*." I'm scared of how intense it is. But he lets out a wordless groan, bites my collarbone, and I know he feels exactly like I do, the pleasure brutal, pulsating, impossible to stop.

"My beautiful mate, coming all over my knot. We're going to do this every day," he husks in my ear. "And when you're ready, I'll bite you where it counts. I'll leave a scar, and I'll lick it every morning and every night. Okay?"

I nod. Wild, bottomless ecstasy pulses sweetly inside me. *It works*, I think. *We work.* But I don't bother saying it, because it's obvious. Instead I ask, "What—what now?"

He shudders and flips us until I'm draped on top of him. His hands shake slightly as he traces the swell of my back. His nails feel . . . no. I must be imagining. "Now . . ." He closes his eyes and arches his hips, as if trying to get deeper inside me. I'm not certain it works, but the knot drags beautifully against my walls. It rides an exquisite line between pleasure and pain, and triggers more spasms on my end. Then on his. "*Fuck*," he mutters briefly. And once he can speak again, he growls, "Now, everything is how it should be. I have you where I want you."

"How long?"

"I don't know." He kisses my temple. "A long time, I hope."

"So, if I really needed to leave to make an important phone call . . ."

His grip tightens on my hips so suddenly, I nearly laugh. Lowe moves down to my lips, kissing me deeply for a moment. "Are you sure it doesn't hurt?"

"No. It's . . ." *Extraordinary. Fantastic. Oddly beautiful.* "I think I like Were sex."

"Not Were sex." His eyes hold mine for a long beat. "*Mate* sex."

I feel myself smile at the word. "Is this going to happen every time?"

"I don't know," he repeats, hand coming up to push my sweaty strands back. "The way I feel, I can't imagine that it won't."

"Because we—" I stop when I notice his hand. Most of it is still in Human form, but his nails are halfway to turning into claws.

"Sorry," he says, sheepish. I watch him make a concerted effort to retract them, amazed by his body. The way it feels inside mine. The things it can do. "I'm not as in control as I should be. It's all really . . ."

"New?"

"Good. Like nothing else, ever."

"Is there something Weres usually do? Something I should be doing?"

He laughs in silent astonishment and shakes his head. "If there were, I wouldn't know. I wouldn't want it. You are perfect, and I . . ." His fingers slide between us, past the sweat of our bellies, making me twitch with more pleasure. My muscles flutter around him, and in response, I feel more liquid flood inside me. And when the new wave of pleasure is over, and I'm gasping on top of him, I realize that Lowe is touching me where we're joined. Where his cock has locked inside me. Like he needs tactile proof that this is really happening.

When he turns us on our sides, one of my long legs hiked on top of his, I can feel his come drip outside of me even past the seal of our bodies. The mess we're making, of the bed and of each other. Somehow, it seems like a good thing.

Outside, the waves crash against the lakeshore. Lowe's fingers wrap around my cheek. I feel the pleasure rise inside me once more, and I settle in for the long haul.

———— ✶ ————

IT'S STILL THE MIDDLE OF THE NIGHT WHEN I WAKE UP. I'M LYING face down on the bed, my cheek buried in a pillow, feeling limp and wrung out, as though a lifetime's worth of sensation has been crammed into and then squeezed out of my body.

It's surprisingly lovely.

Lowe is next to me, propped on one elbow, touching me all over in a way that seems half distracted, half compulsive. Traveling the dip that joins my shoulder blades. Following the round contours of my ass. Combing his fingers through my hair and tracing the tip of my ear. Cupping right between my legs, uncaring, or maybe excited by the slick mess he left there, eager to push his spend back inside me.

I let my eyelids flutter open and observe him observing every curve and angle and slope of my body, entranced by the entranced look in his eyes. He is focused, lost in the simple touch, and several minutes pass before he glances up at my face and finds me awake. His smile is at once reserved and hesitant and proud and luminous.

I want him—I want *this* with him—so much, so forcefully, it's equal parts terrifying and soaring.

"Hi."

I smile back. With fangs. "How long did it take for it to . . . ?"

"About thirty minutes." He leans over to trail open-mouthed kisses across the line of my shoulder. His hand curves around my ass as he murmurs into my ear, "You did so good, Misery. It can't have been easy, but you took me so well. Like you were made for it."

Blood rushes to my cheeks. I shift, savoring the rich soreness within my body. "Considering how busy you are with Ana and your pack, we might have to schedule sex."

It's meant as a joke, but he nods solemnly. "Pencil me into your calendar."

"What about early Sunday mornings? Before ten a.m. though, or I'm going to crash on you."

"Fuck that. Save two hours, every day."

I laugh and stare at the green flush that lingers on his sharp cheekbones, marveling. *Mine*, I think, happy, covetous, greedy. It's a new feeling, belonging. Owning.

"Did I hurt you?" he asks softly, and I laugh once more.

"Do I look like I hurt?"

He hesitates. "It lasted a long time, and it worked . . . maybe it worked a little too well for me. I nearly blacked out for a while there, and I doubt I was at my most observant."

"No, I do not hurt, Lowe." I hold his eyes and ask evenly, "What about you?"

His look is withering, and I feel like laughing again. He and I. Together. The greatest thing of all time that never should have happened.

"Serena might come looking for me," I say. "I don't want her recently traumatized self to stumble upon an interspecies sex moment and get even *more* traumatized, so—"

"She's half Were and half Human," Lowe says. I watch him

curiously until he continues to make his point. "Unless a whole lot of hybrids pop out of the woodwork, she's only ever going to have interspecies relationships."

"Oh." I try to think through the implications of it, but I have to give up. My brain is mushy, mellow with remainders of pleasure, and a loud sort of quiet, and the scent of Lowe's blood. "Either way, I should shower."

"No," he commands brusquely, in his Alpha voice. His muscles coil, like he's getting ready for a fight. Then he must realize the ridiculousness of his reaction, because he scrunches his eyes shut, throat working.

I tilt my head. "You used to be okay with me taking baths."

"It's different. There is a lot going on." He points at his head, but then looks down at his body. *A lot going on inside me*, he means. "I don't think I'm going to be able to let you out of my sight for a couple of days. Or weeks." He sounds unapologetic and remorseful—a combination I did not think was possible. "And right now, you smell like me. Like you wouldn't believe it, Misery. You smell like me from the *inside*, and every damn cell is screaming at me that making you that way is the best thing I've ever done in my life, maybe the only good thing, and I can't let you—"

"Lowe." I shift up to my elbows and lean forward to kiss him on the mouth, stopping the torrent of words. "Will you come take a shower with me?" I pull back and smile. "That way, you can replace the scent right away, and you don't need to let me out of your sight?"

The tension instantly leaves his body. His eyes soften. "That, I can do."

He carries me to his bathroom, and the warm jet of water soothes me as much as his hands following every drop's journey on my body. I close my eyes, tip my head back, and let him touch me in that compelled, absorbed manner that appears to be his new normal. He seems to have accepted this—*us*—effortlessly, unconditionally, but I cannot help but wonder.

"Lowe?"

"Mmm?"

"Since *I'm* your mate, and since I don't really plan to, you know, let go of you . . . you'll never be able to do *this* with a Were," I say without opening my eyes. "You'll never get the hardware experience."

His soapy palms lather my skin, lingering too long on my breasts. "Any idea of doing any of this with a Were died the night I met you." I hear the dismissal in his words. What he adds is a murmur, more for himself than for me. "There wouldn't be anyone else, anyway. Even if you didn't want me, I couldn't."

"But the fact remains that I have way more limitations than you. Is it going to be weird, that we're never going to go for a run in wolf form together? That we'll never take a walk in the sun? Have a meal together? We'll even have to figure out a sleep schedule that fits for both of us."

His thumb and forefinger close around my chin and raise it, gentle but determined, until I'm forced to meet his eyes. "No," he simply says. It's a more potent reassurance than any long speech or vehement denial. Then he pushes a strand of hair behind my ears, and leans forward to suck at one of those spots on my neck that seem to be his magnetic north. He hums and softly begins to scrape over it with his teeth.

"You can go ahead, then," I tell him.

He nips softly. "Mmm?"

"Bite me, if you want." I feel his broad chest stiffen against mine. "Like all the mate scars I've seen."

A deep, resonating rumble rises from his chest. For a brief moment, his grip tightens on my waist almost painfully. Then he lets go, looking as though he's made of steel and restraint. "No."

"If you think I'll change my mind—"

"I don't. But not now."

"Not now."

"There are rituals. Customs. Things that mean something to us. To me," he adds. "I want to see you in those obscene ceremonial marks again. I want to put them on you. Alone, this time—I don't fucking need anyone around to see you like that and get any ideas. And when I finally bite you, it won't be on your neck." He lets out a rueful laugh. "Nothing as dignified for us, Misery."

Oh. "Where?"

His palm rounds my throat. Cups my nape. The pad of his thumb traces down my spine, just one or two vertebrae. "Here. I think I'll bite you here." He says it like it's a secret, filthy plan he's been working on for a while, and then lets out a rueful, frustrated sound. "You'll wear your hair up, and people will see it, and they will know that I took my beautiful Vampyre bride the way wolves do, and that she loved it. And you will be good for me and let me, won't you?"

I would let you right this moment, I think, but don't bother saying it. I know Lowe by now, and the things he's accustomed to denying himself.

"I look forward to that." His pupils widen as though I just promised him riches beyond all comprehension. He deserves the world. He deserves everything he's ever wished for. "In the meantime, would you like *me* to bite *you*?"

He swears softly when my mouth reaches for one of the glands at the base of his throat, and then whispers "Fuck, yes," when my teeth pierce into it. I run my thumb over the gland on the other side, feeling his shudders and hearing the echoes of *please* and *more* and *take all you need*. Lowe was hard before, but now I can taste his impatience in the copper of his blood, and when he slides his fingers deep inside me, when his breath becomes erratic and he orders me to come, come right *now* so he can fuck me again, I can only let my pleasure roll through my body in subsuming waves. After, he picks me up and presses me against the tiled wall. I wrap my legs around his hips and welcome him between my thighs.

He pushes inside, and this time it's as easy as in a dream. I feel the burning stretch and let my nails draw half moons on his solid back. *I can't believe you once thought this wouldn't work*, I almost say, almost laugh, but his blood tastes too good to stop drinking, and I'm mindless from the sensation of him deep inside me, even deeper than before.

"You like this, don't you?" he whispers into my skin, and my responding squeeze around his cock has his mouth falling open against my shoulder. "*Fuck*. I can feel it already. I can feel it swelling again already— Misery, can you—?"

I'm too busy feasting on his blood to tell him how much I *can*, how much I want it. I can show him, though. I suck harder at his gland and he groans and pounds into me so hard and so deep, for a moment neither of us can breathe.

Then I feel the first flutters of pleasure coursing through my body, feel Lowe's knot quickly expand inside me and tie me to him, and under the balmy jet of the water, I smile into his vein.

EPILOGUE

Lowe

S HE MAKES LOTS OF "YOU ARE OFFICIALLY CONDEMNED TO A lifetime of Misery" jokes, and Lowe isn't sure he found them funny at first, let alone now that it's been a week of having her back, but he cannot help being delighted every single time.

Even as he sighs and shakes his head disapprovingly.

"To the right. Actually, to the left. Actually, just let *me* do it," she grumbles, stealing the hammer from his hand. They're hanging a picture on the wall of what's to become Ana's room once again. It's silly, something Lowe drew off the cuff yesterday, because that's what he's been: Spontaneous. Inspired. Happy.

A giant, Godzilla-like Sparkles towering over the Hollywood Sign—that happens to spell LILIANA—is not Lowe's usual artistic fare. And he didn't think the result was *that* good. But when he left his sketch pad open on the kitchen counter, Misery and Serena got a glimpse, and his every protest was met with rolled eyes and accusations that he was fishing for compliments. As soon as the sun went down, they stole his car and drove around for hours just to find the perfect frame.

And while they were gone, Lowe moved Misery's boxes to the adjacent room. She'll just be in Lowe's, since that's what makes the most sense.

Just be with him.

His mate.

With him.

He hasn't quite gotten used to the idea. It's possible that when it comes to feelings like the ones he has for Misery, big and overwhelming and all-encompassing, accustoming is not something that happens, ever. The raw preciousness might never wear off. And whenever he dwells on the future, the possibilities, his heartbeat always picks up like it's in a race against itself.

And Misery always notices.

"What's up with that?" she asks, words mumbled around the nail between her teeth. "Cardiac event?" She gives him a side look with her pretty lilac eyes. Her profile is soft, delicate lines punctuated by the dramatic points of her ear and teeth and chin. It nearly knocks the air out of his lungs.

He doesn't know how to answer her. So he just moves closer, trailing a hand up her back while she hammers into the wall. When that's not enough, he wraps his arms around her torso. Inhales her exhilarating, mind-bending scent. Closes his eyes.

He wasn't alone before her. If someone had asked, he wouldn't have admitted to being unhappy. He had a pack and a sister to see to, things to be passionate about, friends he'd give his life for. He never thought he was missing anything. But now . . .

He's not sure he deserves the warmth of his current life, but he'll keep it anyway.

"Hi," Misery says, as though they haven't been together the entire evening, since the very second she woke up. She sets the hammer and nail down on her dresser. Her pale hand curls softly around his forearm. He feels deep, grounding happiness.

"Hey," he says.

She starts tracing letters into his skin, and he wants to tell her to slow down, to spell the words again. But then he picks up on an L, and a V, and a Y, and he thinks that maybe he can guess—

"The pest has arrived," she whispers excitedly as a car pulls up the driveway under the window. Misery wriggles out of his hug, and Lowe swallows a sullen grunt that he's not his mate's first and only preoccupation. Then he follows her downstairs.

He hasn't seen Ana for over two weeks, but his sister barely gives him a perfunctory hug, too busy showing Miresy and her new friend Serena the new carrier Uncle Koen bought for Sparkles.

Lowe bites back a smile and walks outside just as his closest friend gets out of his car. "Thank you. I owe you one."

Koen snorts. "Bro, you owe me ten. And not because of Ana."

"What else?"

"Emery has been blowing up the family chat. Among other things, apparently." He shrugs at Lowe's lifted eyebrow. "What? Too soon?"

Lowe sighs and gestures him inside. "Come in. I'll catch you up on the shitshow of the past ten days."

"Very excited to hear all about—"

One single step inside the house, and Koen halts as though he just walked into a pile of bricks. His palm reaches for the wall in search of support.

"What the hell?" Lowe stares at him with a frown. When no reply comes, he turns to study his friend. His body is vibrating, ever so slightly. His pupils contract, like they often do when a Were is on the brink of shifting. And his eyes . . .

Lowe follows Koen's gaze. It's trained on a small figure crouched on the living room floor. She's currently scratching the chin of a purring Sparkles and murmuring apologies at him.

Serena.

Koen's gaze remains there for a long time, as though captured, or maybe unwilling to let go.

"Well, well, well," he drawls. His voice is gruff. Too deep. "I'm fucked, all right."

Understanding immediately dawns on Lowe.

This, he thinks, *is going to be an issue.*

ACKNOWLEDGMENTS

Guys, we're doing bullet points again. I would like to thank:

- Adriana, Christina, and Lo, for holding my hand at Comic-Con and encouraging me to write the slightly unhinged book of my heart. Publishing is scary, and I feel so lucky to have you.

- My agent, Thao, and my editor, Sarah, who didn't just *let* me write my knotty book, but fully embraced it. Neither of you know the real color of berries, but I love you anyways.

- Liz Sellers, the assistant editor of everyone's dreams, who always makes me feel like I'm in great hands.

- My publicists, Kristin Cipolla and Tara O'Connor, for being super patient and for putting together the best tour. I deserve you guys less with each book, but I'm so glad I can talk about Taylor Swift with you.

ACKNOWLEDGMENTS

- My marketers, Bridget O'Toole and Kim-Salina I. A million thanks for everything that you do, everything you don't ask me to do, and everything you help me do by holding my hand. You're the best, so I won't steal your Illumicrate editions.

- Rita Frangie Batour and Vikki Chu, for designing the cover (I was so obnoxious for this one, and yet no one has come to my house to murder me yet; thank you for your mercy), and of course Lilith, for being, as usual, the most talented illustrator to ever grace this plane of existence.

- Everyone at Berkley. I had the best time visiting, and I'm so grateful for how incredibly welcoming everyone was! In particular my most heartfelt love to: my grandeditor Cindy, for being, quite frankly, the most formative influence on me before we even met; my grandpublicist Erin; Carly, for calling my book "deliciously filthy" and making my entire year; Gabbie, for asking if my book had knotting in it and making me feel seen and understood; Claudia Colgan, for braving a frigid and hazardous winter.

- My production editor (Jen Myers), managing editor (Christine Legon), copyeditor (Jennifer Sale), and interior designer (Daniel Brount). So sorry I made you read what you had to read.

- My Spanish and Mexican publishers. Special thanks to Marina and Laura at Contraluz; Gerardo, for the best dinner of my life (S. still talks about it every day); and Norma (I am so, so, so sorry about *that* thing).

- My author friends, my fandom friends, my SDLA friends, my Berklete friends, my bookseller friends, my adoptive family friends, my *friend* friends. I'm a mess—thank you for putting up with me.

- My sister, for being cool about stuff.

- AO3 and the Organization for Transformative Works, for my life and my sanity.

- My husband. We're now five books in, and I'm starting to owe some real, not-backhanded-insult-y thanks to him, who will find out about them when his mother sends him a pic of the German edition. Thank you for agreeing to keep Southern European mealtimes, for cleaning the cat poopers when I'm on deadline, and for being proud of me even when I'm not. As usual: IYDIGKM.

I would *not* like to thank:

- Ticketmaster.

If You're Not Reading the Psy-Changeling Series by Nalini Singh, What Are You Even Doing with Your Life?

I'm sorry if the title of this opinion piece sounds judgmental, but let's be real: it kind of is. Nalini Singh is a goddess among humans, and anything she writes is gold, but the Psy-Changeling series . . . the Psy-Changeling series is my mother. It gave birth to me and raised me and packed me school lunches, and I will not rest until everyone in the world is reading it. You haven't picked it up yet? No worries! Here's a handy primer that will catch you up in no time so we can be obsessive and fangirl together.

WHAT IS THIS PSY-CHANGELING SERIES THING YOU SPEAK OF, ALI?
So glad you asked! It's a series of stand-alone romance novels (every book features a different couple, and past/future couples pop up as secondary characters) set in the same universe. Think the Ice Planet Barbarians series (another excellent piece of literature).

BUT WHAT'S SPECIAL ABOUT THIS UNIVERSE?
Everything! But more precisely, here is a brief overview, in which I care more about giving you a quick and dirty idea of the

world-building (so that you can easily jump into the series) and less about being nuanced and accurate.

The Psy-Changeling series is set in the near future, in an alternative reality in which three species coexist on Earth.

THE HUMANS: They're humans like us. Nothing to see here, please carry on.

THE CHANGELINGS: They're basically shifters, humans who can turn into animals at will. What animal? *Any* animal. Leopards. Otters. Cicadas (I'm actually not sure a cicada changeling has ever been mentioned, but you get the gist). Changelings are organized in packs and are generally touchier and more emotional than humans. They tend to live in harmony with nature and can be very formidable in their animal form. It's all very cottagecore, and we love them.

THE PSY: For my Trekkies out there, the Psy are basically Vulcans, but with cooler powers (sorry, Spock, ily). They are gifted with amazing psychic abilities that range from foresight to telepathy to telekinesis to a ton of other stuff that you'll discover as the series progresses (they're so fun!). The problem is, these powers are difficult to control. In order to avoid accidentally killing others, the Psy have to follow a protocol that divests them of their emotions. Basically, they are legally mandated not to *feel*. How's that going for them? you ask. Not super well, my friend.

The changelings and the Psy are not, like, at *war*, but they're not at peace either. Which means we have the species that feels too much on one side, and the species that doesn't want to feel at all on the other.

Honestly, I can't imagine anything worse than a Psy and a changeling falling in love with each other. (Are you evil-cackling with me yet?)

OMG I JUST CHECKED AND THE PSY-CHANGELING SERIES HAS, LIKE, FORTY BOOKS. I CAN'T COMMIT TO THAT???

Listen, I get it. I can't commit to *Grey's Anatomy*. I can't commit to Tolkien. I can't commit to a gym membership. As a Psy-Changeling stan, my gut reaction is to say: READ THEM ALL, THEY WILL ENRICH YOUR LIFE IMMENSELY. But the truth is, you don't have to. While there are overarching plots, you can easily skip books you're not interested in, and you'll still be able to follow along because Nalini Singh is great at catching you up and telling you what you need to know. I promise, you are not signing away your life by picking up this series (unless you're me, in which case you are, but, like, you love it and this is your entire personality).

OKAY FINE YOU WORE ME DOWN CONVINCED ME.

I pride myself on my ability to exhaust people. It's my most useful talent.

OH, SHUT UP. WHERE DO I START?

I gotchu, boo. If I were you, I would start from the first book, *Slave to Sensation*. Not only because it gives you a great overview of the world-building but also because it's truly a masterclass in the black cat/golden retriever trope (grumpy, cold Psy girl/flirty, sunshine changeling guy). Is it my favorite? Well, I would *of course* throw myself under a bus for Sascha and Lucas, but I would throw myself under a *train* for other couples we'll discuss later. Still, it's an excellent book, and it's great to get the lay of the land. Sascha, a Psy woman who never got around to fully developing her psychic power and is a bit of an outcast because of that (👀), finds herself having to collaborate with the alpha of the local leopard changeling pack, Lucas. She is forbidden from feeling emotions. He is into her from the very start and is like, "Babe, you sure you feel nothing? Because I think we have a *thing*." (He is correct.) In the background there is an investigation: a Psy serial killer who's been murdering changeling women. Sascha ends up helping with that and in the process discovers what her real powers are, finds love, and is unconditionally accepted into the most adorable leopard pack ever. I love everything about this book. (Yes, it's steamy; yes, the sex scenes are excellent.)

OKAY, I HAVE NOW PURCHASED AND READ *SLAVE TO SENSATION*, AND MY LIFE HAS CHANGED FOR THE BETTER. THANK YOU, ALI. WHAT ARE YOUR FAVORITE BOOKS IN THE SERIES?
I am so very glad you asked! Of your own free will, no less. Honestly, there is not a single dud in this series, but here are my top four (I tried so hard to pick three, but alas . . .) in chronological order (mild spoilers ahead):

VISIONS OF HEAT: This is the second book in the series, so it's a perfect follow-up to *Slave to Sensation*, especially because you'll see lots of Sascha and Lucas. Faith is very powerful Psy who can see the future. Traditionally, people with her skills have been raised in very sheltered/isolated environments for their own protection (*or have they?*). Vaughn is a jaguar shifter, the only one of his kind, who has a traumatic past and is a bit of a loner (he's also Lucas's BFF). When Faith starts having visions that have to do with murders, he's tasked with keeping an eye on her. He instantly falls for her. She falls for him, too, and discovers what horniness is. Fav part: the first time they bang he's afraid he'll lose control, so he has to be *chained* to the bed. Guys, I'm living my best life.

CARESSED BY ICE: Okay, SO. Here we have our first Psy MMC/changeling FMC couple, and it delivers so hard. Judd is a former soldier who decided to leave Psy society along with the rest of his family to save the life of his young niece, who was being persecuted for her unique set of skills (her name is Sienna; put a pin in that). He lives with the local wolf pack, and there he meets Brenna, a young changeling woman (in STEM!) who almost became the victim of a serial killer (yup, the one from *Slave to Sensation*). She's traumatized and only feels safe with Judd, and Judd clearly loves her *so much* and wants to protect her *so hard*. The problem is, his Psy powers are so lethal he's afraid that if he allows himself to feel emotions he'll end up accidentally hurting her. It's one of those "I'm not good enough for you, this is the skin of a killer" situations, but the worries are very legitimate here. They *want* to be together, but *can* they? (This book also has an incredibly iconic sex scene, in which Judd and Brenna are having sex for the first time, and he ends up destroying all the furniture in the house without even realizing it. Oopsie.)

KISS OF SNOW: Okay, fun story: I literally counted down the days until this book's release when I was in uni. I was *obsessed*. Hawke and Sienna's story was teased for sooo many books, and when it finally arrived, it was everything I wanted and *more*. Sienna is the young Psy who was being persecuted for her powers (Judd's niece). She was trained as a soldier from a very young age, and you can imagine the baggage that comes with that. Hawke, my beloved, is the alpha of the scariest pack in America, and he took in Sienna and her family when they defected. Fun fact: he is fourteen years older than Sienna. Fun fact #2: Hawke believes that his "real" mate died when he was a child and that he's destined to die alone. Yes, this is an age gap story. Yes, it's angsty. Yes, it's delicious, because Hawke tries to deny himself, but Sienna won't have it. And then, when he's all in, Sienna is worried that her powers might kill him. This story is incredibly high-stakes, and I will recommend it till the day I croak.

HEART OF OBSIDIAN: This is a Psy/Psy pairing, and I will never shut up about it. Have you ever heard of the morality chain, that trope in which one character is fully ready to go berserk and destroy the entire universe, but they decide not to do it because their significant other tells them "It would make me kinda sad if you did it"? This book is the gold standard for that! Kaleb Krychek, the husband of my heart, was young when his even younger closest friend, a girl named Sahara, disappeared. He never believed that she was dead, and in the intervening years he's been accumulating a truly indecent amount of power and money, and he never stopped looking for her. At the very start of *Heart of Obsidian*, he finally finds her and *OH. MY. GOD.* Guys, we're talking about the most powerful dude in the universe, very ready to just wipe out every living being and only stopping because he knows that it would make Sahara pout. He is so whipped it's not even funny (jk, it *is* funny).

OKAY, THANKS. I'M GONNA GO READ. BYE.
Byeeee! Have fun 💜 💜 💜

Justin Murphy of Out of the Attic Photography

ALI HAZELWOOD is the #1 *New York Times* bestselling author of *Love, Theoretically* and *The Love Hypothesis*, as well as a writer of peer-reviewed articles about brain science, in which no one makes out and the ever after is not always happy. Originally from Italy, she lived in Germany and Japan before moving to the US to pursue a PhD in neuroscience. When Ali is not at work, she can be found running, eating cake pops, or watching sci-fi movies with her three feline overlords (and her slightly less feline husband).

VISIT ALI HAZELWOOD ONLINE

AliHazelwood.com

AliHazelwood

AliHazelwood

LEARN MORE ABOUT THIS BOOK AND OTHER TITLES FROM *NEW YORK TIMES* BESTSELLING AUTHOR

ALI HAZELWOOD

SCAN ME
or visit
prh.com/alihazelwood